A hunt through the Scottish Highlands for a hidden cache of gold draws in three passionate couples—who discover that love is the greatest treasure of all—in the thrilling new trilogy from *New York Times* bestselling author

CANDACE CAMP

Secrets of the Loch

Praise for Book One
Treasured

"Sweet. . . . Entertaining. . . . A Highlands version of small-town charm."

—*Publishers Weekly*

"*Treasured* demonstrates Candace Camp's ability to draw her readers in with strong, well-drawn characters. A legend of hidden treasure, a man who hides behind many façades, and a woman who fights for her birthright form the tapestry of this poignant, sensual, and emotion-packed romance."

—*RT Book Reviews* (Top Pick)

And praise for Candace Camp's acclaimed trilogy Legend of St. Dwynwen

The Marrying Season
A Summer Seduction
A Winter Scandal

"Sensuality, intrigue, and Camp's trademark romantic sparring. . . . Delightful."

—*Publishers Weekly*

"A delightful romp. . . . Camp has a way with truly likeable characters who become like friends."

—*Romance Junkies*

"Where the Bascombe sisters go, things are never dull. Candace Camp delivers another witty, heartwarming, and fast-paced novel."

—*A Romance Review*

A Lady Never Tells

"This steamy romp . . . will entertain readers."

—*Publishers Weekly*

"Well-crafted and enchanting."

—*Romantic Times* (4½ stars)

"Superbly written and well paced, *A Lady Never Tells* thoroughly entertains as it follows the escapades of the Bascombe 'bouquet' of Marigold, Rose, Camellia, and Lily in the endeavor to make their way in upper-crust London Society."

—*Romance Reviews Today*

"One of those rare finds you don't want to put down. . . . Candace Camp brings a refreshing voice to the romance genre."

—*Winter Haven News Chief*

"Filled with humor and charm. . . . Fine writing."

—*A Romance Review* (4 roses)

CANDACE CAMP

PLEASURED

POCKET BOOKS

New York London Toronto Sydney New Delhi

Pocket Books
A Division of Simon & Schuster, Inc.
1230 Avenue of the Americas
New York, NY 10020

This book is a work of fiction. Any references to historical events, real people, or real places are used fictitiously. Other names, characters, places, and events are products of the author's imagination, and any resemblance to actual events or places or persons, living or dead, is entirely coincidental.

First Pocket Books paperback edition April 2015

POCKET and colophon are registered trademarks of Simon & Schuster, Inc.

For information about special discounts for bulk purchases, please contact Simon & Schuster Special Sales at 1-866-506-1949 or business@simonandschuster.com.

The Simon & Schuster Speakers Bureau can bring authors to your live event. For more information or to book an event contact the Simon & Schuster Speakers Bureau at 1-866-248-3049 or visit our website at www.simonspeakers.com.

Manufactured in the United States of America

10   9   8   7   6   5   4   3   2   1

ISBN 978-1-4767-4109-3
ISBN 978-1-4767-4113-0 (ebook)

For Elijah Moersch,
the newest member of the clan

Acknowledgments

Thanks, as always, to my wonderful editor, Abby Zidle, whose sense of humor makes revisions so much easier, and to the team at Pocket. Also to my agent, Maria Carvainis, and her team, who deal with all those things I hate to do. And, most of all, for the folks here at home, who help me in ways too numerous to list.

PLEASURED

Prologue

1746

Her eyes flew open at the sound of the knock. She waited, tense, until the faint rap came again. She slipped out of bed, picking up the iron poker beside the fireplace, and on silent feet crossed the floor. The door was sturdy and would hold, but it was old, and a bit of space was between it and the frame, enough to look out.

All she could see in the moonless night was darkness. She stood, barely breathing, considering. Who waited outside—some poor soul needing her assistance in the middle of the night? A Highland fighter running from the British? Or even worse, a British soldier, roaming the countryside to loot and plunder and kill?

When the tap came again, she spoke up boldly through the crack. "Gang away from this hoose. I hae my musket primed and aimed at your heart."

Astonishingly, her words brought forth a chuckle on the

other side of the door, and a low masculine voice said, "Ah, but I have no heart and well you know it, for it's been long in your keeping."

For a moment the voice, so dear and so familiar, froze her. Tears sprang into her eyes and clogged her throat. "Malcolm!"

"Aye, it is I. Will you not open the door, then, my love?"

Her paralysis broke, and she shoved up the bar and pulled back the door, her heart pounding like a mad thing. It was Malcolm, tall and wide-shouldered, his blond hair shaggy, the Rose tartan wrapped around him and slung over his shoulder. The tears she had held back for months gushed forth, and with a choked cry, she dropped the poker and leapt forward into his arms.

"Oh, Malcolm, Malcolm." She wrapped herself around him and pressed her face into the crook of his neck, drinking in his scent, her tears flowing.

"Here now, lass, you'll get me all wet," he protested, but only rich satisfaction was in his voice as he squeezed her to him, moving out of the doorway into the shadows.

"I missed you sae." She gulped back her tears and pressed her lips to his neck. "I feared you wouldna come back."

He nuzzled into the thick fall of her hair. "You cannot get rid of me that easily; you should know that." He raised his head. "I dare not kiss you, or I'll never stop."

"There's nae need to stop." A wicked smile crossed her face. "My mither's gane to our cousin's. I'm here alone all night and more."

She slid out of his arms and took a step toward the doorway, looking back at him with a glinting smile. "Will ye come inside, then?"

"Aye." His grin was wolfish. "You know I'd follow you anywhere, love."

He closed the door behind them, settling the heavy bar in its slot with a soft thud, and bent to pick up the poker she had dropped. "We'll need to get you a better weapon than this. Take my dirk."

"Nae. Not your dirk. Are you mad? It's got your rose all over the hilt."

"Not that one." He reached down to the top of his stocking and pulled out a smaller knife with a black hilt. "I carry more than the one, you ken."

"I ken you're a dangerous man," she retorted, setting the knife on the table. Taking his hand, she started toward the bed in the far corner of the cottage.

But he pulled her the opposite way to the fireplace, where he used the poker to prod the peat into renewed life. "Wait. I need a proper look at you. I've been thinking of this face for so long; I want to see if I've remembered you right."

Suiting his actions to his words, he set down the poker and tilted up her chin. The firelight played over her features, lighting her eyes and caressing the curves of her face.

"And do I look the way you remembered?" she asked saucily, her lips curving in an inviting way.

"Nae. You're even more beautiful." He stroked his knuckles down her cheek. "Softer. More enticing. You've cost me many a sleepless night the last few months."

"Did I?" She slid her hand beneath the edge of his tartan and under his shirt, her fingertips lightly teasing his skin.

"Aye. And more than a little pain as well."

"I would hae thought you'd find many a French lass to ease your pain."

"You know none of them will do." His voice thickened. "I want no one but you." He grazed his fingertips across her breasts, and his eyes darkened as her nipples tightened in response. "Did you miss me at all?"

"All I could think of was you." Her voice was low and threaded with emotion. "All I wanted was to hae you here again with me. To taste your lips . . . feel your touch . . . to hae you deep inside me."

Hunger flared in his blue eyes, and he pulled her up into him. As he had warned her, once he kissed her, he could not stop. They sank together to the floor, kissing greedily, frantically, their hands neither gentle nor patient as they shoved aside their garments and found the naked flesh they craved. He kissed the soft mounds of her breasts, the flat plateau of her stomach, the silken skin of her thighs. Lifting her hips, he plunged deep into her, and the moan of her satisfaction was echoed in his throat.

"Mo leannan." His breath was hot against her skin.

She trembled under the force of her passion, and just when it seemed she could not bear the sweet strain of anticipation a moment longer, pleasure broke over her in a great wave, and she clung to him as he, too, shuddered.

Long afterward, they lay twined together, too weary and replete to move, his tartan wrapped around them for warmth, until finally the chill sent them to the comfort of the bed. There they cuddled under the thick layers, lazily stroking and kissing until their passion swelled once more, and they made love again, this time with the care and patience of those who had loved often but never enough.

"Hae you been to the hoose?" she asked at last as they lay in dreamy contentment.

"Nae." She felt the rumble of his deep voice in his chest, a sound at once infinitely reassuring and stirring. "I had to see you first." He sighed. "But I must get to the castle before dawn breaks. They say there are lobsterbacks roaming all about."

"Aye, you must no' let them see you." She sat up and looked down at him, her voice urgent. "They will kill you if you're found. Oh, Malcolm . . ." Her voice caught. "You shouldna hae come here. You should hae stayed in France."

"While my people fought and died? Nae, how could I?" He sat up, his eyes bright. "It isn't all lost, my love. We can turn the tide with what I've brought back."

"You brought an army?"

"Nearly as good. I brought the means to raise an army."

"Malcolm!" She stared. "Dinna tell me. You got the gold?"

"Have you no faith in me, lass? You think the Baillannan would come skulking home empty-handed?" He grinned.

"I should have known—no French king could match Malcolm Rose for stubbornness." She glanced toward the door. "But where is it? Dinna tell me you left it on the ship. Can you trust those men?"

"Of course not. I trust no one." He took her hand, his face sobering. "No one but you, *mo cuishle*."

"Me?" She stared. "What do you mean?"

"I have to find the prince, and I dare not carry a chest of treasure while I run about the Highlands searching for him. I stowed the treasure in our place. Where we leave our messages. You must keep it safe for me."

"I? But I am no warrior. How can I protect it?"

"That is why you would not be suspected. If the English

thought it was in Baillannan, they'd tear the house apart, looking for it. There's my brother's home in Kinclannoch, but I don't know where Fergus is or if he even survived. I had no idea what had happened until we landed and learned of Culloden. In any case, Fergus is exactly where they'd look if Baillannan gave up no treasure. But you . . . a mere slip of a girl . . . they'd not suspect you. No one knows what you are to me."

"But I am not—"

"You are a clever woman who knows these woods and caves and all the ancient places better than anyone. If there is a safer place to hide it, no one would ken better than you where that is. The gold is in bags. Easy enough to transport one at a time if you need to." He smiled and smoothed his thumb across her wrinkled forehead. "Don't look so worried now, love. You won't have to hide it long. I'll find the prince and be back before you know it."

"I'll know every minute you're awa'." Her fingers dug into his shoulders as she pulled him to her.

He kissed her, his hands gliding down her body, but after a moment, he let out a soft noise of frustration and pulled away. "You are too tempting. I must go if I'm to get across the loch before dawn comes."

She let out a sigh but did not protest, only rose, wrapping the blanket around her for warmth, and watched him dress. Belting his tartan again, he adjusted the sword and dirk and glanced toward the table. "I meant it about the dirk. Keep it close to you. You don't know when one of the bloody English might pop out of the woods." He dropped a kiss on her forehead, then leaned his head against hers. "I'll not see you again before I go. 'Tis too risky. I wish . . . och, no time to be wishing." He shook his head and kissed her hard. "Take care, my love."

She followed him to the door, but when he opened it, she let out a low cry and flung her arms around him. "Don't leave, Malcolm. Please. I canna part with you again."

"Ah, lass, you tear my heart out." He wrapped his arms around her waist, nuzzling into her hair. "I canna stay, you know that. My prince needs me. My people. The Baillannan doesna shirk a fight."

"*I* need you, too."

"Aye, and glad I am of it. I need you as much. But in no time I'll be back, and we'll have the rest of our lives together."

"Will we?" She pulled back and pinned him with her fierce gaze. "You know we canna. It's no' our fate. I will never live with you, Malcolm. I'll never have your name."

"I know, *mo leannan*, I know." He raised her hand to his lips and kissed it, gazing deep into her eyes. "But you will always have my heart."

He turned and walked away, and with dread knotting in her chest, she watched him vanish into the dark.

August 1807

The wheel of the carriage hit yet another rut in the road, jerking the Earl of Mardoun awake. He glanced across at the opposite seat, where his daughter sat with her governess. Miss Pettigrew was awake, and she cast her eyes down quickly, doing her best, as always, to blend into the upholstery. Lynette, however, had obviously been dozing, for she straightened up, running her hands over her face and yawning. Reaching out, she pushed aside the curtains.

"Look! It's beautiful!" Lynette cried, sticking her head out the window. "Papa! It's like a carpet of flowers."

"Miss Lynnette, be careful," the governess fussed. "You might catch a chill." She hastened to spread a carriage rug over the girl's lap.

"'Tis nearly August," Damon commented drily. "I think Lynette is unlikely to catch cold." The woman's constant caution and fussing wore on his nerves. He was beginning to wish he had sent her ahead to Duncally with the servants.

He glanced at his daughter and saw that her dark eyes, so like his own, were lit with laughter. "It's good to see you smile."

"Yes, poor dear," Miss Pettigrew agreed, tucking in the robe more securely. "It has been hard, losing her mother. Such a saint as Lady Mardoun was. And, of course, Miss Lynette is a very sensitive child."

"Mm." Damon had no idea how to respond to that statement, given that he had felt more relief than sorrow upon hearing of his wife's demise. But then, he was neither sensitive nor saintly. He cast a glance at his daughter and saw that the smile had vanished from her face. Blast the woman—Lynette's governess seemed to have a perfect knack for casting gloom on every situation.

He pushed aside the window curtain on his side of the carriage. "Your 'carpet of flowers' is heather. It was not out when I was here before, though one and all, they assured us it was too bad we missed it. It seems they were right, doesn't it?"

"Oh, yes! I am so glad we came to Scotland. Are we getting close? I see some buildings ahead. Is that part of Duncally?"

Damon craned his neck in the direction Lynette was looking and chuckled. "No, that's not Duncally, not even the gatehouse. You'll know Duncally when you see it."

"But how? I've never been there before." Lynette spoke

with a shyness that never failed to send a pang of regret and guilt through him.

He smiled at her. "You will see."

"Is it like Edinburgh Castle?"

"No, it's not grim. It looks—oh, like a castle on the Rhine, I suppose. Or a drawing in a book. My grandfather apparently had a sense of the dramatic. Those buildings you see ahead are, I suspect, the village nearest the castle. Kincannon, Kenkilling, something like that."

"Kinclannoch," Lynette corrected him, then looked a trifle abashed. "I looked it up when I learned we were coming here."

"Yes, you are right. Kinclannoch. Not a very prepossessing village."

"No. But look at the thatched roofs. They're quaint, aren't they?"

"Yes. I can see you are prepared to like the place."

"Yes, I am." His daughter blushed faintly. "Are we Scots, then?"

"I suppose. Partly. My grandmother, your great-grandmother, was Scottish, the last of her line. The Countess of Mardoun in her own right, so when she married, the title came to her husband, Lord Rutherford, and then to their son. But Grandfather was English, of course, and my mother, as well."

"And mine." Lynette sighed. "So I am only . . . an eighth Scottish?"

He nodded. "You sound disappointed."

"A little." Color tinged her cheeks. "It seems very romantic. Tragic Queen Mary, fleeing with Bothwell and riding through the night. Bonnie Prince Charlie."

"Also fleeing. Not exactly comfortable fates."

"No. I suppose not."

"But decidedly exciting."

Damon was rewarded by the way her delicate face lit up again. "But, look, we are stopping. Is this an inn? Will we not reach Duncally today?"

"No, it's not far. I suspect the coachman's gone to ask directions. The roads are rather ill marked." He leaned across to look out the curtains on the opposite side of the carriage. His hand stilled on the drapery.

A woman stood across the narrow street, chatting with a young gentleman. She was attired in a simple blue cotton dress, a little too low-waisted to be fashionable, and not even a ruffle around the skirt for adornment—but then, that sweetly curved body needed no adornment. Her arms below the short cap sleeves were bare—white and soft and shapely—and she wore no gloves. Her head, too, was bare and, in the glint of the afternoon sun, was a riot of thick, red curls. Her face was heart-shaped, with rounded cheeks and a firm little chin.

She turned and looked toward the carriage and her eyes met Damon's. For an instant it seemed as if his heart stopped. Her eyes were glorious—large and wide set and rimmed with thick, dark lashes, and their color was stunning, a brown so light, so clear, they appeared golden.

"Oh, Papa, look at that lady," his daughter said in a hushed tone. "Isn't she beautiful?"

"Yes," he agreed, his voice a trifle husky. "Yes, she is."

Meg Munro turned toward the noise of horses' hooves, and her eyebrows rose at the sight of the elegant black vehicle and matched team of four coal-black horses. "Look at that."

Beside her, Gregory Rose looked in the same direction. "Well, well."

"The Earl of Mardoun, do you think?"

"I'd guess. All of Kinclannoch has been buzzing ever since his staff arrived last week. Still, I never thought he would actually come. Ah, look, the lord is surveying the peasants."

A man's face appeared in the carriage window. Thick, black hair swept back from a square-jawed face, his skin as fair as his hair was dark, his eyes under the prominent ridge of his brow echoing the jet black of his hair. Arrogance and boredom colored his expression in equal measure, but neither could detract from the handsomeness of his face.

He stared straight at Meg. She was accustomed to men's stares. What was unfamiliar to her was the visceral pull she felt in return. She was suddenly, acutely aware of the sun's warmth on her arms, the touch of the air on her face, as if her senses had awakened from a deep slumber. Even the scents carried on the breeze were suddenly sharper, the sounds brighter. Yet at the same time the world around her seemed to retreat, her focus narrowing to the carriage window.

"Meg? Are you all right?" Gregory's voice pulled her from her trance.

"What?" She pulled her gaze away and looked up at the man she had known since childhood. "I'm sorry . . . what did you say?"

"Nothing important. Just wondering how long the earl

would last this time." Gregory gave her an odd look. "Is there something amiss? Do you feel ill?"

Meg forced out a credible laugh. "Do I look so bad as that?"

"You never look bad, as you are well aware," he retorted. "You just seemed . . . very far away." He glanced over at the carriage. The man in the carriage had pulled back and was now only an indistinct form in the shadows of the interior. "I thought—I wondered—do you *know* that chap?"

"The Earl of Mardoun?" Meg's voice dripped with scorn. "Oh, aye, I know him. I've never seen the man before, but his deeds speak for him. Tossing all his people out of their homes without the slightest thought for how they will live or where they will go, all so that he can make a few more pounds profit raising sheep instead. He's a coldhearted devil." No matter that he was a handsome one as well.

"Perhaps he is unaware of his steward's actions," Gregory suggested mildly.

Meg sent her friend a speaking glance. "It is like you to hope for the best in people. But I have dealt with too many of his sort to hold a rosy view of him. He is the sort Andrew was wont to bring home with him from Oxford—English 'gentlemen'—haughty and fine and unaccountably full of themselves, certain that everyone else was put on this earth to serve them. Remember, it was the earl who hired MacRae as his steward, and I doubt that worm of a man would do aught but his master's bidding."

"No doubt you're right. I wonder Mardoun dares to come here. Surely he must know how everyone around the loch despises him."

"I doubt he cares. Or perhaps he is like MacRae and

he enjoys watching firsthand the misery he inflicts on the crofters."

"MacRae." Gregory made a disgusted noise. "That man is a snake."

"Aye." Meg's jaw hardened.

"Has MacRae been bothering you?" Gregory narrowed his eyes at her. "If he has, I'll have a word with the man."

"Don't you begin, as well." Meg rolled her eyes. "I can handle MacRae; he is a pest, nothing more."

"Very well. I shall not plague you . . . as long as you promise to tell me if the man needs a more physical reminder."

"Yes, yes." Meg heaved a martyr's sigh. "I promise I will tell you if MacRae grows too difficult. At least I can count on you not to send the man to his grave, which is not something I can trust with my brother."

"'Twould be no loss if he died."

"It's not MacRae I worry about. I don't want to see Coll in gaol." Behind them came a shout and a slap of the reins, and they turned to see the earl's carriage rumble off.

"Well sprung, isn't it?" Gregory said in an admiring voice. "Though I'd prefer something a little more flash myself."

Meg chuckled. "The Highlands roads will put those axles to the test well enough." She made a face and waved her hand in a dismissive gesture. "Enough about the Earl of Mardoun. How do you fare?" She tucked a hand into Gregory's arm as they strolled down the street. "How is your father? I heard you visited him last week."

"Aye." Gregory sighed, his face falling into unaccustomedly sober lines. "He seems better. The couple who look after him are good to him, but they understand they must not let him out of their sight. Orkney is not far enough away, I know, but it seemed unwise to move him to a city. Jack has been very agreeable about the matter, more so than my father deserves."

"Jack is not like most gentlemen. And your father is family to him now, after all."

"True." Gregory grinned. "I suspect the man would do most anything Isobel asked."

"And vice versa." Meg laughed. "They are almost enough to make one decide to marry."

"No!" He put on a shocked expression. "Surely not you."

"Nay, not I. Nor you, I'll warrant. How are the happy couple? Have you heard from them?"

"Aunt Elizabeth received a letter from Isobel, and it seems they are enjoying London very much. Still, I think they miss the Highlands. I would not be surprised if they return soon."

When they reached the edge of the village, Meg parted from her friend, following the road the carriage had taken until, after a few minutes, she came to an intersecting path. She paused for a moment, as she always did, to take in the landscape before her.

To her left along the path lay the woods and her home and the loch, though from this vantage point she could not see the water itself. At the farthest end of the loch, dominating the countryside around it, was Duncally, the seat of the earls of Mardoun. It rose in manicured layers of gardens and terraces up the hillside, crowned at the top by the magnificence of the castle itself. No medieval fortress, the Earl of Mardoun's home was more akin to a palace, all narrow towers and turrets and spires and terraces, sparkling white in the sun.

But Meg's eyes were not drawn to this opulent sight. What always brought her to an admiring halt was the green clearing before her and the towering stones that stood in the center of it. Each weathered white rock was twice Meg's height or more, and together they formed a massive oval with a gap here and a tumbled-down stone there that had once made the figure complete. In the distance was the grassy hump of a barrow, and on either side of the stone circle, but clearly apart from it, were two other standing stones, one smaller than the others and with a curious hole through the center.

Meg drew in a deep breath and closed her eyes, the familiar sense of peace settling over her. Sometimes here among the "old ones" she could almost believe the tales her mother and Elizabeth Rose told, legends of the fey folk and mystical beings. She could almost believe the whispers about the Munro women and their uncanny knowledge of the forest and caves, their special skills with herbs and potions. Isobel Rose had once said that Meg was "one with the land," and standing here, Meg knew she was.

Until she opened her eyes and let out a sigh, and once more this was merely a lovely, peaceful spot, a bit of land special to the people of Kinclannoch, however little they knew now of what it had once been. And she was simply a woman who had grown up roaming the area and learning all its secrets, the descendant of a long line of women who were herbalists and healers.

She made her way around the stones to take the path home, and as she turned, she cast a glance up toward the castle that dominated the horizon. She wondered if the carriage had made it to Duncally yet; it was a long way round the loch to the mansion at the far end. Why had the earl decided to grace the glen with his presence? She wondered if Lady Mardoun had been in the carriage beside him. He looked the sort of man whom a wife would be foolish to let out of her sight.

Meg clicked her tongue with annoyance. What was she doing, thinking about Mardoun or his lady? The gentry were nothing to her—especially someone as vile as Mardoun. The earl was not the only one evicting his crofters from the land their families had lived on for hundreds of years. Landowners such as Isobel Rose and her new husband who cared more for their people than for gold were in the minority, and all over the Highlands, the Clearances were tearing people from their land, setting them on the road, with no place to go and only the clothes on their backs and the goods they could carry. But Mardoun, as the largest property owner in the area, was responsible for more of the displacements, and worse, he was notorious for the cold and callous way he tossed his crofters out with little notice.

She had despised the man without ever laying eyes on him—which made it all the stranger that when she had seen him today for the first time, she had felt such a strange, strong frisson of excitement. Meg thought again of that lean, compelling visage—the dark, intense eyes beneath the ridge of his brow, the thick, black sweep of hair, the arrogant tilt of his head, the sensual curve of his mouth. Amazingly, her insides warmed again at the thought of him.

Her reaction astonished and appalled her in almost equal

measure. Meg had never been one to swoon over any man. She had been the object of male pursuit for years—she was too honest to pretend she did not know that men found her desirable. As far as she was concerned, her friend Isobel's elegant blond beauty was more attractive than her own flamered hair and too-wide cheeks, but her looks had a certain flamboyance that drew men, which was only enhanced by the reputation the Munro women had always carried. Many men assumed that a woman who lived freely was free with her favors, as well.

Meg had always been quick to dispel that notion. Meg Munro was not a woman to settle for anything less than the deepest of feelings, and no man had managed to disrupt her thoughts, let alone capture her heart.

It was ridiculous to think that a strange man sitting in a carriage—a man, moreover, whom she considered a blackguard—could so immediately, so effortlessly, stir her blood. It was more than ridiculous; it was impossible. Whatever strange sensation had run through her, it could not have been desire. She had not even gotten a proper look at him. It had been a mere glance, no doubt a trick of her eyes that made her think he was far more handsome than he was. The idea of some sort of immediate visceral connection between them was ludicrous, the stuff of the Gothic novels Isobel's aunt was fond of reading.

A closer look would no doubt have shattered that first illusion. The mystery had intrigued her—that momentary glance, the deep, dark eyes, the way the sun had highlighted the fair skin of his face amid the pool of shadow inside the carriage. If he had stepped out, she would have seen . . . what? Perhaps he would have proved to be shorter than she and potbellied. Or a vacuous fop, dressed in a chartreuse jacket and sporting a gigantic posy in his lapel.

She giggled at the image. But, no, she could not believe that the lean, strong features and proud head indicated anything but an equally powerful frame. And it was hard to picture that burning gaze turning blank and vacant.

It was easier to imagine that mouth in a hard, cruel line, disdain etched upon his features. Yet, just thinking of him, she felt a treacherous warmth twining through her again. With a disgusted noise, she shook the image from her mind and strode briskly to her cottage.

She had things to do—those mushrooms she'd spotted on her way to the village earlier and vegetables to harvest, not to mention the tonic for Aunt Elizabeth and a poultice for Ben Fleming's gout. And old Mrs. McEwan was in need of something for her lumbago.

Meg's steps slowed. Mrs. McEwan's daughter Sally was cook at Duncally, and it would be easy enough to take her a pot of salve for the old woman. Sally would no doubt welcome some fresh herbs as well, now that the earl was there and expecting tasty dishes. The cook was always eager for a good gossip. Perhaps this was a good time to visit the castle.

———

Early the next morning, Meg plucked handfuls of herbs from her garden, mint and rosemary and thyme, and tucked them into a basket along with a bag of fresh mushrooms, a pot of salve, and a bottle of her best plum cordial, which was Granny McEwan's favorite. Then she set out for the

Duncally kitchen. It was a pleasant walk up the hillside to the castle if one knew the way through the woods, and the last climb up the steps and terraces of the gardens offered a sweeping view of the loch, where one could see the jumbled ruins of the old castle and the gray bulk of Baillannan across from her.

Meg passed the Duncally mews with a wave to the falconer as he stood, heavy glove on his hand, waiting for a hawk that swept in on wide wings. She then walked through the wide, manicured sweep of the lowest garden and started up the steps to the higher levels. Duncally was usually a quiet, deserted place, with only a skeleton staff about to keep the gardens and house neat and ready for the master's potential arrival. But now it hummed with activity, though conducted in a hushed and unobtrusive manner.

"Meg Munro!" Sally McEwan cried as Meg stepped through the door. "Bless us, child, you maun hae read my mind." Sally bustled forward to take the basket from Meg's arm. "I was just about to send Josie to your cottage. Here is himself, saying we maun hae mushrooms with the chicken tonight, and me thinking if I sent Josie to pick them, we'd find everyone dead in their beds tomorrow morning. Oh! And fresh rosemary!" Sally held up one of the small sacks and sniffed dramatically.

"This is for your mother." Meg dug the pot from the basket.

"You *are* an angel." The older woman popped the small jar into one of her capacious pockets. "Come, sit doon. I hae not seen you in this age." Sally took the basket and handed it to a kitchen maid, saying, "Here, lass, put these awa' and fetch a cup of tea for us."

"Are you sure you're not too busy?" Meg glanced around at the bustling kitchen.

"Och, we've been nocht but too busy for the week past, and I see nae hope of it getting better. Take your moment while you can, I say." Sally steered Meg out of the busy room and into the servants' dining room, where Sally sank down on a chair and fanned her red face. "How did you ken my mither was down in the back? Sometimes I think you maun hae the sicht like your gran."

"No." Meg smiled. "I heard it from Mary Grant. Is she in much pain?"

"She'd not be feeling bad at all if she hadna tried to lift a sack of meal all on her ane," Sally retorted unsympathetically. "I told her I'd send Tommy to help her, but, no, she maun do it richt that morning 'fore he got there." Sally shrugged. "Well, you ken how she is."

"Aye, I do." One of the kitchen maids brought in a pot of tea and cakes, and as Sally went about pouring it, Meg went on, "Who is 'himself' that must have mushrooms with his chicken? Mardoun?"

"Nae, not the earl. I've not seen that one since we lined up for our curtsy yesterday. 'Twas Hudgins." Her sour expression left little doubt as to her feelings for the man. "That fancy Sassenach butler who came to set us all in order. Och, it would break that man's face to smile. It's for the little missy, says he, she's partial to mushrooms. And there'll be no more haggis at their table—Hudgins tossed it on the dust heap last night. The poached salmon will do, ye ken, but his lordship's 'palate' is too 'refined' for blood sausage. I ask you, what sort of man does no' like a bit of blood sausage with his breakfast? And what is a *palate*? Some fancy English thing, I suppose."

"Mm." Meg hid her smile.

"And if *he* isna bad enough, here's Mrs. Ferguson aye-ways popping in to check on everyone."

"The housekeeper? But she is always here."

"Aye, and I've learned to put up with her sermons and her rules. But now she's worried this English butler will find her wanting. So she's forever sticking her nose in, harrying the maids and telling everyone they're taking too long to do their jobs. Well, they'd do them much faster, wouldn't they, if she were not here bleating at them?"

Meg did not bother to hide her smile this time. She had been on the receiving end of Mrs. Ferguson's sermons a time or two. "Who is 'the little missy'? Surely he was not talking about the countess."

"Nae, the countess passed on nigh a year ago. It's the earl's daughter I mean—a pale, little thing, trailing about with that woman hovering over her. She maun hae the windows closed lest she catch cold. She canna do this and she maun be careful there—"

"The earl's daughter is sickly?"

"Aye, it seems so." Sally frowned. "Though it's not the lass, ye ken, who does all that fussing. It's the governess. The woman seems to think the Highlands are full of wild creatures out to gobble the lass up. She frets when Miss Lynette gies oot to the gardens or doon to the falconry. Fair taken wi' the birds, Miss Lynette is." Sally paused, considering. "The lass was lively enough when she was talking to Jamie."

"They are in mourning, I take it."

"Aye, I suppose—though I canna say *he* looks grief-stricken." Sally leaned forward confidentially. "I hear Mardoun dinna live with his lady and the lass. He wasna even in the country when the countess died." The cook leaned back, giving a shrug. "Course, they're English."

Meg took a sip of her tea and said casually, "What is he like—the earl, I mean?"

"He's a good-looking devil. Dark as Lucifer and just as handsome. But beyond that, I dinna know."

"Well, you know he does not like blood sausage." Meg grinned.

"Aye, there's that." Sally chuckled. She paused, cocking her head to one side, listening to noises in the kitchen. "Och, there's Mrs. Ferguson now. Best get back to the chopping board or I'll no' hear the end of it." Sally shoved herself up from the table.

Meg hopped to her feet as well. "I'd best leave, or she'll be asking me why I was not at kirk on Sunday."

"Aye. Thank ye, lassie, for the medicine for Ma." Sally took Meg's hand, squeezing it. "Ruth will hae set your basket by the door."

Meg escaped with only a dark scowl from the housekeeper, who was more intent on scolding one of the housemaids than tending to Meg's morals this morning. She picked up her basket, now filled with vegetables from the cook's garden and a little pouch of coins, and slipped out the rear door.

She glanced to her right where another set of steps led to the main terrace. It was empty, as was the garden below, apart from a pair of gardeners trimming the hedges. Not that she had really expected to see the earl—or anyone else. She started along the flagstone path leading to the lower gardens. She had not yet reached the stairs when the sound of footsteps behind her made her stop and turn around.

There, at the edge of the terrace, stood the Earl of Mardoun.

2

Meg's *stomach lurched as if* she had gone down a step she had not realized was there, and suddenly her muscles seemed not to work. Any thought of the earl's being too thin, too fat, too anything other than brutally handsome, was instantly, clearly wrong. His wide shoulders filled out a plain but exquisitely cut black jacket, and his equally well-tailored fawn breeches left little doubt as to the musculature of his long legs. Gleaming boots, a snowy-white shirt, and an artfully tied neckcloth completed the picture of a London gentleman. But such elegant details scarcely registered. It was his face that held her captive.

No shadows, no dark recesses, obscured him here; he was bathed in the golden morning light. His square-jawed face was just as compelling as it had been yesterday—strong features sharply etched, as if cut in marble by an expert hand, and eyes dark and fathomless, their depths pulling her in.

"I can see that tales of the beauties of Scotland are not exaggerated."

At the sound of his voice, something hot and thick and unfamiliar uncurled inside Meg. She realized, a little appalled, that her fingers were trembling. She clutched the handle of the basket more tightly to still them as her mind scrambled for a reply. Normally words came easily to Meg, but at this moment, she had been rendered mute.

Embarrassed by her unaccustomed ineptitude, she dropped a hasty curtsy and whirled, hurrying to the steps. Head down to watch her footing as she rushed down the stairs, she mentally castigated herself. How could she have stood there, dumb as a sheep, and then curtsied to the man like a scullery maid? She was Meg Munro, an independent Highland woman, not some serf to bow her head when a lord passed by.

As she reached the bottom of the steps, she lifted her gaze, and an absurd, annoying shiver went through her as she saw the earl trotting down a set of stone steps at right angles to the one she took.

"No, stay," he said, striding toward her, and he smiled.

His smile was a fearsome thing, she thought, lighting his dark eyes and softening the sharp angles of his face. No doubt it had conquered many a girl's virtue over the years.

"I did not mean to frighten you away," he went on, slowing as he came closer, like a man approaching a scared animal.

His words struck a nerve. Meg faced him. "I don't frighten that easily."

"That's good to know." The curve of his lips was more intimate now, and his eyes swept down her in a swift but unmistakable glance. "Then you will not be too timid to tell me your name."

Meg was not a novice at parrying a gentleman's advances. Over the years more than one of Sir Andrew's friends visiting at Baillannan had assumed she would succumb to his flattery or be bought by his coin, and she had given them swift, sharp setdowns. Today, however, instead of telling this man that he had no need to know her name, she merely lifted her chin in a challenging way and said, "I am Margaret Munro."

"Margaret Munro." He rolled the words in his mouth as if they tasted sweet to him. "'Tis a lovely name. It suits such a lovely woman."

"I am glad you approve," she retorted tartly.

His eyes widened slightly, a little breath of a chuckle escaping him. "Do compliments raise your hackles, Miss Munro? I shall have to be careful, then, for the sight of you spurs compliments." He moved a trifle closer. "I saw you in town yesterday."

"And I saw you."

"So you did. What good fortune, then, that you should visit Duncally today."

She stiffened. Did he mean to imply that she had sought him out? "'Twas not good fortune brought me here. It was business." She lifted her basket a little higher on her arm and gave him a cool smile. "Now that business is done, I'd best leave. Good day, sir."

"But wait, you cannot leave yet," he protested in a light, flirtatious tone. "I have learned nothing about you save your name."

"Dinna worry," she tossed over her shoulder as she

walked away. "I am sure any number of people will be happy to tell you about Red Meg Munro."

———

Damon watched Meg stroll off, taking the curving path past the roses. He followed at a leisurely pace, stopping at the stone balustrade to watch her move down the long slope to yet another level, where grand stone steps split and cascaded on either side down the last steep drop.

The wide, green swath of the lowest level of gardens lay before him, ending at the dark gray waters of the loch. But he did not study the magnificent view of land and water, only the small feminine figure striding along the promenade dividing the formal garden in half. She wore no cap or kerchief; the sun turned her hair to fire.

Red Meg Munro. He smiled to himself. The name suited her, all heat and boldness and allure. God, she was beautiful! In her simple, slightly faded dress, without artifice or adornment, she would cast into the shade the most fashionably dressed, coiffed, and elegantly jeweled lady of the *ton*.

The plain dress was not revealing, but neither could it conceal the sweet swell of breast and hips, and his hands itched to slide down her, discovering each curve and dip of her body. Only a saint would not feel lust stir at the sight of her vivid hair piled on her head in a thick, haphazard mass of curls.

But it was her eyes—huge and clear and astonishingly golden—that pierced a man to his very soul. He had been struck by her beauty yesterday, so much so that when he'd seen her from his study window this morning, he had bolted out of the house like a green youth to intercept her in the gardens. Then she had looked up at him, the sun full on her face and her eyes the color of molten gold, and the flood of desire that surged through him had been so swift and fierce it was all he could do to remember how to speak.

What he had seen of her after that—the eyes and face and figure even more alluring up close, the soft fragrance that clung to her, the creamy voice with its soft hint of Scottish burr—had done nothing to lessen that desire. And her bold manner in speaking to a strange man, without blushes or shyness, the flirtatious challenge to find her that she had tossed over her shoulder, hinted of a woman well aware of the response she called up in a man . . . and perhaps willing to answer that response. Unconsciously, his fingers curled around the lapels of his jacket, gliding up and down the material as he watched Meg disappear around the corner of the falcons' cages.

The prospect of meeting with the estate manager in a few minutes was even less appealing now. With a sigh, Damon went back to the house. As he stepped inside, he caught sight of the housekeeper bustling down the back hall toward the servants' stairs. MacRae could wait.

"Mrs. Ferguson."

The plump, gray-haired woman whirled around at the sound of his voice and hurried toward him, her forehead creased. "My lord! Is aught amiss? What can I do for you?"

"No, everything is fine. Excellent. I merely had a question—it occurred to me that you would be the person who would know most about the locals."

The woman preened a little. "Indeed, sir, though I am

from Glasgow originally, I have been here at Duncally nigh on twenty years, so I know the area well. Is there some service you require? Some place you wish to visit?"

"No. But I wondered what you know of Miss Margaret Munro."

"That one!" The housekeeper puffed up like a pouter pigeon. "Did the girl bother you, sir? Indeed, I must apologize. She should not have ventured into the house."

"No, no," Damon assured her hastily. "She did not bother me." That was a lie, but he did not think his middle-aged housekeeper would appreciate hearing exactly in what manner Meg Munro had disturbed his peace. "I ran into her in the gardens."

"She should not go through the gardens." Mrs. Ferguson tsked. "I shall have to speak to her. She has always been a wild thing—bold as brass. I hope you were not offended."

"No, no offense, nothing of the sort. I simply wondered who she was. If she, um, was employed here?"

"Oh, my, no. You must not think I would hire such a hussy!" Seeing the earl's raised eyebrows, she went on hastily, "I beg your pardon for my blunt speech."

"No, please, go on."

"Meg brought herbs and such for the kitchen. No doubt she had some tonic or other. It's all nonsense, of course, but the people of the glen are a superstitious lot, and they believe she can cure them of ills. It's the devil's business, I say. I have tried to help the lass, I can assure you. 'Tis not her fault that she was brought up the way she was—born on the wrong side of the blanket and all." The housekeeper leaned forward and lowered her voice confidingly.

"Ah, I see."

"Her mother was raised the same before her. The Munro women have a long history of being headstrong and wayward. 'Tis said they never marry. Certainly her mother did not. They live all alone at the Spaewife's Cottage."

"Spaewife?" Damon repeated blankly.

"Aye, sir, it's a word for a woman who has the sight. They say that one of the Munro women was a spaewife— well, more than one. The Munros roam about, plucking up leaves and roots and who knows what to make their godless potions. It was no surprise to me that some of them were burned at the stake in years past—though, of course, I cannot hold with that. It's a matter for God himself to judge, I say."

"People think Miss Munro is a witch?"

His skepticism must have come through in his tone, for Mrs. Ferguson straightened and drew her mouth into a prim line. "Nae, not a witch. But to hear the folks around here tell it, it's her that cures those who are sick, not the grace of God. It's why few condemn their licentious behavior. For generations they have been, well, the sort of woman that I cannot bring myself to name." She gave him a significant look. "They have always had a 'special relationship' with the lairds of Baillannan."

"The lairds of Baillannan? That gray-stone manor house?"

"Aye, my lord. Sir Andrew and before him Sir John. Meg's mother, Janet, was Sir Andrew's nurse when he was a babe, and Janet was *uncommon* close to Sir John. I would not like to think there was anything to the rumor, but given the circumstances . . ." Mrs. Ferguson's voice trailed off. "Well, you can see that she is not the sort whom I would allow to work at Duncally. Why, she would have the men all in an uproar, a lass like that. Our servants are of the highest character, I assure you."

"I have no doubt of that, Mrs. Ferguson."

Damon dismissed her and stood there for a moment longer, a faint smile on his lips. So Red Meg Munro was a mysterious, wild woman of the woods, gathering plants and making potions and doing as she pleased. All his housekeeper's remarks concerning Miss Munro's lack of suitability had made her more appealing to him by the moment. Clearly she was no blushing virgin, but a woman of experience.

He was beginning to think that this trip to the Highlands might just turn out to be quite entertaining.

⎯⎯

Meg hardly noticed the woods around her as she walked back to her cottage, nor did she stop even once to take in the view of the loch or Baillannan, for she was far too busy arguing with herself. Why had she tossed that parting comment over her shoulder at the earl? She had meant the remark to be needling, but somehow it had come out almost flirtatious. She was not above a little harmless flirtation; but that had been with Gregory Rose, or the shopkeeper's son—men who knew her, men who understood that it was a pleasant little game and nothing more.

Mardoun was another matter altogether. He was a stranger and, worse, an aristocrat. Accustomed as he was to being pampered, flattered, and pursued by eager women, he would doubtless assume she had been throwing out lures to him.

Which she most assuredly had *not*. Meg Munro did not pursue any man—least of all someone like the Earl of Mardoun. Titles and wealth did not fill her eyes with stars. She had, she would admit, felt a quiver of attraction when she saw him. But that did not mean that she *liked* him. Anyone would feel a little jolt upon seeing so handsome a man.

Meg thought of his eyes, dark and unknowable, like bottomless pools. She remembered the quirk of his mouth and the tiny scar just above his upper lip that made her imagine pressing her lips to it. The square set of his jaw and the jet-black hair. His voice, deep and rich, which had seemed to vibrate in her. She remembered the way he had looked at her and the way he had smiled.

Glancing up, she saw her cottage at the end of the path in front of her, and she realized that she had been so deep in thought she had forgotten to check her beehive on her way back as she had intended. She let out a sigh. Well, it would just have to wait until tomorrow. She had baskets of plums waiting for her in the kitchen, newly picked, and she must start making her cordial and preserves.

She worked steadily all through the afternoon and even managed to keep her mind off the Earl of Mardoun—at least most of the time. She was still stirring the pots in her kitchen late in the evening, the air of her cottage filled with the sweet scent of plums, when she heard a rattle and a thump at the back of the house. Startled, Meg poked her head around the corner of the small alcove that was her kitchen and workroom just in time to see a man crawling through the open back window.

"Well," she said sternly, crossing her arms. "So now you've taken to climbing in windows, I see."

"Aye, I have—though I wish your window were not so wee," her brother, Coll, answered imperturbably, contorting his long frame to pull it through the small, open square.

"I'm sure our great-great-gran would have made it larger if she'd known you'd be wanting to use it for a door," Meg retorted. "Would you care to tell me why you are doing so?"

"Donald MacRae is watching the path to your door." Coll came toward her, tall and wide-shouldered, his shaggy blond hair catching the low light in the cottage.

"Oh, Coll, what have you gotten yourself into now?"

"Sorry. I would not have pulled you into it, but it's Young Dougal; he has a wound needs tending." As Meg reached back to untie her apron, Coll held up a staying hand. "Nae, you need not come. He has a burn, the fool, nothing you can do except give me some ointment to soothe it—and maybe a tonic for the pain."

Meg sighed and went over to her cabinets, pulling out mortar and pestle and several packets of herbs. "How bad is it? My ointment will help, but if the burn is severe . . ."

"It's all down one arm. But they put it out quickly." Coll followed her into the small workroom, ducking his head with the ease of long practice to walk through the low door-way.

"I'll send something for infection as well, just in case." Meg handed him a long wooden spoon turned dark from the simmering plums. "Here, stir that while I make this."

"Smells good." He sniffed the air appreciatively. "Will I be getting some plum preserves then?"

"Aye, you might. And plum wine as well, if you've a mind to it." Meg's fingers flew as she ground and stirred, filling a small pot with a thick ointment. "What have you done—no, I don't want to know. I wish you would stop all these things you've been doing. I understand; I laughed, too, when Mardoun's lackey got tossed into the lochan. No one can blame the lads who tried to block MacRae's men from pulling Mrs. Sinclair from her cottage. But it dinna stop them, did it? And some of the things that have happened lately—stopping Jack on the road and robbing him, breaking into the granary—what does that have to do with fighting the Clearances? You're going to get caught!" She stabbed her forefinger at him. "What if you get transported? Or hanged?"

"We dinna know it was Kensington till after we stopped him, and we let him go." Coll held up his hands in an exculpatory gesture as she drew breath to argue. "I know, I know. You're right. The lads have gone too far. I told them we are not reivers. It's that Will Ross. I knew he would be trouble from the first. He's hotheaded and none too honest. The way I see it, he joined more to get into mischief than anything else." Coll shook his head. "I wasna there; I told them the idea was foolish. But Ross got in their ear this afternoon and convinced them I was too cautious. They only came to me afterwards because they need your help."

"Well, they'll not be getting my help ever again if they land you in gaol!"

"Ah, my fierce Meg." Coll grinned at her, his blue eyes dancing. "What a terror you are."

"You'd do well to remember it." She gave him a sharp nod and turned to pull down a burlap bag hanging from a hook on the wall.

A loud *thud, thud, thud* sounded, and they froze, their eyes darting to the barred door.

3

MacRae," *Meg breathed, and glanced* toward her brother.

The door handle rattled and a hand banged against the stout wooden door again. "Meg Munro! Open up!"

Coll ground his teeth and started forward, but Meg caught his arm and motioned him back. "Nae, stay here. I'll get rid of him."

She crossed the floor to the front window and peered out. As she expected, the narrow form of Donald MacRae was on her doorstep. "It's late to be paying visits, Mr. MacRae."

He turned toward the window. "Open the door, Meg."

"I'm not in the habit of opening the door to men at this hour," she told him, crossing her arms.

"You know you need not fear me, Meg. 'Tis only affection I have for you."

"Affection? Is that what you call it now?" Meg snorted.

"Aye." He stepped closer. "You could have whatever you wanted, you ken, if you'd say the word."

"The word would choke me." Meg regarded him stonily.

His mouth tightened. "You'll change your tune one day. It'll be your ill luck if I don't want you any longer."

"Why are you here, MacRae?"

"Someone set fire to the storehouse tonight."

"Well, it was not I."

"I did not think it was." He smiled thinly. "I am looking for your brother."

"My brother? What does Coll have to do with your storehouse catching fire? Are you needing his help to put it out?"

"The only help I need from your brother is to find out who set the fire."

"I don't know if you're mad or a fool, MacRae, but I—"

"Leave off, Meg," her brother interrupted. She whipped around to see him stride past her and shove up the wooden bar on the door. He yanked the door open and stood towering over the other man.

MacRae gaped at him, and Meg turned away to hide her smile. Coll looked ludicrous. He had pulled one of her aprons, liberally splattered with plum juice, over his head. The garment was far too short and too small, the sash barely meeting behind his broad back. In one huge fist, he carried a wooden spoon, which he now pointed at MacRae as if it were a dagger. "What do you mean, MacRae, hanging about my sister's cottage this late?"

The estate manager straightened, trying to recover his air of authority. "I was looking for you, Munro."

"And you found me." The two men glared at one another.

"Well, then," Meg said crisply, "if all you wanted is to look at Coll, I'd say you've accomplished your goal." She put her hand on the door as if to close it.

MacRae threw up his hand to block the door and turned his sharp gaze on Meg. "You expect me to believe he's been here all evening?"

"I don't waste my time contemplating your beliefs on anything. Coll is helping me make my plum preserves. If it's proof you need, you have only to look in my kitchen."

MacRae shoved past them, stalking into the kitchen. Meg followed him, casting a quick glance at the worktable. She saw that Coll had shoved jars of preserves, bottles of various tonics, and empty containers around the things she'd prepared for Dougal, effectively concealing them. The cramped room was hot and thick with the scent of stewing plums, the pot bubbling away merrily on the fire.

"Satisfied?" Meg asked scornfully, planting her fists on her hips. "Now, I'll thank you to take your suspicious mind elsewhere."

MacRae turned a look filled with frustration and anger on her, then strode back into the main room of the cottage. Turning slowly, he cast his eyes over the entire room. His gaze lingered for a moment on Meg's bed, tucked into a corner of the room and partially hidden by a wooden screen, and Meg's skin crawled.

"Time for you to leave, MacRae." Coll clamped his hand around the other man's bony arm and steered him toward the front door.

MacRae jerked his arm away. "I intend to find the men who started the fire tonight."

"Aye? I guess you'd best be about it, then, hadn't you?"

"You can hide behind your sister's skirts all you want, Munro," MacRae sneered. "But I know you're involved."

"Don't be a fool." Coll loomed over him. "I never touched your storehouse. But you'll have the devil's own work finding the man who did. There's no friend to Mardoun in this glen, only those who work for him and those whom he's beggared for the sake of his profits. Now get out of my sister's house, and if I learn you've been back here bothering her, I can promise you, you won't be finding those men or anything else ever again. Now go!"

Coll closed the door on MacRae's retreating figure, then slammed the bar back into place. Coll turned to her, scowling. "Has MacRae been bedeviling you? Does he dare to come here?"

"Pffft." Meg made a dismissive gesture. "MacRae is a worm."

"More like a snake, I'd say." His hand clenched around the spoon so tightly it snapped.

"Och, Coll . . . now look what you've done." Meg plucked the pieces of the spoon from his hand, shaking her head.

"It's what I'll do to him if I find him nosing around you again."

"Fine. But I would like to keep my utensils in one piece, if you don't mind. I've a great more fondness for them than I do for MacRae." Her lips twitched. "And take off that apron. You look ridiculous."

He grinned back at her. "Nothing convinces people of the truth like making yourself look a fool."

"Ah, no wonder everyone thinks you're sae honest," Meg shot back, and reached out to pinch his arm. "Stop scaring me like this, Coll, I mean it. I could not bear to lose you."

"I know." He sighed. "It's just—what will happen to the men? I worry what mad thing they'll get into if I am not there to persuade them otherwise."

"It doesn't sound as if you kept them from doing it tonight."

"Nae, you're right." He ran his hand back through his hair. "I wish there was some other way to help them. I feel guilty, you ken, safe and secure, working at Baillannan, while they are getting run out of their homes."

"I know. But it isn't your fault; it's MacRae's doing. And Mardoun's," she added darkly. That was just one more reason she needed to stop thinking about the man.

———

It was a good idea, but easier said than done, Meg found. She awoke the next morning from a delicious and disturbing dream about the tall, dark-eyed earl. To make it even worse, her mind kept returning to the dream throughout the morning.

In an effort to distract herself, Meg took her hat and gloves and went to tend the beehive. When finished, she strolled back through the dappled woods in a more peaceful frame of mind, but as she drew close to her cottage, she was brought up short by the sight of a stranger standing at her cottage door.

The man was dressed in severe black and white, like the minister of a kirk, and his pale face looked as if emotions were foreign to it. As Meg watched from the edge of the clearing, the man knocked on the door again, then began to walk around, craning his neck around the corner of the house, even shading his eyes to peer into her window.

"Good morning to you, sir." Meg had the satisfaction of seeing him jump and whirl around at her words.

But the face he presented gave little away, and he nodded to her without any seeming dismay at being caught snooping. "Good morning. Margaret Munro, I presume?" His crisp British accent identified him immediately as one of Mardoun's entourage.

"Aye. And you are?"

"Blandings, miss. I have been entrusted by the Earl of Mardoun with delivering this to you." He reached into the pocket of his jacket and pulled out a folded piece of paper, extending it to her.

Meg's brows rose and she came forward to take the note from him. The paper was sealed across the fold with a blob of red wax, stamped with something that looked rather like a lion standing on its back legs. She looked at it, then back up at the man. "Mardoun wrote me?"

"Yes, miss. His lordship instructed me to read it to you if you were un—that is to say, if you wished it."

"No doubt it will surprise *his lordship* that even though I was raised this far from civilization, I can manage to bumble my way through a few lines of script." Meg snapped open the seal and unfolded the note.

My dearest Miss Munro,

I pray you will allow me to further our acquaintance by granting me the pleasure of your company this evening for a late supper in the south tower.

Yrs,

Mardoun

The paper trembled slightly in Meg's hand as fury flooded her. How dare the man! He had already scheduled an assignation for them and sent a servant to inform her of it? Nothing could have told her more clearly what the earl thought of her.

"I shall be pleased to return to escort you to the castle this evening," the man went on.

Meg's head snapped up and she fixed the earl's servant with so daggerlike a look that the man took a startled step backward. "I dinna need the flunky of some Englishman to lead me about my own woods any more than I need some arrogant lecher's summons to his bed." Meg's accent thickened with her anger. "Mayhap the English lasses dinna mind being treated like one of the muslin company, but not I." Meg raised the note and ripped it in half, then tore the halves again. "Here is my answer to the earl."

Blandings's jaw dropped. "Miss! You cannot mean—it is an insult!"

"Insult, is it? And what do you call this?" She shook the torn invitation at him, then shoved the pieces into his hand.

"Any woman would be flattered—he is the Earl of Mardoun!"

"Well, I am not any woman. And I dinna care if he is the Prince of Wales. Now be gone with you. And tell Mardoun that he can choke on his 'flattery.'"

4

Damon gazed down in astonishment at the torn pieces of notepaper his valet held out to him somewhat hesitantly. "Well. I presume Miss Munro was not interested in dining with me this evening."

"She is a foolish girl, sir." The valet lifted his chin in such a haughty manner that one might suppose he was the nobleman, not Mardoun. "And may I say, sir, I think you would have found her much too coarse."

"You are, as ever, loyal, Blandings. However, you need not soothe my wounded feelings. I have been turned down before." But in truth, Damon would be hard-pressed to remember such a situation. Women of any class were not likely to reject a wealthy earl. It was, in fact, so unusual and unexpected that Damon was not sure exactly how he felt.

There was the bite of disappointment—not of any great consequence, but he had been looking forward to the evening's diversion. He had hoped that Meg Munro might prove to be a continuing entertainment during his stay here. Probably a country girl had little to hold his interest other than beauty, but this woman was extraordinarily beautiful.

Had he misread Meg? It was difficult to reconcile the shredded invitation with the saucy rejoinder she had thrown at him in parting. It occurred to him that perhaps this rejection was simply a coy maneuver. His lips tightened. If Meg Munro thought he would dance to a tune of her making, she was sadly mistaken. Damon enjoyed a chase as much as any other man, but he was not about to let some slip of a girl dictate terms to him.

"Well, 'tis a matter of little importance." He tossed the pieces of paper into the fire. "I did not travel to the Highlands to dally with a female." However attractive she might be.

His daughter was what was important; his purpose in coming here had been to spend time with her, to reestablish the relationship they had once had. From the moment she was placed in his arms as a red-faced, squalling infant, Lynette had captured his heart. But after his wife's death, he had realized that he had over the years become something of a stranger to his daughter. It was far better, really, now that he thought about it, that Meg Munro had not accepted his invitation—though perhaps he would have preferred it done in a less insulting manner.

"I believe I shall take a ride around the estate with my daughter this afternoon." Damon turned toward his desk. "But first, send for the estate manager. I want to hear an explanation for this fire last night."

MacRae, however, seemed uneager to provide one. A few minutes later, when he stood in front of Damon's desk, he shifted from foot to foot, turning his cap in his hand. "It's all under control, my lord. No one was harmed."

"That is fortunate, but I would scarcely describe the place burning to the ground as 'under control.'"

"It's just a few ruffians, sir. I will sort them out soon enough."

"*What* is 'just a few ruffians'? I heard nothing about 'ruffians' in your report yesterday. As I recall, you spoke only of the profitability of turning the land over from raising crops to raising sheep." And a damned tedious report it had been, too.

"There have been some incidents, hardly worth mentioning, my lord."

"Why don't you mention them now," Damon suggested, keeping a rein on his temper. It was not the man's fault that Damon was already in an irritable mood.

"These Highlanders are an unruly lot. They took exception to my bringing in men from the Lowlands, and they tossed one in a lochan. The brigands attacked one of the wagons, but now I send armed guards with any supplies coming in or money going out."

"Attacked a wagon?" Damon's brows rose. "Are you saying these miscreants are armed?"

"I believe so, sir." The man shifted, his brown eyes taking on a muddier hue. "No one was injured either time. They are more bluff than anything, and I assure you I have taken steps to find these men and punish them. There won't be any more incidents."

"Good. I should hate to have an insurrection on my hands," Damon said drily.

"Yes, sir. Of course, my lord."

"You might find it useful to do something to calm the troubled waters. Perhaps if the citizens are resentful of the men you brought in, you could hire some of the locals."

"I have, sir. They are all too apt to be laggards."

"Then I suggest you find something that works." Damon stood up, fixing the manager with a cool stare. "My daughter is with me. Whether it's ruffians or brigands or a whole bloody band of Scots, I will not have my daughter exposed to danger."

Dismissing the man, Damon went in search of Lynette. A ride would improve his spirits, and it seemed a good way to begin to reestablish his relationship with his daughter; horses had long been a bond between them. He found Lynette walking in the garden, her governess scurrying along beside her, attempting to shield the girl from any stray touch of the pale northern sun.

". . . but I won't get lost," Lynette was saying as Damon came up behind them. "I'll take a groom."

"But it is so wild up here," the governess said with something of a whine in her tone that set Damon's teeth on edge. "Think, Miss Lynette. Almost anything could happen. You and your groom could be set upon."

"By whom?" Lynette flung her arms wide out to the side. "Why would anyone attack us?"

"I'm sure I don't know why, but I have heard such tales about the Highlanders! Did we not read about the massacre of the MacDonald clan at that place, Glencrow?"

"Glen *Coe*, Miss Pettigrew," Lynette corrected. "But that was ages and ages ago; everyone seemed to be murderous back then. Anyway, it wasn't near here, and I don't think there are any *Campbells* around. In any case, my great-grandmother's family were MacKenzies, Papa said." Lynette turned and saw her father. He was gratified to see that a smile brightened her face. "Papa! I was just talking about you."

"So I heard." Damon's face softened as he looked at her. "You are right; your ancestors were MacKenzies. And I think we need not worry about any blood feud here."

"Then it would be perfectly safe for me to ride, wouldn't it?" Lynette went on triumphantly.

"But what of your horse, Miss Lynette?" Miss Pettigrew's forehead creased with worry. "Your Freya is still at Rutherford Hall; there may not be one suitable for you."

"Freya is like a rocking chair," Lynette said somewhat petulantly. "I can handle a more spirited mount."

"I should think you could," Damon agreed. "Do you mean to tell me you are still riding your old pony? I thought I put you up on that bay mare a couple of years ago."

No, he realized, it had been more like three years now. Lynette's tenth birthday. He remembered cupping his hands to vault her up onto the horse's back and the way she had trotted around the yard, showing off her skills, black braids bouncing on her back. Something in his throat tightened. That had been the week before that last bitter argument with Amibel that had sent him back to London. Guiltily, he realized he had returned only at Christmas since then.

"Guinevere!" Lynette's fine-boned face lit up. "That is what I called the mare. She was beautiful!"

"You don't ride her now?"

"I—I had to stop." The light in Lynette's face died.

"Miss Lynette was injured," the girl's governess explained in a hushed tone. "Lady Mardoun could not let her get on such a spirited animal again."

"I did not know you had been hurt." Damon frowned in concern.

"I broke my arm." Lynette looked away with a stubborn jut to her jaw. "But it was not Guinevere's fault. I rushed the fence."

"We all come a cropper at one time or another," Damon replied easily. "Best thing is to get back on. I would have thought Ned put you up on her again once your arm was mended."

"He wanted to. I wanted to. But Mama—" Lynette stopped and swallowed. "She did not want me to continue to ride; she thought it was too dangerous. Finally she agreed, but only if I would go back to Freya." Lynette turned entreating eyes to Damon. "But I can ride a better horse than Freya, I know it."

"Of course you can." Damon tamped down his irritation. Sometimes it seemed to him that Amibel had done her best to turn Lynette into a fellow invalid, but it would do no good to criticize the girl's dead mother. "There is a mare in the stables that would be just the thing for you. Her name is Pearl, and she is indeed a jewel. Hudgins had the head groom procure mounts for us, and the man did a good job of it. What do you say you and I try them out?"

"Could we? Really? Oh, Papa!" Lynette reached out to curl her arm through his, squeezing it. "I would love it!"

"So would I." Damon smiled at his daughter, ignoring the wrinkling of concern on the governess's face. "Why don't you and I go down to the stables so that you can meet Pearl? I am sure Miss Pettigrew will excuse you from your studies this once." He cast a glance at the governess.

"Yes, of course, my lord." Miss Pettigrew gave a bob of

acquiescence before turning to Lynette. "Have you your handkerchief, Miss Lynette? Perhaps a wrap against the chill . . ." The governess dug into her pocket. "Here are your smelling salts, just in case you feel faint, and—"

"I am sure Lynette will be fine." Damon covered Lynette's hand on his arm with his hand and, giving a dismissive nod to the governess, started away. "I believe the stable yard is in this direction." In an undertone he murmured, "Is that woman always so anxious?"

A burble of laughter escaped Lynette. "Sometimes even more so. I think she worries that she will be blamed when I fall ill."

"Are you ill so much?"

"I suppose I am." Lynette sighed. "I try not to, I really do. I used to—to find it hard to breathe sometimes. I would cough."

"I remember." He could recall all too well Lynette's small, pale face, the fear that tainted her eyes as she struggled to breathe. "I held you upright; it seemed to help you."

"Did you?" She looked at him with rounded eyes. "I don't remember."

"No, I don't suppose you would. You were a mite of a thing then. Three, I think, that winter when you had such a terrible cough." He saw no sense in bringing up the terror he had felt as he held the child in his arms, hearing the rasp of breath in her throat, afraid the spark of life in her would dim and disappear altogether. "As I remember, your nurse rather resented my presence there, but it seemed to quiet you."

"It scared me when I couldn't breathe," Lynette said in almost a whisper. "But once when I fell off my pony, Ned told me to let go and be easy, trust that the breath will come back. It worked then, so afterward I tried it whenever I had one of my 'spells,' and it helped."

"Clever girl."

"Miss Pettigrew shoves those foul-smelling salts at me, but I do not think they work." Lynette looked up at him earnestly. "I don't have those attacks often, not anymore. I really don't. I *can* run without having an attack. And I have never had one when I was riding, I promise."

"Good." He looked down at her, touched again by the uncertainty that had come to him more than once the past few months. Was he looking after Lynette properly? If she did come home wheezing after their ride, it would be his fault.

Amibel had told him more than once that he expected too much of their daughter, just as he did of Amibel herself. "You have no idea what it is like to be delicate," she had said, her voice filled with resentment. "You're so big and . . . and robust." Her tone had made the word sound like a sin. "Lynette will ruin her health trying to please you, just as I have."

He had retorted that he had never noticed Amibel's attempts to please him, and their row had progressed in its customary bitter way. But he could not forget her words, now that he was his child's only parent, the one entirely responsible for her well-being and happiness. He had never experienced ill health, at least in any serious or lengthy way. Was he wrong to dismiss Lynette's governess's warnings of cold drafts and open windows and too much excitement? Would Lynette suffer for it?

"You must promise me you will not overdo it," he told her now. "When we go out, you must tell me when you are tired."

"I won't be tired." Again that smile flashed like the sun. "I know I won't. I don't get tired when I am riding."

Damon chuckled. "You were an eager little horsewoman. You never wanted our rides to end."

"Did you ride out with me?" she asked, amazed.

"Of course. 'Twas I who put you on your first pony."

"Really? I don't remember."

"I should think not, as you were only two at the time."

Her eyes widened again. "Mama must have been very upset."

"Indeed." His voice was dry. "But you loved it. Do you not remember our rides?"

"I remember when you brought home Guinevere. And I remember one Christmas when we rode in the snow. I had on my favorite scarf."

"I recall. It was bright red." His smile was bittersweet. "I did not realize . . . how quickly children forget."

"Are you sad?" Her brow creased as she looked up at him. "I shall try to remember more."

"No, no, you have done nothing wrong. There is no reason you should remember what happened years ago. Lynette—" He stopped and turned to look into her eyes. "I want to apologize to you."

"Apologize!" She gave him a puzzled look. "Whatever for?"

"Because I . . . have been too little with you in recent years. I should have come home more often. I should have stayed longer." He gave her a rueful smile. "Perhaps interfered more. I can see now that I chose the easier path. It was wrong of me."

"You and Mama did not get along."

He cast her a startled look, but did not argue the point. "That had nothing to do with you. I told myself I was doing what was best, that a girl should be with her mother. That you would be happier without our quarreling. But I think I failed you."

She was quiet for a moment. "But you came for me after Mama . . . was gone."

"Yes, of course. Did you think I would not?" He saw the flash of uncertainty in her eyes, quickly concealed, that told him she had indeed wondered exactly that. He bent down so that his face was level with hers. "I would not abandon you. It was never that I did not want to be with *you*. You must believe that."

"I know, Papa. Mama and Aunt Veronica thought you would not come for me . . . afterward. I heard them talking about it. But I knew you would." Lynette smiled a little shyly and slipped her hand into his, and Damon experienced the sensation in his chest that he had never felt for anyone but his daughter, the tendril of emotion that curled around his heart, part pleasure, part pain, and entirely vulnerable. She added encouragingly, "I remember that you brought me Pudgie."

"Pudgie?" He gave her a mystified look.

She giggled.

"Yes. He was brown and had big, black button eyes and he was ever so fun to squeeze. You brought him to me when you came back to the hall one autumn. I still have him."

"A bear. I do remember him." Damon laughed. "I bought him for you in Germany."

"He slept on my bed for years. Well, actually, sometimes I get him out still," she added confidingly. "When it's stormy.

He's rather a sad sight, though. One eye is all scratched, and there is a patch on his arm."

"Perhaps I should buy you a new one?"

"No," she said scornfully. "I'm much too old for one now. I'm almost grown."

"At thirteen?" He smiled. "Well, then I suppose Pearl will have to suffice." He gave her hand a squeeze. "Come, let's visit your new horse."

They started forward again, and despite being thirteen, Lynette gave a little skip as they walked to the stables.

———

Meg scrambled higher on the rocks, the basket on her elbow banging clumsily against her leg. She paused, poking about, searching the crevices. Turning, she took a look at the sliver of beach between the rocks and the ocean. The tide was starting to come in. She would have to hurry. Gathering her skirts to her knees, she tied them in a large knot, set down her basket, and clambered up.

She was rewarded for her effort by finding bearberry growing between the rocks. Snipping off a clump of the plant, she began to climb back to the shelf where her basket sat. As she set her foot down, the whicker of a horse and the accompanying jingle of its bridle startled her, and she whipped around to see a rider on a large bay horse gazing up at her from the foot of the rocks. The Earl of Mardoun.

"Oh," she said, stiffening. Her nerves danced, and she clenched her hands in her skirts in an effort to control them. "You."

"Yes. I."

Blast the man; he managed to look elegant and cold and powerful despite the wind's having ruffled his hair. Her fingers twitched to reach out and smooth the strands back into place. What an idiotic notion! "What are you doing here?"

Her comment sent the dark slash of his brows higher. "I might ask you the same thing, as it is my beach."

"*Your* beach?" The arrogance of his words, delivered in that crisp accent, the aloof, haughty set of his face, all raised her hackles. "Och, I see." Her accent thickened. "You own the shore. Nae doot all the rest of it is yours, as well." She flung her arm out, pointing to the gray, rolling water. "The ocean maun belong to you. Aye, and the sky, too. Should I ask your leave to let the sun shine on me? Will you take me in for poaching these sprigs from your rocks?" She flung the branch of bearberry in her hand down into the basket at her feet.

His eyes widened a fraction, and his horse danced beneath him. She braced for him to blast back at her in anger, but he only studied her for a long moment, then said, "Clearly you have taken a dislike to me, Miss Munro, though I fail to underst—"

"You fail to understand!" Anger surged up in her so fast and hard it was a wonder she didn't leap off the rock at him. "Aye, what right would I have to be insulted just because you treat me like a doxy? I'm not a lady, am I? Being born in a cottage instead of some fine house makes me of no more notice than the dirt beneath your feet."

"I would say rather that you were of a great deal of notice to me," he shot back. "And my invitation had nothing to do with your birth."

"I'm sure you would have sent an invitation to your bed to some duchess you just met."

"Frankly, I would not send an invitation to my bed to *any* duchess I've met." For an instant humor glinted in his dark eyes.

"It is all a fine jest to you. Would you feel the same if a man had made that sort of suggestion to your sister? Your daughter?" She felt a spurt of satisfaction when his mouth thinned, his face turning to granite. "But a common lass like me, that's a different story."

"It had nothing to do with your station, I can assure you." She had finally goaded him into raising his voice. "I asked you because I found you desirable, though at the moment I cannot imagine why."

"And because you desired me, I must jump into bed with you? I should feel gratified that you dispatched your servant to fetch me, as if I were a dog or horse you had purchased?"

"I sent Blandings because I believed it would create a good deal less stir than my riding up to your door for all to see. I apologize for thinking you might appreciate the discretion."

"You thought I would appreciate your thinking I was a common whore?"

He blinked. "Clearly I do not understand how things are done here, but I assumed that since you were, um, the sort of woman that you are, you would not be averse to—"

"The sort of woman that I am! What *sort of woman* would that be?"

He looked at her oddly. "The sort who—" He made a vague gesture. "Damnation! The sort of woman who lives alone in the woods and does not marry, but takes men into her bed as she chooses."

She clenched her fists, her back rigid. "So because I am

a free woman, I am a trollop? Because I do not choose to shackle myself to a husband, because I choose what man I wish, I am—what did Gregory call them?—ah, yes, Haymarket ware."

"What else do you expect me to think?" he snapped back. "The bold way you look at a man, the way you speak, the way you go about dressed like that." His eyes flickered down to her legs, bare and shapely below her hiked-up skirts. Suddenly the heat in his eyes was different, just as his voice had changed, growing lower and softer.

The air, moments earlier simmering with tension, was now charged with something more than anger, an unmistakable sexuality weaving through the heat of their emotions, intensifying, altering, confusing. Meg was conscious of her heart pounding in her chest, the flush rising up her neck into her face, the breath moving through her throat. She could feel the warmth of the sun on her legs, the ocean mist on her face, the breeze that teased at her curls.

She realized that, amazingly, insanely, she wanted him to rise up in his stirrups and pull her down onto the horse with him. With an effort of will, she jerked her eyes from his and stepped back. Avoiding his gaze, she pulled at the knot she had made in her skirts, usually such a loose and easy thing to undo and now tightly twisted. Or perhaps it was that her fingers had become uncommonly clumsy.

It came loose at last, and she twitched her skirts down. The silence stretched, underscored by the steady rush of the ocean, and she cast about for something to say, some way to end this awkward situation. She thrust her feet back into her shoes and picked up her basket. Looping it over her arm, she forced herself to lift her head. Mardoun was watching her, had been watching her, she knew, the whole time. Meg did not often felt embarrassed, but she did now. Though she didn't know why—he was the one in the wrong, not she. But somehow, knowing that in his eyes she was a low, licentious woman, she felt the sting of shame at the way he looked at her—and even more shamefully, she was aware that something in her stirred at the touch of his gaze.

And *that* was such an irritatingly, unthinkably wrong thing that it gave her the impetus to turn her head away from him, seemingly cool and unconcerned.

"The tide," she gasped. She had been so distracted by their argument that she had not paid attention to the water's moving closer, and now it lapped around his horse's legs, his hooves entirely immersed. "The tide has come in. We must leave. Now."

5

Meg put her hand on an outcropping of rock and
started to climb down.

"Here!" Damon coolly assessed the situation
and edged closer, holding up his free hand while with the
other he controlled the now-restless horse. "Ride with me."

"No!" She stiffened. "I can walk. 'Tis not yet deep."

"Don't be nonsensical. Your shoes and skirts will get
soaked."

"I have been wet before."

His eyes darkened and his face subtly shifted, and she
knew that she had misstepped. Now she was picturing herself in soaked clothes, the material plastered against her
body. She felt sure he was envisioning the same thing. His
voice was gruff. "Get on. Devil take it, woman, I will not
ravish you."

He thought she was scared of him? Meg had too much
pride to let that stand. Avoiding his hand, she crouched close
to the edge of the rock and slid onto the horse behind him.

It was awkward, made even more so by the basket slung over her arm, and she could not avoid grasping his shoulders to steady herself.

The earl turned the horse, heading back in the direction from which he had come minutes earlier. The hoofprints were gone, covered by a steadily rising water. Whether it was the encroaching water or the extra passenger, something made the mount skittish, and he danced sideways from the surf rolling in, so that Mardoun had to rein him in. Meg could not avoid wrapping her arms around the man to stay on the jittery animal.

She clung to him, pressed against his back, terribly aware of the heat of his body, the scent of him, the rise and fall of his chest as he breathed. She could feel the movement of the horse beneath her. She had gotten on astride, as it was easiest, so her legs were immodestly parted as she sat behind him, and she could not keep from thinking about how Mardoun was seated between her legs, flush against her, in as intimate a way as she could imagine—well, not the *most* intimate fashion, but that thought made her flesh heat even more.

Meg had ridden once or twice behind Andrew or Gregory, but it had not felt like this. Indeed, this embrace seemed closer, more sensual, than any of the times when a man had taken her into his arms and sought to kiss her. On those occasions, it had been easy to push away from the man with a laugh or a scornful remark. Her insides had not turned to warmed, malleable wax; no ache had been deep within her. Her skin had not tingled everywhere it touched the man.

It was absurd to be thinking of such things. The earl's opinion of her was worse than low, and she viewed him with equal contempt. He was the last person for whom she should feel a physical response, and yet her body traitorously softened as she clung to him.

Their mount came to a halt, and when the earl tapped his heels against him, it only made the horse shy to the side. Meg felt the muscles of Mardoun's back move beneath his jacket as he tightened his control of the reins, forcibly turning the horse's head. Meg peered around his broad back. They had reached a large boulder that jutted out from the base of the cliff, narrowing the beach to a sandy strip. The horse had to edge around the boulder, stepping into deeper water, and that obviously unnerved him. For a moment, Meg thought the animal would simply balk and they would have to ride back in the other direction, from which there was no easy path up the cliff.

However, the earl's will proved stronger than the animal's, and after a shake of his head, the horse started around the rock, stepping cautiously into the rolling water. A larger wave crashed in, hitting the mount's belly. He reared, and Meg felt herself sliding backward. She clutched at Mardoun, but the panicky jumping and kicking of the animal tore her hands from his jacket, and as the horse leaped forward, Meg went flying backward.

She saw a fleeting glimpse of the gray sky above her before her back hit the water hard, knocking the breath from her, and a wave rolled over her, sending her under.

———

Damon had spotted Meg Munro as soon as he rounded the outcropping, her red hair a streak of color against the gray cliff. He had known he should turn around. The woman had made it clear she wanted no part of him, yet he had let the horse have its head, unwilling to turn away from the sight of her climbing over the rocks, skirts pulled up to her knees, exposing her shapely calves.

The horse had ambled on under Damon's loose hold until he'd pulled it to a stop at the base of the rocks, enjoying the view as she made her way back down. He had seen a number of female legs, and her trim ankles and leanly muscled calves were among the best. Indeed, he thought, they might very well be the winner. And the rounded derriere above those lovely legs was an even more enjoyable sight. She had pulled the skirt forward tightly when she knotted it above her knees, and the fabric was stretched across her buttocks, showing each delectable movement as she climbed down.

Then she turned around, and he had been struck all over again by the beauty of that face, those large, golden eyes. He had realized that he had no idea what to say. He must look a fool, gaping at her like a callow youth even though she had rejected him as surely as if she'd slapped his face.

She had no such problem, immediately lighting into him, and her sharp antagonism had set the fire to his own temper. The ensuing row had been in equal parts confusing, enraging, and arousing, the heat of it all swirling in him until he was unsure whether he wanted to shake her or pull her into his arms and stop that luscious, provoking mouth with kisses.

God, but it was annoying to have her rail at him and yet all the while feel that rich voice with its soft brogue creep through him like honey, thick and sweet. How could he defend himself when he was too entranced by the shape and movement of her lips or the tantalizing view of her legs bared to the knees? He had been relieved—no, it was nearer to elation than relief—when they noticed the tide and he had had a good excuse to get her onto the horse with him. He had intended to cradle her in front of him, his body already tightening in anticipation of that firm bottom against him, but she had thwarted him—of course—by sliding onto the animal behind him. Still, it had been delicious in its own way to feel her tight against his back, her arms circling his chest, her thighs opening around him.

He had been hard as a rock as they rode away, his mind frantically searching for some way out of this situation that would end with her in his arms in a bed. No doubt that distraction had contributed to his losing command of his mount for an instant when the thing reared and bucked in fear. But that arousal had vanished, his body turning ice-cold as he felt Meg's grasp on him slip, then break, and she flew out into the water.

Cursing, he yanked the horse's head down, hard and sharp, and jumped off even as the animal's hooves returned to the ground. The water broke around his knees as his eyes searched the gray water. He saw her bright head come up, and she struggled to stand, the water not yet waist deep around her.

"Meg!" He started toward her as another wave hit her from behind, knocking her legs out from under her and sending her beneath the water again. It was too slow, too cumbersome, trying to run toward her through the waves, his boots filling with water, and he leaped forward into the water in a shallow dive and swam toward her.

The water was murky with sand stirred up by the crashing waves, and his boots and jacket were heavy encumbrances, but he found her. Grabbing her hair, he hauled her up by her arm. They floundered to their feet, lurching and stumbling, spluttering. His arm around her, Damon started toward shore, but once more a large wave struck them, sending them under, and he felt the fierce tug of an undertow dragging them out.

Damon struck out to the side, not fighting the pull, but moving across it. She was swimming, too, but he dared not let go of her lest he lose her again. Her soaked skirts dragged at them. So did his jacket and boots, and he cursed himself for not pulling them off before he plunged in. But how could he have taken the time?

They slipped away from the undertow, and he turned toward the beach again, going with the water, letting it lift and carry them in until he could stand once more. They waded in, falling down on the wet sand not far from the rocks where they had originally set out. He staggered to his feet, reaching down to pull her up, but Meg was already rising. He looked up the beach and saw that the outcropping of rock that had proved their undoing was now lapped with water, blocking the beach in that direction. No doubt his riderless horse was halfway back home by now. He whirled, searching the other direction.

"Where's another path up?" he asked, starting that way though he could see nothing but cliffs and rocks.

"You'll only find the channel to the loch that way. Come! Follow me!" She grabbed his hand and darted up the beach. He followed, his boots squelching and sloshing with every step.

She slanted across the sand to a jumble of rocks and began to climb. He heard the rip as she stepped on her skirt, and she reached down, impatiently grabbing up the hem and continuing to climb, the torn piece of her petticoat trailing along behind her.

He looked up at the sheer cliff face above them as they climbed. "Where the devil are we going? Do you plan to perch on the rocks like seagulls through high tide?"

"You'll see," she panted, not stopping.

When they topped the last boulder, Damon saw a hole behind it in the side of the cliff, dark and half his height. Meg plopped down on the rock, catching her breath. She skimmed her wet hair back from her face, twisting and squeezing the mass, dark now with moisture. He dropped down beside her.

Even after the tumble in the water, she was beautiful, drops clinging to her lashes and skin. He watched a stray drop trickle from her temple down over the curve of her cheek, traversing the soft skin, rosy from exertion. He thought that if he drew his finger across her cheek, she would feel like rose petals. His groin tightened.

Damon looked quickly away. What a foolish thing to be thinking, stuck on top of a pile of rocks above the ocean. He pulled off his boots and dumped the water from them, setting them aside. He ran his hands through his hair, dispelling the water, and glanced at Meg again, squeezing water from her skirts. Her fingers were long and slender, and he could see their strength as she wrung out the fabric. It was easy to imagine those fingers on his skin.

If he continued to think like that, it would prove a trying time as they waited out the tide. He wondered how those hours would unfold. Would they sit here in silence? It would be pleasant to look at her, but equally difficult to keep his thoughts from straying to the erotic. If she had not taken such a dislike to him, the hours could have passed quite enjoyably, but he doubted that he could repair the damage done.

Clearly he had taken a serious misstep with the woman, but he was confused as to exactly where he had gone wrong, much less what it would take to melt her resentment. He should not have sent her an invitation via his valet, of that much he was certain. But had the offense lain in sending Blandings? Had Blandings said something insulting? Done something? Damon had to admit that his valet could be something of a snob.

Or was it the note itself? Had his wording been clumsy? He could not remember precisely what he had said, but he was certain it had not been anything blatant or crude. It struck him as decidedly peculiar that she would resent an attempt to be discreet, but what seemed to anger her most was that he had sent her a note at all instead of showing up at her door. Was it that she wanted others to know he desired her, that it gave her a certain cachet to be the object of an earl's attention? His assumption that she was a woman of easy virtue had infuriated her, yet she had readily admitted that she wanted no husband, that she chose men as she pleased. So it was not actually an issue of her virtue, but of the way he'd acted regarding her virtue. Perhaps she wanted him to play a game, pretend that he thought her a maiden who must be seduced into letting him into her bed.

He cast another look at her through his lashes. He did not like to engage in pretense, but the thought of seducing Meg Munro struck him as delightful. Unfortunately, he had already put himself at a grave disadvantage. She despised him, and whatever he said to her only seemed to make the situation worse. What was it she would want? He counted himself a sophisticated man, and it was rather dismaying to find he wasn't sure what to do when it came to a simple country girl.

"Are you all right?"

"What?" He turned toward her in surprise.

"Any cuts? Sprains? Anything broken when your horse tossed you off?" She surveyed him assessingly.

"I wasn't 'tossed off,'" he corrected, affronted. "I dismounted so I could save you from drowning."

"Save me?" She raised her eyebrows. "I didn't need 'saving.' I am quite able to swim out of three feet of water."

"Yes, no doubt that is why I saw you go under twice." Sweet heaven, this girl was prickly. "Clearly the undertow had no pull on you."

"Yes, well . . . it was rather forceful." Meg looked abashed. "I was frightened." She paused, then added in a softer voice, "Did you really jump into the sea to help me?"

"Yes, of course." He looked at her, puzzled.

"Oh. Well . . . thank you. That was kind of you."

"Did you think I would not?" He scowled. "That I would have ridden off and left you to drown?"

"I don't know. I don't really know you." She turned away, smoothing at her skirts.

"Yet, not knowing me, you are ready to believe the worst of me."

What was he doing even contemplating trying to win this woman over? Tempting as she was, she could not possibly be worth the trouble. Meg Munro was prickly and baffling and odd. She made him feel off-balance and . . . foreign. Those flickers of hunger whenever he looked at her could easily be fed when he returned to the city. He would be here only a month or two; he could live that long without a woman in his bed. After all, he had had no expectation of bedding anyone while he was here.

He changed the subject, determined to be civil during the time they had to spend together. "How long will it be before the tide goes out again? I assume we must wait here until that happens. I see no way up this cliff."

"There's not, unless you can climb like a cat. But we don't have to wait. I know another way out." She pointed at the opening in the face of the cliff.

"That hole?" he asked doubtfully. "A cave? But how—"

"You'll see." She stepped over to the opening and dropped down on all fours. "Follow me." Tossing him a mischievous grin, she crawled into the darkness.

6

Damon stared at her retreating back. Then, with a sigh, he grabbed up his boots and crawled in after her.

He was relieved to find that after the first two feet, the rock above his head sloped up at a sharp angle so that he was soon able to stand. He peered around him. The area was sunk in gloom, the only light the slanting pool of sun coming through the low entrance behind him. He could see no sign of a wall in any direction, only darkness. The stone floor of the cave was fairly level and dusted with fine grit. A boulder loomed to his right, and across from it a thick stalagmite thrust up from the floor, looking like a huge, milky icicle in the midst of melting.

"Miss Munro." He turned to Meg. She stood in front of the boulder, her face pale in the velvety dark, her eyes large, their amber color seeming to pull in all available light. "How does this cave offer a way out?"

"These cliffs are honeycombed with caves. Many of them

interconnect, and it is possible to pass through them and emerge on the other side. One exit comes out above my cottage, and I know the way."

"In the dark?" he asked skeptically.

"Come, my lord." Her smile flashed teasingly. "Do not tell me you are afraid of the dark?"

"I admit I have a healthy fear of running into a rock wall or tumbling into a hole because I cannot see in utter blackness."

"We can keep from doing either." She stepped around the boulder and bent down, then turned back, holding up a lantern. "I have this."

He stared. "You so often traverse the caves?"

"I don't usually go all the way through them, as it's a twisty, up-and-down route, longer than the cliff path. But I do go into a number of the caverns often enough, searching for moss."

"Moss? What on earth for?"

"There are several lichens that are useful." She squatted down and busied herself lighting the lantern. "Iceland moss. Irish moss, which I find in one of the lower caves; it grows on rocks submerged in water. Very helpful for coughs."

"Ah, yes, potions and such." Amusement tinged his voice. "I was told you were a witch."

"You seem to have been told a great many things about me." She fixed him with a steely gaze. "I do not practice witchcraft. I find that magic is what ignorant minds attribute to skills they do not understand. I am a healer; I create teas and tinctures and balms to help with a variety of ailments. There is no sorcery involved, only knowledge of plants and illnesses, passed down through hundreds of years."

"I beg your pardon." He nodded his head to her gravely. "I have clearly been misinformed on a number of topics."

"Yes, you have." She shrugged and stood up. "There are many people who are too 'modern' or 'scientific' to believe that my 'wee folk cures' can heal a person. That is fine. I help those who come to me and do not worry about those who do not." Meg picked up the lantern, clearly dismissing the topic. "Come. It's this way."

Hastily he pulled on his soaked boots and hurried after her. The boots, squishing unpleasantly as he walked, were also gritty with sand from his dousing in the murky ocean— as was seemingly every other part of him, from his hair to his toes. The first thing he would do when he got home, he decided, was to get into a tub of warm water and wash away all the sand and salt.

"Is that how you live?" he asked, faintly intrigued by the thought, as he followed her up the path. "Selling your, um, tonics and tinctures and such? That is how you are able to, ah . . ." He trailed off, suspecting he was about to raise her ire again.

"Aye." She glanced over her shoulder at him, her eyes dancing with amusement. "That is how I am able to survive without payment from a man. There are some ways, you see, for a woman to make money without lying on her back."

"Miss Munro," he said somewhat stiffly. "I do apologize for impugning your character. I did not intend to insult you, I assure you."

"I know." Again she shrugged, her voice light and care-less. "It is not the first time I have been accused of selling my body rather than my remedies."

He felt a twinge of guilt, perversely strengthened by

there being no complaint in her voice as she said it. He should not have acted so quickly, he thought, should not have relied on the word of his housekeeper, whose nature, he had known from the way she spoke, was sanctimonious. He had been, he thought, all too eager to have Mrs. Ferguson brand as licentious the woman for whom he lusted. If he had approached Meg himself, if he had played the game of discovery and desire, he would have realized how little she was like any other women he had known.

She baffled him. What, he wondered, would it be like to pursue a woman who was not angling for some form of payment, whether marriage, a carte blanche, or coins in her hand? A woman who could choose to let a man into her bed without considering what he would give her in return. How would it feel to kiss lips that sought pleasure instead of doling it out? How differently must her moans of passion ripple through him when she had no need of anything from him except himself?

He had never considered this before, and the notion stirred him—a response, he suspected, amplified by the sight of Meg's form in front of him, the curves of her body delineated by the wet garments that clung to her. His eyes dropped to the movement of her hips beneath the material, the muslin rendered almost translucent by moisture. Her enticingly rounded bottom flexed and contracted as Meg walked up the rising path.

His gaze slid down her legs, ankles bared as she held up the skirts to walk. Meg's feet were bare, her shoes having been torn off in the roiling sea. Her pale feet were long and elegant, like her hands, and he thought how it would feel to glide his fingers over her legs, to take that narrow, arched foot in his hand, to drag his thumbnail along the sole and watch the shiver run up her body.

Damon realized that despite his good intentions a few minutes earlier, he was once again tempting a lust that was all too easily aroused by Meg. Blast it, he normally had more control. But when it came to Meg Munro, nothing seemed to be as normal.

He tried to concentrate on his surroundings. They passed through tunnels and caves, some cavernous, some so narrow it felt as if the walls might close on him at any moment. In minutes he was turned around, with no idea how to retrace his steps. He sincerely hoped Meg's confidence was not misplaced.

The walls oozed moisture, their surfaces rippled and slick in the lantern light. He saw stalactites and stalagmites, some thick and others no larger around than his wrist. Here they might appear as dry and grainy as a salt pillar; there they resembled a melting candle; still others looked like a sheet of water frozen as it ran. Most were varying shades of white and tan, but in one low-ceilinged cave, the rippled sides were a muted rainbow of colors. It would be a wonderful place to explore . . . when he was not wet and filthy. And cold.

Inside the caves, out of the sun, the temperature was constantly cool, pleasant enough if one was dry, but enough to make one shiver when covered in sodden clothes. Still, even the chill could not thwart the lust rising in him. Indeed, everything about their circumstances seemed to arouse him. Their situation was intimate, alone together in the quiet dark. He could not drop back lest he lose the narrow circle of light cast by her lantern. Her scent teased at his nostrils; he could feel the warmth of her body. If he stretched out his hand, he could slide it down her back and over that tempting derriere. Once thought, that vision was difficult to banish.

She turned to caution him about a low tunnel ahead, and he could not keep his eyes off the wet cloth that molded to her breasts, clearly outlining the thrusting points of her nipples, sharpening in the cool air. The folds of fabric draped from the gown's high waist normally concealed the shape of her body, but plastered wetly to her skin as they were now, he could follow every dip and curve—the narrowing of her waist flowing out to feminine hips, then down to thighs and calves. Her body was revealed, yet still concealed in a fashion more titillating than bare skin. His fingers itched to reach out and pull that fabric aside, to slide down her bare skin, slick with moisture. The mystery of her made him ache to explore her, to find out what shade of pink her nipples were and whether that bright flame of her hair was echoed farther down, to map the curve of her back and steal between her legs, seeking the heat.

Desire throbbed in him, a sweet pain that made it difficult to think of anything but her body and all the ways he wanted to discover it, the secrets he wanted to know. It only increased when they reached a ledge and she pulled up her skirts to climb up on it, exposing her legs all the way past her knees. He could not keep himself from reaching out to give her a helpful boost, one hand at her waist and the other under the tantalizing curve of her buttocks, and it was all he could do not to let his fingers roam farther afield.

She scrambled quickly onto the rock, turning her head to shoot him a warning look. But he saw that her chest was rising and falling more quickly, too, and he smiled to himself as he climbed up after her. A short passage followed in which they had to crawl their way along a tunnel, presenting Damon, behind Meg, with an entertaining view. They emerged in a small chamber where, amazingly, clear water fell from a small ledge higher up, cascading into a wide, shallow cup of rock and running off in a stream.

"A waterfall!" Damon stared at it in amazement. "Here in the depths of the rock."

She nodded, smiling. "Yes. I took a small detour to reach it. I could not pass up the opportunity." She started toward the shallow pool. "Come."

"What?" He gaped at her. "You expect me to stand beneath a flood of cold cave water?"

"Unless you enjoy having sand all over you," she tossed back as she stepped beneath the waterfall.

He stared at her, struck dumb and motionless by lust. She stood in the crystal cascade, water sluicing over her hair and body, plastering her clothes even more tightly to her form. He watched, his throat dry, as she turned her face up to the spate of water, eyes closing, and let the water flow over her. She turned, reaching up to hold the neck of her bodice away from her back so that the water poured over her skin inside the gown.

Cold be damned, he thought, and yanked off his boots, dropping them onto the floor of the cave. He stepped into the waterfall with her. There he received his second shock. "It's warm!"

Meg laughed, turning toward him. "Yes. It's fed by a hot spring. There's another spot higher and farther along where it runs quite hot, but by the time it reaches here, it's a wonderful temperature."

He had to agree. It was like being bathed in warmth and comfort. Except that there was no comfort to be had, not when he was standing a foot away from Meg Munro, watching her comb her fingers through her hair, separating the strands to let the water wash the sand from it. He tried to be practical and mature, but the knowledge that he was essentially bathing with her even though they wore all their clothes was almost too much for his control. He felt the water running over him, warm and sensual, sliding beneath his clothes, and knew she was experiencing the same sensations.

His eyes roamed her body, feasting on her with his gaze, and hunger thrummed in him, hot and heavy. The touch of his eyes was not nearly enough. He craved to feel her, hold her, have those legs wrap around him and that softness press into him. To steal the water drops from her lips with his tongue, to open her mouth to his and taste its sweetness. Hunger quivered in him, need rushed through his veins.

Damon took a long, quick step and pulled Meg into his arms.

———

Meg saw the flare of heat in his eyes and knew what he was about to do. In an instant, his body was against hers, his mouth taking hers. She felt the heat. The urgency. Everything within her surged in response. Men had grabbed and kissed her before, but she had never felt anything like this.

This was no drunken pawing, no clumsy groping by a callow youth. This was a man who knew how to kiss, who, no matter the eagerness with which he kissed her, moved his mouth against hers in a seductive, expert way. Her lips parted before his, and she heard the satisfaction in the soft noise he made. Then his tongue was in her, exploring, arousing, and she could not hold back a quiver at the pleasure in it. One of his hands fisted in her hair, the other clutched the fabric on her side, holding her in place.

The waterfall poured over him, breaking over and sliding down his head and neck and onto her cheeks, warm and sensual. Meg curled her fingers into the lapels of his jacket, holding on to him as her muscles melted. She had never imagined such bright frissons of sensation shooting along her nerves, had never dreamed what need, what fire, could explode in her belly. His kiss brought up a deep, primitive ache in her, and she was aware of a shocking urge to rub herself against him. Heat blossomed between her legs. He changed the angle of his kiss, and his hands slid down her back, firm and sure, and rounded over her buttocks, his fingers digging into the soft mounds and pressing her into him. She could feel the hard length of him against her. That, too, had happened a time or two before, when she had not been able to evade one of Andrew's aristocratic, young friends who thought she was there for his pleasure, but she had felt no excitement then. Her abdomen had not turned achy and malleable as hot wax as it did now.

Damon tore his mouth from hers, kissing her cheek, her jaw, her throat, his breath hot upon her trembling flesh, until he came to her ear and took the lobe teasingly between his teeth. Surprised, she could not hold back a little moan, and at that, the heat in his body flared. He murmured something low and throaty, her name, she thought, and his tongue traced the delicate whorls of her ear. She shivered, fueling the throbbing ache deep within her.

"No . . ." she murmured weakly, though she could not have said whether the remark was intended for him or for herself.

"Yes." His voice was as low and shaken as her own. "Oh, yes."

He cupped her breast, a movement so unexpected, so tantalizing, it brought a gasp from her. His thumb stroked across her sensitive nipple, separated from his touch by only a layer of wet cloth. She might as well have been naked to him, she thought, and somehow that idea, too, sent shivers through her.

As if he knew what she was thinking, his fingers slipped beneath the neckline of her dress, gliding down across her bare skin, delving beneath her chemise. Light as a feather, his fingertips eased over her until they found the hard button of her nipple. His forefinger circled it, so gently she could almost believe she imagined it. But she was certain she could never have imagined anything so piercing and sweet, so el-emental. His mouth moved downward, taking its delightful teasing over her neck and onto her chest until at last his lips reached the swell of her breast. His breath came hard and fast, and she could feel the tension in his body, taut as a bowstring though his mouth moved so leisurely, softly, as if he had all the time in the world and was willing to spend it all on just this. He nuzzled aside the neckline of her dress, nudging it downward, skimming it over her breast, until at last the nipple popped free. He let out an odd little noise, faint and indistinct, half sigh, half groan, and his tongue delicately circled the tip.

Meg jerked, startled by the intensity of the sensation that shot through her. She felt too hot, too breathless. Her head swam, and she thought that at any moment she might simply break apart and fly off in all directions. It was exhilarating. Terrifying.

With a small, strangled cry, Meg pushed away. Whirling around, she ran from him.

7

Scooping up the lantern, Meg threw herself back into the low tunnel. Behind her she heard Mardoun let out a low curse. She did not pause or look back, just crossed as fast as she could and swung herself over the ledge to the path below. She slowed then, for she could not run away, leaving the man alone in the dark. But she did not turn to look for him, only loitered until she heard him jump down from the ledge behind her.

"Meg, wait."

She ignored him, too rattled and embarrassed to even look at him. All she wanted was to leave behind this tangle of heat, confusion, and desire.

"The devil! Stop running away."

"I dinna run away!" That pierced her pride, even more so because his aim was far too accurate, and she stopped to face him.

"You did a bloody good imitation of it."

"I am trying to get us out of here. I thought that was what you wanted."

"Of course it is, but"—he took a step forward—"back there—"

"This is scarcely the time for dalliance," she said sharply. "Now I'm going home. I suggest you follow me."

He looked as if he would like to say more, but he swallowed his words. "Of course. Lead on, Miss Munro." He gave her a sardonic bow, sweeping his arm out as if ushering her through a doorway.

Meg made her way unhesitatingly through a series of caves, each one dropping farther below the last one, in reverse of the rising path they had climbed earlier. At last she could detect the glimmer of light before her, and she ducked under a rock overhang to emerge into a vaulted cave. A slice of sunlight from a high, narrow split in the rock brightened the chamber. Boulders of varying sizes dotted the floor, and Meg went straight to a tumble of rocks at the foot of the cave wall. Dousing the lantern and setting it aside, she climbed up the rocks until she reached a point where only the sheer cave wall rose above her. There, a thick, knotted rope dangled from the narrow entrance near the top of the cavern.

Mardoun followed her. "You mean to climb that rope?"

"Of course. It's the way out." She narrowed her eyes at him. "Are you unable to do it?"

"I believe I can manage it," he told her drily. "It was you I was wondering about. A lady's skirts would scarcely—"

"We have already established that I am not a lady." She reached down and swept up her skirts, knotting them as she had earlier. Grasping the rope with both hands, Meg planted her feet flat against the cliff wall and began to scramble up, hand over hand.

Below her, Mardoun grasped the rope, holding it steady. As Meg crawled over the lip of the cave, she heard Mardoun start up the rope behind her. Standing up, Meg pulled in a lungful of air and looked around her with the faint sense of relief she always experienced when she left the caves. She had never feared them, but she far preferred the sun and earth and trees.

"My home is not far," Meg said as Mardoun came up behind her. She realized belatedly that her words sounded too much like an invitation, so she added quickly, "The way to Duncally is easy after that."

Meg wound through the trees, coming out on a path so faint that few but she would have recognized it as such. Mardoun kept pace beside her, not saying anything—for which she was grateful, as she was far too jangled and edgy to speak. Really, what was there to say?

She could not explain, even to herself, why she had melted in the man's arms. After all her anger and resentment, she had given in to him without a second's hesitation or protest, no doubt proving to him that his low estimation of her was accurate. She despised her weakness. More than that, she was stunned by it.

Meg Munro was accustomed to being in control. She went where she wanted, she did as she pleased. She made her remedies from precise recipes; she measured, never estimating, never substituting or deviating unless she had thoroughly tested it. When she birthed a babe, she gave orders and others followed. She set the limits for her suitors with equal certainty.

But this afternoon, she had been swept away by his kisses, swamped by sensations and emotions she'd never known. She had been a stranger to herself, not a reasonable, intelligent woman, but a roiling mass of need and desire. She had wanted, she had ached, she had rushed on thoughtlessly. It was not that she had not heeded her wiser instincts—she had not even considered them. She still tingled with energy, every sense awakened, her body alive and hungry. And what she hungered for was *him*.

Meg cast a sideways glance at Mardoun. He was a handsome devil, she'd give him that. He had the sort of jaw a man should have, and long, mobile fingers that caused her insides to dance just looking at them. His thick, black hair, those dark, piercing eyes, deep set beneath fierce slashes of brows, the long torso, tapering into narrow hips. She had never posited what features in a man appealed to her, but she knew now, looking at him, that he possessed them.

She wanted him; it would be foolish to deny it. She ached to feel again the storm that had rolled over her when he kissed her: the rush of heat and excitement, the pure pleasure that had invaded every inch of her from head to toe.

But that was impossible. In those moments with his mouth on her, his heat and scent enveloping her, she had thought of nothing else. If the power of her feelings had not been so strong that they frightened her, she would have gone further, deeper, more headlong into the passion. If she kissed him again, if she let him glide his hands over her, she knew it would not end until they were in bed.

But she refused to sleep with him. She wasn't about to give Mardoun the satisfaction of proving his assumptions right. More than that, she could not allow herself to *be* the kind of low, loose woman he thought her—and wasn't that exactly what she would be if she tumbled into his bed? She could not give herself to a man who clearly held her in contempt.

Her mother had raised her to be a strong woman, powerful and independent. It was the way of the Munro women, and Meg embraced the philosophy. They did not abjure men. Nor were they the sirens of some folks' telling, luring a man just to get with child, then casting him aside. Her mother had loved her father all her life and had borne him two children. She rejected only the shackles of marriage. Meg had never expected to do any different—though, now that she was almost twenty-eight, she was beginning to wonder if such a thing would ever happen to her.

Meg wanted a man and intended to give herself to one someday. But she also wanted love. Or at least respect and affection. She would not sell herself cheap, would not squander herself on some tawdry fling with a man who desired only to relieve his boredom for a week or two.

Her cottage came into view, a low, brown, thatch-roofed house, snuggled into a curve of pines and silver birches. An ancient yew guarded the cabin, spreading its branches over the roof. In the dappled shade beneath the trees grew ferns and tall stalks of foxglove, their vivid purple, bell-shaped flowers trembling in the breeze. A neat herb garden was laid out beside the house and further sheltered by a low stone wall, rosemary, sage, and lavender lightly scenting the air. A larger vegetable garden lay in the flat, sunny glade beyond the house. Roses climbed up the dun wall on one side of the wooden door, and on the other, colorful flowers added another splash of color. In the distance, among the willow trees, one could hear the burble of the burn that ran down to the loch.

"Is this your house?" Mardoun asked.

"Aye, it is." Meg braced for his comment. Her home was lovely to her in every way, but she thought it must seem small and insignificant to the Earl of Mardoun. It could fit in its entirety into a drawing room at Duncally, with room to spare. But when she looked over at him, she saw nothing on his face but intent interest.

Meg opened the door and stepped inside, Damon ducking his head to follow her through the low door. She went straight to the fireplace and stirred the fire to life, adding more blocks of peat before she turned back to Damon. He was simply standing there, gazing around curiously. It occurred to her that he might never have been inside a cottage of this size, with the rough plastered walls and the well-worn furniture, everything—for eating, sitting, and sleeping—lumped together in the same room.

His eyes roamed the walls, taking in the cabinets of jars and pots and herbs, the small fireplace, and settling finally on the bed in the corner, only partially separated from the rest of the room by a folding wooden screen. Something in his face changed subtly, and Meg felt a blush rising in her cheeks, her abdomen suddenly flowering with heat.

Annoyed with both him and herself, she gestured toward the fireplace. "No doubt you'll wish to warm yourself by the fire. If you hang your jacket on the chair, it will dry a little."

She crossed to the sleeping area and pulled dry clothes out of the chest of drawers. Behind her, she could hear Mardoun moving about. She stepped behind the screen and hesitated. It was incredibly awkward to change clothes not twenty feet away from him, separated only by a screen. Even if he acted like a gentleman—not a certainty, given how he regarded her—the situation was inherently suggestive. He would know she was naked. He would hear the sounds of her undressing and could visualize her stripping off her dress and undergarments, just as easily as she could imagine him shrugging out of his jacket. Would he take off his wet shirt as well? His breeches? Surely not, despite the discomfort.

Meg skinned out of her dress and let it drop to the floor, followed by her petticoats and undergarments. She was in too much haste to don a chemise and petticoats, so she merely pulled on an old, simple sacque dress that hung straight down and was fitted to her only by pulling the sash tightly around the waist and tying it.

She stole a peek through the narrow crack where the sides of the folding screen joined. Mardoun had removed his jacket and the waistcoat beneath it as well as the sodden stock around his neck. His fine lawn shirt was plastered against his skin, practically transparent. She could see his skin and the shape of the muscles beneath it, the dark blur of the hair on his chest tapering down to his waist, the brown circles of his nipples. He tugged his shirt out of the waistband of his breeches, and Meg held her breath. He unbuttoned his shirt, though he did not take it off but opened it wide and turned to face the fire.

Meg swallowed, her hands clenching in her skirt. She was a terrible hypocrite, thinking the earl might not respect her privacy, yet here she was, staring at him avidly. Disgusted with herself, she turned to the chest and picked up her comb to untangle her wet hair. Thank heavens she had washed the sand and salt from it in the cavern waterfall.

And that, she thought, was a dangerous thing to contemplate. Better to forget altogether that moment when she had been so close to him, the warm water streaming over them, the look in his eyes, the searing touch of his hand.

Meg closed her eyes. When she opened them again, her gaze went to the mirror, and across the room she could see Damon in front of the fireplace. He stood facing her, his shirt hanging open and loose, revealing a strip of bare skin down the center of his torso. He was watching her, and the heat in his eyes was enough to take her breath away.

"Meg . . ." he said, his voice low and rasping, and the timbre of it seemed to vibrate through her. "Come stand with me. 'Tis warmer here."

His gaze tugged at her, but she said faintly, "I am fine here."

"Much easier to dry your hair by the fire." A smile hovered on his lips, inviting and challenging. "I'd be happy to help you untangle it."

"I can manage it myself," she retorted, but started forward anyway.

"Ah, but my way is much more . . . entertaining." He watched her walk toward him, his gaze as tangible as a caress on her breasts, her hips, her legs.

She stepped up to the fire, keeping a careful distance between them, and crossed her arms over her chest. "Lord Mardoun, you seem to have the wrong impression."

"Have I?" Now, to her irritation, amusement tinged the sensual heat in the man's eyes.

"I did not change my mind. I have no intention of getting into your bed."

He reached out and took a strand of her hair, assuming a

thoughtful expression as he slid it through his fingers. "One has to wonder, then, why you invited me into the waterfall with you."

Meg flushed. "So you could wash the sand and salt off you. That's all."

"Really?" He smiled into her eyes. "It had nothing to do with curiosity? With desire? With wanting to feel this?" He stroked his knuckles down her cheek. "Or this?" He leaned in and brushed his lips across hers.

She knew she should pull back. Should tell him to stop. Something, anything but stand here mutely, staring into his eyes and trembling. Yet she could not seem to move, even when he boldly plucked the comb from her to slowly work it through a handful of her hair, watching the strands separate and fall in the glow of the firelight.

"It's like the sunset," he said softly. "Red as fire but filled with light as well." His gaze shifted to her face. "But it cannot match the brilliance of your eyes." He took her chin between his thumb and forefinger, tilting it upward. "Nothing could. They're like the sun, your eyes; they could melt a man where he stood."

He bent and pressed his lips to hers again, not briefly now, but taking his time with it, luxuriating in the pleasure of the kiss. Passion sparked in Meg, as hot and fast as it had in the waterfall—no, even more than that, for the memory of it simmered in her, flaring up now with greater fury. She felt her skin heat, and his flesh responded. His hands were on her, not pressing, not gripping, but skimming up and down her body with the lightest possible touch, bringing every nerve in her to clamoring life.

Meg moved closer to him, wanting to feel his hard, male

strength against her, yearning to have his arms wrap around her like iron, but he held back, possessing her with his lips while his caresses stayed agonizingly light upon her. With one hand, he twitched open the bow of the sash behind her back, so that the dress fell loosely about her.

Damon's hand slid under the neckline and onto her breast, and his breath chuffed out in satisfaction. His fingers moved across her flesh, finding the buds of her nipples and teasing them to hardness. The wide neckline was easily shoved down, exposing her breasts. Meg was too lost in the delights of his mouth to feel embarrassment. When his mouth left hers to move to her breast, she could only gasp at the pleasure blossoming in her.

The gentle suction of his mouth seemed to pull all the way through her, tugging at the deep, dark heat pooling low in her abdomen. Clenching one fist in her skirt, he bunched it up, until finally his fingers found the bare skin of her thigh. Meg shuddered at the touch, and he smothered a low groan. His fingers traveled up her thigh, sliding onto the rounded curve of her buttocks, then, shockingly, stole between her legs.

"Ah," he breathed, nuzzling into her neck. "You're like the sun here, too, blazing hot." Meg gasped at the unexpected touch of his fingers on such an intimate place. "Shh, now," he soothed, pressing his lips to the tender flesh of her neck. His voice had a hint of a chuckle, a rich, ripe masculine smugness, as he went on, "Yes, heat in plenty, and sweetly wet, as well." He nipped at the cord of her neck as he stroked her.

She dug her hands into his arms, rocked by the sensations flooding her. Feeling his fingers upon her there was shocking, yet no disgust or repulsion rose in her, only a need to have more. She wanted to move, to grind herself against him, to part her legs and bring him flush against her. Her breath came raggedly, and she had to bite her lip to hold back a moan. His mouth returned to hers; his hands came up to yank down the neck of the loose dress so that it hung down around her arms, and her breasts were bared to him. He cupped his hand around them, thumbs stroking across the soft flesh.

A whistle sounded in the distance, sharp and distinctive. Meg jerked back, staring at him in frozen horror. A moment later there was a shout, faint but plain: "Meg!"

"Oh, my God!" she exclaimed. "Coll!"

8

Meg jumped back as if she had been shot, hastily pulling her clothes back into order. Mardoun simply stood, staring at her dazedly. She darted to the window to peer out, retying her sash as she went.

"Coll?" Damon repeated. "What—who—" His brows rushed together. "Who the devil is Coll? The man I saw with you in the village?"

"What? No." Meg turned back toward him, her voice a mixture of puzzlement and panic. "Get dressed. Quickly. He'll be here any moment."

"Who is Coll?" The heat was still in his voice, but from an entirely different source now. "Your lover?"

"What?" Meg gaped at him. "No! Get dressed, you fool!" She ran to the bed and grabbed up a blanket.

"Is that why you refused me the other day?" He took a long stride toward her. "Because you already have a lover?"

"Oh, yes! Of course! That had to be the reason I turned down someone as magnificent as you. Because I belonged to another man." She hurled the folded blanket at him. It would have hit him straight in the face if he had not reached up to grab it. "I don't have a lover, and I turned down your 'gracious' offer to bed me because I did not want you!"

His eyebrows shot up. "I believe we just answered the question of whether you want me." He gestured toward the spot in front of the fire where they had just stood. Jamming the blanket beneath his arm, he strode to the window, buttoning his shirt. "What in the—" He swung back to her, his dark eyes hard as slate now. "That's not the man you were with in the village!" He started toward her. "How many men do you *have* dangling on a string?"

Meg planted her fists on her hips. "A hundred! A thousand! I cannot count the number!"

Before Damon could answer, the door swung open, and Coll stepped in, carrying a brace of pheasants in one hand. "Meg, what are you shout—" Coll halted abruptly, his mouth dropping open. His gaze went from Mardoun to Meg, then back to the man standing in Meg's house, jacketless, shoeless, and damp. Coll dropped the birds and started forward, his hands bunching into fists. "Who the devil are you? What are you doing here?"

Unsurprisingly, the earl did not answer Coll's questions, but merely assumed as haughty and disdainful an expression as Meg had ever seen. Mardoun shifted subtly into a wider stance, his hands curling into fists as Coll's had done. "I might ask you the same question—but it's obvious what you are about." Mardoun nodded toward the birds Coll had dropped on the floor. "Poaching my game."

His words checked Coll for an instant as his eyes widened

in understanding. "You're the bloody earl!" Fury flooded his face. "It's not your game. And neither is Meg!"

Coll charged Mardoun.

Meg sprang forward and planted herself between the two men, holding her hands out warningly toward each. "Stop! Coll!"

Coll did as she said, but, his expression murderous, he started to slide around her as his eyes remained on the earl. "Get out of the way, Meg. You canna think I'll stand by and let this lord make sport of you."

"Move, Meg," Mardoun said behind her, his voice ice to Coll's fire, but no less deadly. "I've a mind to teach this oaf you do not belong to him."

He, too, made to bypass her, but Meg moved with them, keeping her body between them. "Stop it! Both of you. I do not belong to either of you." She shot the earl a furious glance, then turned the same angry gaze on her brother. "Coll, step back. I will not have you shaming me in my own house. I was on the beach, and the tide caught me on the rocks. The earl rescued me. He came into the sea after me when I fell in; he saved me from drowning. We had to come back by the caves. He is here to dry out a bit. That is all."

Coll glowered, shooting a suspicious look at Mardoun, but he relaxed his fists and stood still.

Meg swung around. "And you! Coll is my *brother*. He is the gamekeeper for Baillannan, and what he brought me he has permission for from the Roses. You do not own everything here, me, least of all. Now . . ." She looked back and forth between them, giving them equal doses of her scorn. "Listen to me. I am my own woman and the property of no man, be he earl or brother. This is my house. And whomever

I choose to invite into it is no concern of either of you. Have I made myself clear?"

"Indeed." Mardoun folded his arms, his voice as aloof as his expression.

"Good." Meg looked at Coll inquiringly.

"Oh, aye, Meg." He let out a gusty sigh and stepped back. "You always do."

"Very well, then." She swiveled back to Mardoun. "Thank you, my lord, for helping me. I imagine you are eager to be on your way home. Just take the path that way." She pointed in the opposite direction from which Coll had come. "When you reach the standing stones, take the path to your left, and—"

"I am sure I can make my way home from there," he told her stiffly. He snatched up his wet garments and boots, then inclined his head toward Meg. "Good day, Miss Munro." His glance flickered toward Coll, but he said nothing, merely gave him a short nod before he strode out of the cabin.

Coll waited until Mardoun was gone before he swung back to his sister. "Now, would you mind telling me what that man was doing here?"

"I did so already. Did you think I was lying?"

"I'd like to see the day when *you* get caught by the tide."

"Well, here it is, so I suggest you enjoy it."

"Why were you on the beach with that villain anyway? And what were you doing to make you forget about the tide?"

"We were having a row, not that it's any of your business."

"And the tide washed you off the rocks?"

"No, of course not, I was on his horse and the thing

reared and sent me into the water. The undertow took me, and—"

"You were on his horse? What the devil were you doing on his horse?"

"Trying to escape the rising water, you fool!" Meg stamped her foot down hard, though since it was unshod, it failed to make her point. "What do you mean interrogating me like this? I am a grown woman and have been for many years. You have no reason to know every detail of my life, much less any right to it."

"I know full well you're an independent sort, and I dinna pry into your business," Coll said loftily. Meg rolled her eyes. "Not as much as I'd like to, at any rate." His face relaxed into a small smile, and Meg had to do the same.

"I can take care of myself, Coll. You know that."

"Aye, I do." He nodded and picked up the birds he had dropped, carrying them into the kitchen. "But this is the Earl of Mardoun we're talking about."

"Do you think I'll be so dazzled by his fine name that I'll lose all good sense and leap into his bed?"

"No, of course not. I know you care nothing for a title or wealth or any of that. But he's a powerful man, and his sort is used to taking what they want. Just think what he's doing to his crofters! That tells you what manner of man he is."

"I know that full well. Do you think I'm daft? I have no interest in jumping into his bed." That, she reflected, was a lie, so she added, "I won't sleep with him."

"And what if he doesn't care what you want, only what he wants? He's an English lord, and they're accustomed to doing whatever, however, they please to the Highlands, and never being punished for it."

"Och, Coll, you need not worry about that. The man is too used to crooking his finger and a woman running to him for him to chase a lass who's unwilling."

"Some men prefer a chase," Coll told her darkly.

"I know how to discourage them." Meg smiled and linked her arm through his. "Here, sit and talk with me. I was about to fix a cup of tea to warm me up. Will you have some?" As he nodded, she went on merrily, "And we can talk about what lass *you're* chasing now."

"Meg . . ."

"Hah! Now the shoe is on the other foot, eh?" She filled up the kettle with water and hung it over the fire to boil, then plopped the teapot onto the table and measured out the tea. "I hear you've been courting Dot Cromartie up the glen."

"I may have danced with her once or twice at Danny's and Flora's *réiteach*."

"Walked her home, was the way it was told to me."

"That, too. She is a bonnie lass."

"She is."

Coll heaved a great sigh. "But the fact is, you might as well talk to a stump. Better, really, for at least a stump disnae giggle and say, 'Oh, ye're so clever, Coll!'"

"Some men like a bit of admiration, I understand," Meg told him drily.

"As do I, but it disnae mean much coming from one who knows so little."

Meg laughed. "I could not see you being content with her. You've always had a liking for bluestockings. As I recall, you were quite smitten with Isobel's governess."

"Aw, Meg . . ." His voice turned plaintive as a dull flush rose up his neck.

"You used to bring her nosegays, I mind. The gardener was furious with you for snipping off the roses."

"I was twelve at the time."

"And so earnest."

"I am glad I was able to afford you so much amusement," he told her sourly.

"And Isobel, too." She reached out and patted his hand, saying more soberly, "Sometimes I think it was not fair to you for us to be taught with Isobel and Andrew and Greg. I don't know how you'll find any woman around here who can converse with you about your books and such."

He shrugged. "I'd rather have the knowledge. You'd have the same problem, I think."

"I am not as fond of books as you."

"A bonnie face can make up for not loving books."

"So I've heard."

"All I ask is more curiosity and intelligence than Dot Cromartie."

"That's setting a low standard." Meg grinned, and stood up as the kettle whistled.

When she returned from the kitchen and poured the water into the pot, Coll changed the subject. "Alan McGee is back in the glen."

"Da's home?" Meg smiled and returned the kettle to its place. "Have you seen him?"

"No. He will pay me a visit as soon as he needs something."

"Ah, Coll." Meg made a little clicking noise with her tongue. "Don't we all come to you when we need something? Me? Isobel? Half the glen, in fact. You are too hard on him."

"*You* are too easy on him, and so was Ma. I cannot fathom why women are always so foolish about the man."

Meg chuckled. "Look in the mirror and maybe you'll understand. He's a fine-looking man, our father, and charming, as well."

"And rootless. And feckless. It scarcely makes me proud that I resemble him."

"Still, he is your father. And we've little enough family." Meg's voice turned a little wistful. "We never met out grandmother. Ma did not even know her father's name. And Ma herself died far too soon."

"We have each other. And growing up as we did, the Roses are almost family."

"Almost. But that's not the same. I love Isobel, you know that, and yes, we are close as sisters—closer than many I've seen. But Baillannan is not our home. And their past is not our past. Did you not ever feel, growing up there, that we did not truly belong? That we were always different . . . apart . . ."

"Aye, they're not our family by blood. And we *are* different—from everyone, really. The Munros always have been." Coll frowned. "I'm not sure what you're saying, Meg. Do you—do you wish you were something other than a Munro?"

"No! Oh, no, never that." Meg reached out and took his hand. "I'm proud of our family, and I would never have wanted anything other than the life we have had. I don't want any brother but you—or sisters or cousins, either. I just wish . . . wouldn't you like to know more about us? About the Munros who came before us? For all that was handed down throughout the years through generations—the remedies, the cottage, the way we live—we really don't know about the *people*. Our grandmother, for one. Do you know aught but that her name was Faye and she died giving birth to Ma? I don't. What was she like? How did she look? Who did she love? Wouldn't you like to know who our grandfather was? Sometimes I think there may be people somewhere about here, people I've walked past all my life, and we've got the same blood running through our veins, but I'll never know."

Coll looked at her, considering. "Truth is, I've never thought about it. I suppose I'd like to know who our grandfather was, but it does not trouble me. Most like, he was another such as our father." Coll shrugged. "Here and then gone. Never there when he was needed."

Meg's eyes softened, and she reached over and laid her hand upon Coll's. "But *you* are. Da is a will-o'-the-wisp, and I take him for what he is—loving the music and laughter in him and expecting naught else. You are my rock and always have been. Never think I dinna treasure that."

"Even when I poke my nose into your business?" Coll quirked an eyebrow at her, the beginnings of a smile tugging at the corner of his mouth.

"Even then." She laughed. "But I'll still ring a peal over your head when you do."

———

What a bloody irritating female! Damon started down the path, pulling on his boots as he went, half hopping along. He was too furious, too in need of movement, to stop and pull them on rationally, though he had little doubt that he looked like a buffoon. But then, he had looked like a buffoon with this woman at every turn.

She had dismissed him—*dismissed* him, like a servant or

a guest who had outstayed his welcome. Just sent him on his way—after she'd tied him up in knots. Teasing and arousing him until he was ready to burst, then shoving him aside at the sound of another man's arrival. No wonder he was wound like a too-tight clock, ready to spring apart in every direction.

Jealous! Him! It was absurd. Devil take it, he was the Earl of Mardoun; he had never felt jealousy over a female a day in his life. Women were easy to come by and easy to let go. When a mistress had sought to rouse his jealousy, threatening to give her favors to another gentleman, he had merely smiled and wished her Godspeed.

But there he had been, jealousy spearing him like a red-hot lance when the man had casually entered Meg's cottage as if he owned the place and everything in it. Fury had swept over Damon, all his frustrated, pent-up hunger swirling into a chaotic need to strike out. He had been eager to fight, wanting to smash his fist into the fellow's face, some deep, primitive instinct in him hungry to draw blood.

He thought of Meg throwing herself between them. It had given his heart a lurch, knowing that if he had already started to swing, he might have hit her. Then, bizarrely, lust had shot through him anew at the sight of her, standing her ground as fierce, as haughty, as demanding, as a warrior queen. How strange that her denial of any obligation or tie or subservience to him should make him desire her even more.

He had also felt a fool to learn the fellow was her brother. How was he to have guessed that? The big, blond bear of a man looked nothing like Damon's golden-eyed, fiery-haired Scottish temptress. He could not blame her brother for lashing out at him. Who wouldn't, upon finding a half-dressed stranger in his sister's house? And if the man—what had she called him, Coll?—and what sort of name was that?—if Coll was in the right of it, that meant Damon was in the wrong, and that was another position he was unused to occupying.

Then, as he stood there, roiling with unspent anger and unsatisfied lust, Meg Munro had told him to leave her house. Crisply, coolly given him his congé. He ground his teeth just thinking about it.

The only thing to do was to avoid her. If she thought to make him dance to her tune, she would find out she was sadly mistaken—though God knew, Meg was bloody good at playing the tune. She blew hot and cold, beckoning then retreating, building one's frustration to a snapping point. He was not one to delude himself that no meant yes. If a woman did not cast out lures, he did not follow. He had not, after all, pursued her after her blatant rejection of his invitation. He had done nothing . . . until she stepped under that waterfall in the cavern.

She had to have known the picture she presented, standing there with the water sluicing over her, the hunger it would pull up in a man. Then—sweet Lord—she had invited him into the water, too. Asked him to join her. Urged him to stand only inches from her in that warm stream, her mouth close to his, her body ripe and temptingly revealed in the garments clinging to her.

When he had kissed her, there was no denying her response. She had kissed him back, rising on her toes to deepen the kiss. He had felt the response of her body beneath his hands. Then, as the need had surged up in him, she had broken off and run away.

It had been hellishly frustrating. But only minutes later, when he had kissed her in front of the fire, no reluctance had been in her, no shyness or rejection. She had been eager, hungry. He remembered the moan that had escaped her when his fingers found her center, the sweet pooling of desire there. The scent of her was still on his skin.

His steps slowed, heat rising in him again at the memory. He realized suddenly that he had come to a complete stop, standing there daydreaming about the woman like a moonstruck calf. His jaw tightened. It was best he remember that right after that kiss, she had sprung away from him, turning once more into a sharp-tongued virago.

Meg Munro was playing him like a fish on the line.

"Lord Mardoun! Sir!"

Damon turned and saw the head groom riding toward him down a narrow path he had not even noticed.

"Thank heavens you're all right, sir!" The groom pulled the horse to a stop and jumped down. "You are all right, aren't you, my lord?"

"Yes, I'm fine. I wasn't paying enough attention and got tossed off." He wasn't about to go into what had actually happened. Noticing the man's gaze going to his damp clothes, Damon added, "Into the sea."

"Aye, weel, makes for a softer landing, that. Red Ryan's a good horse, though. Not usually sae skittish." His tone was anxious, and Damon knew he was afraid Damon would get rid of the animal. It increased his respect for the man, already bolstered by his ability to judge horseflesh.

"No, it was not his fault. You're right; he's a good horse."

"Guid, then." The man brightened, then hastily added, "I mean, it's guid to see you're unhurt, my lord."

"I trust Red Ryan returned home."

"Oh, aye, my lord. Joseph found Red grazing in the pasture. I dinna ken what had happened to you, but I dinna want to worry the lassie, so I went looking for you first."

"Exactly right."

The groom extended the reins of the horse to him. "Just tak that path up to the house, sir. It cooms out below the gardens. It's faster that way, you ken. Not well marked, so it's easier to wander astray there, but Goldie knows the way well. Gie her her heid, and she'll tak you there true enough."

The man was right. Goldie was a bit of a plodder, but she was certain of her route. And if Damon had not been damp and increasingly cold as the afternoon slid away into the half-light they called gloaming here, he would have enjoyed the view of the loch and the large, gray house on the other side, of his own Duncally rising above him in a way that lifted the heart.

Predictably, his valet was aghast at the damp, dirty state of Damon's clothes. As Blandings directed the servants to fill up the tub with hot water, he picked up the garments one by one, tut-tutting over their state. Damon had to smile at the horror on the man's face as he inspected the earl's boots.

Damon sank into the bath with a sigh of satisfaction, leaning back to soak, letting the heat seep into his bones and banish his weariness and aggravation. A faint, pleasant scent of pine permeated the water from some oil Blandings had put in. It made Damon think of Meg's cottage, nestled among the Scottish pines and white birches.

It had been a relief to see that cottage as it carried the prospect of warmth and rest, but something more had tugged at him. Quaint and charming, it had fit into the curve of the trees as if it had been there always, the dun hues of its stone walls and thatched roof blending into the browns and greens of the landscape around it. Flowers of all sorts were bright splashes of color against its dull walls. On the lift of the breeze came the scents of pine and rosemary and sage and half a dozen other smells he could not identify, mingling pleasantly in his nostrils. Even still charged with lust and bound with sexual frustration as he had been, his first thought had been of peace and contentment. Of welcome.

He had followed her into the tiny house, and it had wrapped around him, dizzying his heightened senses. Dim and warm and redolent with herbs and spices. He had looked around him, surprised by the cabinets and row upon row of shelves lining the walls, filled with jars and bottles and bags, some empty, others filled to varying degrees with herbs or liquids or creams. Plants of all sorts hung in bunches from the ceiling on one side of the room, and the entire place was permeated with odors, some sharp and pungent, others mellow or sweet or richly, darkly earthy. He had been drawn to it, as he usually was by the foreign, the unfamiliar. It was intoxicating. Exotic.

Damon drifted on the memory. He thought of looking across the room and seeing Meg's bed, half-hidden from the rest of the cottage by a wooden screen. The partial concealment only added to the allure, lending an air of secrecy to the soft, inviting expanse. Impossible not to think of sinking into the bed with Meg beneath him, naked and eager.

Meg had gone behind the screen to undress, and though she had been invisible to his eyes, his mind had seen her well. Each plop of a sodden garment on the floor had carried through the silence of the room and vibrated within him.

He had imagined her white body revealed inch by inch—the full globes of her breasts, rosy-tipped, the sweet curve of her body, in at her waist then out again to her hips, the indentation of her navel, beckoning the touch of his fingers, the soft triangle of hair, as fiery as the locks on her head.

Even now, as he remembered the moment, the hunger that had gnawed at him all afternoon sprang again to full, clawing life, and he knew he was a fool to think he could ignore Meg Munro. He wanted to see her again, to be in that bed with her, to explore and taste her. To sink into her heat and softness until he was mindless with pleasure.

What did it matter if it took a little time and patience to win her over? He had plenty of time here and little to do. He need not give over his power by pursuing her, but he could wait and watch. He could woo. He could let her lead him on or he could pull her back.

But before this was over, Damon promised, he would have Meg Munro.

9

Meg woke up, her heart pounding, her skin dewy with moisture. She sat up, shoving the thick braid of her hair back over her shoulder. Strands had tugged out of the braid and coiled damply all around her face. She had been dreaming. She wasn't sure about what, but she knew it had left her hot and sweating and breathless, a deep, sweet ache between her legs. And she knew it had featured the Earl of Mardoun.

She flopped back against the pillow. Outside, the sky had lightened, so that her room was dimly visible around her. It must be near dawn. Any thought of falling back into slumber was useless. What a nuisance that man was; now he was invading her sleep.

The Earl of Mardoun. Master of Duncally. Her mouth twisted wryly. He had kissed her senseless, had made her ache and yearn and feel all sorts of sensations she never had before, and she did not even know his first name. Indeed, she was not sure of his last name. The family had been MacKenzie once, long ago, before the last female heir had married an Englishman. She wondered what the women he took to his bed called him. Mardoun? My lord?

A little giggle escaped her lips at the absurdity. She could not imagine a man of his importance, his stature, his hauteur, allowing some ladybird the use of his given name. But, in retrospect, he had little hauteur in him yesterday afternoon when he had hauled her up against him and kissed her so deeply, so fiercely, that she had felt it down to her toes.

Letting out a low noise of frustration, she sank her fingers into her hair, shoving it into further disarray, and slipped out of bed. Whatever was the matter with her? How had she come to this—twisted into knots over a man, so twisted that she dreamed of him? And over such a man!

Going over to the window, she shoved it open and let the cool morning air wash over her. The sounds of the birds waking came to her, the familiar scents of trees and plants perfuming the air. In the morning silence she could even hear the distant trill of the burn tumbling over the rocks on its way to the loch. It was home, familiar and wonderfully peaceful, but for once the sight and sound of it did not ease the tangle of feelings inside her.

What was she going to do about the Earl of Mardoun?

She wanted him. He was a wonderful thing to look at, with that long, muscular frame and the intense dark eyes, the thick sweep of black hair. From the instant she saw him, just the look of him had stirred something deep within her. And if she was honest—as Meg prided herself in being— more than that drew her. He was unlike any other man she had ever known.

Meg had told Gregory that she knew the earl's ilk, that

he was the same as the young aristocrats Andrew would bring home with him on holiday, but it had taken only a few minutes with the man to know that was not true. Aye, pride was in him in full measure, an arrogance that scraped at her nerves. But he had none of the bumbling or uncertainty of those callow youths, made no attempt to impress or intimidate. Instead, power and certainty radiated from the man, a casual acceptance of his place in the order of things.

God help her, that quality drew her. He knew the world, had seen things Meg had never known or even heard of. He was polished and sophisticated, with a dry wit and a voice as smooth as silk. He was unknown, unfamiliar, and he challenged her, rousing some deep and primitive instinct to bring him to heel, to pierce that cool and confident exterior and bring forth the heat that lay beneath. To find the fire in him that matched her own.

But being attracted to a man and letting him into her bed were far different things, and until yesterday Meg would have said she had no problem keeping a man at a distance, however sinfully enticing he was. But yesterday's kisses had shown her weakness. His touch, his mouth—Lord, the very scent of him, it seemed—set her afire. She wanted him with a fierce hunger she had never before experienced, never even realized she could have for a man.

But how could she give herself to such a man? How could she lie with someone who had no thought for others, who was capable of callously tossing out his own crofters because he saw more profit without them? A man who valued gold over people and himself over everything. She had seen for too many months now the results of Mardoun's orders—the families cast adrift, old women and men expelled from the homes they had lived in since childhood, and children torn from the only world they knew—to believe he was a man of character. He was cruel and thoughtless, and a devastating smile could not change that.

Some would argue that passion did not require love or even liking, that all that mattered was seizing the pleasure she craved, even if only for one night. Indeed, many around the glen believed that was precisely Meg's pattern and that of the Munro women before her—taking and discarding lovers as the whim moved them.

But in fact the Munro women, while they valued their freedom from the constraints of men and marriage, believed in love and fidelity. Her mother, Janet, had taken no other mate than Alan McGee, and she had loved him till the day she died. Meg had always assumed she would do the same. She had begun to think that she would never fall in love, but even if that was not her destiny, it did not mean that she should lower her standards.

If she gave in to her desires, if she lay with such a man, without any sort of affection or even respect between them, then she would be exactly the sort of low creature Mardoun had assumed she was. She would not, could not, do that. It seemed the worst sort of jest that the one man whom she had ever wanted was the one she wanted least to be with.

Thank heaven Coll had come along when he did. From the look on the earl's face as he left, Meg suspected that Mardoun would not be importuning her again. She only needed to avoid Duncally while he was here. He would soon return to London, and her problem would be solved. The key, she knew, was to keep busy.

Over the next few days, Meg threw herself into drying

and grinding, mixing and distilling. She visited a mother with a sick child. She went to the caves seeking replacements for the mosses she had lost in the fiasco at the beach. She made Susan Murray an infusion of Our-Lady's-thistle for her man, not saying (since she was sure Susan knew it full well) that the best solution to Duncan Murray's stomach ailments was for him to limit the whiskey he imbibed. And if Meg's busy fingers could not keep her mind from straying to thoughts of hot dark eyes and a smile that would lighten one's heart, well, surely that would pass.

One afternoon she heard a tuneful whistling coming toward the cottage, and she smiled, setting aside her work. She knew that merry lilt, the tone, the tune. The man walking up the path to her door was tall and handsome, his thick, blond hair shot through with streaks of gray and worn a bit too long and shaggy. That casual, careless inattention to his grooming was, she reflected, one of the similarities to his son that would make Coll scowl if she pointed it out.

Their father's square-jawed face was another, though on him the lines were softer. Alan McGee's eyes were not so vivid a blue, and far more wrinkles ran out from his eyes and alongside his mouth. The hands, too, were different, not wide and work-scarred, but with long, sensitive, agile fingers capable of coaxing the saddest, merriest, loveliest of notes from the strings of a fiddle.

"Meggie, my love," her father said, stretching out his hands and taking her into a hug. He was warm and smelled of aromatic pipe tobacco, his rough wool jacket scratchy against her cheek.

"Da." She went up on tiptoe to kiss his cheek. "I'm so happy to see you. Come in and sit. Let me make you some tea."

"Nae, no more tea, lass, though I'd take some of that fine plum cordial of yours."

"Then you shall have it." She linked her arm through his and led him inside. "Coll told me you had returned from Edinburgh."

"Did he now? Haven't seen the lad. Don't expect I will 'less I beard him in his den."

"I don't think Coll will eat you," she tossed over her shoulder as she pulled a bottle and cups out of a cabinet.

"Aye, weel, he'll roar loud enough, I expect." Alan shrugged philosophically. "I canna blame him. I was no' the father I should hae been to him." He took a sip of the cordial and let out a sigh of satisfaction. "Ah, that's it, lass. There's none can touch your plum cordial . . . though I wouldna hae said so to your mother. Proud of her cordial, Janet was."

"And rightly so. She taught me how to make it, after all."

"Aye, she did. And though she'd hae had my heid if I'd agreed, she said yours was sweeter." His eyes twinkled. "I would tell her I preferred a bit of bite with mine."

"I'm sure you did, you old flatterer." Meg patted his hand.

"It's ayeways been easier with you. It's that way with dochters, I'm told. Sons, now . . ." He shrugged. "No doot that's why you dinna see a flock with two rams, do you?"

"I suppose." Or perhaps, she thought, she had just not needed as much from him as Coll had. She changed the subject. "How was Edinburgh?"

"Grand as ever. There's ayeways somewhere that needs a fiddler, you ken." He began to talk of the dances he'd played, both large and small, the pipers he'd joined, old friends he had seen again. Finally, with a sigh, he said, "Still, it wears on you, the noise and the people. A body canna find a spot to be quiet in. And the Highlands call you back." He settled back in his chair and took another drink.

"I don't think I could stay in the city as long as you."

"Och, no, you couldna. Your ma would hae run from it screaming, as well. There's some as are made for the braes and the burns. I expect you're one of them."

"I might like to see the city sometime," Meg protested. "I would like to travel."

"Aye, you micht, true enough, but I wager it wouldna suit you lang."

"You're probably right." Then, because it had been on her mind recently, Meg said, "Da . . . did Ma ever tell you aught about her mother?"

"Faye?" He looked at Meg in surprise. "Nae, not much. She never knew her, you ken. Faye died bearing her, and her gran brought Janet up."

"I remember Gran a little. She had a cloud of fluffy, white hair, and she liked to slip us a sweet when Ma wasna about."

"Did she now?" Alan laughed. "I thought she was a fearsome woman. Course I was courting her granddochter and she dinna favor me much." He chuckled. "Gran Munro did not favor anyone, as I remember." He shook his head, his eyes lit with a distant fondness. "But Faye, now . . . there was a beauty."

"You knew her?" Meg straightened. "You knew Ma's mother?"

"Oh, aye. Weel, Janet was eight years younger than me, so I was a lad when she was born. And everyone round the loch knew Faye Munro. Och, but she was beautiful. I remember I thought she must be an angel. You favor her, lass."

"Really?" Meg leaned forward, intrigued.

"Indeed. Though her hair was black as a winter night, not flaming like yours. But she had those same shining gold eyes. I mind Gran Munro saying once, when you were wee, that you had Faye's bright eyes. Fair made her cry, that. Only time I saw tears in her, I'll tell you." He gave a sharp nod.

"I didn't know," Meg said wonderingly.

"Janet's gran wasna wont to talk about Faye, and Janet dinna like to press her, for it made the old woman sad to speak of her. She was young to die, Faye, and oh so bonnie." His face was tinged with sadness. "I maun write a lament for her. That would hae pleased your ma. I'll play it at Janet's graveside."

That was, Meg thought, exactly the sort of sweet, artistic, and theatrical thing that was typical of her father, the sort of gesture that brought a wistful smile from most women—and earned a roll of the eyes from Coll. Meg's reaction was usually a bit of both.

"Do you know who Ma's father was, then?" Meg asked, pulling him back from his bittersweet reverie.

"Oh, nae! None do. If Gran knew, she never told. That woman was silent as the grave if she took a mind to it. Everyone wondered, even years afterward. No one could name any man she favored, you ken, and Faye never spoke of him. The Munro women were ayeways something of a mystery to the rest of the glen—and all the more alluring for it." He gave her hand a pat. "There were rumors, of course. Some said it was a British soldier after Culloden, that one of them found Faye in the woods one day and had his way with her. It wasn't an unlikely story, and you could see why she and her ma wouldn't have spoken of it. Others were more romantic—a lover who died in battle. Even Bonnie Prince Charlie himself."

"That seems a bit unlikely for a man running for his life from the British, I'd think."

"Aye." Alan grinned. "That's what your ma said, too. You Munro women are a sadly unromantic lot. There were other tales, even more fanciful—they said he was a selkie or maybe a fairy king, drawn by Faye's great beauty. Janet suspected her father was one of the MacLeod brothers, from sooth of Baillannan. The MacLeods had flaming hair, you ken, like your ma and you."

"The MacLeods." Meg narrowed her eyes, considering. "Robert MacLeod?"

"Nae; he's their cousin. There were two or three of those lads, all gone by the time I was wooing your mother. David was the one Janet thought, for he moved away after Faye died."

"Where did he go?"

"I dinna know." Alan tilted his head, considering. "You should talk to Angus McKay if you want to find out anything there."

"Old Angus?" Meg lifted her eyebrows. "Why?"

"Weel, he's a cousin to the MacLeod lads on his mother's side, you ken, and he and David were great friends as I remember."

"I'm not sure my curiosity is enough to make me beard Angus McKay in his den." Meg chuckled. "Still . . . he does like my comfrey cream when his joints are aching. Perhaps a pot of it would make him a wee bit friendlier."

"Aye, there you are. You can sweeten even old Angus." Alan drained his glass. "Ah, weel, I maun be gaun. I maun practice if I'm to fiddle at the Grieg girl's wedding tomorrow. Will you be there?"

"Of course, especially if you will be playing."

"Miss Meg!" The urgent, high-pitched voice made Meg stop and glance toward the window. "Miss Meg!"

Meg jumped up and went to the door, her father on her heels. Tommy Fraser was running toward them, his arms waving wildly. He stumbled to a stop before them, bending over and gasping for air.

"Ma . . . says . . . to come."

"Is she ill? What's wrong?"

"Nae. No' that." He went on in bits and spurts between his gasps. "'Tis the stones. Mardoun's man means to pull them down."

"What!" Meg stared at him. "Are you sure?"

"Aye, my uncle Ronald hires out to him now and then. They need the coins something fierce, you ken. MacRae's man coom by and told Uncle Ronald to coom help. They're tearing down the circle, and the Troth Stone's first. Ma said you'd care about the Old Ones."

"She'd be right," Meg said grimly. She turned toward her father. "Da, give Tommy a drink and one of the oatcakes."

Lifting her skirts, she took off at a run for the ring of standing stones.

W ill we pass by the ring of stones as we go to the beach?" Lynette pulled her mare up beside Damon's horse as they picked their way down the rocky slope. "I can see them from some of the terraces."

"We could go that way if you wished. I believe there's a path from the circle to the sea." Or they could take another path from the circle, one that led to a snug, brown cottage set among the trees.

But they would not. Damon refused to make a complete cake of himself. He had already laid his plans to see Meg without arriving like a supplicant on her doorstep. With any luck, that would occur tomorrow evening. Anticipation fizzed in him at the thought.

"I would like to see the standing stones," Lynette went on. "I've read about Stonehenge, and they seem much like it. It makes one wonder, doesn't it, how people raised them so long ago? And why."

"It does indeed."

"Miss Pettigrew says they are heathen things."

"No doubt they were. They have been there since long before Christianity came to these shores. Though I don't know why that matters." Damon glanced at Lynette thoughtfully. "Perhaps it's time you had a more educated tutor. Someone who could provide you some challenge."

Lynette turned to him, her eyes lighting. "Truly? I would like that. There are so many things besides needlework and poetry. I am a very poor poet." She hesitated, some doubt creeping into her expression. "But what of Miss Pettigrew? Would you send her away? I should hate for her to be without a position."

"If you wish to, I will keep her as well to teach you comportment and painting and such and add a tutor for the more difficult subjects."

"She fusses a great deal. But Miss Pettigrew means well. She was most devoted to Mother."

"Naturally."

"She writes to my aunt, you know," Lynette offered.

"What? Who? Miss Pettigrew?"

"Yes." Lynette nodded. "She corresponds with Aunt Veronica."

"I see." He didn't really. Amibel's sister Veronica was not so dedicated to having delicate health as his wife had been, but she was equally proud and stiff, narrow in her thinking and utterly without humor. He could not imagine why anyone would wish to write to her, much less have to read her replies. "No doubt Lady Veronica enjoys getting news of you."

"I think it is more news of you she wants."

"What? Why on earth would she want news of me?" He turned his head. His daughter was watching him with mischief in her eyes.

"It's my opinion Aunt Veronica has designs on you." Lynette giggled as he gaped at her.

"It's *my* opinion you are trying to cut a sham with me," Damon retorted.

"No! Truly. When Aunt Veronica called on us before we left, she was dressed very smartly, and whenever you spoke, she was rapt with attention. You probably did not notice because women frequently act that way with you. You're quite a catch, you know, being a widower."

"And I thought it was my charm"—he laughed—"when it's only my marital availability. But I think you must be mistaken about Lady Veronica. I doubt I could meet her standards."

"We shall see," his daughter told him airily.

"I believe this path will cut across to the stones." Damon turned his horse's head, pushing aside a low-hanging limb.

They passed through a copse of trees to the edge of a broad clearing, and Damon pulled his mount to an abrupt halt. The ring of tall, narrow stones lay before them. Damon felt an odd atavistic tug in his gut at the sight of it.

But a scene nearer to them captured his attention. Another stone stood on this side of the circle, half the height of the others. In the middle of the rock a round hole had been hollowed out—whether natural or man-made, he could not tell. Two men were wrapping a length of rope around this peculiar stone, watched over by Mardoun's estate manager, who sat nearby on a horse. Several more men stood a few feet away from the stone, shifting on their feet uneasily. The cause of their unease, Damon assumed, was the crowd of on-lookers, sullenly watching and muttering among themselves.

"Papa! What are they doing?" Lynette turned toward him, puzzled.

"I haven't the faintest notion." He started to nudge his horse forward, but he stopped as a woman burst into the tableau, bare legs flashing beneath her raised skirts, red hair streaming out behind her.

"Papa! It's that beautiful lady again!"

"So it is," Damon murmured.

"No!" Meg Munro planted herself in front of the rock, arms outspread. The beauty and fury blazing out of her face were enough to stop any man in his tracks. "You willna do this!"

"Out of the way, Meg!" Donald MacRae rode forward on his animal. "We're taking down that rock."

"I'll see you dead first," she tossed back.

"Are you threatening me?"

"Nae. I'm telling you straight out, if you tear down that stone, you'll rue it the rest of your short, miserable life."

The estate manager's face flushed. "You cannot stop us. Move or we'll pull it down atop you."

"Are you planning to do the pulling yourself? For if you're counting on this lot doing it, I'd think again." She swept her hand across the array of workmen, turning the full force of her blazing gold gaze on them. "Which of you will pull down the Troth Stone, that's stood here for more years than anyone can tell? This is *our* ring and *our* stone." She swung around to face the watching crowd behind her. "Will you let them? How many of you pledged your troth here?" As she rolled on, her voice slipped deeper into a rich burr. "How many of your mithers and faithers? Your grans? Will you let this soothlander, this tool of the English, coom in and tear doon our stane? Is it sae easy for you, then, to gie up your birthright?"

The woman was a natural rabble-rouser, Damon thought, as several of the crowd responded with an angry "No" or "Never" or "Damned Sassenach."

"Damn it!" MacRae snapped, gesturing at the men in front of the stone. "Take the ropes. Pull it down."

The men gaped at him, shuffling their feet as they looked from him to Meg to the crowd and then to each other.

"Will you topple it on me, Ewen?" Meg pointed to one of the workers. "Who was it birthed your bairn last winter—that was turned around wrang and your Nell screaming with the pain? John MacKenzie, dinna I gie you salve for your da's cankered legs? And you"—she swung the other way, singling out another man who was studiously avoiding her gaze—"Colin Grant. Tell me who gaed to your croft when your wee laddie's lungs were laboring for air. Do you want to cross me? Do you want my blood on this sacred ground and me cursing your name with my last breath?"

The men edged backward, eyeing the ropes as if they were snakes lying on the ground.

"And you—you ootlanders"—Meg turned her fierce gaze on MacRae's other men—"do you think you can wreck these stanes and not answer for it? Do you think because you're frae the Lowlands, you willna suffer the consequences? This is where the ancients danced. It has been holy ground since time began, afore there were Gaels or Scots, afore the Norsemen came, and long, long afore the English ever set foot here. The auld ones guard these places still. I would not want to be the one who disturbs their spirits. Do you think *he* will protect you when they come for you one nicht?" She gestured scornfully toward Donald MacRae. "Nocht can save you frae the Old Ones' curse."

It was not, Damon thought, the Old Ones' wrath that should strike fear into them, but Meg's. Her gaze was enough to turn a man to ash. God, but she was stunning! Everything inside him rose up in response to her, and instinctively he started forward.

MacRae's men glanced uneasily toward MacRae and away. The hue of the manager's face deepened to almost purple. "What the devil are you standing there for? I told you, pull it down!"

"Stop," Damon's voice rang out, crisp and clear, as he rode forward. Everyone there, including Meg, turned toward him.

"You!" Meg's golden eyes narrowed, her voice soaked with scorn. "I might have known you'd come to see your handiwork. No doubt you own this as well."

"As a matter of fact, I do." Amusement tinged Damon's voice. "We are on my land, after all. However, I did not realize this spot lay under your protection."

"The Ring belongs to no man." Meg crossed her arms. "If you destr—"

"No, no, you can hold your curses, delightful as they are." He raised his hands pacifically. "I have no intention of tearing down the circle." He turned to his manager. "The stones remain." Ignoring MacRae's outraged expression, Damon looked back at Meg, the faintest trace of a smile on his lips. "There, Miss Munro. Will that do?"

"What about when we leave? When no one is watching?"

"I swear it to you on my honor. I will not tear down this stone or any of the others. Neither I nor anyone who works for me. And anyone who does will have to answer to me."

"No. Wait." MacRae urged his horse closer to Damon's. When Damon turned a cool face to him, eyebrows slightly raised, he added quickly, "Sir. My lord. Please do not be hasty. These stones are a nuisance. They attract the locals and encourage them to trespass on your estate."

Damon gave him a long look. "I believe I made myself clear."

"Certainly, my lord." MacRae swallowed whatever else he might have been about to say and turned, gesturing to his men. "Take the ropes and leave."

As the men scrambled to unwind the ropes, Damon doffed his hat to Meg. "Good afternoon, Miss Munro." He nodded a good-bye to the crowd beyond her and went back to rejoin his daughter. "I believe it would be best if we took another route to the beach this time, Lynette." He turned his mount toward the main road.

MacRae caught up with them. "My lord."

Damon suppressed a sigh. "Yes, what is it?"

"I beg you to reconsider, sir. You do not understand what the people here are like. How they—"

"I *understand* that I did not give you leave to remove those stones. I *understand* that you did not consult me about it."

"Forgive me, my lord, I did not mean to presume," the man groveled. "When we discussed turning the crofts from farming to raising sheep, I was under the impression that you did not wish to be bothered with the details of running Duncally."

"Of course not, but what the devil does raising sheep

have to do with dragging down a monument that has been standing for centuries?"

"They are only rocks, my lord. Primitive superstitions. And it causes the locals to trespass on your land. Couples go there when they plight their troth; they walk through your property to reach the circle. Allowing them to continue to do so encourages them to believe that the land belongs to them."

"What nonsense. Of course they know that the land belongs to me; it has for generations."

"Old ways die hard, sir," MacRae replied portentously. "Giving in to these people will only reinforce their resistance to progress. Highlanders are hardheaded and contentious. Look at what the rabble has already done—stealing, intimidating my workers, burning down the storehouse. Your own life could be in danger. I have spent years trying to control them. You must rule them with an iron fist. If you back down, they will view you as weak and only demand more—"

"Mr. MacRae," Damon interrupted him sharply. "I am not new to the task of overseeing an estate."

"But, sir, these are—"

"I feel sure that Scots, underneath it all, are much the same as anyone. I see nothing wrong in their attachment to the standing stones, and I don't mind that they come onto my land."

"But we could—"

"Moreover," Damon plowed on over the other man's words, "it seems foolish to introduce a new provocation into an already volatile situation. We are trying to eliminate the local unrest, not increase it. In the future you will bring it to my attention *before* you undertake such drastic action."

"Of course, my lord. As you wish." MacRae inclined his head in acquiescence and excused himself, turning back toward the castle.

"I don't like that man," Lynette said quietly as she and her father resumed their ride in the opposite direction.

"Neither do I, particularly."

"Then why do you keep him on?"

"He is the best manager I've had for Duncally, the first one who has turned any sort of significant profit." Damon shrugged. "A pleasant demeanor is not necessary for the job. And, fortunately, we don't have to be friends with him."

"Was that true what he said? That you are in danger? Would those people try to harm you?"

"No." Damon cast a sideways glance at his daughter. "Do not worry about that. He exaggerates to make his point."

"The storehouse did burn down. I saw the flames from my window."

"You watched it? Miss Pettigrew assured me you were sound asleep."

"Miss Pettigrew was," Lynette answered simply.

"Setting fire to a remote storehouse is a far cry from attacking a British landowner. They know the trouble in which they would find themselves if they attempted to harm me. No doubt it is a small number of malcontents, anyway. I will give you a bit of advice in handling tenants. MacRae's sort of heavy-handed methods are not the best. It shows fear, which is never advisable, and it can turn indignation or resentment into a veritable storm of opposition. Far better to get along with one's tenants. You have seen our Rent Day celebrations, the Christmas tradition of handing out wassail. I have now and then paid a visit to a local wedding or some other sort of village festivity. I am sure your mother visited the sick—" He stopped. "Well, perhaps not that."

"No. But the housekeeper did. And Mrs. Pennington, the estate agent's wife."

"Exactly. Those are the things one does as a landowner; it is part of one's duty to the estate and the title. It's a simple enough thing."

"Then why did Mr. MacRae try to tear down the stone?"

"Shortsightedness." Damon shrugged. "He is fearful of losing control, so he clutches at it harder."

"But why are the people angry to begin with? Why would they wish to harm you?"

"MacRae has instituted a number of changes to make the estate more profitable, mostly bringing in sheep instead of farming. Change is hard; many people resist it. And apparently they consider him an outsider even though he is Scottish. And he is working for an Englishman, which would not make him popular."

"But you will change the situation, won't you? You will turn them around and they will be more like the people at home."

The unquestioning confidence in Lynette's face as she looked at him made his heart squeeze in his chest. "I shall do my best. I plan to put in an appearance at a wedding celebration tomorrow night."

"And you were on their side this afternoon."

"Hopefully that will repair some of the damage, though I would have done so in any case. History has value, even when it's not your own."

"Papa, who was that woman? The one at the stones? Do you know her?"

"I have met her a time or two."

"Is she Red Meg? I heard one of the maids talking about Red Meg; it was something about a toothache. She said Red Meg was a witch."

He shrugged, a smile in his voice as he went on, "I have been told that ignorant people attribute to magic what is in reality skill."

"Oh, I don't believe in witches. Anyway, she is far too pretty."

"Witches cannot be comely?"

His daughter laughed. "Of course not. They must be old and have warts and such. Did you not know?"

"My education is obviously lacking." Damon smiled at her.

Every day Lynette's manner with him had changed further, becoming warmer and more at ease. Coming to Duncally had been the right thing to do; he was sure of that now. In a new place, without the reminders of her late mother, he had been able to recapture his relationship with his daughter. Amazingly, he found that she had become dearer to him than ever. The daily rides with her had revealed Lynette to him as a person in her own right, not just the sweet child who was his daughter, but a girl almost on the verge of womanhood, bright and witty and wonderfully interested in everything around her. It chilled him to think of what their relationship would have become as time made them ever more strangers to one another. He had almost let the most precious thing in the world slip through his fingers.

"They have so many wonderful tales here!" Lynette went

on. "I found a book in the nursery about the first Baillannan."

"The house across the lake?"

"No, the laird. That's what they call him, too. There was a spirit in the loch and she fell in love with him."

"Ah, yes. Of course. The spirit in the pond back home took a terrible fancy to me."

Lynette's laughter trilled out. "It's a legend, Papa. They are always like that. There's lots more—faeries and trows and kelpies and selkies."

"Good Lord. You are speaking a foreign language."

"They're magical beings. Cook told me all about them. There's even a story of a treasure."

"A treasure! What sort of treasure?"

"I'm not sure. It happened during the rebellion, you see—the Uprising, they call it. She mentioned it, but then I think she remembered, you know, that I was a Sassenach, because she started talking about something else."

"A Sassenach! I can see that you have become quite the Scotswoman."

"Well, we are that as well. She told me about our family, too."

"Cook seems a veritable fount of information."

"She says there's nothing about this glen she doesn't know. Cook's very nice. She gives me a treat when I go down to the kitchen." Lynette cast him a twinkling smile. "I always make friends with the cook."

"Wise girl. Then tell me, what did you find out about our ancestors?"

"One of them drowned his nephew in a vat of wine. The nephew was plotting to overthrow him, you see."

"A pleasant lot. Perhaps we should go back to those trews and sulkies."

"*Trows* and *selkies*, Papa." Lynette laughed. "They're strange, magical beings. And at night they come creeping out. . . ."

II

M*eg hummed along with the* familiar tune as she glanced around the people gathered in the Griegs' barn. There were two fiddlers, one of them her father, as well as a drummer and a piper, and dancers moved nimbly across the floor. The bride had taken to the floor with Gregory Rose, and the groom was in a cluster with Coll and a number of other men, laughing and downing "wee drams" of whiskeys that grew larger with every round. Poor Mary would be lucky if her Sam was able to carry her across the threshold at the end of the evening.

Away from the dancers, people gathered in knots of conversation, and laughter rang out now and again even over the music. Everyone, Meg thought, was eager for a chance to celebrate, including Meg herself. Ever since the confrontation the day before at the Troth Stone, an unspent energy had fizzed inside her, seeking release. She looked forward to an evening of dancing and conversation.

She wore her best blue gown, with ruffles of precious lace

along the neckline and edging the short, puffed sleeves. In her hair she had fastened a delicate comb of twining stems and flowers, her prized possession, not only for its beauty but because it had once belonged to her grandmother.

The reel wound to a close, and couples trailed off the floor. A soft ripple of sound near the doorway caught Meg's attention, and when she turned to look, she saw that the Earl of Mardoun had just walked in. He was the picture of elegance and taste in his exquisitely tailored jacket and breeches. Nothing was too formal or showy about the severe black-and-white garments, and even the onyx tiepin nestled in the intricate folds of his snowy-white neckcloth was subdued so that he did not look too out of place among the other guests.

Meg took a quick breath, her pulse suddenly loud in her ears. The earl was the last person she expected to see tonight. She wondered if his presence here indicated courage or stupidity.

Bustling forward to greet him, Mr. Grieg wiped his hands down his front and bobbed his head in a succession of uncertain bows as he stammered out greetings and thanks to the visitor. Mardoun replied with a smile and a few words, then turned to make his bow to the bride's mother. Meg wondered if the earl thought that after unceremoniously tossing half his crofters out of their homes, he could now win them all over with his charm? She had to admit that he seemed to be doing an excellent job of it with the Griegs.

Nor could Meg deny that she, too, was shamefully susceptible to the man. Unconsciously, she rubbed her thumb across her fingers, remembering his touch upon her hand.

She thought of the other afternoon in her cottage, of Damon's hands on her, his mouth. She recalled the heat in his eyes. The heat in her.

"Sae that is himself, eh?" a voice sounded in her ear, and Meg jumped. She whirled around to see that Dan Grieg, the bride's brother, had come up behind her. "My faither will be talking aboot this for weeks. I wonder why Mardoun is here."

"I wondered the same thing."

As she watched, the earl turned his head, his eyes sweeping the room. When his gaze fell on Meg, he stopped, his eyes locking with hers. Meg swallowed and forced herself to turn her head away. "Take me out for the next reel, Danny."

Dan blinked in surprise, but recovered his wits enough to take her hand and lead her out onto the floor. Throughout the dance, Meg kept her eyes firmly on the other dancers, determined not to look for the earl. But when the reel was over and she turned to walk off the floor, there he was, only feet from her, his lips curved into that ghost of a smile that did odd things to her stomach.

"Miss Munro." He bowed and came closer.

"My lord," she replied stiffly. Beside her, Dan Grieg—*the coward*—slipped away into the crowd.

"My lord?" Mardoun repeated, shaking his head. "Surely we have progressed further than *my lord*." He offered her his arm, and Meg could see no way out of taking it.

"I do not know what else to call you." Her voice came out shaky, and she only hoped he could not feel a similar trembling in her fingers on his arm.

As they strolled away, he bent his head closer to hers and

murmured, "Usually when I have bathed with a woman, she calls me Damon."

Meg pulled in a sharp breath. "We have not—I have not—"

"Been with me while warm water poured all over us?"

"That is not the same as bathing—you make it sound terrible."

"I did not mean to. I assure you I found it delightful."

Meg was certain her cheeks were bright red now, and she could not meet his gaze.

"Your face is flushed," he went on smoothly. "It *is* rather warm in here. Perhaps a bit of evening air to refresh you?"

She realized that Mardoun was steering her toward the wide doorway. "No. I am fine right here."

"Do you think I am trying to lure you outside for carnal reasons? I am not . . . though I must say it is rather an enticing notion."

"Perhaps for you." Meg jerked her hand from his arm. "But not for me." She turned away, heading for an empty spot along the wall, but maddeningly he followed her.

"I am crushed. Have you not even a word of kindness for me after I ensured the preservation of your—what did you call it, a truth stone?

"It's the Troth Stone. Couples used it to become betrothed. They stand on either side and clasp hands through the hole in the stone, then pledge their vow to marry."

"It sounds a delightful tradition."

Meg frowned at him, suspecting that he was mocking her. She crossed her arms, her jaw setting pugnaciously. "Am I supposed to be grateful to you because you did not destroy a sacred place?"

"No, I do not expect your gratitude, I assure you—though it might surprise you to learn that there are some who would, in fact, feel some appreciation for my deciding in their favor." Annoyance edged his voice.

"We should not have to beg you for the favor. The ring is not yours. Those stones belong to the earth."

"And that piece of earth belongs to me."

"Oh, yes, I know. As does everything else—and that is all that is important."

"Not *all*." His eyes glinted suggestively as he leaned in toward her. "I value some other things as well." He straightened, going on lightly, "I have no interest in destroying an antiquity. Indeed, my old professor would have had my head if I had let MacRae tear down something so old and meaningful." He paused. "I do apologize that my man tried to tear down the stones. I promise you, I did not order it; I did not even know what he was about. And I have made it clear that he must obtain my approval before he does any such thing in the future." He smiled at her. "Come, Meg, could we not call a truce? This is a party, after all."

"Very well. I will agree to a truce," she said stiffly, though she was reluctant to lower the shield of her antagonism.

"Perhaps we could seal our agreement with a dance." He glanced toward the couples in the center of the floor.

"You don't know how."

"It sounds not unlike a waltz."

"It's a strathspey."

"I believe we could make a waltz out of it. 'Tis an elegant dance. I could teach you." He reached down and took her hand in his. "I hold your hand, thus. And put my other hand on your waist." His fingers curved around her side.

Heat stole through Meg, and her heart gave a crazy, little leap. She stepped back, pulling her hand from his. "It does not matter. The next dance will be a reel."

"What you were dancing earlier with that most fortunate man? A country dance, I think; I can manage that as well. Still, I can see that you are quite set against dancing. Do you not care for music? I confess I have no ear for the bagpipes, but I thought the fiddler seemed rather accomplished."

"The fiddler is my father." She had the satisfaction of seeing she had surprised him.

Damon turned to look at the musicians. "Is he now? Then he has more than his music to be proud of." Studying Alan, Damon went on, "Ah, yes, I can see the resemblance to your brother."

"Do not say that to Coll."

He glanced back at her curiously. "Yet I would think your father is a man most would term handsome. Your brother is not fond of him?"

"Da is . . . a wandering sort of man. We did not see him much."

"Some would consider that an advantage in a father."

What was she doing, standing here talking about her family with the Earl of Mardoun? Coll would be furious if he knew she had revealed anything of him to a stranger, much less to a man he held in contempt.

"Yes, well, excuse me, but I must, um . . ." She turned aside, glancing vaguely around the room. "I should go," she finished lamely.

"I can see that you have urgent business . . . somewhere."

Meg narrowed her eyes in irritation. "I don't know why

I bother with courtesy for you. Shall I just say that I do not wish to talk to you?"

"You may say that, yet I would swear it is not true. But I will not argue the point." He shrugged. "You do not wish to talk. Nor does dancing please you. There must be other things we could do." He slanted a sideways glance at her.

"There are not," Meg told him firmly.

"We managed to find some the other afternoon." His low voice curled through her like whiskey. He reached out to take her elbow, then with a feather touch ran his fingertips down the underside of her arm. "I could remind you."

Meg was jolted by the unexpected heat that shot straight into her abdomen and blossomed between her legs. She pulled away. "No." Meg heard the hitch in her voice, and she mentally cursed the weakness. "Lord Mardoun—"

"Damon."

"Lord Mardoun," she repeated firmly. "Other women may be flattered to receive your attentions, but not I. I am not some dangling fruit to drop into your hands at the slightest wind. I am not loose or weak. I am not easy."

"I do not think you are easy." A smile tugged at the corner of his mouth. "Indeed, I believe you are quite difficult. But the hardest fruit to reach is often the sweetest, is it not?"

"I am sure I wouldn't know." She lifted her chin. "I do not know what you hope to obtain by plaguing me like this. Indeed, I cannot understand why you came here at all, since you are clearly a man who values sheep more than human beings. Perhaps you should try conversing with them instead."

It gave Meg some gratification to see Mardoun's eyebrows shoot up in astonishment. Without waiting for him to recover enough to respond, she whirled and strode off.

Heading straight for her brother, she grabbed Coll's arm and pulled him onto the dance floor. Coll, nimble on his feet despite his size, was happy to oblige, and he'd downed enough whiskey to then be cajoled into singing a lament with their father.

By the time Meg looked around the barn again, the earl had gone. That was a relief, she told herself. But she found that the evening had lost its sparkle.

———

Damon stood on the upper terrace, gazing out across the gardens. He took a last sip of his brandy and contemplated going back inside to pour another glass, but he found himself reluctant to leave the view. Drenched with moonlight, the gardens dropped down the hillside, revealing a view in the distance of the narrow slice of road to the village. The scene was lovely and peaceful . . . and Meg Munro would take the road on her way home from the wedding celebration.

He had, he thought, played his hand well tonight with Meg. He had teased a little, but not pressed. Reminded her of the passion between them the other afternoon, but had not acted like a man desperate to bed her—no matter how hot his blood had been humming through his veins. They had actually had something resembling a conversation. But that tart remark at the end from her about people and sheep had left him floundering. He'd never before had a woman criticize him about his estate practices—and what the devil did his decision to bring in sheep have to do with her, with them? Meg seemed to be grasping for reasons to resent him.

But that was better, surely, than indifference. Meg had responded to him physically; he was certain of the light that had sparked in her eyes, the shiver that had run through her when he slid his fingers down her arm. He had left the festivities early instead of making a cake of himself by hanging about watching her, as he had been tempted to. It had been a beginning.

The trouble was, he wanted so much more than a beginning. Damon shifted, one hand absently rubbing his chest. A breeze wafted over him, lifting his hair and teasing over his torso, cool and soft. He had removed his jacket and waistcoat and the constricting neckcloth when he came home, but still he was warm.

Damon set his glass aside on the balustrade and wandered down the steps, restless. It would be easier to see the entire road from the lower terrace. He had stood there looking out often enough these past few days, especially in the evenings when the soft half-light of the gloaming turned the landscape dreamy and seductive, and he had caught sight of Meg once or twice. He was acting a fool, he knew. Had anyone told him a month ago that he would be loitering about the gardens, hoping to catch a glimpse of a country girl—indeed, of any female—he would have laughed. Still, he could not leave just yet.

Meg had worn blue tonight, a more stylish dress than he had seen on her before. Dainty, puffed sleeves left much of her arms bare, and blond lace edged the neckline, drawing the eye to the soft, curving flesh beneath—as if his attention needed any push. Her hair was done up in a sophisticated manner and secured with an elegant comb—a delicate tracery of gold, leaves, and branches twining, with little green leaves and flowers formed of peridot and citrine. His first thought had been how beautiful it looked nestled in her thick, red hair, the citrine echoing the gold of her eyes. His second had been that the ornament was too expensive to have been within the reach of a rural healer and midwife.

A man had given it to her. A lover. Jealousy pierced him at the thought. Damon pictured some other man sliding the comb into her hair, brushing his fingers over the lush red curls, bending to place a kiss upon her lips. It was what he would have done.

Bracing his arms against the wide stone railing, he stared out, wishing he had maneuvered Meg outside the party for a stolen kiss instead of striving to maintain the image that he was in control of his relationship with Miss Munro. It would be far more appealing, he thought, to actually *have* a relationship. Pride was a cold companion.

He stiffened and leaned farther out, peering through the darkness. A woman in a light-colored gown was strolling down the road, too far away, unfortunately, to tell whether her hair was brown or a flaming red.

Damon hurried along the terrace and down another set of stairs. Frustratingly, he found that though he was closer, his view of the road was blocked. He strode to the opposite end, where another flight of stairs descended to the large formal garden. It was, he realized, an absurdly long flight of stairs.

When he reached the stone balustrade at the far end of the garden, he could see that the figure was indeed Meg. He watched her turn onto the road that led to the stone circle, abnormally aware of the beat of his pulse in his throat. Unconsciously he rubbed his hand over his chest again.

He trailed along the balustrade, keeping her in sight, until he reached the end of the terrace and she vanished from his view. He trotted past the mews, ignoring the interested yellow gaze of an owl on its perch, and took the final set of stairs two at a time. He saw her in the distance. Soon she would be gone again, for the stone circle and the path beyond it were hidden from the castle by the copse of trees. He loped down the narrow dirt path to level ground and through the copse, emerging at last at the edge of the clearing.

The stone circle lay before him, and Meg was strolling toward it. Her skirts fluttered a little in the breeze, the moon highlighting her pale skin and leaching her hair. As he watched, Meg entered the ring of stones. Her face raised to the moon, she reached up and pulled the jeweled comb from her hair, shaking her head to release the glorious red curls. Lifting her arms, she spun in a slow circle, face tilted up and eyes closed.

Damon moved forward, drawn inexorably to the elemental beauty of the woman and the scene.

She must have heard him, for her hands dropped and she whirled to face him. "What are you doing here?" Though her voice was breathless, no fear was in it.

"Watching you," he replied candidly. "Dancing amidst the stones in the moonlight. Have you come to call down your powers? To cast a spell?"

"Only to enjoy the night. I have no magic."

"Do you not? I believe you have ensorcelled me." Damon started toward her.

12

Meg watched Damon come to her, her breath catching in her throat. She wanted him. Against all reason, all propriety, all intention, she wanted him.

His long legs ate up the ground between them, and he stopped inches from her. The breeze lifted a curl and blew it against her cheek. Damon reached out to gently push it back, his fingertips grazing her skin. She could feel the faint tremor in them, and it did something hot and peculiar to her insides.

"Why are you here?" she managed to ask, but her voice sounded too high, too quick. "Are you following me?"

"I saw you from the terrace." His fingers, having tucked the wayward curl behind her ear, trailed down the line of her jaw. He was, she thought, breathing harder than normal, and she wondered at what speed he had come down from his terrace. The thought that he had hurried to catch her only added to the prickle of heat and excitement.

"But why? What do you want?" Meg was not sure why

she was forcing the issue. Better by far to let the matter die, bid him good-night, and go home. But she wanted his answer.

A fragment of a chuckle escaped him. "I should think that was clear." He slid his fingers along the cord of her neck onto the ridge of her collarbone, his eyes following their path. "I wanted to see you. I wanted . . . to kiss you." His mouth softened sensually, and his eyes came back to hers, intent and mesmerizing. "To touch you." He leaned in, heat radiating from his body, and his breath was a caress upon her forehead. "To bring that delectable little noise from your throat once more."

His words should have made her blush with shame, but Meg knew the flush that swept her was more arousal than embarrassment. "Stop," she said shakily. "You are mad."

"Yes. You have made me so." He nuzzled into her hair. "You smell like heaven."

"Anyone coming along could see us," she protested.

He pulled her deeper into the shadows, behind a towering stone.

"I don't like you," she grated out, clutching at the last remaining threads of her resistance.

"I know. I don't care if you like me as long as you kiss me."

His mouth found hers, drawing from Meg such a rush of desire it made her tremble and sag against him. His mouth moved to her neck, exploring it with soft, languorous kisses. One hand at her back, pressing her to him, he drifted slowly down her body with the other, fingertips tracing the line of her backbone, the curve of her buttocks, slipping along the cleft between. She remembered when his fingers had dipped lower, finding the deep, wet center of her.

"Damon . . ." The sweetness of his name on her tongue amazed her.

She could feel his smile against her skin, and he lifted his head. "I like to hear you say my name." His thumb came up to drag softly across her lower lip. He followed the movement with a light kiss. "Say it again."

"Nae," she teased, twining her arms around his neck and smiling up at him. "'Twould be too familiar of me." He waited, his eyes consuming her as a smile played upon his lips. "My lord." The light in his eyes flared higher. He kissed her. "Mardoun," she whispered. The sensuality in his smile deepened, and he kissed her once more, his lips slow and soft and thorough, moving with a lazy assurance that made desire swell within her. When he lifted his head this time, she breathed, "Damon."

His mouth settled on hers, his arms wrapping around her like iron, as he ravaged her senses, sparking a hot, hungry need inside her. Meg strained up against him, sliding her fingers into his hair and clenching them in her fervor, pulling him closer. He sank to his knees, carrying her with him, and stretched out on the ground. He took her mouth as if he would consume her, sinking his hands into her hair and cupping her head as if to hold her prisoner to his kisses.

Meg felt no desire to escape, wanting only to feel more, taste more, of him. The clothes between them frustrated her. She wanted to have his flesh beneath her hands, to wrap her legs around him, but she could not pull her hands away from their greedy exploration of his body long enough to remove the garments.

He rolled onto his back, pulling her on top of him, and his hands went to the hooks fastening her dress. His fingers were clumsy with haste and need, and she heard a rip of fabric, but she did not care, for then his fingers were on her skin, sliding under her chemise, and she shuddered beneath the touch.

Damon sat up, pulling away from her, and tore at his own buttons. Meg shoved her dress down and untied her chemise, pulling it over her head and tossing it aside. The evening air caressed her naked breasts, nipples tightening. She saw that Damon's fingers had stilled on his shirt as he watched her. She saw the passion on his face, the slackening and softening of his lips, the hunger that heated his gaze. Meg felt none of the shame or embarrassment she would have supposed she would at baring her breasts to him, only pleasure and a kind of power, even pride, that she could affect him so.

With a huff of breath, he yanked off his shirt and spread it out on the ground, then lowered her to it. Lying down beside her, propped up on one elbow, he laid his other hand upon her and moved over her. His hands were surprisingly gentle, given the avidity in his eyes, as he traced the lines of her collarbone and ribs, curved over the swell of her breasts, and trailed onto her stomach.

"I have never seen aught so beautiful," he murmured, and leaned down to kiss her breast, the upthrust nipple, the quivering flesh of her stomach.

With the tip of his tongue, he traced one nipple, startling a shiver of pleasure from her. When he pulled the nub of flesh into his mouth and settled down to suck at it, Meg gasped and reached out blindly, digging her fingers into his shoulders. His mouth was hot and wet and insistent, a wealth of extraordinary new delights, and some invisible cord running through her throbbed at the pull of it.

Eyes closed, she struggled to suppress the moans that sought to rise to her lips, but then his hand delved down beneath the waist of her dress and under the thin cotton of her underclothes, slipping between her legs, and at the touch, she could not hold back a soft cry of surprise and pleasure. Digging her heels into the ground beneath her, Meg bowed up against his hand.

Damon's mouth turned searing, and she could feel the tension in his muscles beneath her hands, the taut coiling of leashed strength, as his fingers gently explored her, opened her, teased rippling threads of desire through her. He lifted his head and Meg opened her eyes to find him watching her. She saw the quickened rise and fall of his chest and the flame in his eyes, the raw need that stamped his face, and the sight of his hunger only deepened her own.

Reaching down, he hooked his hands in her garments, shoving them down in a quick, impatient movement. Meg kicked them off as Damon stood up to peel off the rest of his clothes. He loomed above her, magnificently naked, and Meg thought perhaps she should feel scared, appalled—something more maidenly than the eager surge of lust that rose in her at the sight of him in this pure, raw state. She reached out a hand to curl it around his ankle and slide it up his calf, letting the rough, curling hairs tickle her palm. The gesture sent a visible shiver through him, and he came back down to her.

Meg sat up to meet him, sliding her hands up his arms and across his shoulders. She sank her fingers into his thick, dark hair and pressed her lips to his. A low sound shuddered out of him as his mouth melded with hers. He slid one arm behind her, cushioning her head as they lay back on the ground. His other hand moved over body, caressing, kneading, exploring every inch of her. Damon released a noise of deep satisfaction as his hand slipped between her legs and found the damp heat that waited for him there. He slid between her legs, and with his hands beneath her buttocks, lifting her, he moved into her.

She let out a sharp gasp and braced herself at the flash of pain. Damon's head shot up and he stared at her in shock. "Meg!"

"No, don't stop," she whispered. Digging her fingertips into his hips, she pushed up to meet him, and slowly he buried himself in her. A deep, primal satisfaction swept through Meg as he filled her, and for that moment she was lost in him, joined in a way she had never imagined. Tears filled her eyes, not from pain, but from a joy so sharp, so piercing, she knew she would never be the same.

She heard his ragged breath, felt the strain in his arms around her, cradling her as he stroked in and out, and his care, his restraint, touched her even as his movements aroused her. She turned her head to press her lips against the side of his head, and he shuddered at the touch, his movements growing harder and faster. Meg sucked in a breath at the need rising in her, frantically reaching for something she didn't know. She ached to seize it, to claim it, and she dug her fingertips into his back, aware on some deep level that he could bring her to what she wanted.

A harsh groan burst from him and he moved wildly against her, and in that moment she was lifted up and over, pleasure exploding deep within her and rippling out. She let out a sharp sob and went limp in his arms as he collapsed onto her.

Meg lay trembling in his arms, unable to speak or move or think, drained and replete and teetering on the edge of laughter or tears, she wasn't sure which. Perhaps it was both.

"Sweet bleeding Christ," Damon mumbled, and rolled off her. For an instant she felt the loss of him, but he immediately cradled her against his side and kissed the top of her head. He ran a gentle, caressing hand down her back and along her thigh. "Are you all right?"

A giggle escaped her. Apparently laughter had won the day.

He tilted his head toward her. "Are you laughing?" he asked in some astonishment.

"No! Yes. I mean . . ." How could she explain how absurd it had seemed to hear him ask if she was all right when she was filled with the most amazing, buoyant happiness . . . as well as feeling as if every bone in her body had melted? Finally she said, "I feel very all right."

She snuggled into his side. He continued to slide his hand idly up and down her. "Cold?"

"No." The night air was cool on her skin, but the blood still sang through her veins, and Damon was like a hot stove.

"Did I—were you—Meg, why did you not tell me?"

At the concern and puzzlement in Damon's voice, she lifted her head to look at him. "Not tell you what?"

He frowned. "That you had never . . ." He stroked his hand down her side again. "That you were untouched."

"Oh. That."

"Yes, that."

"I never said I was otherwise." She fisted her hand atop his chest and propped her chin on her fist, gazing at him with wide eyes across the expanse of his chest.

"No, but I thought—"

"I know what you thought." Her voice sharpened, and she started to turn away, but he took her chin in his hand and held her.

"No," he told her firmly. "I knew you were not as my housekeeper told me. I did not hold you cheap or easy, I swear it. But I thought you had lain with a man before. You told me you chose a man as you pleased."

"I do. I did . . . tonight." She looked at him unwaveringly. "Does it matter? Would you not have . . . done this tonight?" She trailed her fingers down his chest.

"I would have." His eyes lit as he wrapped his hand around hers and raised it to his lips. "You must know I would have. But not this way . . ." He gestured vaguely around them. "I would have moved more slowly. Been gentler. Not taken you here on the ground. You should have had a soft bed and wine and time."

Meg's lips curved in a smile, and she lay back, gazing up at the sky above them. "I like it here. Beneath the stars and the moon, with the stones standing guard all around us. 'Tis a lovely place. I will cherish the memory."

He went up on his elbow. "I will give you more memories." He bent to kiss her eyes, her nose, her mouth. "Sweeter, hotter, longer." He trailed his thumb over her chin and down the center of her body, stopping teasingly just before he reached the juncture of her legs.

"My. Such lofty promises." She smiled teasingly. "Are you sure you can meet them?"

"You think I cannot?" He grinned back. "I will. And more." He kissed her until she was breathless and tingling, then rose lithely to his feet and offered her his hand. "But right now I think we should get you back in your house, snug and warm, before someone else takes it into his head to visit the circle in the full moon."

They pulled on their clothes, Damon dressing in his shirt and breeches more quickly than Meg could pull on all her undergarments and dress and hook the fastenings. Damon stepped over and finished the last few hooks, adding a soft kiss where her neck joined her collarbone.

Reaching down, he picked up Meg's elegant comb and rubbed his thumb across it. "'Tis a lovely object." He slid it into her curls. "Almost as lovely as its wearer."

"Flatterer." Meg wrinkled her nose at him, but she could not deny that she warmed inside to hear him say it—warmed even more at the look in his eyes. "But thank you—it belonged to my grandmother."

"Ah. Then beloved as well as beautiful." He pulled on his boots and started along the path to Meg's cottage with her.

"You need not walk me to my house."

Damon turned his raised-brow, haughty expression upon her, saying, "Is that what you think of me? That I would not see you safely to your door?"

"I have nothing to fear from these woods."

"Then perhaps I should be the one seeking your protection." He curled his arm around her shoulders.

Meg leaned into him, enjoying the moment. Time enough tomorrow to think about the future and possibilities . . . and consequences.

Their steps slowed as they approached her snug, dark cottage. Damon's arm tightened around her a little more; Meg snuggled a trifle closer to his side. She did not want to part from him; she wanted to continue to drift in this dreamy warmth, spent and fulfilled. To lie in the shelter of his arms, his strength and power enveloping her. Filling her. Meg blushed at her thoughts and reached for the handle of her door. Damon wrapped his hand around it and pushed it open for her. She turned in the doorway, gazing up at him, as he braced the door open with his arm.

Damon brushed his fingers down the side of her face, watching their movement on her skin. Meg saw desire darken his eyes. He bent to kiss her, then kissed her again. He raised his head. "I must go," he said hoarsely. "Or else—"

"Or else what?" She slid her hands up his chest and linked them behind his neck, watching him all the while.

He spread his hands out on her sides and slowly moved them down until they rested on her hips. "You know what." He stepped closer, pulling her against him so that she felt the hard, pulsing evidence of his desire. "I will want to make love to you all over again." His fingers curled up, gathering the material of her skirts in his grasp. He dropped his head to rest against hers. "To be inside you again. To feel you hot and tight around me."

The huskiness in his voice, the little hitch in his breathing, sent heat spiraling through her. Boldly she pressed herself against him. "Then surely you should stay, not leave." She went on tiptoe to kiss him.

Letting out a low noise, half laugh, half growl, he swept her up in his arms and, kicking the door shut behind him, started across the room.

13

Damon set Meg down beside the bed and peeled her clothes from her piece by piece, caressing and kissing her flesh as if she were a rare treasure. When she was completely bare to his gaze, her skin rosy with rising ardor, he dropped his hands and stood, watching Meg with a hot, hungry gaze as she unbuttoned his shirt and pulled it off, then roamed his chest with hands and mouth and tongue. His skin flared with heat beneath her touch and the muscles of his stomach quivered, but he made no move to hurry her untutored exploration. She used her tongue and lips and teeth on his flat, masculine nipples as he had on hers and was rewarded by the low growl of pleasure from his throat, the fierce surge of his flesh against his breeches.

When her fingers went to the buttons of his trousers, he drew in a short, sharp breath. Meg slanted a teasing look up at him, and though she knew the answer from the unmistakable reactions of his body, she asked, "Am I too bold? Would you rather I did not?"

"Bold women suit me well." He slid his hands over her hair. "You may torment me at your leisure."

Meg smiled and continued, sliding her hands inside the breeches and pushing them down as she curved her hands over his buttocks. She had never dreamed how exciting his body would feel beneath her hands, the pleasure of learning the different textures of his skin, of seeing his arousal deepen with every movement she made. She lowered his breeches, her body sinking with them, so close her full, loose hair brushed over him. Damon hauled her to her feet and kissed her deeply.

He laid her on the soft bed and leaned over her, bracing his arms on either side of her. "I have been dreaming for days about lying in this bed with you."

He slid in beside her and began to make love to Meg with slow, patient deliberation. What had before been a feverish, hungry explosion of sensations was now a long, delectable slide into pleasure. Taking his time, he moved with painstaking care, seemingly determined to arouse every inch of her body into a fervor. Desire ratcheted up inside Meg, growing and spreading in a way she had never imagined, until she dug her fingers into the sheets beneath her, her body bowing up to him, as small, breathy whimpers fell from her lips.

Then, at last, he entered her with the same maddening, delightful care, magnifying their pleasure with each slow stroke until it seemed almost too much to bear, and finally they tumbled over the edge into a dark, blissful chasm of release.

When Meg awakened the next morning, she lay for a few minutes, gazing up at the ceiling and trying to pull some order out of the myriad thoughts and emotions tumbling about in her. Even though she had expected Damon to have gone back to Duncally, she had a little sting of disappointment that she lay in her bed alone. But beyond that, she felt—well, no use denying it—she felt wonderful. Every inch of her body was warm, relaxed, and pleasurably alive. Awakened. It seemed as if until this day, the world had, unbeknownst to her, been tinged with grayness, and only now did everything blaze forth in its full color. Her cottage was beautiful. She was beautiful. Damon was beautiful.

Laughing at the absurdity, she sat up, curling her arms around her jackknifed legs and resting her head upon her knees. Damon would no doubt bridle at such a description of him, but he was beautiful. It wasn't only his handsome face or the strength and grace of his long body, though those things were excessively appealing. It was the way he touched her, kissed her, the desire that shone from his eyes, the gentleness that leashed his hunger. At times in the past she had wondered if she was too particular, if she was waiting for a perfection that would never come, but she knew now that she had been right in doing so. Nothing else could have matched last night.

Even the twinges of soreness seemed exactly right, eloquent reminders that she had entered a new world. In the past she would have scoffed at such thoughts. Perhaps she was being a bit extravagant, but she had no desire to temper her emotions. It was all far too enjoyable.

Rising and stretching languidly, she grabbed one of the

sweet-scented soaps she made and walked down to bathe in the secluded cove on the other side of the burn. Even in August the water was chilly, but she liked the feel of it on her skin. Lathering her hair and body, she washed off the soap, then floated languidly for a few minutes, thinking of the night before.

Before long, however, less pleasant thoughts began to slip in. As amazing as their lovemaking had been, Meg could not avoid that she had given herself to a man she should have despised. However skillful Damon was, however gentle he had been with her, he had not shown kindness elsewhere. He was still the man who had turned a third of his crofters out of their homes—and there was no reason to think the number would stop there. What kind of person would that make her if she ignored all that because of the pleasure she found in his arms?

Excuses for him bubbled up in her mind. Damon had assured her last night that he had not even known that Mac-Rae planned to pull down the Troth Stone. So perhaps he had not ordered the clearances, either. It was possible, was it not, that an estate owner living in England would not be aware of what his estate manager was doing? It was tempting to think so.

Meg let out a disgusted noise and left the water, chastising herself as she dried off and dressed. Whatever was she doing, sitting about mooning over a man? Weaving daydreams about him and concocting reasons to exonerate him from guilt? She had always prided herself on being realistic and practical, not the sort to indulge in pretty fantasies.

The truth was, though she had known him intimately last night, she did not really know him at all. She must not whitewash the man simply because his kisses turned her inside out. Indeed, it was idiotic to even be contemplating the future with him. For all she knew, she might never see the man again.

The differences between them were vast. What had been a rare, magical experience for her, ushering her into a new world, was probably a commonplace encounter for him. The Earl of Mardoun would have had countless women at his beck and call. How many times had he taken some opera dancer to bed, then returned to his mansion the next morning, never to see her again, leaving behind some little bauble as a token of his appreciation? Damon had pursued Meg eagerly before, but now that he had achieved what he desired, he might well be content and move on to chasing another.

It dismayed her to realize how much she did not want that to happen. She, the always-confident, ever-independent Meg Munro, was suddenly vulnerable and uncertain, dependent on a man's desires, his decisions. Well, she certainly was not going to sit about, lost in memories of the night before or fretting over whether she would see him again. She would get dressed and be about her daily business.

After breakfast, Meg set out for Wes Keith's croft. His mother was ill, and though Meg suspected that she could do nothing to defeat the specter of death that hung over the woman, she could at least give her something to soothe the pain. When she arrived at the Keiths' croft, however, she was brought up short by the sight of Donald MacRae and his men grouped outside the small farmhouse. Wes Keith stood blocking his doorway, arms crossed and face grim. Behind him, Meg could see a child peeking around his leg.

"I've told you many a time," MacRae said, his face growing red, "you canna stay here."

"I canna leave!" Wes shot back. "I shouldna hae to. This is my faither's croft and his faither's afore him. We were here lang before any Englishman."

"I dinna care if you've been permitted to stay here for four hundred years! That ends now. The Earl of Mardoun owns this land."

"My mither is sick and like to die. Hae you no heart?" Catching sight of Meg hurrying toward them, Wes pointed to her. "Ask Meg. She'll tell you how it is with Ma."

MacRae whipped around. "You again! Dinna think you can stop me. There's nae earl here for you to work your wiles on."

"Mrs. Keith is quite ill," Meg went on, ignoring the man's words. "Surely you canna force a dying woman out of her home. Where will she go? What will happen to her?"

"That's not my concern."

At MacRae's cold words, Wes Keith charged him, but two of the manager's men grabbed Wes and held him back. "You think to hit me?" MacRae shouted, his face suffused with color. "You're asking for transportation. How do you think your wife and wee children would do with you being sent to Australia?"

A gasp and a shriek came from the doorway of the house, and Wes's wife cried, "No! Wes! Dinna do it."

Meg went to Mrs. Keith and took her arm, turning her back into the house, saying in a soothing voice, "Here, the children are frightened." She pointed to the young boy and the girl only slightly older, holding the baby of the family.

Millie Keith, tears coursing down her cheeks, took the

baby, jiggling her to hush her cries. "I dinna ken what we'll do, Meg. My brother will tak us in, but he canna feed us all. And when will they force him off his land, too? Nae, it's the end of us."

"Come, let's see to Wes's ma." Hoping to distract Millie, Meg took her arm, steering her into the next room, a cramped, dark space where an old woman lay on a narrow bed. Meg's heart sank at the sight of her, but she said only, "Good day to you, Mrs. Keith. I brought you something to ease the pain a bit."

The woman, who Meg knew was not as old as she looked, peered at Meg. "Janet?"

"Nae, it's me, Meg, Janet's daughter."

"Oh, aye, Meg."

Meg managed to coax a sip or two down her. As Meg stood up and handed the bottle to Millie, shouts erupted outside. Whirling, they hurried into the next room. "Get out!" Wes shouted, pelting through the front door. "Get the children out! They've set it on fire!" He shoved past them, going to his mother.

Meg snatched up the little boy, grabbed the girl's hand, and ran for the front door. She could hear the wicked whisper of fire on the thatched roof above her head. Neighbors had gathered outside, and two men ran into the house to help Wes. Meg handed the two children off to one of the waiting women and turned back to see Millie emerge from the house, followed by Wes, carrying his mother. The other two men stumbled out after him, arms filled with the few bits of bedding and furniture they had managed to save.

The roof was blazing now, and fire had begun to eat its way down one of the supporting beams. Meg ran to MacRae and grabbed his arm. "Stop this! How can you do such a thing!"

He turned his cold gaze on her. "Too late. We could nae stop it now if we tried."

"You are a monster!" Meg was rigid with fury. "That woman is dying! You could have at least waited, let her end her life with a bit of dignity. It is inhuman to turn her out— and three children as well. Mardoun could not have wanted you to—"

"The earl? Hah!" MacRae let out a crack of laughter, his eyes glittering with malice now. "Whose orders do you think I act on? Did you think he would stop the clearances just to get under your skirts? All that matters to him is profit." Mac-Rae shrugged. "Anyway, there's no need for him to please you now, is there? He got his reward last night."

"What!" Meg sucked in her breath, the blood draining from her face. MacRae could not know about Damon. How could he?

"You've played out your game there, Meg. You'd have done better to turn to me. I'll be here long after the earl has returned to London."

Meg drew back, fury and disgust swirling in a turmoil inside her. "You are a vile, despicable man. I would say I hope you rot in hell, but there's no need. That is clearly your destination."

14

Meg could do little enough for the Keith family. The roof of their house collapsed in flames, and they could do nothing but watch as their possessions and home burned. Glancing at the others around her, Meg saw not only sympathy and grief for the Keiths, but also a panicky fear. If the Keith croft had been taken, how long would it be before the earl took their homes away as well?

Meg had awakened this morning in such happiness that the world had sparkled. Now she felt hollowed out, spent, wrung dry by her impotent rage and bitter sympathy. Mac-Rae was scum and Meg took nothing he said for truth, but she doubted that he had lied to her just now. How would the man know Damon had lain with her unless the earl had told him? She pictured Damon tossing off a careless remark about her, the two of them laughing in that way men had when talking about sex, and her heart twisted at the thought.

Reason also told her that Damon must have approved

MacRae's plans to oust the crofters. Damon had assured her last night that the estate manager would not act again without Damon's permission. She had been a fool, letting emotions and passion color her thinking.

Meg stayed to help care for Mrs. Keith until Millie's brother arrived to carry the family and their few possessions back to his farm. When Meg approached her home, late in the afternoon, her heart was heavy within her. Her happiness of this morning had been shattered, and though she could not completely drive out some small, stubborn flicker of hope deep inside that Damon would come to her and explain, somehow set things right, she knew that was mere foolishness. As she walked into her bedroom, her eyes immediately spied the small, flat box lying on her pillow. She came to a dead halt, her stomach clenching. She had to force herself to pick up the calling card that was tucked beneath the box. Across the ornately printed title was penciled the single word *Damon*.

Inside the box, resting on a cushion of black velvet, lay a necklace of gold and amber, lovely and elegant and worth more, probably, than anything else in her cottage. At the sight of it, something hot and choking pushed up in Meg's throat, anger and shame mingling with a bitter disappointment. Here was the answer to any lingering hopes she had about Damon. He had dropped off his payment for sleeping with him. This was the bauble she had imagined him tossing to some ladybird in London as he left her after a satisfactory night. Did the man carry such things about with him on the chance that he would need to compensate some doxy on his travels? She wondered whether he had brought it over himself or handed it to his snooty valet to deliver. Her cheeks burned at the thought.

Meg closed the box, her fingers tightening around it until her knuckles went white. Turning, she slammed out of the cottage.

Her fury did not dissipate as she hurried up the path to Duncally. If anything, it grew, gathering strength with every step, each bitter remembrance of Damon's arrogance and cruelty. And her own blind passion. She did not pause as she crossed the terrace and walked through the back door of the elegant house.

"Meg!" A footman, one of the locals hired from Kinclannoch, goggled at her as she strode down the hall. "What are you doing here?"

"Where is he?" She pinned the young man with a look that would have given pause to a far more confident man than he. "Tell me where Mardoun is."

"I . . . uh . . . his study." The footman pointed down a side hall. "What—wait—"

Meg took off down the corridor he'd indicated, ignoring his weak protest. The door to Damon's study stood open, and she saw him at his desk, a quill in his hand and paper before him.

"Meg!" He looked as astonished as the hapless footman as she entered, and he jumped to his feet. A variety of emotions flitted across his face too quickly to discern, ending in a slight frown, as he dropped his quill and came around the corner of the desk. "What is it? What's the mat—"

"There!" Meg slung the box down on the floor at his feet. His stunned expression gave her some small measure of satisfaction. She rushed on, "How dare you? How could you believe that I would accept—that this was why I—" She broke off, her voice too clogged with outrage to push out the words.

"What the devil?" He gazed with a stupefied expression at the box, which had popped open and was spilling out the amber necklace. "Meg—"

"I don't want your bloody trinkets!"

"Trinket?" Damon raised his head, irritation edging his voice. "You call this a trinket?"

"I don't care if it's the queen's necklace. I am not for sale. You are a vile and heartless man, and it sickens me that I let you into my bed last night. It will not happen again."

Damon went white around the mouth and his eyes blazed. He drew himself up to his full height, setting his chin at that contemptuous tilt she had seen before. "I see. Then I must apologize for presuming too much. I assure you it will not happen again." His voice dripped scorn. "There are doubtless an ample number of women here who will warm my bed as well as you."

Meg felt as if he had slapped her. That was silly; he was merely putting into words what she had already known was his opinion of her. There was, she realized, nothing else to say. She whirled and fled from the room.

———

Damon stood staring at the open doorway as Meg's footsteps retreated down the hall at a run. What the devil had just happened? He had set out this morning in buoyant good cheer. This was the last way he would have expected the day to end.

It had been damned difficult to pull himself out of Meg's bed before dawn. He'd been tempted to snuggle down with her in the soft, warm darkness and wake up to make love to her again. But he could not. If he was seen exiting Meg's cottage in the morning light, it would further damage her reputation, which had already been unfairly impugned. Besides, he could not stroll into breakfast with his daughter dressed in only his shirt and breeches from the evening before.

Despite the unaccustomed tug of reluctance at leaving Meg, it had been a most pleasant walk home, the dark damp air tinted with a woodsy scent. He had even stopped to enjoy for a moment the sight of the misty loch as the sun rose behind him, slanting light on the great gray stretch of Baillannan on the other side. Unfortunately, he had run into MacRae as he started the trek through Duncally's garden. Though MacRae had been his usual obsequious self, Damon had, with irritation, caught the knowing glint in the man's eyes. Damon had been quick to nod and send the manager on his way as MacRae began to drone on about turning some croft or other to sheep.

But even that encounter had not been able to dampen Damon's mood long. As he went through the routine of washing, shaving, and dressing, he happily contemplated what he might give Meg, some jewel to express his admiration, his gratitude—all the things bubbling inside him. If they were in London, he would go out this morning and find a necklace or bracelet that was adequate for her beauty. He would have been able to stop by a flower market as well and buy a posy, just for the opportunity to watch her eyes light with pleasure as she took it and drew in a deep breath of its scent.

Since he was here in the wilds of Scotland, that was impossible. In any case, she was surrounded by flowers. But it occurred to him that some jewelry might be stored away here that would do—surely at least a brooch or cameo or bit of ornamentation she would like. After he returned from his ride with Lynette, he had gone through the safe in his study. Nothing there seemed right. But upstairs in his bedroom safe he had found exactly what he wanted: a lovely creation of gold and amber that would echo the radiance of Meg's eyes. He pictured it around her creamy throat and regretted the lack of matching earrings to grace her earlobes.

He had been restless after that, unable to settle to anything, and finally, deciding it was foolish to wait until evening, he had set out for Meg's cottage. He had found the place empty, and he'd waited a while, roaming around the place, going down to the loch and back. Finally, feeling a bit odd at intruding, but not willing to leave yet, he went inside. As it had the other day, the snug place closed around him warmly. He felt Meg in every part of the room—the scents, the herbs, the bottles and jars of mysterious substances, the soft, welcoming bed, the brush lying on her dresser along with the elegant comb she had worn the night before. He sat down and passed the time daydreaming about Meg.

It had struck him that he was acting like an adolescent in the first throes of infatuation. Indeed, he did not think he had been so callow even when he was nineteen and over the moon about the actress who had become his first mistress. It was absurd. Besides, Meg might not return for hours. She did as she pleased, not answering to anyone. And what would a woman as independent, as fierce, as desired, as Meg think when she returned and found Damon cooling his heels, waiting for her? Might she not find him weak? Lacking in dignity? Something of a fool?

He was, after all, the Earl of Mardoun. Perhaps he ought to act more like it. Finally, he had given up and returned to Duncally. He had debated whether to take the gift with him or leave it as a pleasant surprise for her, until finally, disgusted with his indecision, he set the gift on her pillow, signing one of his calling cards with a pencil he found lying about and tucking it under a corner of the box.

Next thing he knew, Meg was storming into his study and throwing the thing at his feet as contemptuously as if he'd offered her a rag. She had called him vile. Heartless. Her words had stung—no, more than stung, they had cut him—though fortunately he had managed not to show it.

The woman was mad. Utterly, howlingly mad. There was no other explanation. What other woman would have acted, not just unimpressed, but absolutely *offended* at the gift of a necklace of such beauty? The piece would not have been appropriate for a young girl whom one was courting, at least not until one was engaged to her. But why would Meg have been concerned about the propriety of it when she had slept with him the night before?

Damon thought of Meg as she had been the previous night, warm and pliant in his arms. He had been shaken by her innocence, her passionate response. This afternoon, she had changed into a termagant, raging and furious. She had acted as if she hated him—no, there had been no acting about it; she *did* hate him.

With a twist of his mouth, Damon bent down to pick up

the box and shove the necklace back inside. His finger trailed over the cool, smooth ovals of amber. It was just as well, really, that he was rid of a woman so unstable, so impetuous and changeable. Her absence would not change his life. It had only been one night of passion, after all.

Still—he snapped the box shut—Damon could not deny the empty feeling in the pit of his stomach.

15

Meg *tied her dory to* the dock and started up the path to Baillannan. Though some would consider the looming gray-stone house gloomy, the sight of it lifted Meg's spirits. It would be good to see Isobel's sweet, if somewhat vague, aunt, and perhaps Aunt Elizabeth would have word of Isobel. More than ever, Meg wished Isobel were here.

Yesterday evening, back at home after her confrontation with Damon, Meg's anger had given way to a flood of tears. Not over the Earl of Mardoun, she told herself, but the realization of how foolish she had been, the death of that fanciful dream she had inhabited for one night. That had not made the pain and regret any less piercing.

This morning she found herself turning toward the comfort of Baillannan. Her friend might not be there to hear her woes, but still, she had spent much of her childhood there, sheltered within its thick walls from the sting of gossip as much as from the cold and wind.

She entered through the kitchen, pausing for a bit of gossip with the servants and to listen to various complaints regarding their health. Passing into the main part of the house, she took the staircase to the pleasant sitting room. Elizabeth Rose, a graying woman with the tall, spare build common to the Rose family, came forward to greet Meg, her face wreathed in smiles.

"Meg! Hamish told us you were here. Come, sit down and talk to us. How pretty you look." Elizabeth took Meg's arm, leading her over to the chairs by the fireplace where another middle-aged woman sat.

"Meg." Millicent Kensington also set aside her embroidery and rose to kiss Meg's cheek in greeting. Jack's mother was a short, plump woman, pretty of face and fluttery of movement.

"I hope you are well," Meg told them both, and handed Elizabeth a small sack. "I brought you some more of your tonic, and also a tin of the chamomile tea for you both. I believe that you enjoy it as well, Mrs. Kensington?"

"'Tis most soothing for my poor nerves," Millicent responded. "Almost as effective as your delightful plum cordial, though of course I don't drink that any longer."

Her avoidance of the cordial, as well as any other alcohol, Meg knew, was due more to Isobel's edict than to any restraint on Millicent's part. Still, the woman did try, and she had managed to repair, at least to some extent, her relationship with her son, Jack.

"Thank you, dear. You are so sweet." Elizabeth beamed at Meg. "Barbara and I were just talking about you."

"Millicent, dear," the other woman corrected.

"What? Oh, yes, Millicent, I mean. Did I say Barbara?

How silly of me." Elizabeth's memory had been slipping for some time now, but Meg's tonic had helped her over the past few months, as had, apparently, Isobel's marriage to Jack and the addition of his mother to the family group. As dissimilar as the two women seemed in personality and background, they had quickly become friends, united not only by their enjoyment of needlework, but also their love of romantic tales.

"We wrote you an invitation and were going to send it over, but now we can give it to you," Millicent told Meg. "Just let me fetch it."

"Isobel and Jack are on their way home," Elizabeth went on.

"That's wonderful!" Meg had already heard the news in the servants' hall, but she was not about to spoil Elizabeth's surprise.

"Yes, isn't it?" Elizabeth's cheeks were pink with excitement. "Millicent and I have decided to have a party to celebrate their return. It is Saturday; do say you will come."

"Of course. I would not miss it for the world."

"Here it is." Millicent hurried back, waving the white square. "Jack and Isobel will be so surprised, don't you think?"

"I am sure they will be very pleased, as well." Meg only hoped the two women were not off in their estimate on the couple's arrival. Travel through the Highlands could be difficult to calculate.

"Now tell us what is going on in the world," Elizabeth said.

"Have you seen the earl?" Millicent added breathlessly. "What is he like?"

"Yes, I have seen him," Meg said carefully. She should

have known that the two women would be eager to talk about this.

"I have heard he is very handsome," Elizabeth went on. "Is that true?"

"He is indeed handsome." Meg smiled determinedly, leaching all her emotions out of her tone. "Black hair. Black eyes. Tall. He came to the Griegs' wedding celebration."

"Really?" Elizabeth rounded her eyes. "They were always such a snobbish lot at Duncally before. We sent him an invitation, too, of course, but I don't expect him to attend our little party."

"Mm." Meg's stomach clenched. She hoped Elizabeth was right. Damon was the last person Meg wanted to see, but she could not forgo the celebration for her dearest friend's arrival home.

"Ooh, I hope he does," Millicent breathed. "I have never spoken to an actual earl—indeed, I do not think I have even seen one."

She prattled on merrily, and Meg resigned herself to a long discussion of the Earl of Mardoun. Fortunately, neither of the women needed much help from her to keep the conversation going, and they did not seem to notice Meg's lukewarm participation. Meg allowed herself to be persuaded to stay for luncheon, then dropped by her brother's cottage on the estate. Coll was not at home, which was something of a relief. It would be much more difficult to convince Coll that she was in good spirits than it had been Elizabeth and Millicent. And she absolutely could not talk to her brother about Damon.

She rowed back across the loch and tried to work, but her mind kept drifting back to Damon. Whether she thought about the pleasure of the night they had spent together or the pain of her confrontation with him yesterday, it brought her no joy. She could not even maintain her sense of satisfaction at telling him what she thought of him yesterday. He plainly had not cared. No regret had been on his face, no unhappiness—not even anger. He had merely been stiff and arrogant and oh so polite in that maddening British way. As if her wrath were a minor annoyance. The strongest reaction from him, she thought, had been his indignation at her calling the necklace he'd given her a "trinket." Clearly the piece of jewelry held more value to him than her opinion of him. No doubt he had already found some other local girl to take to his bed, just as he'd told her he would.

This entirely wasted day was followed by a night spent tossing and turning. When she arose the next morning, finally having fallen to sleep not long before dawn, she decided that she would be better served to spend the day outdoors. She tended to her garden in the morning and early in the afternoon set out to gather plants in the woods.

Grabbing up a basket, Meg started up the trail toward Duncally, but soon turned aside and wound deeper into the woods. In the cool, green, peaceful dimness beneath the trees, she found it easier to escape her thoughts as she poked about, searching for flowers or seeds or leaves she could use.

She raised her head when she heard a crackle of twigs. A scuffling of leaves followed, then a little thump, and a female voice exclaimed, "Drat it!"

Curious, Meg started in the direction of the sound, her own steps silent. She spotted a girl among the trees ahead, swiping at the dirt and leaves that dotted her skirts. Meg had seen this lass riding with Damon that day at the Troth Stone—his daughter.

The girl's black hair was fashioned into long braids, but strands of it had pulled free and straggled around her face. A ribbon had come loose from its bow on one side and dangled from the end of the braid; the ribbon on the other plait was missing entirely. Dirt smudged her cheek; a ladder climbed one of her stockings; and dirt and leaves clung to her skirt despite her efforts to brush them off.

"Hello," Meg said quietly, trying not to frighten her, but the girl jumped at the sound and whirled around.

"Oh!" She peered at Meg. "Oh," she repeated, this time in relief. "You're that lady. The one at the stone."

"Yes." Meg came forward. "I am sorry if I startled you. My name is Meg Munro."

"I know. I mean, I've heard your name." The girl blushed. "I'm sorry; I'm a bit . . . rattled. I think I am lost. Indeed, I am quite certain I'm lost." She came toward Meg, saying again, "I'm sorry. I am Lynette Rutherford. How do you do?"

"I'm very well, thank you." Meg took the girl's hand.

Lynette was a slip of a girl, fine-boned, with none of her father's height or strength. But Meg could see something of Damon in her dark hair and eyes and even, a bit, in the set of her far daintier chin and firm mouth.

"I am Mardoun's daughter."

"Yes, I thought you must be." Meg smiled and turned to lead the girl back to the path. "Come, I'll show you the path to Duncally." She meant to take Lynette to the trail and set her on her way, but after a glance at the weary sag in the girl's posture and the clear track of tears through the dirt on her cheek, Meg went on, "My house is near here. Perhaps you'd like to rest a bit before we start up to Duncally. Have a cup of tea? Or will they be searching for you at the house?"

"That sounds lovely!" Lynette brightened. "I should love some tea; I am rather parched." She paused, considering Meg's question. "I do not think they will be worried. Miss Pettigrew was taking a nap; that is how I was able to slip away. She never wakes up before three. And if she does, she will assume I have gone out to the gardens. I guess it is fortunate that I got turned around rather soon after I left." She grimaced. "It is so difficult to tell which way is which in the midst of all the trees."

"It is indeed."

"But *you* don't get lost."

"Oh, I have done so once or twice. But over the years, I've come to know this place well. Fortunately, the woods are not large. When you get lost, the best thing is not to twist and turn about, trying to retrace your steps. If you but go straight, before long you will come out of the trees. And from most clear spots, you can catch sight of Duncally or the loch or the circle of stones, and you can orient yourself from that. Ah, here is the path. If you continue in that direction, you will reach Duncally, but my cottage is this way." She turned and led the girl toward her house.

"It's very pretty here. You must like living in this place. Are your parents here as well? Or, I suppose perhaps you are married. You are much too pretty not to be." Lynette cast Meg an apologetic look. "I'm sorry. Miss Pettigrew says I should not ask personal questions. It's just that I always want to *know*. . . . I am a terrible snoop, aren't I?"

Meg could not help but laugh at the girl's artless questions. "I don't mind. I understand just how you feel; I have always been curious, as well. Many people have deemed it a fault. Anyway, it is difficult to get offended by such a compliment. But to answer your question, no, I am not married. My mother is dead, but my father is still alive. I have a brother as well, but I live by myself."

"Truly?" Lynette looked at Meg with wide eyes. "You must be very brave. I think I should be scared, all alone out here."

"I have lived here all my life." Meg shrugged. "I've never been afraid in the woods."

"I wish I were like that." Lynette's smile wobbled. "You will think me a terrible rabbit."

"Yet I saw you riding with your father. That would frighten me, being up on a horse." Meg flashed a smile at Lynette, but thought of the moments when she had been on a horse behind Damon, clinging to him. There had been no fear then.

"A horse?" Lynette was the one who chuckled now. "Oh, no, horses don't frighten me. Riding is like flying, as close as one can get to that, anyway. The ground rushing beneath you, the wind whipping past your ears, that lift when he jumps a wall."

"I would say you are not a rabbit at all." Meg liked the girl, who displayed none of her father's arrogance. Indeed, Lynette seemed most friendly and eager to please.

When they drew close enough to see Meg's home, Lynette clasped her hands together with a soft cry. "Is that your house? What a cunning cottage! The flowers and, oh, that tree that spreads out over it as if it is protecting it—it's all perfect."

"Thank you." Meg smiled at the girl's enthusiasm. "That is how I have always viewed it."

Meg opened the door and ushered Lynette inside, and the girl stared with wonder. Meg could not help but remember the way Lynette's father had glanced around when he entered the house, as if he had stumbled onto something foreign. Meg showed the girl the washstand, then went to boil water for tea. When Lynette finished washing up and tidying her clothes and hair as best she could, she wandered around the room, taking in all the jars and bottles and sacks, the bundles of drying herbs, the unguents and tonics and teas, the spices and honey. Meg wondered what she was thinking.

Lynette turned to Meg with a smile. "It smells wonderful here. Like—I'm not sure what—the kitchen, the stillroom, the outdoors, all in one."

Meg chuckled. "Aye, I always loved the smell of the cottage, especially when Ma was baking." She added cups and spoons and little plates to the table, along with a tin of biscuits. Lynette's eyes widened in appreciation, and she was quick to take a biscuit when Meg offered her the tin.

"These are wonderful." Lynette giggled. "I keep saying that, don't I? But everything is so . . ."

"Cunning?" Meg suggested, her eyes twinkling.

Lynette laughed, blushing a little. "I am acting like such a wet goose. You must think I have never been out of the house before. It's just—everything is so different. Are all the houses in the Highlands like this?"

"Nae. I am the only one who deals with plants and such."

"One of the maids said you were a witch, but Papa said that was nonsense."

"Your papa is right," Meg replied lightly.

"Cook says that you heal people."

"I try to. Sometimes I cannot."

"And you use all these things? What are they? How do you get them?"

"I will show them to you, if you like."

"Oh, yes, please."

Meg took her on a tour of the cabinets when they'd finished their tea and biscuits. She expected Lynette to grow quickly bored, but the girl intently followed Meg's words, asking questions and peering into the containers, breathing in their scents.

"Do all of these come from the woods?"

"Some of them grow wild, and I gather them. Boneset, eyebright, bryony, hawthorn berries, and such. But other things I have to purchase. The ginger, for instance, comes from far away. I raise many of the herbs and flowers— marigolds, roses, onions, rosemary, lavender, and so on. The honey and wax come from a hive nearby."

"You use the wax, too?"

"Aye, for my salves and balms and candles."

"Could I go with you sometime? Or watch you make something?"

Meg glanced at her, surprised. Something in Damon's daughter, not shyness exactly, for the girl talked to her too easily for that, but a hesitancy, an uncertainty, touched Meg. The child was lonely. Meg started to agree, then hesitated. "I would be happy for you to return. But I am not sure your father would like it."

"Papa? But why?"

Meg could scarcely tell her that she doubted the earl would approve of his daughter associating with a woman with whom he had dallied.

Fortunately Lynette did not wait for an answer but went

on earnestly, "Papa is rather imposing, but he really is not a stuffy man. I was a little unsure, at first, what to say to him after . . . after I went to live with him. I was afraid he might say I was a chatterbox, for you can see, I do talk a good bit. It was wont to give Mama a headache. But he does not mind, and he listens, you know, and even asks me things. I am sure he would not mind. He thinks it is good that I am curious about things."

"Then I would be happy to show you some of the woods and the plants." Meg smiled at the girl. "But only after you have asked your father. If he does not know where you are, he will worry."

"I will." Lynette nodded.

"And speaking of worry, I think it is time I took you back up to Duncally, before they start hunting for you."

Lynette agreed and they set out, Lynette peppering Meg with questions all the way up the path. When they paused for a moment at the clearing overlooking the loch, Lynette gazed across the serene water at Baillannan on the other side. "Where do you think the treasure is?"

"You know about the treasure?" Meg asked, surprised.

"Oh, yes, Cook told me. She's told me lots and lots of stories."

Meg chuckled. "Well, Sally McEwan would be the one to know all of them."

"She didn't say much about the treasure, though, only that it was at Baillannan, and it was after Culloden." Lynette turned to Meg. "Do you know more about it?"

"I don't know that there was ever any treasure. It's been said for years and years that Malcolm Rose, the Laird of Baillannan, returned from France with a chest of gold from the French king, to help Prince Charlie in the Uprising." Meg paused and glanced at Lynette. "You know about the Uprising?"

"Oh, yes; I've read about Culloden. I read a great many books on Scotland when Papa said we were coming here. I think Cook was hesitant to say much about it because we're English, you see. But we're Scots as well."

"Aye, I suppose you are. Well, the story was that Malcolm Rose returned too late, after Culloden was over, but he had the treasure, and when he saw the state of things, he hid the gold nearby and went off to find his prince. But no one ever saw him or the treasure. I always thought it was only a legend."

"But it wasn't?"

"I don't know about the gold. But Malcolm returned. They know that now, for only a few months ago they found Malcolm's body in a secret room beneath the old castle."

"Ohhh." Lynette sucked in a breath. "Truly? A secret room? Had he been murdered?"

Meg hesitated, saying doubtfully, "Perhaps this is not a tale I should be telling a young girl."

"No, you must," Lynette cried. "You cannot stop now! I won't be scared, I promise, even at night. Papa's just down the hall, you see, so I know nothing bad will happen, really."

Meg smiled, feeling a wistful pang at the girl's trusting surety in her father. "You are right. You'll be safe as can be in Duncally. And yes, Malcolm Rose had been stabbed to death. But they did not find the gold with his body."

"So he had hidden it?"

Meg shrugged. "No one knows. Perhaps he had. Or perhaps it was stolen. Or perhaps it never existed at all."

The rest of the way to the castle, Lynette continued to ply Meg with questions about the treasure, the murder, and the discovery of the body. As they neared the gardens, Lynette ended her queries abruptly, exclaiming, "Oh, look! There's Papa." A smile burst across the girl's face as she pointed up.

Meg's head snapped up. There, above them at the long, imposing stone balustrade that edged the gardens, stood the Earl of Mardoun.

16

The late-afternoon sun behind Damon glinted on his raven hair and cast his face into shadow. But Meg did not need to see his face; she knew that long, lithe body, the straight, imperial stance.

"I shall take my leave, then," Meg said hurriedly. "Goodbye, Lyn—"

"Oh, no, stay." Lynette laid a hand on her arm. "My father will want to greet you. See, he is coming down now."

Meg glanced at the stairs. Damon was indeed walking down the steps toward them. He looked, she thought, every inch the aristocrat, from his starched and intricately wrapped neckcloth pierced with a stickpin of the deepest red ruby down to his gleaming Hessian boots. Meg braced herself, her stomach churning. She dreaded the anger she knew would be in his eyes, the biting words that would dismiss her from his daughter's presence.

But only coldness was there, she saw as he drew closer,

the remote, impersonal gaze of a stranger. Somehow that was even worse.

"I see the prodigal daughter has returned," Damon said to Lynette, warmth and humor touching his eyes as he smiled at her. "You had Miss Pettigrew worried; you will have to apologize."

"I will, Papa, I am sorry. I went for a walk, and I got terribly lost. But fortunately I ran into Miss Munro. See?" She gestured toward Meg as if presenting a prize. "She showed me the way back, and she took me to her house to rest and have tea."

"Did she?" Damon turned to Meg. "Then I must offer you my gratitude, Miss Munro." He gave her a stiff nod.

"It is unnecessary, I assure you." Meg was pleased to find that she was able to match his polite detachment despite the cold clenching of her stomach.

"Papa, Meg said that I could visit her. She said she would show me where she finds the plants she uses and how to make things."

"Did she now?" His eyes studied Meg assessingly. "That is very . . . kind of her, no doubt, but we must not put Miss Munro to any trouble."

Damon's dismissive tone raised Meg's hackles. She lifted her chin. "I assure you, Lord Mardoun, it is no trouble. I would be quite happy for Lynette to visit me."

Now something moved in those dark eyes, and Meg felt a flicker of satisfaction, though she was not sure what emotion had sparked there.

"There, Papa, you see?" Lynette told him happily.

"Miss Munro, I am aware that you are a most *kind*

and *tactful* woman." His tone put an ironic emphasis on the words. "But I could not impose on you so. Thank you again." He gave her a brief bow and turned away, taking his daughter's elbow. "Come, Lynette."

"But, Papa . . ." Lynette began as they walked toward the stairs. She looked over her shoulder at Meg. "Good-bye! Thank you."

"Good-bye." Meg smiled at her, but as the girl turned away, Meg's eyes went past her to her father's straight, unyielding back as he walked away without a backward glance. She had known he would not want his daughter visiting her, but still it stung. Meg realized belatedly that if he did glance back, he would discover her staring after him. She whirled and walked away, careful to keep her pace unhurried and casual, as if she were not twisted and burning inside.

———

A jolt had run through Damon when he saw Meg walking up the path with Lynette. The immediate leap of excitement he felt each time he saw Meg was mingled with a subtler warmth at seeing her with Lynette, Meg's bright head bent toward his daughter's dark one, a bittersweet pang of recognition of something he had not realized he wanted and now knew he would never have.

On the heels of that immediate response came another, more worrisome one: What the devil was Meg doing with his daughter? He had not been worried by Miss Pettigrew's hysterics concerning Lynette's absence. He did not think Lynette had been spirited off or fallen into the loch or any of the hundred other dire things her governess described. But this—seeing Lynette smile so trustingly up at a woman who clearly despised him—was troubling.

Why had Meg taken up with Lynette? What did she want? Could she hope to use Lynette to draw him back into her web? No. He sharply suppressed the little rise of eagerness in him at that thought. The last two days had been torment enough—remembering everything about the night they had spent together, aching to hold her again, fighting the urge to go to her and somehow win her back. It would be the height of folly to throw himself back into that fire.

Or did she hope to hurt him through his daughter? Remembering the fury in her eyes, Damon could well believe Meg wished him harm. He was reluctant to think she would stoop to use a child to do so—but then, he clearly understood Meg Munro not at all.

Fortunately, by the time Lynette and Meg looked up and saw him, he had had time to recover his wits and put a firm damper on his emotions. He managed to carry on a cool, polite conversation without revealing that inside him a battle raged between the hunger to pull Meg into his arms and the urge to rail at her for rejecting him.

Meg, of course, did not even look uncomfortable. She was the picture of calm, rosy cheeked and bright eyed— clearly *she* had not spent the last two nights tossing and turning, sleepless, in her bed. No doubt he looked pallid and hollow eyed since he had spent the previous two nights doing precisely that.

Damon ended the conversation as quickly as he could, finding it increasingly difficult not to blurt out something he shouldn't. He steered Lynette toward the steps, refusing to give in to the impulse to turn for another look at Meg. He would not give the woman the satisfaction of knowing how much seeing her had shaken him.

By the time they reached the top of the stone stairs, Damon could restrain himself no longer, and he turned to look back. Meg was still in sight as she walked down the path. He wondered how a woman could possibly look so alluring at such a distance. He wished he knew what was in her head. He wished . . . oh, the devil with it.

"Do you not like Miss Munro?" Lynette asked, startling Damon from his reverie.

He glanced over to see her following his gaze. "No, I do not dislike Miss Munro."

"She was very kind to me. She gave me tea and very tasty biscuits. And she told me all kinds of things. Her house is marvelous."

"Yes, it is."

"Have you been there? Have you seen it? All the jars and bottles and bowls . . ."

"Yes. I have, um, seen it." Damon turned toward the gardens.

"It smells wonderful."

"Lynette . . . I do not think it is a good idea for you to go there again."

"But why? I wasn't a bother, I promise. Meg said it was fine if I came. She wasn't upset by my questions. She told me all sorts of things, and she talked to me as if—as if I were a regular person."

"A regular person?" Damon lifted his eyebrows.

"Yes, I mean—she didn't talk to me as if I was 'my lady' or 'Miss Lynette' but just like, you know, the way people talk to each other."

"Ah . . . I see." A faint smile curved his lips. "Yes, you're right. That is pleasant."

"I enjoyed talking to her. And she knows so much—she told me all about the treasure."

"Treasure?"

"Yes, you remember, I told you Cook had said there was treasure hidden here."

"Ah, yes, the fellow at Baillannan. During the rebellion."

"Yes, it was French gold, and no one knows what happened to it. *I* believe it's still around somewhere." Lynette took her father's arm, saying earnestly, "Meg wouldn't have told me all that, would she, if I was being a bother? It was fun. I *liked* her."

"I am sure you were no bother. But . . ." Damon raked a hand back through his hair. "Sometimes even though you may like someone, it is better not to spend time with them."

"But why? What is wrong with Meg?"

"People may be exciting and . . . fun, but . . . they are not people you should be with." He sighed. "It ends badly. And you know it will end badly, so it is better not to continue."

"I don't understand." Lynette stopped walking, and Damon turned to see that she was staring at him, frowning. "What would end badly?"

"I'm sorry." Damon gazed at her in frustration. Surely Meg would not intentionally harm Lynette; he could not believe he was that wrong about the woman. But there were other ways of being wounded. Meg was volatile, as he knew full well, and if Meg should turn against the girl, Lynette would be crushed. But he could hardly tell his daughter about the situation between Meg and him or his fears of what could happen. He could not explain that to see Meg with Lynette twisted a knife in his gut—indeed, he could not explain that even to himself.

"Please, Lynette, just accept this," he said finally. "Stay away from Meg Munro. It is better this way."

—

Saturday evening Meg walked into the ballroom at Baillannan on her brother's arm. She had barely stepped inside when Isobel called out her name and hurried toward her. "Meg!"

"Isobel!" Emotion welled up in Meg at the sight of her friend, and unexpectedly, she had to swallow against the tears in her throat. They hugged for a long moment, then stepped back, grinning at each other. Meg gave a watery, little laugh. "Look at me; I'm about to cry."

"Och, now don't turn into a watering pot on me," her brother protested.

Isobel turned to hug Coll as well. "Hush, you!"

"You look lovely, Isobel," Meg said, no less than the truth.

Isobel's dark blond hair was done up in an intricate array of curls, a midnight-blue ribbon to match her dress woven through the arrangement. Her tall, sylphlike figure was set off perfectly by her London-made gown. High-waisted in the latest style, with the slightest of trains in the back, the dress was simple, elegant, and expensive, and its color deepened the gray of her eyes. A strand of pearls that Meg recognized as Jack Kensington's wedding gift to his wife graced Isobel's throat, matching the pearls at her ears. Even if Isobel had acquired other necklaces on the trip—and Meg, knowing Jack, suspected that he had indeed lavished more elegant jewels on her—this set would remain her favorite.

"She is always lovely." Jack Kensington came up beside his wife, sliding his hand around her waist. His hair was dark and thick, and his soaring cheekbones and unusually dark blue eyes lent his face a faintly exotic look. "Isobel outshone all the ladies of London. I am sure they were shouting hallelujahs because she left the city."

Isobel rolled her eyes. "If they were, it was only because you were buying up every gown in London for me."

"That is hardly my fault. You looked far too beautiful in every one of them." He bent closer and whispered something in her ear, and Isobel's cheeks turned pink.

She gave him a playful tap on the arm with her fan, saying with mock sternness, "Stop that. Go off and talk with Coll. I intend to have a nice coze with Meg." She linked her arm through Meg's and drew her away. "It has been ages since I saw you last. I enjoyed your letters, but it isn't the same, is it? You must tell me everything that has been going on."

"You want news of Kinclannoch?" Meg laughed. "You are the one who has been to London; you should be telling me of your travels."

"I am sure I will, and at boring length. But right now I want to hear only of home. I understand things have been exciting."

"Mm. No doubt you have heard about the arrival of the earl."

"Aunt Elizabeth and Millicent have been full of nothing else but the Earl of Mardoun—though as best I can tell, neither of them has ever met him. They are atwitter with excitement, hoping that he will come tonight. Do you think he will?"

"I have no idea." Nerves danced in Meg's stomach. She fervently hoped he would not, yet her eyes kept straying to the door, and she knew that part of the jangle inside her was anticipation.

"I remember years ago when he was here, they did not deign to mingle with any of us."

"He is proud, but he was at the celebration when the Griegs' daughter married."

"That is what Millicent said, but I could scarce believe it. Did you see him? Is he all they say he is?"

"I doubt it." Meg had been aching for days to spill out her heart to her friend, but the middle of their welcome party scarcely seemed the time and place to do it. She went on lightly, "It would be hard to measure up to the gossip that has flown around about him. He is handsome, certainly, though he has an arrogant tilt to his head. I am sure women swoon over him regularly." Meg heard the faint touch of bitterness in her voice despite her best efforts to sound dispassionate. She saw Isobel look at her more closely and hurried on before Isobel could ask any probing questions. "And, of course, he still continues the clearances. But enough about Mardoun. I don't want to waste breath talking about that man. Tell me about London."

"It was mad. So crowded and noisy and dirty, you cannot imagine! But, oh, my, the number of things to do and see . . ."

This safe and nearly inexhaustible subject was easy enough to listen and reply to even though Meg was distracted by the arrival of each new guest. Before long Isobel was pulled away to converse with another friend, and Meg moved over to chat with Elizabeth and Millicent. Meg's father was there, and soon the fiddles tuned up and began to play.

Meg danced a reel with her brother and another with Gregory, then stood aside and clapped along with everyone else as Isobel took the floor with Jack, who had clearly been tutored in Scottish dances since their wedding celebration. Meg took another quick look around the room. Damon was not there. Well, that was good. Surely he would not arrive this late, and she could stop worrying about what she would do and say if he did. She wondered when the party would be over.

Isobel and Jack came off the dance floor, flushed and laughing, and joined Meg at its edge. While Jack wandered off in search of drinks, Isobel and Meg walked away, finding a cooler spot by the open doors leading out into the garden. Isobel waved her fan as she related in comic detail the afternoon she had spent giving dance lessons to her husband. Suddenly a hush fell over the chattering crowd, and the two women turned. The reason for the sudden silence was immediately obvious: the Earl of Mardoun stood in the wide doorway.

Meg's heart stumbled, and her hands went cold. She stared at Damon glancing around himself, as beside her Isobel murmured, "Oh, my. Aunt Elizabeth and Millicent did not exaggerate."

Jack went forward to greet Mardoun, and Damon's face relaxed just a bit as he nodded. Meg thought he was probably relieved at meeting another English gentleman, someone of his own kind, and she wondered what Damon would think if he knew that Jack came from the streets and had made his fortune with his wits, adopting the speech and air of a gentleman to ease his way into card games with the wealthy.

As she watched, the two men started across the room toward them. Meg froze. Of course Jack would bring his titled guest to meet Isobel immediately. She cursed herself for not leaving Isobel's side as soon as she saw Damon. Now if she walked away, it would be far too obvious that she was fleeing. Clasping her hands in front of her, she did her best to appear impassive while inside her thoughts scuttled about, desperately searching for a way out.

"Isobel, my dear," Jack said as the two men reached the women. "Allow me to present the Earl of Mardoun."

Isobel held out her hand, inclining her head, Meg was sure, to exactly the correct degree. "My lord."

"Mrs. Kensington." Damon bowed over her hand. When Isobel introduced Meg, he gave her a punctilious nod, his face that of a stranger as he said, "Miss Munro and I have met. Good evening, Miss Munro."

"My lord." Meg was sure her response was as imperfect as Isobel's had been polished. For the next few minutes, the other three kept up a polite chat regarding the weather, the Highlands, and London. Meg said nothing, busily working at not looking at Damon. She felt his gaze upon her, but she was not sure if the feeling was real or only in her imagination. Another tune was struck up, this time on the piano. Jack flashed a smile at Isobel.

"I believe you promised me a waltz, my dear."

"Jack! You never told them to play a waltz, did you? I shall never hear the end of it from Mrs. Grant."

He grinned, unrepentant, and extended his arm to her.

Just like that, the other couple were gone, and Meg and Damon were left standing in awkward silence. She glanced up at him, and it gave her some degree of satisfaction to see that a flare of panic lit his eyes, too, at least for an instant, before it was firmly pushed aside. Still, he seemed more ill at ease now than indifferent, which sparked Meg's courage.

"I hope your daughter has suffered no ill effects from her adventure the other day."

"No, she seems well enough, though less than happy with me." He shifted his position, turning outward to gaze across the room, and folded his arms across his chest. He went on in a goaded voice, "Apparently I am a villain not to let her roam free about the countryside."

"Not to visit me, you mean," Meg amended crisply. Resentment settled in, making it easier to talk.

"Yes, not to visit you." His voice took on a grating quality, like the rub of metal against metal.

"I imagine it would be difficult to explain to one's daughter that she cannot mingle with my sort of woman."

"What is that supposed to mean?" He glanced at her, his brows drawing together sharply.

"It means that an earl's daughter cannot associate with the earl's doxy, but 'tis awkward to explain that to your daughter."

"That is not why!" He whipped back around to face her, his voice rising. He seemed to realize that he had spoken too loudly, for he cast a look toward the nearest guests, then lowered his voice to a hiss. "Do not lay this at my feet. As if I am being—" He made a vague gesture with his hand.

"Arrogant?" Meg supplied. "Snobbish? Rude?"

"Unreasonable!" he snapped. "As if I disdain you, as if I had mistreated you. Blast it!" He glanced around again, then wrapped his hand around her arm and stepped through the closest door, pulling her with him onto the flagstone path outside, away from the noise and light of the ballroom.

"What are you doing? Let me go." Meg jerked her arm from his grasp.

He faced her. "What the bloody hell are you playing at with Lynette?"

"Playing at?" Meg's eyebrows sailed upward, and she planted her fists on her hips. "I found her wandering in the woods, lost, and I brought her home. Oh, and I also committed the unpardonable sin of giving her a cup of tea and a biscuit and the opportunity to sit a bit at my table."

"I will not have you hurt her. I will not let you win her admiration, her friendship, and then abandon her."

Meg gaped at him. "Why would I do such a thing?"

"I have no idea! Because you wish to hurt me, to use Lynette against me? Because it amuses you? Because you are utterly mad? I have no idea why you do any of the things you do. I have done naught but think about it for the past week, and I still cannot understand you." His words tumbled out, his face a study in frustration. "You came to my home and railed at me. Reviled me, with nothing but hatred and fury in your voice. Yet only the night before you were kissing me, wrapping your arms and legs around me as if you could not get close enough." He came a step closer, his voice lowering. "Melting into me like warmed butter."

Meg turned her head away, her cheeks flushing with shame at his description of how easily he had aroused her, how wantonly she had responded to his kisses. Worse, she could feel herself responding even now, her senses reeling at the closeness of him, her blood thrumming with the sensuality of his words. Her knees trembled, a heavy ache forming between her legs. Even knowing his opinion of her, knowing how hard and selfish a man he was, she hungered for him.

He leaned in, wrapping one hand around her wrist. "You wanted me, I will swear you did."

"I did not! I don't! Not anymore," Meg whispered, and even to her own ears her protest sounded feeble. She lifted her chin to glare at him, but she realized immediately that it was a mistake. His dark eyes locked with hers, his gaze so intense she felt as if it reached to her very center.

"I think we both know that is a lie." He jerked her to him, and his mouth came down on hers, hot, hard, and hungry.

17

D*amon's kiss proved every word* she had just said false. Meg wanted to press herself against him, to wrap herself around him and take him into her. The desire she had felt that first night had swept her away, but it had been only a foreshadowing of what she felt now. She knew what lay before her—the sensations his supple fingers could draw from her, the scorching arousal of his kisses. She knew the thundering satisfaction when he filled her and the deep well of pleasure awaiting them. And she wanted, almost unbearably, to have that again.

In another instant she would throw away all scruples and pride; she would shame herself by pulling Damon down to the ground right here and giving herself up to him. A will-less, spineless slave to her desires.

"No!" Meg jerked backward, planting her hands flat on Damon's chest and shoving him.

His arms fell open, releasing her, and he took a step

backward. His eyes were dark and wild, his chest heaving, his face stamped with heavy desire.

Meg knew that she must look much the same. "Yes, I wanted you," she snapped. "But that was before I knew what you were! I was weak and foolish. I let myself believe that you were different. I told myself I could not be attracted to a cruel man."

"Cruel? Bloody hell, in what way have I been cruel to you?"

"Not to me! I do not care only for myself, as you do! I was there at the Keith croft that day. When you had your man MacRae throw them off their land."

"A croft?" His voice rose in amazement. "Who is Keith and what does some croft have to do with anything? What does it matter?"

"It doesn't matter to you! That is the point! Nothing matters to you except your own wishes, your own desires. We are not worthy of your consideration; our birth makes us something less than people to you. Perhaps we are useful to clean your house or cook your food or groom your horses. Or to grace your bed. But our lives mean nothing to you if we interfere with what you want. You want to bed a girl, so you do, then toss her a bauble to silence any chance of scandal."

"What? That wasn't—"

"Oh, yes, I know, it was not a mere bauble," she said, plowing on through his attempt to speak. "I don't care if it was the crown jewels. I am not something you can buy and sell. But that does not matter to you any more than it matters if the crofters are turned out of their homes, so long as you can make a profit. People or sheep, they're all the same to you."

"That is what you are angry about? You loathe me and my touch because I gave you a present? Because I have moved tenants off my land? Because I wish to raise sheep instead of tilling poor soil?"

"They are not just tenants! They have lived there all their lives. Those crofts have belonged to their families for generations. The Keiths were there long before your family ever married yourselves into Duncally. You may have some fraction of MacKenzie blood in you." She held up her finger and thumb, measuring the tiny amount. "But you are all English."

"The devil!" Whatever passion had pulsed in Damon before, Meg could see that now it was nothing but anger. "I own Duncally, and I will do with it as I see fit. Those crofts are *my* property."

"Aye, but they are their *homes*. What do you think they will do now? Where are they to go?"

Damon looked at her blankly. "I don't know. Someplace else. They'll get other employment."

"Where? Where in the Highlands will they find work? And doing what? They have spent their lives here tending to the land."

"There are other kinds of work. Factories or the docks or . . . I don't know. They make a meager enough living here digging peat and raising potatoes amongst the rocks."

"I see, they can go to Glasgow or Edinburgh or London and live with thousands of other people in wretched houses, never to see the sun or the mists or the heather as they toil inside a factory sixteen hours a day! That is, if they can wrest the jobs from the men and women and children who already work there. If not, they can, of course, take to begging on the streets."

"I am responsible for what happens to every soul who lives here? I must see to it that they all have full bellies and places to live? Good God!" he shot back in a goaded voice. "Why don't they emigrate to Canada or Australia or some such place?"

"Aye, they can leave Scotland forever—if they have sufficient money to do so. But where are poor crofters with only the clothes upon their backs to get money to pay their passage? Some few landowners have enough kindness and fairness to give them some compensation for taking away their homes. But certainly not you. *Your* crofters are lucky if they are given enough time to move out their possessions. And if they are not fast enough, you set fire to the place."

He stared at her, then grimaced and shifted his position. "Nonsense."

"Nonsense, is it? I was there; I saw it with my own eyes. I was *in* the Keiths' cottage when MacRae threw a torch on the roof. We had to grab the children and run before it collapsed on us. Wes Keith's mother was on her deathbed, and Wes had to carry her out and lay her on the ground." Meg's eyes glittered with tears. "The woman is dying, and she would have no place to lay her head but for the charity of relatives. But how are those relatives to feed six extra mouths, and them only scratching out an existence themselves? And what will happen to them when you decide you'd like to have their croft for your sheep as well? You would not treat a dog that way. You are a cold, hard man, Mardoun. There is no heart inside you. And *that* is why I loathe you. 'Tis a good thing you have your land and your wealth, because you'll never have love."

Meg whipped around and ran out into the garden, leaving Damon staring after her.

—

She took the path that ran behind Baillannan and up to the promontory. There beneath the spreading oak tree was a stone bench where one could sit and gaze out over the loch. Though not much was to be seen at night, it would give her time to settle her nerves and wait for Damon to leave the party.

Meg wiped the tears from her cheeks and tried not to think about Damon. As she had learned over the last few days, not thinking about Damon was no easy thing to do. For twenty-eight years she had never seen the man, had barely known he existed, and now it seemed he intruded upon her every thought. She shivered. The chill of night was creeping in along with the mist.

"Meg?"

Meg turned, startled, and saw Isobel walking up the path toward her. Her friend had been wise enough to throw a wrap around her shoulders, and Meg was glad to see that she carried Meg's shawl in her hand.

"Isobel." Meg stood up and took the shawl Isobel handed her. "Thank you. How did you know I was here?"

"I looked for you," Isobel answered simply. "I could not find you when we left the floor after the waltz. I thought perhaps you'd gone into the garden, and then I saw you sitting up here. I thought you might be cold. Is something wrong? Do you feel unwell?"

"No. I'm fine. I was just . . ." Meg sighed. "I argued with the earl, and I was waiting for him to leave."

"Mardoun?" Surprise rang in Isobel's voice.

"Yes. Is he still there?"

"No. He left some time ago. He did not seem angry, just . . . stony. I thought he was probably bored. Or maybe just British."

The corner of Meg's mouth quirked up. "No doubt he was."

"Why on earth did you quarrel with the Earl of Mardoun? Did he say something to offend you?"

"He does not have to say anything. *He* offends me." Meg sighed. "Oh, Isobel. I slept with him."

"Mardoun?" Isobel's voice vaulted up and her jaw dropped so comically that Meg let out a ghost of a laugh.

"Yes, Mardoun. I have been such a fool." The whole sorry story tumbled out of her, from his insulting invitation delivered by his valet and their later encounter at the beach clear through to the amber necklace he had left upon her bed.

"Oh, Meg!" Isobel reached out to take Meg's hand. "I am so sorry he came to our party. If I had known—"

"No, do not trouble yourself over that. You couldn't have ordered him not to come. And I would not have you at odds with the only person of your station close by."

"My station! As if I care a fig about that. We certainly shall not continue our acquaintance with him."

"No, pray, do not ostracize him or say anything. Coll cannot know about this; he would be bound to do something foolish, and I will not have my brother transported to Australia over my folly." She gave a little smile. "Perhaps

Jack can befriend Mardoun and take his money at whist. That will be adequate penalty. Mayhap he will win Duncally as well."

Isobel chuckled and gave Meg's hand a squeeze. "Just so." After a moment Isobel went on, "But, Meg, are you sure he meant an insult with the necklace? It is the way of men, I've found, when their affections are engaged. Jack came home every evening in London with something, it seemed— a ring, a cameo, the most amazing sapphire necklace!"

"Jack loves you, that is the difference. He is your husband. But it is also the sort of thing men give their mistresses. A parting gift when the lure of the chase is over and their interest wanes."

"An amber necklace sounds a rather expensive payment for one night."

"Mardoun is a wealthy man." Meg shrugged. "He is very discreet. He would consider my silence worth it, I imagine. And perhaps he did not intend it as a parting gift, but a payment for an 'arrangement' throughout his stay here." Meg turned to her friend. "You don't understand, Isobel; it isn't the same if you are not born a lady. None of Andrew's or Gregory's friends would have tried to give you a ring or a bracelet or anything like that; they would have considered it an insult to you and to Andrew. But that wet goose Harry Hazelton offered to give me his tiepin if I would slip up to his bedroom with him."

"You're joking!"

"No. Worse than that, it was a dog's head pin!" Meg giggled, and Isobel joined her, their laughter spiraling until they were both holding their sides. When they finally quieted, Meg said with a sigh, "It does not matter, really, whether

Damon meant to insult me or not. I canna give myself to a man who has done what he has to his crofters."

"'As ye have done it unto one of the least of these my brethren . . .'" Isobel murmured. "Yes, you are right."

"I hate that I feel this way for a man who is so ruthless. But there was no pity in his face. No regret. All he cared about, all he kept saying, was that it was *his* land, *his* right to do with it as he willed. And it is, I know, but . . ."

"You could not love a man so callous."

"I do not expect love from a man of his station. But I must have respect and liking, at least. Both for him and from him. Neither are here. Only lust." Meg sighed. "I cannot rid myself of that, it seems. I didn't—I never realized what it would be like. To have a man make love to me, I mean."

"Oh."

"Yes, oh. It wasn't that I scorned it. I knew many women enjoyed it. I knew you seemed happy with Jack."

Isobel's smile was sensual and secretive. "Yes, I am happy with Jack."

"I hoped I would feel that way myself someday. But I have always been a realist, I suppose one might say a cynic. I have seen far too much suffering and pain—women bloodied and bruised by their men, tearful brides reluctant to return to their husbands, girls scorned after giving themselves to a man. I could not hold a starry-eyed view of coupling with a man. But with Damon, it was so . . . there was such excitement, such intensity and pleasure and . . . and *closeness*. I had never dreamed I could feel so much, so deeply—not just passion but a sense of joining with another, of completion." Meg cast an embarrassed glance at her friend.

"Yes, I know what you mean. It *is* rather spectacular."

"At that moment, I felt we were meant for each other. Perfect." Meg sighed and shook her head. "I don't love the man. How could I? I barely know him. And so much of what I know I do not like. But I keep thinking about that night and wishing that it would happen again. I want him still. Tonight, before we had the row, he kissed me, and I didn't want him to stop. Despite everything that happened, I wanted him. What does that make me?"

"Probably quite human," Isobel replied drily. "If it were easy to be holy, we all would be."

"Yes, I suppose so." Meg gave her friend a wry smile. "What am I to do?"

"I don't know, Meg. Live through it however you can." Isobel squeezed Meg's hand. "Whatever you do, it will be the right thing. Whatever the Earl of Mardoun may be, *you* are a good person. You'll see your way clear." Isobel put her arm around Meg's shoulders and hugged her.

Meg leaned her head against Isobel. "Och, I hope you are right." Meg straightened, drew in a breath, and stood up, extending her hand to her friend. "Come, then, I'd best get to it."

———

Damon crossed his arms, staring broodingly out into the dark night as his carriage jounced along.

Damn it all! Why had he come tonight? He had known Meg might be there. It would have been unthinkable at home for a woman like Meg to mingle with the local gentry. But this place was odd. And, really, there was no woman like Meg at home—or anywhere else that he had seen. The last thing he had needed was to see her, though questions had teased at his mind all day: What color dress would she wear? Would it be the same blue one with the lace that flirted across her breasts? He could picture her in gold to match her eyes. He had decided not to attend—what use was it to meet the local gentry when he would be leaving in a few weeks? There was little point in staying; the closeness that he had established here with his daughter had been set back by her fascination with Meg Munro.

Lynette did not argue or pout, but he could feel her withdraw, once more uncertain of her step around him.

That, too, was Meg Munro's fault, as were the long, sleepless nights and the heated, vivid dreams when he did manage to sleep, dreams that always ended with his waking up sweating and hard and surging with lust. In those early mornings, desperate and hungry, it had taken all his will not to rise and go to Meg, to beg her to relent and take him into her bed again. He knew he would probably have done so if he had had the least idea what Meg wanted from him, what it would cost him to win her.

Despite his firm intentions, he had in the end gone to the party, telling himself he should get out of the house. It had been agreeable to meet another Englishman adrift among these Highlanders. Jack Kensington was pleasant, easy. Familiar. Then Kensington had led Damon across the floor to meet his wife, and there was Meg Munro, standing beside her. He had barely noticed the tall blonde beside her. How could anyone make an impression next to Meg's vivid beauty?

Damon's heart had skittered in his chest, and he had known that, no matter how he tried to deny it or hide it, she was what had brought him to the party. The nagging, restless itch that ate at him. Desire for Meg was a fever in his blood. And she hated him.

She was the most difficult, impossible, frustrating woman he had ever met, as foreign to him as the farthest star. He ought to be glad to never have anything to do with her again. Yet even as he walked to her, even as he braced himself to face her wrath, her coldness, her indifference, whatever she chose to fling at him, deep inside him hope whispered that he could find what had turned her against him and make it right.

Well, he had certainly found out the answer tonight, and it gave him no peace. Damon let out a low groan and sat forward, bracing his elbows on his knees and sinking his head onto his hands. The vehicle rolled between the magnificent open gates at the entrance to his castle grounds, and Damon sat up abruptly and rapped on the ceiling. The coachman pulled the team to a stop.

"No. Do not get down." Damon motioned to the coachman as he stepped down from the carriage. "Drive on to the house. I will walk from the gatehouse."

"Aye, my lord." If the coachman thought the earl's command was peculiar, it did not show on his face.

As the carriage rolled away, Damon turned toward the small stone cottage. The gatehouse was dark, but Damon rapped on the door anyway, then again, with more force. "MacRae! Answer the door, man. It is I, Mardoun."

There were noises inside and a moment later a bolt slid on the door, and it opened. MacRae had taken the time to pull on breeches and a shirt, but his feet were bare and his hair stuck out in all directions. In one hand he carried an oil lamp. "Come in, my lord, come in." He stepped back, gesturing inside. "Pray, sit down." He set the lamp on a table and turned the wick higher, illuminating the room.

"I'll stand. This should not take long." Damon leveled a cool gaze at MacRae. "Did you burn a tenant out of his home last week?"

MacRae shifted, his eyes wary, and he said in a careful tone, "I evicted Wes Keith from the croft he worked, aye. He was stubborn. Defiant, so I took steps to make him leave."

"And those steps were to set a torch to the thatched roof while the family was still inside?"

"Sometimes it is the only way, sir."

"You have done this before? You have burned the homes of several crofters?"

"Those that wouldna leave, aye. As I told you, sir, they are a stiff-necked lot. I have had to use force to evict them."

"Burning their homes and all their possessions? Lighting a fire while there are still women and children inside?" *Meg.*

MacRae set his jaw mulishly. "Sir, you dinna know how these people are."

"I am learning how *you* are." Damon took a step forward, looming over the man. "There was a dying woman in that house."

"These people are wily, sir. Deceitful. They always have some excuse not to go, some reason you must wait."

"I should think that a woman on her deathbed would be sufficient reason to hold off."

"How was I to know she was dying, my lord? Like as not, the whole thing was a pretense, a delaying tactic. Indeed, we still dinna know."

"Miss Munro told you she was dying."

"Miss Munro." The other man's eyes were suddenly bright with fury. "That's it! It's her that told you! She's wrapped you around her finger, and you're so hot to have what's between her legs that you'll believe the whore's li—"

Damon's fist landed squarely on the man's chin, knocking him to the floor. "You are through here, MacRae. I want you out of this house and off my land tomorrow."

MacRae reached up a hand to wipe away the blood trickling down his chin. "My lord," he whined, "I was doing what you wanted. You told me to clear them out."

"I did not tell you to burn people out of their homes!" Damon thundered. "Or to haul a woman off her deathbed and leave her lying on the ground. You have attached my name to your contemptible actions and made *Mardoun* a byword for cruelty. I will not stand for it."

"You were happy enough to get the money from it." MacRae scrambled to his feet. "I never heard you asking any questions before about how it was done. Not until Meg Munro threw out her lures to you. You will live to regret this. You'll learn what she's like. What she's after. She'll lead you around like a bull with a ring through his nose, and all the while they'll all be laughing behind their hands."

Damon's eyes were cold and flat. "Well, you will not be here to witness it."

18

The walk up the long driveway to the house was not enough to ease the jittering nerves in Damon's stomach, so he turned to his study and the decanter of brandy that waited there. Stripping off his jacket and slapping it down on a chair with a good deal more force than was necessary, he poured a large glass of brandy and sank down in the comfortable chair behind his desk.

Dismissing MacRae had relieved some of Damon's pent-up emotions—and planting a facer on him proved even more satisfying. But it did not stop the images that preyed on him: the burning house—with Meg inside, a thought that turned his gut to ice; the old woman, wasted and weak, pulled from her bed and laid on the ground like some broken chair; the family cast adrift, torn from all they had known.

Damon wanted to protest that it was not his fault. He had not known his manager was shoving people out in such a manner. He would not have permitted it if he had been aware. He would certainly never have ordered his manager to do so. He was *not* the ogre that Meg had painted him.

But that did not change what had happened. Nothing could. In the end, was it not his responsibility? MacRae had acted in his name. Damon had told the man to continue with the clearances. Indeed, that very morning of the eviction MacRae had told Damon he was going to clear out some crofts, and Damon had nodded and dismissed him, too caught up in the afterglow of his night with Meg to pay attention to the man. His ignorance of MacRae's methods was no excuse, for surely he should have known what was happening on his own estate.

But MacRae's words haunted Damon the most—he had been pleased enough to have the profits, and he hadn't inquired too deeply into how that was accomplished.

Even with the aid of the brandy, sleep eluded him the rest of the night. For days, frustrated desire had made his sleep fitful, but this night—even though passion had flared up in him like a volcano when he kissed Meg—that was not what kept him awake. That hunger only thrummed on a lower level, a background to the endless circling of his thoughts.

Dawn found him the next morning standing on his balcony, a whimsical walkway connecting the bedrooms on this side of the hall, its primary purpose being to echo the identical stone balustrades edging the varying levels of garden far below. Damon had frequently haunted it since discovering that from it he could see all the way down to where the trail emerged at the bottom of the hill and joined with the path to Meg's cottage. God, what a fool he was, drawn to her like iron to a magnet, no matter how fiercely she rejected him.

Damon turned away from the view and went back inside. His valet waited for him there, his expression an expert rendering of resignation and disapproval at Damon's disheveled appearance. "I know, I know, Blandings." Damon held up a hand to stop his valet's words. "I look like hell."

"Far be it from me to criticize your lordship." That meant, Damon knew, that Blandings was about to do exactly that, and at great length. "But you cannot go on without sleep."

"I sleep."

"This is the fourth time in the past week that I have come into your room of a morning to find you already awake."

"Maybe it's the Highland air."

"Indeed. And no doubt that is why your plates return to the kitchen half-full every meal."

"No, *that* is the Highland food."

"Ah. Which leads one to wonder what the explanation is for the substantial decrease in Duncally's supply of brandy."

"Oh, Blandings, do leave off. The fact that I have neither wife nor mother does not mean that you must fill the void."

With a sigh of martyrdom, the man fell silent and set about doing what he could to remedy Damon's appearance. When he was done, Damon went downstairs to the dining room. When he saw Lynette at the table, he paused, then, straightening his shoulders, he went forward and took his seat.

"Lynette, I have changed my mind." She looked over at him in surprise. "I was . . . under a misapprehension concerning Miss Munro. I learned last night that I have misjudged her. You have my permission to visit her . . . as long as she wishes it, of course." He could only hope that Meg would be fond enough of his daughter not to mention her opinion of the girl's father.

Having taken care of the first and mildest of his duties this morning, Damon went to his study after breakfast and removed a small bag from a drawer, pocketing it, then set out for Baillannan. It was a shorter trip across the fields to Baillannan than all around the loch, as a carriage would travel, and before long the massive, gray house loomed up before him. A groom ran out to take the reins of his horse, and Damon turned toward the house. He caught sight of a man striding up the path to the house from the other direction, and Damon stopped, letting out a low curse.

Coll Munro.

Damon clenched his jaw and waited. Coll lifted his head, saw Damon, and also came to a stop.

"You!" Coll spat, and charged Damon. Damon did not move aside, just knotted his fists and waited. He could not fault Munro for disliking him, but he'd be damned if he would back down before the man.

Coll was faster than Damon would have thought a man his size could be, and Damon barely had time to raise his fists to block a blow before Coll slammed into him, knocking him to the ground. Damon tasted blood as Coll's fist landed, but Damon blocked the next blow and launched his own fist back into the other man's face. They rolled across the ground, punching and grappling. Damon barely felt the blows; it was wonderfully gratifying to be able to hit something, even to take a punch in return.

Neither man heard the shouts behind them. When someone grabbed Damon's arm, he surged up and back to fight off this new opponent. The other man blocked his blow with an upraised arm, then neatly grabbed Damon's arm with both his and twisted it up behind his back. A small man grabbed Damon's other arm, and though he shook him off, a second groom joined him, and Damon staggered back under their combined weight.

"Bloody hell, man!" Jack roared. "Will you stop!"

Damon ceased struggling, the fever of battle cooling. He looked across to see Coll Munro in the grip of the Kensingtons' squarely shaped butler and a groom, with Isobel Kensington standing in front of Coll to block him.

"Stop it, Coll!" Isobel snapped. "Will you shame me in my own house?"

"Ah, Izzy," the big man said sullenly, sounding so much like a scolded boy that Damon let out a little chuckle.

"I'm glad you find it so amusing." Isobel swung around to face Damon. "I fail to see the humor in going about starting brawls in front of my home."

Jack's grip on Damon's arm relaxed and he shrugged out of Jack's grasp. Straightening his jacket, Damon swept Isobel an elegant bow. "I sincerely apologize, Mrs. Kensington. In truth, I did not come here today to start a fight."

"You've got a great amount of gall showing up here, Mardoun," Coll said, shaking off the others' light holds on him.

"I did not come here to see you, Munro."

"I'm not sure why you *are* here, my lord," Isobel interrupted crisply. "But if you have business with my husband, I'd suggest you get it over with and quickly. Coll is right. You are not welcome at Baillannan."

Damon's brows lifted as Isobel turned, taking a firm grip on Coll's arm, and steered him to the house. Damon glanced over to find Jack regarding him expressionlessly. "Well. Mrs. Kensington is very, um, forthright."

"'Tis her nature." Jack almost smiled. He regarded

Damon thoughtfully for a long moment. "I must ask what you intend to do about Coll."

"Do?" Damon blinked. "I have no intentions regarding Coll Munro other than to stay as far away from the bloody madman as possible. Every time I've seen him, he's tried to hit me."

Damon's words surprised a short laugh out of Jack. "I understand the problem. Still, I should not like for him to be arrested."

Damon scowled. "Do you think I would bring the law down on him for getting into a mill with me?"

Jack shrugged faintly. "You are a nobleman and English."

"Well, I'm not the sort to press charges because a fellow drew my cork." Damon realized that blood was trickling down his face, and he pulled out his handkerchief to wipe his face. "You talk as if you were not also those things."

"Oh, I'm English enough, but no nobleman." The brief flash of Jack's smile held no warmth. "I am not a 'member of your club,' if that is what you thought."

"I know that."

"You do?" Now it was Kensington who looked surprised.

Damon shrugged. "Don't worry; you're quite good. But one can tell—your demeanor, while impassive enough, lacks that certain quality of utter indifference that is essential to a British gentleman." Damon grinned, then winced at the pain it caused in his upper lip. "Ow. Bloody hell, that Munro has fists like rocks."

"He is someone I prefer to have on my side. I assume you had a reason for coming here today."

"Yes." Damon folded his handkerchief, keeping his eyes on his hands. "I—Miss Munro advised me of some things, practices of my steward . . . that I was not aware of. I—there is a crofter. Wes Keith. I wanted to talk to the man, but I realized that I had no idea where to find him. I did not like to ask one of the servants." Damon shoved the piece of cloth into his pocket and lifted his head, jaw set. "The only person I could think of who might know the area well enough and who would be likely to tell me was you."

"I see."

"I was, you see, unaware that Mrs. Kensington would be, um . . ."

"My wife is very fond of Meg Munro. Everyone here is."

"So am I. Unfortunately, she is rather less fond of me." Damon took a step forward, fixing his eyes intently on Jack. "If you don't wish to tell me where Keith is, it does not matter. I can find out another way. But I'm damned if I'll let you think that I would ever in any way have intentionally hurt Meg Munro. I have—she is—oh, bloody hell, I'm not discussing her with you or anyone else." Damon turned and started toward his horse, still held by the highly interested groom.

"Mardoun. Wait." Jack started after him. "I have no idea where Wes Keith lives. I've barely been here long enough to know the names of my own crofters, let alone yours. But I shall ask Isobel; there's no one in the glen that she and Coll don't know. I'll have my horse saddled; there's no hope of me giving you directions."

Damon thought sourly that neither Coll nor Isobel would be likely to help, but to his surprise Jack emerged from the house a few minutes later and mounted the horse that had been led out of the stables for him.

They rode in silence for the most part. Kensington

seemed to have no need for social chatter, and Damon found that the burst of energy from the fight was swiftly draining from him. His jaw was beginning to ache, and the sleepless night was catching up with him. The narrow track they followed widened out, revealing a distant vista, one of the bleak and oddly beautiful views of hills and glen that one happened upon so often here. Closer to them, dwarfed by the magnificence behind it, stood a low, thatch-roofed house of the same dun color as the landscape around it.

As they approached, a man stepped out of the door, another man right after him. A curious blend of defiance and resignation was on their faces, and their postures were those of men braced for the worst.

Jack nodded to them. "Good day to you, sir. I am looking for the house of John Grant."

"I am Grant," the man in front said tersely.

"I am Jack Kensington. My wife sends you her regards."

Grant nodded, though his gaze lost none of its wariness. "She is a fine lady, and we thank her for the things she sent." His gaze slid over to Damon.

"The Earl of Mardoun asked me to guide him to your croft."

"Aye, I see him."

"I am looking for Wes Keith." Damon dismounted, turning toward the other man.

"I'm Keith." He crossed his arms, regarding Damon stonily. Behind him, two women and several children had begun to trickle out the door. One of the women held a baby in her arms, and a toddler had a hand firmly clenched in her skirts. One and all, their faces were etched with dread.

Damon, looking at the house, at the man, at the clump

of people, was suddenly at a loss for words. He cleared his throat. Finally, simply, he said, "I have come to apologize to you, Mr. Keith."

Had the situation not been so grim, Damon thought he would have laughed at the stunned expressions on the faces before him. "I have been . . . lax in my oversight of my land. I chose a steward poorly and did not inquire too much into how he was governing Duncally. As a result, things have been done in my name"—Damon's voice hardened under a fresh spark of anger—"things that were wrong, that I would not have had happen." He took a step forward, his eyes on Keith. "I am sorry for your loss. For the house, the possessions, the uprooting of your family."

"It's little help now, is it?" Keith's voice held more despair than accusation.

"No, you are right, it's not." Damon reached into his pocket and pulled out the bag of coins he had taken from his office earlier. He held it out to Keith, who gazed at him blankly. "Take it, man." Damon waggled the bag impatiently, then thrust it into Keith's hand. "It will not bring back what you lost, but it can, at least, help you to replace your possessions. If you wish to return to the croft and rebuild, you may. If you would prefer to emigrate, I will provide your passage."

"I . . ."

As Keith continued to stare at Damon in shock, one of the women stepped forward and took possession of the bag, thrusting it into her pocket. "We thank you, my lord. Wes . . ."

"Aye, we do."

"And pray give my best wishes to your mother," Damon went on awkwardly, starting to move back to his horse.

To his dismay, Mrs. Keith invited him in to speak to Wes's mother in person. Damon could see no way out of it, so he followed the woman into the hut, ducking his head to pass through the low doorway. Inside, the hut was dark, airless, and cramped; his head almost brushed the ceiling. His gaze went to the corner of the room, where a woman lay on a pad on the floor. She was pale and gaunt, so still and lifeless that he would have taken her for a corpse already were she not watching him. His gut clenched, but he strode forward and squatted down beside her.

"Mrs. Keith, I am Lord Mardoun."

"Aye, I ken . . . an earl . . . in my hoose." Her skeletal face held a look of wonder. She gave a little laugh, which turned into a cough.

Alarmed, Damon reached out and put his hand under her back, lifting her up to aid her breathing. Her bones felt horribly fragile and exposed. "Ma'am." He turned his head toward the other woman uncertainly.

"Nay," the old woman murmured, and drew a shaky breath. "'Tis done now. I shouldna laugh, you ken." Damon laid her back down as gently as he could, and she gave him a faint smile. "Thank you."

"I wish . . ." His throat tightened.

"Och, there's nocht you can do. Life is what it is, and it's all too short at that." She smiled faintly, and her eyes closed as she drifted back to sleep.

Damon stood up, nodding to the other Mrs. Keith, and left the house. Jack, chatting amiably with the men, straightened when he saw Damon and quickly made their goodbyes, following Damon as he mounted and rode away.

Damon wanted to race away, to ride as if the hounds

of hell were after him, aching to put the house and the people—his *thoughts*—far behind him. Prosaically, though, he pulled up, realizing that he could not find his way back on his own. Jack caught up with him, and without comment they rode on.

"I've never known, I've never seen—" Damon burst out, then stopped.

"How other people live?" Jack's inflection was faintly sardonic.

"Yes. No. I mean, I have seen the houses, I have seen the East End; nothing could be worse than parts of London. But not on my own lands; my tenants at home are not so . . . hopeless."

"This is a hard land. And they have been treated harshly."

"I know. I know—and it was by my hand. You need not tell me. But what is one supposed to do?" Damon turned toward Jack. "The crofts are small, the land is poor. MacRae was right about that; it's neither efficient nor profitable. The crofters are able to live only hand to mouth. They'd be better off to leave, to do something else."

"But what? And where?"

"I don't know," Damon shot back in frustration. "But does that mean I must leave everything as it is, forget progress, forgo the profits of wool, give my lands over to these people so they can continue to scratch out a miserable existence here? Is that what you have done? How do you manage it?"

"I cannot claim credit for anything done at Baillannan. I am only lately come to it. It is my wife and Coll who have managed the estate, and they have been able to turn a profit. But to Isobel, the crofters are 'her people.' They are as important to her as the money she makes. She loves Baillannan in a way I cannot quite understand; I certainly cannot explain it. The loch, the glen, Kinclannoch—it's all her home."

"And it is not mine."

After a long moment of silence, Jack said quietly, "Are you doing this to win Meg back?"

Damon let out a short, harsh laugh. "No. There's nothing could change Meg's opinion of me now."

"You could try talking to her."

"Go begging to her?" Damon wasn't about to admit he had thought of doing just that, of going to Meg and pleading with her, apologizing, begging, whatever she asked. He wanted nothing so much right now as to lose himself in her, to feel her arms wrap around him and her warmth envelop him, giving him comfort, soothing away the tumult inside him. But surely he must preserve some tattered shred of dignity.

"I have found that groveling works wonders with a woman," Jack said mildly.

Damon let out a dismissive grunt. "It's much harder to grovel when you actually mean it." He gave a weary sigh. "Handing Wes Keith a bag of coins cannot undo the past. Or change all the previous clearances. I am still the Earl of Mardoun, a man who cared more for profit than people. No, I fear I am firmly entrenched as the villain of this story. Meg Munro is lost to me."

He would have to learn to live with that.

—

Meg dug the fork deep into the ground, prying up the onion. She had spent the day harvesting her crops, striving to keep her mind off last night and the Earl of Mardoun. At the sound of a voice in the distance, Meg looked up.

A slim girl was hurrying up the path toward her. "Meg!" The girl waved her hand, breaking into a trot.

"Lynette?" Meg blinked in surprise and stood up, stripping off her gloves. "Hello! How are you?"

"I am just perfect, thank you!" Lynette beamed. "Isn't it a lovely day?"

"It is, indeed. Does your father know you are here?"

"Yes, he told me I could come. Isn't that wonderful?" Lynette paused, adding candidly, "Well, at least for me. Is it all right with you if I visit you? I wouldn't want to be a bother."

"You're no bother. I was just about to stop for tea. Would you like some?"

"Oh, yes." Lynette followed her inside, chattering away happily.

Meg put the kettle on to heat and measured one of her teas into the teapot, her mind churning with speculation. Why had Damon suddenly changed his mind? "How is everything at Duncally?" she asked casually as she set out the dishes. "Your father is well, I trust?"

"Oh! Have you not heard the news?"

"What news?" Meg's heart began to pound. Had something happened to Damon? But, no, his daughter would not be so cheerful.

"Mr. MacRae is gone."

"Gone?" Meg stared. "What do you mean?" The awful thought that one of Coll's men had done something dreadful to the man leapt into her head. "Where has he gone?"

"I don't know where he went." Lynette shook her head,

taking a bite of one of the oatcakes. "Papa dismissed him. MacRae cleaned out his things from the gatehouse and left."

"Damo—I mean, the earl let him go?" Meg set down the teapot with a thump and dropped into her chair. "Really?"

"Yes. I don't know why. Everyone shuts up when I come around, but all the servants are talking about it. One of the maids said the dairyman told her he saw Mr. MacRae this morning loading things into a wagon, and he had a big split lip."

"Oh! My. What do you suppose happened?"

"I think MacRae got into a fight with someone, and Papa must not have liked it. The coachman said he let Papa out at Mr. MacRae's house last night when he came home from the party."

"He did?" Realizing she was gaping, Meg collected herself and smiled. "You certainly seem to have heard a great deal for someone around whom no one will talk."

Lynette's eyes twinkled. "I am very quiet. And if I am in the library reading, the chair back hides me."

Meg laughed, turning her attention to the tea to hide her thoughts. Damon had gone to MacRae as soon as he left Isobel's? And MacRae was sporting the hallmarks of a fight this morning? She did not think Lynette's guess was accurate, but neither could she believe the scene that was unfolding inside her head. "What will your father do now?"

"I don't know. I suppose he must hire a new estate manager, mustn't he? Do you think that will take very long?"

"I don't know."

"I hope it does. I worry that Papa will want to leave soon."

Meg's head popped up, then hastily went back down as

she finished pouring the tea. "Why do you say that?" It was doubtless terrible of her to pump the poor child for details, but Meg could not help herself.

"I'm not sure—he is bored, I think. He rides out a lot—even when he and I have already gone out in the morning. And I hear him walking about late at night sometimes. I was glad he went to the Kensingtons' party last night. He used to go to his club when we were in London; I think he must miss it."

"No doubt. Well, perhaps he will become friends with the Kensingtons." Not if Isobel had anything to do with it, Meg thought. And really, it should not give Meg this sick, cold feeling to think of Damon's departing.

"I hope so. I don't want to leave. I like it here."

"I'm glad."

"It's ever so much better than London. Better than home, too. I can ride, and there are all those rooms to explore—and the mews. We did not have birds of prey at home. Jamie said he would teach me how to hawk. And Papa sometimes overrules Miss Pettigrew. He lets me do things. He doesn't *hover*."

"Ah. And Miss Pettigrew does?" It was better, Meg thought, to keep the conversation to such subjects as the governess. She should not use this friendly, sweet girl to get information about Damon.

"Yes." Lynette nodded. "It drives me mad sometimes. She . . . she means it for the best. She worries about me. So did Mother." Lynette frowned. "I was sickly when I was young—coughs and catarrh and such. But I am much better now." She gazed at Meg earnestly, as if Meg might dispute her words.

"Yes, I have seen that happen."

"Really?"

"Yes, children sometimes grow out of such things."

"I knew it!" Lynette's smile was dazzling. She polished off the rest of the cake and said, "What are you doing this afternoon? Will you make something?"

"I was thinking of starting on a cream for Angus McKay."

"Who is that? Why does he need a cream?"

"He's a cantankerous old fellow. His joints hurt, and as I want a favor from him, I intend to sweeten him up with something to make him feel better. I have been experimenting with different recipes."

Lynette was eager to help, and they spent the rest of the afternoon on the cream. It was easy working with the girl, who was both quick of mind and carefully precise. Varying the recipe each time, they produced three small bowlfuls, which Meg deemed an adequate trial.

"I'll take him all three and let him test them for me," Meg said. "It will make it easier for his pride if I tell him it is a favor to me."

"You mean because he can't pay for it."

"Aye. Angus bristles at the idea of charity—and a number of other things as well."

"Papa has a friend like that, a man who used to teach him. Papa has to disguise the things he does to help him."

"Does he now?"

"Yes, I've met the man." The girl giggled. "Mr. Overton is very sweet, but he'll walk out without his hat if you don't watch him. Papa says his head is occupied with more serious matters, like the Punic Wars."

"The what?"

"I don't know, either, but it sounds funny, doesn't it?"

Lynette sighed and reached up to untie her apron. "I'd better go now. Miss Pettigrew will worry." She looked at Meg a little uncertainly. "May I come back another afternoon?"

"Yes, of course. I enjoyed having you here. I will walk with you toward Duncally."

"Thank you, but I know my way now. Anyway, one of the grooms will be waiting for me where the path splits. Papa insisted I bring him with me."

Meg saw Lynette to the door and watched her start off down the path, then turned back to the cabinet and began to clean up the remnants of their experiments. At the sound of a knock on the door, she stopped and glanced over, thinking Lynette had returned. But it was her brother who opened the door and stepped inside.

"Coll! This is a sur—" She stopped, registering that one of Coll's eyes was swollen and red and his cheek was scraped. "Coll! What happened?" She rushed to him, taking his hand and pulling him over to the table so she could inspect his wounds.

"Ah, Meg, dinna start to poke and prod at me. Isobel's already done enough of that."

"Sit." She gave him a push, and he sat down at the table. "Was it *you* who got into a fight with MacRae?"

"MacRae? No. I have not seen the man. Why would you think that?"

"Lynette told me he had a cut lip. She thought he'd been in a fight and her father had dismissed him for that."

"Lynette? Her fa—you dinna mean the earl's daughter, do you?" Coll heaved a disgusted sigh. "So now you've taken up another of the Rutherfords?"

Meg rolled her eyes. "She is a sweet girl. Only a child. I

found her wandering about lost one day, and she was interested in what I do, so she came to visit me. I think she's a mite lonely up there in that grand house, no other children around."

"No doubt she is, but I don't see why you have to be the one to take her in." Meg bustled about, picking up supplies and bringing them back to table. "She said Mardoun let MacRae go?"

"Aye. This morning, apparently. Had you not heard? It seems he tossed the man out. MacRae loaded up all his possessions this morning and left. And he was sporting a split lip."

"So Mardoun popped him, too," Coll mused.

"I think—wait." Meg grasped her brother's chin none too gently and turned his face up to her. "'Too?' Are you saying it was Damon who did this to you? Coll! What have you done?"

"Why must it be me who did something? It might have been Mardoun who caused it."

"So you're saying the Earl of Mardoun sought you out this morning so he could start a fight with you?"

Coll glowered. "He showed up at Baillannan. There he was, just strolling up to the front door as if he was welcome there."

"Well, he was invited to a party there last night."

"Why are you taking up for that man? You think just because I said nothing I dinna see your face last night? That I could not tell that you'd been crying over the man?"

"So you saw Damon in front of Baillannan and you hit him."

"It wasn't like—well, yes, I did."

"Oh, Coll, have you no care for yourself? What will I do if he sends the magistrate for you?"

"He won't. Jack asked him, and he said he would not. At least he was man enough to take his lumps without whining." Coll paused, considering. "And he has a good right jab, as well."

"Och . . . men!" Meg poured a dark liquid onto a cloth and began to clean the cut on his cheek. "No doubt now that you've beat each other about the head, you will become friends."

Coll snorted. "Thank you, no. One Sassenach is enough for me. Ow!" Coll sucked in his breath. "Have a care, Meg, that stings."

"You might think of that before you start swinging." Meg began to grind up herbs with a mortar and pestle.

Coll eyed the mixture suspiciously. "What do you mean to do to me now?"

"Don't be such a bairn. I'm making a poultice to reduce the swelling. You will thank me tomorrow." She paused in her work and reached out to stroke her hand lightly across his head. "You're a good brother, Coll. I dinna like to see you hurt."

"I feel the same for you."

"I know. So for my sake, please try not to run afoul of the earl again. You are my family." She shifted and turned back to her task, briskly crunching up the dried herbs. "Which reminds me . . . I've decided to visit Angus McKay."

"Old Angus? Good Lord, why?"

"It's my hope he will tell me more about our grandmother—and the man she loved. Da told me I should ask Old Angus about her. I'll take him some balm for his aching bones to sweeten him up."

"Hah! It'd take more than that to sweeten that one. What would Angus know about Faye, anyway—" Coll stopped, an appalled expression crossing his face. "Nae, Meg! You're not saying Angus MacKay is our grandfather!"

Meg burst into laughter. "No. At least, I hope not. Da told me the other day that our mother suspected her father was David MacLeod."

Coll frowned, thinking. "I don't know him."

"That is because he moved away right after Faye died. His family is all gone. But Old Angus was some sort of cousin to the MacLeods, and he and David were friends. He might know whether David MacLeod was our grandfather. And if he's still alive, maybe even where he is."

"Ah, lass, why do you keep poking and prodding at that?"

"I'm just curious." Meg did not add that the project would help keep her busy—and her mind off the Earl of Mardoun.

"Mayhap you'll find out something you'd rather not know. The man took off with never a thought to the child he left behind. What sort of man does that make him?"

"But at least I'd know. Right now all I can do is wonder. I would like to know who he was, what he was like. Why he never acknowledged his child. What happened to him? Did he watch his daughter growing up and never say a word? Was it someone Ma knew? Someone we know? Aren't you curious?"

"Well, I am *now*." Coll was silent for a moment, tracing a pattern absentmindedly on the tabletop. "I wonder if that was his sgian-dubh." At Meg's questioning glance, he explained, "You know, the sgian-dubh, the knife Ma left me.

You remember, she gave you that fancy hair comb and she gave me a knife." He reached behind him and pulled a small knife from the scabbard at his belt, laying it on the table before him. Old, with the black hilt that gave the knives their name, Scotsmen had long ago worn such a knife at the top of their sock, a smaller, secondary weapon. A symbol was carved into this one's handle.

"Oh, yes, I remember. Ma said it was Faye's, like my comb."

"I always thought it an odd thing for our grandmother to have owned."

"Aye, it would more likely have been a man's." Meg set aside what she was doing and sat down, reaching out to trace the engraving on the hilt. "I wonder how she felt about him, what she thought. To keep something of his like that, she must have treasured it. Wanted the reminder of him. Yet she was so secretive . . . maybe she kept his knife as a reminder of how foolish she had been to care for a man like that."

Coll studied Meg's pensive face. After a moment he said quietly, "Mardoun came to Baillannan today to find out where Wes Keith and his family were."

Meg's head snapped up, her gaze suddenly piercing. "Why? What did he want with them? Why ask at Baillannan?"

Coll shrugged. "I think he felt more at ease talking to Jack. You know—someone who was his own kind."

"Did Jack know? Did he tell him?"

"Isobel knew and she told Jack how to get there. Jack took the earl to them." Coll leaned back in his chair, crossing his arms. "Mardoun gave Keith money, Jack said. I don't know how much. He said . . ." Coll cleared his throat, then said a little grudgingly, "Mardoun apologized, and he told

Wes he could come back to his croft and rebuild or he'd give him passage if Wes wanted that. He even went inside to speak to Wes's mother."

Meg stared at Coll, her thoughts churning so much that for a moment she could not speak. "Did Damon not know?" she burst out at last. "Do you think he really did not know what MacRae was doing?"

"Perhaps." Coll shrugged. "Jack believes him. He says Mardoun seemed . . . troubled by it all."

"Oh."

"Or perhaps the earl just now realized how much he is despised throughout the glen and decided he'd best do something to deflect people's anger."

"Och, you're a cynical man, Coll."

"Just one who does not want to see you hurt. Mayhap the man is sorry; maybe he was not aware of how much misery he was spreading. Jack says that men so wealthy and high like that don't really understand what life is like for ordinary folks, of what losing their croft means to someone. I am willing to believe he was shocked at MacRae's methods. Even surprised to find that evicting his crofters left them with no choices. I'll take Jack's word for it, for Jack's not one to be easily duped."

"I would be glad to think I was not that wrong about him."

"Have a care, Meg. Dinna get swept away because the man is probably not a monster. He'll hire another estate manager, and that one will advise the same thing. It's happening all over the Highlands, not just here. And when it comes down to the question of his profits, Mardoun will choose his pocket, not his sympathy."

"You don't know that," Meg insisted.

"I know you canna trust men like him. He is a British earl and he has no reason to love the Highlands. He does not care for any of us; we are here but to serve him. If you put your faith in the Earl of Mardoun, it will only break your heart."

Indeed, Meg thought, she was afraid it already had.

19

Lynette returned to Meg's cottage often during the days that followed. Meg was careful not to inquire about Mardoun, for she felt it would unfairly be using the man's daughter. However, Lynette's conversation was frequently sprinkled with comments about him, so Meg learned that Damon had not yet hired a new estate manager, that he went out riding or walking much of the time, and that Jack Kensington had once come to call.

Meg did not see Damon. That was good, of course. Still, she had to wonder where he rode and walked all those days, for Meg had not caught sight of him when she went to the shore or the stone circle or anywhere along the path from her house to Duncally. Clearly, she thought, he was avoiding the places she was apt to be. And that was a good thing, as well. Coll was right; it was better to forget about Mardoun.

It surprised Meg when Lynette did not come to see her for two afternoons in a row. It felt a bit odd to go about her tasks alone; Meg had grown accustomed to Lynette's presence. She thought about putting off her visit to Angus McKay the next day, thinking Lynette might come and she would be gone, but she decided to go early in the morning so that she would be back in plenty of time for Lynette, who never arrived till after noon.

As she neared McKay's house, Meg was relieved to see that the old man tromped out onto his porch without the musket he sometimes used to greet visitors. "Meg Munro."

"Angus. How are you?" Meg said cheerfully as she came to the porch steps.

"Well enough." The old man beetled his brows. "Whit are you doing oot here, bothering an auld man?"

"Autumn's coming, and the weather will be getting cold soon. I thought you might want a pot of balm to warm your joints."

"I don't ken why you'd hae thocht that. Hae I ever asked you for a pot o' balm?"

"No, you have not." Meg put her hands on her hips and scowled back at him. "Because you're a thoroughly thrawn, bull-heided old man, and you wouldna ask for a hand out of the loch if you were drowning."

"Whisht. I wouldna be fool enough tae fall into it in the first place."

"I've made three pots, and I'm not sure which is best. It's nae use to test it on myself. If you were to try them all, you could tell me the good and the bad of them all."

"Sae you want to experiment on me?"

"You wouldna be my first choice," Meg snapped. "There are many more agreeable."

"Then why come tae me?"

"Och, for pity's sake. Because I want you to tell me

something, and I thought I could trade you the cream for information."

"Weel, why dinna you say so tae begin wi'? Here, gie me those and sit doon." He gestured toward the two stools on the porch of his cabin. "I suppose you'll be expecting me tae gie you tea as well."

Meg had to chuckle. "Nae. I'm not wanting any tea."

"I do, sae you micht as weel hae it." He clumped back into the house, and Meg settled down on the stool to enjoy the view.

Before long he returned with two mugs and thrust one at her. Meg took it, trying not to think of how clean any of the old man's dishes might be, and took a sip. It was hot enough to scald her tongue and far too sweet, but at least the honey countered the bitterly strong brew. From the smell that wafted through the air to her, Meg surmised that Angus had added to his a healthy dose of the whiskey he distilled out back.

He took a deep swig, not seeming to notice the scorching heat of the liquid. "Weel, then, whit hae you coom tae hear?"

"My da told me—"

The old man immediately interrupted, "Och, Alan McGee, noo there's a will-o'-the-wisp. Whit your ma saw in him, I canna ken. But women are foolish over a pretty face."

Meg kept a rein on her temper. "He said you knew my grandmother."

The old man's face softened, surprising Meg. "Ah, Faye Munro. She was a bonnie, bonnie lass. You favor her, but you'll never match her, I'll tell you that. Not that I was fool enough tae try to catch her eye, you ken. There wasna a lad in the glen that dinna wish she'd choose him. She knew it, of course, but she wasna a tease. She dinna gie anybody false hope."

"But she must have chosen someone. Who did she love?"

"You're wanting to learn who was your grandda, then."

"Yes. Do you know? Da said you were good friends with David MacLeod, and my mother thought he was probably her father."

"Weel, Davey loved her, that's a fact." Angus nodded, gazing pensively off into the distance. "And he would hae liked tae be her man. When she was carrying your ma, he hung aboot up there. He cut peat for them and brocht her meat. I mind he took a goat over, so she would hae the milk. A lot of folk thocht he was the faither, and he was happy tae let them think it. He hoped she would let him act the faither to the bairn, that if he did, she micht tak him tae be her man. But it wasna Davey she loved. She dinna get that look on her face that a woman does, you ken, when she sees the man she loves."

Who would have thought this testy old man could wax so poetic, Meg thought. "Who do you think she did love? Do you know?"

"She dinna tell me, you ken. But she was sad all that time she was carrying your ma. I'd see her walking, just walking, and she'd hae this look in her eye, this deep, lost darkness. She would sit up on the cliffs and look oot to sea, as if he micht coom back to her."

"You think he left her, that he sailed away?"

"Nae, not sailed. Just that he was never coming back. I think 'twas Davey's brother, Jamie, she loved. He was older, and a braw-looking man. All the lasses sighed over him. Faye was a woman grown, you ken, not just some lass. She would hae wanted an older man, not a stripling like our Davey. But he went off, not to sea but to fight for the prince. No one knew whit happened to him. But he dinna return, and I think that is why Faye Munro was sae sad."

Meg felt tears well in her eyes for the grandmother she had never known.

"It's my thocht she was happy to pass on, but it struck poor Davey hard. I thocht he micht stay, just tae look in on the bairn, but he couldna do it. He left, you ken, and he never came back either." Angus let out a sigh, his rheumy eyes sorrowful.

Meg sat for a moment, absorbing what she had learned. "Where did David MacLeod go? Is he still alive?"

"I dinna ken. I've never heard aught else from him. Their mither and faither are both dead these many years, as well as one of their sisters. Mary, though, is still alive; she meritt Tom Fraser. But, och, they say her mind's no' richt anymair."

And that, Meg thought, was that. She thanked Angus for the tea and the conversation. Talk of his old friend seemed to have mellowed him a bit, and he actually tipped his hat to her as she left and said quietly, "Ah, weel, there willna be another as bonnie as Faye, but in truth, you have her eyes, lass."

It was, Meg reflected, as nice a compliment as one could hope to receive from Old Angus. She returned to her cottage in a wistful mood, thinking about her long-dead grandmother and her ill-fated love, imagining the woman sitting on the cliffs, gazing out at the gray sea and mourning the man who had gone off to war. Poor David MacLeod, as well, loving the woman who loved only his brother. It appeared Meg was not destined to find out the identity of her grandfather. It made her ache a little.

The sky overhead was a sullen gray, reflecting Meg's mood, and by the time she got back to her cottage, it had begun to drizzle. Lynette did not come again, and even though it was not surprising, given the gloomy weather, worry tickled at Meg's mind. Had Damon once again forbidden the girl to see Meg? The drizzle stopped, then started, and by the time night fell, it began to rain in earnest. Banking the fire, Meg went to bed early, and with the comforting noise of the rain falling on the roof, she fell asleep.

———

Meg awoke with a start. She could hear the rain clattering against the roof and the windows, much harder now. Had thunder awakened her? As she sat up, the *thump-thump-thump* came again. Not thunder, but someone pounding on the door. A voice sounded, but she could not distinguish it in the noise of the rain.

Meg was accustomed to people coming to her in the middle of the night, needing help. She slipped out of bed and pulled on a robe, lit a candle from the glow of the embers in the fireplace, and started toward the door.

"Meg! It's me. Open up."

She stopped, her throat going dry. She was close enough to recognize the voice now, even muffled by the rain. Her heart began to pound, and she hurried forward.

"Damon?" She stopped at the door, her hand on the bar, suddenly scared—not of him but of the feeling surging in her, the mingling of hope and despair and sheer vibrating lust.

"Yes. Please, Meg, open the door. I'm not here to importune you, I swear."

She broke from her momentary trance and lifted the bar to swing the door open. Damon stood before her. He wore no jacket, his lawn shirt soaked by the rain into transparency, its loose folds clinging to his chest. His eyes were huge and stark, dark blue smudges beneath them like bruises, and his cheeks were hollowed out. His head was bare, and the rain sluiced over him, plastering his hair to his head.

"Damon!" Meg gasped, stunned by his appearance.

"Don't turn me away. I know that you despise me. But, please, just listen to me." Desperation was in his eyes and voice. "Lynette is ill. I need your help. Come with me. Please. I am begging you."

20

Meg *whirled and ran to* her dresser, shedding her robe as she went. She jerked open a drawer and pulled out her sacque dress, just throwing the loose dress on over her nightgown and tying the sash. Leaving her hair as it was, she wrapped her hooded cloak around her and stepped into her slippers, then hurried to her cabinets.

Damon still stood in the doorway, taut and still, out of the rain but not really entering the room.

"What is wrong with her?" Meg took out a small chest. "What are her symptoms?"

"She is burning with fever." He ran a hand back through his hair, looking as if he was trying to collect his scattered thoughts. "And coughing. She had terrible coughs when she was young."

"What are they like?" Meg grabbed up supplies as she talked, stuffing them into the small chest. "Dry? Wheezing?"

"Not like when she was young." His eyes focused more

sharply. "Not those deep, barking sort of noises. But not wheezing either. She sounds . . . as if she is drowning."

Meg continued to ask him questions as she filled the case; it seemed as if answering them settled him a bit, pushed back the lurking terror in his eyes. After a final glance around, Meg tucked the box under her arm and followed Damon out of her cottage.

Damon lifted her onto his horse and swung up behind her. His arms went around her as he gathered the reins in his hands, and he bent his head toward her, his voice low and unsteady. "Thank you."

"Of course," she said simply.

The path through the trees was too dark to ride quickly, particularly with the rain turning the track to muck, but when they reached the clearing, Damon dug in his heels, and the horse leaped forward. Meg let out a squeak and grabbed at his shirt.

Damon wrapped his arms tightly around her. "It's all right. I have you."

Clutching the small chest to her with one arm, Meg leaned into him, closing her eyes. She relaxed, and for those few moments there was only his warmth and solidity against her, the well-remembered scent of his skin, the encompassing strength of his arms around her. Nothing else—neither the swift pace of the horse nor the rain soaking her, not even the fear in the pit of her stomach—mattered. When they clattered onto the stones of the drive in front of Duncally, a waiting groom raced out to take the horse's reins. Damon dismounted and hauled Meg down, then, tucking the small chest under one arm, he pulled her up the front steps. The heavy door opened before them, the butler standing aside.

Meg did not waste time taking off her cloak and handing it to the man, just ran with Damon toward the stairs. The butler bustled after them, keeping up surprisingly well.

Candles burned low in sconces along the wall, lighting the massive hallway. Damon strode through an open door with Meg on his heels. A small, brown wren of a woman sat beside the bed, her hands clenched in her lap. Her eyes were closed and she mumbled under her breath. At the sound of Damon's entrance, her eyes flew open.

"Oh, my lord. Thank heavens you are back. She—she is unchanged." Tears sparkled in her eyes and spilled over. She moved out of Damon's way, wringing her hands. "Oh, dear, poor girl, poor man."

Damon went to the bed, reaching down to take his daughter's hand. Lynette looked small and frail lying there. Her cheeks were flushed and her hair lay damply against her head; her breath rasped in the silence.

"Lynette, sweetheart. Look who has come to see you. It's Meg." Damon's tone was gentle as he laid his other hand on her forehead, brushing back her hair. His hand, Meg saw, trembled faintly.

Meg reached up to untie her cloak, and as she took it off, she was surprised to find the butler behind her, whisking it away. She moved forward, and Damon stepped back to give her room. As he did, the butler wrapped a blanket around him, saying, "Here, sir. I've sent for hot drinks for you and Miss Munro."

Damon nodded absently, and a shiver ran through him. Meg felt Lynette's forehead, then bent to lay her head against the girl's chest. As Meg straightened, Lynette's eyes opened hazily. "Meg! Have I missed—" She lost the thread of what she was saying, her gaze drifting beyond Meg. "Papa. I don't feel well." Her eyes welled with tears. "I'm sorry."

Meg heard Damon's choked breath behind her, speaking of his pain more eloquently than any words. Hastily Meg said, "No reason to be sorry, pet. We all get sick. I'll warrant even your papa has run a fever a few times in his life."

"Yes," Damon agreed, forcing a light tone. "Dozens of times. Blandings will tell you."

"Your papa brought me here to help you get better," Meg went on. "So that is just what we are going to do."

"Good . . ." Lynette's voice trailed off on the word, her eyes fluttering closed, but her mouth curved up faintly.

Meg went over to the dresser, where the butler had set her box, and poured a bit of brown liquid into a little tin cup. Sliding her hand beneath Lynette's head and lifting it, she coaxed her to drink, then wet a rag and wiped down Lynette's heated face and throat. Rearranging the pillows to prop Lynette up, Meg turned to Damon. She could see that he was braced for what she would say, his face like stone.

"That should help her breathe, and I have given her something for the fever. She should rest a little easier. Now I must go down to the kitchens and make a few things for her."

Damon nodded numbly and followed her out the door, reaching out to take Meg's arm. "Can you help her? Please tell me if—"

Meg wrapped her hand around his wrist and stared straight into his eyes. "I will do everything I can to help her. I promise you. Now you should go change into dry clothes."

"I cannot leave her." He turned back toward the room.

"Damon." Meg kept her voice crisp, letting none of the

emotion she felt show in her face. "You will be no help to Lynette if you come down with a fever as well. Put on some dry clothes, and then you will be able to help me when I return."

"I shall see to it, miss," said a voice. A man she had not seen standing on the other side of the hall stepped forward, the servant who had delivered Damon's invitation to her that first day. No snobbery was in him now, nothing but concern as he turned to Damon. "Come, sir, I have clothes laid out for you, and we'll have you back in a trice."

"Yes, very well." Damon shoved his wet hair back again and, with a last glance toward Lynette's room, went with the valet.

Meg followed the butler down the back stairs and into the large kitchens. The cook, sitting in a chair and dozing, awoke with a snap at their entrance and rushed forward.

"Och, this is a terrible business, Meg. I was so glad when I heard he went to fetch you. Can you help the poor child? What can I do? I've been giving her warm teas with a bit of thyme, but I dinna ken what else to do."

"No doubt that helped," Meg assured her. "Right now, I need to make an infusion as well as a cough syrup. Have you any raspberry vinegar for the syrup? And honey. Hot water for the infusion."

"Of course. The kettle's on; I'll fetch you the vinegar and honey. Bowls?"

"Aye." Meg opened her chest and began to lay out herbs on the worktable. "I'll need cool water, too, as cool as you can get it."

"I'll draw up a bucket and put it in the cold cellar."

Meg worked quickly and carefully, measuring out fennel, hyssop, and elfwort. She made a decoction, pouring a small amount of hot water over the ground ingredients and setting them aside to soak. She put more herbs together into a small sack and mixed yet another batch into a small jar of oil. When Sally brought her the raspberry vinegar, she added honey and poured in the strained decoction of herbs to complete the syrup.

Followed by a maid with a kettle of steaming water, Meg carried her remedies up the stairs, where the waiting valet hurried forward to take Meg's bottles. Damon was inside the room, now clad in dry clothes, sitting in the tall wingback chair beside Lynette's bed. His head rested against the back of the chair, and Meg saw that he had fallen asleep as he waited for her. Meg tiptoed to the bed to check on her patient, and Damon stirred, opening his eyes blearily.

For an instant, a smile touched his face, an expression so open, even boyish, that Meg's heart turned in her chest. "Meg," he said softly, and reached out to take her hand, pressing it against his cheek. His eyes cleared, and he released her hand and stood up. "I beg your pardon." He cleared his throat. "I'm not sure I—thank you for coming. For helping Lynette."

"Of course I came. Did you really think I would not?" She looked at him searchingly.

"No. I hoped—I counted on your heart." He glanced away. "But I feared you might refuse. I know how you feel about me." He shrugged as if shoving the topic aside. "What can I do to help?"

Knowing he needed to be useful, she told him to raise his daughter to a sitting position. He hastened to do so, lifting Lynette as if she were a fragile piece of glass. Meg coaxed the girl into taking a spoonful of the syrup, though Lynette's mouth twisted at the taste, then stuffed more pillows behind Lynette so that she lay at a steeper angle. Next, Meg rubbed some of the pungent-smelling oil on Lynette's chest, covering it with a piece of wool. Pouring out a small handful of her dry mixture into a bowl, Meg placed the bowl on the table beside the bed and poured hot water over the herbs. Aromatic steam rose from the bowl.

"That will help her breathe," she told Damon. "It will also help her to cough, which is all to the good."

He nodded and gave the waiting servants a brief nod of dismissal. What must it be like, Meg wondered, to have such authority? It was no wonder that he carried such an air of arrogance. Or that he did not understand the position of his crofters, who had so little power, even over their own lives.

"Blandings should go to bed," he said, glancing around vaguely. "But he will not, of course." Damon rubbed his hands over his face.

"What about you?" Meg asked. "How long have you been up?"

"It seems forever. Lynette took ill Sunday, and then she began to cough. She was restless, could not sleep well for the coughing, so I sat with her last night. She just got worse all through the night and today." He paused. "I guess that was really yesterday now, wasn't it? It must be the middle of the night."

"Yes. And you have apparently not slept for a day and a half. You should get some rest. I will look after her."

"I cannot." He cast a glance toward the bed. "I cannot leave her alone." Damon pushed his fingers back through his hair in the same weary, restless gesture as before. "I feel so bloody useless! I sent for the blasted doctor; I never dreamed there would not be one for miles and miles. I was a fool to bring Lynette up here. We should have gone back to the Hall or stayed in London, where we could get a doctor. I should at least have brought her old nurse. She is the one who always cared for her in her illnesses. Miss Pettigrew is worse than useless."

He paced away, then back, caught up in his wretched regret. "I should have thought Lynette might come down sick. But she seemed so much better. I told myself it was just Amibel's hysteria. That she was so enamored of her own fragility, she sought it out in her daughter as well. I flattered myself that Lynette would be better with me. I let her do too much. I was sure it was good for her to ride and walk and be outdoors." He turned tortured eyes to Meg. "I was so arrogant, so foolish, so certain I was right."

"Aye, you were arrogant, I've no doubt, and you are that way still if you think you should have known the future. Are you so godlike? All-seeing, all-knowing?"

His mouth thinned and his expression turned annoyed. "You are certainly a dab hand at making one feel better."

"I am not here to make you feel better," Meg retorted. "I'm here to help Lynette, which I can tell you true I'll do as well as any of your doctors, who would likely decide it would help to leech her or some such nonsense. She may be small, but Lynette is a sturdy girl for all that, and she has a lot of spirit. She'll fight for every breath, and so will I. And anyone here will tell you that there are few as stubborn as Meg Munro."

"I am well aware of that," he murmured, his features lightening a little.

"You could not have known Lynette would fall ill here and now. It is not as if you took her into some pestilence-ridden area. It may be that Lynette would not have been ill if she had not come here, but it also may be she would have gotten sick in any of those other places as well. She told me herself that she coughed more in London than she did here. Lynette loves it here! She has been happy to be around you, to go riding with you each day, to have you treat her as if she is not a fragile, useless creature."

"Do you really think so?" Hope pierced the pain in his eyes.

"I know so." Meg gestured firmly toward the chair. "Now, if you will not sleep, at least sit down. It will be a long wait."

"No. You sit here." He stepped aside politely. "'Tis more comfortable."

"Mayhap. But I do not think this other little chair is meant for someone your size." Meg pulled out the dainty chair in front of the vanity and carried it to the other side of the bed. "I will do quite well here, and it is closer to the water, in any case."

Lynette's fever continued to rage through the night, and Meg and Damon kept watch. Now and then Lynette was racked with spasms of coughing, and Damon would hold her until the spell passed. Blandings made frequent trips downstairs to replace the kettle with another steaming one and fill the pitcher again with cold water from the cellar so that Meg could renew the aromatic steam and continue to bathe the girl's feverish face.

Meg's back grew tired from bending over the bed, and her eyes grew heavy. Once she jerked upright to find that she had fallen asleep beside the bed, her head resting on the mattress.

"Meg?" Damon's hand was on her shoulder. "Meg, wake up." He leaned over his daughter, gently wiping Lynette's face with the cool, wet cloth. "She is hotter, and her breathing—her breathing's changed." He turned to Meg, his face tight with tension, his eyes deep wells of pain. "I cannot lose her, Meg." His voice was thick. "I have always had whatever I wanted—but none of it is worth a damn if Lynette . . ." He pressed his lips tightly together, as if to prevent the word he dreaded from even slipping out.

Meg jumped to her feet and went to the head of the bed. Lynette's face was red, and she moved her head restlessly. Her breathing was labored, each breath seeming more difficult.

"Her fever has spiked. She is growing worse."

21

"Q uick," *Meg went on.* "*We* must make her a tent for breathing. We need material."

"Blandings!" The valet popped into the room, and Damon repeated Meg's command.

"And more water—hot and cold." Meg gave Lynette another spoonful of tonic to reduce her fever and wiped down her face and chest with the cool water. "Here." She turned to Damon. "Raise her up and hold her." She handed him a small towel. "I have to clear her lungs."

Damon leaned his daughter against his chest, and Meg cupped her hand and laid it on Meg's back, just above her shoulder blade. Keeping her wrist on Lynette's back, she began to clap her cupped hand against Lynette's back. It made a loud popping sound, and Damon winced.

"It doesn't hurt her. It sounds loud, but it's only a tap." Meg continued to move her hand up and down. "Now, Lynette, take a breath. Do you hear me, sweetheart? Take a deep breath."

Lynette drew in a bubbly breath and began to cough.

"There, that's good. That's my girl." When the spasm ended, Meg moved to the other side of Lynette's back, following the same routine. After that, she went through the same treatment on either side of the girl's upper chest, urging her to breathe in deeply after each set of tapping. She followed up with a final set of claps on Lynette's lower back.

Blandings returned, and Meg instructed the two men to drape a sheet over the head of the bed, forming a tent. She replaced the herbs in the bowl with a fresh mixture, crumbling up a few new leaves and adding them. With the makeshift tent now in place over Lynette's upper body, she set the bowl down on the small table and poured steaming water over it. Bathing the girl's face again with the freshly cold water, she closed the tent around Lynette and the steaming bowl and stepped back.

As Blandings slipped out of the room behind them, Meg turned to Damon. He was still as a rock, gazing at the tent as if he could will his daughter to breathe. Without thinking, Meg took his hand, and he closed his fingers tightly around hers.

"Is she better? How can I tell?" His voice was low and raw.

"We must wait." They stood that way for what seemed forever, but finally Meg straightened. "Listen." She pulled him a step closer to the tent, bending her head toward Lynette. "There. Can you hear it?"

"Her breathing is easier."

"Yes, the heat and herbs have opened her airway. She does not have to labor so to breathe."

Damon looked over at Meg, a glimmer of tears in his

dark eyes. "Thank God! Meg . . ." He pulled her to him, wrapping his arms around her and resting his head against hers. "I thought she was going to smother. I thought I had lost her."

Meg wound her arms around him, holding him tightly, as if she could pour her comfort into him. She felt Damon press a kiss to her hair and say her name again in a voice choked with emotion. In that instant she felt joined to him as surely as they had been joined that night in her bed. She knew his pain, his dread, the relief and hope that flared inside him now, and it was sweet, so sweet, to hold him. So right.

Then his arms loosened around her, and she looked up at him. He held her for a moment longer, his eyes gazing into hers before he stepped back, releasing her. Clearing his throat, he said, "Thank you."

"There is no need to continue to thank me, Damon. I am happy I was able to help her. Lynette is dear to me. And even if I did not know her, I would not have refused."

"Thanking you is a necessity for me, I think." He let out a long breath. "She is better now, isn't she?"

"She is better," Meg said carefully. "There is still a long way to go, but for the moment, she is responding to the remedies. Her fever has dropped and her breathing is clearer. Her lungs are still very congested. There may be another crisis. But I am hopeful. I meant it when I told you that Lynette is stronger than she looks."

"Good. That's good." He repeated his words almost as if to convince himself. "What do we do now?"

"Wait," she said prosaically, and returned to her chair. "We will probably have to cup her back again in a few hours. You should sleep while you have the chance."

"I cannot." Damon went to the window and pushed aside the curtain, looking out. "It's dawn," he said as if surprised to find the world still moving. He stood for a moment, gazing out, before he turned and prowled restlessly about the room, finally returning to his daughter's side.

The upper part of Lynette's body was hidden beneath the tent, her form barely visible through the material. Damon brushed his fingers across her hand on the sheet.

"She is so small," he said quietly. "She always was." A smile of reminiscence touched his lips. "I remember the first time I held her. She was tiny and red, squalling, wrinkled, with an astonishing amount of black hair standing out all over her head like a cat with its back up. I looked at her, screaming and flailing her arms around, and I thought she was the most beautiful thing I had ever seen. She was perfect, such tiny fingers and toes, miniature nails. When I held her, I felt—I cannot even describe it. I had never imagined that I could feel so proud and so fierce. So . . . entranced."

Meg's throat closed with tears. She swallowed hard. "Bairns are the most perfect creatures."

He nodded, tracing his forefinger down a line of bone and tendon on the back of Lynette's hand. "I was not the father I should have been. Well, nor the husband either, no doubt, but that is neither here nor there. I should have stayed there with her, but as Lynette grew older, I let my feelings for her mother drive me away. Amibel did not like London, and I ran to it to get away from the arguments—no, not even arguments—the complaints, the incessant need to be coddled and cajoled, the endless perusal of symptoms and maladies and evaluations of how anything that happened would affect her. I went there more and more often and found it harder and harder to come back." He grimaced. "I was selfish. Stupid. How could I expect a child of four to remember me? To see me a few times each year and yet feel the way a daughter does about her father? I realized too late what I had done. When her mother died, I was a stranger to her."

"Damon . . ." Meg could no longer sit still. She went around the bed, taking his arm and turning him toward her. "Lynette loves you. You are her father, and she has been delighted to be here with you." She took his other arm as well and gave him a shake, though it did little to make him move. "Dinna drive yourself mad thinking what you might have done differently. Whether you should have come here, whether you should have lived there more. It is in the past, and all that is important is that you have each other now. Lynette loves you; indeed, she idolizes you."

"You are a kind woman."

Looking up into his eyes, she felt a visceral tug, the urge to wrap her arms around him and comfort him. And that, she thought, presented an even greater danger to her heart than any passionate embrace. She dropped her hands and stepped back. "'Tis not kindness, only the truth." She turned away and busied herself with dipping the cloth in the water and washing Lynette's face again.

It would be easier, she thought, if all she had to combat was the sensual lure of him. If only she could continue to despise him as she had that day she had flung the necklace back at him. If he had not shown compassion or remorse for the things his steward had done. If she could not feel the pain in him, the fear of losing his daughter, the regret and guilt with which he grappled. And why did she have to remember the exhaustion on his face as he slept in the chair, the artless smile when he woke up and saw her, before he remembered what lay between them? Or that moment in his arms a few minutes earlier, which had felt like coming home.

———

The morning wore on, and Lynette continued to sleep. Meg cooled her and kept a close watch on the girl's breathing. Lynette awakened once or twice, still feverish, and Meg was able to get a few sips of water down her before she fell back asleep. Damon stayed by her side, sometimes pacing the room restlessly, then coming back to sit. Now and then Meg saw that he had dozed off in his chair, but then he would awaken with a jerk and a quick, anxious look toward his daughter's bed. The butler brought in a tray of food for Damon and Meg, and though Damon waved it away, Blandings managed, with an expert combination of pleas, hurt feelings, and complaints, to bully his employer into agreeing to eat. The day wore on, and though Meg, at Lynette's bedside, caught a few minutes' sleep, she grew increasingly weary. It was a wonder, she thought, that Damon could stay upright, since he had lost more nights' rest than she.

As evening fell, Lynette's cough worsened, and they increased the number of times they cupped her back. They had done it so many times now that they were able to work together with easy efficiency. By the time the sun rose again, Lynette's breathing was noticeably easier.

"I'm hot," a plaintive voice sounded from beneath the tent. Meg and Damon both sprang to their feet. "Papa? What—" Lynette pushed weakly at the material hanging in front of her.

"Lynette!" Damon lifted the material.

Lynette started to speak, which dissolved into a cough. Damon lifted her up, bracing her until at last she quieted. As she lay back down, Lynette smiled weakly at Meg. "Meg! You *are* here. I thought I dreamed it."

"Yes, I am here. I have been giving you some of the herbs we talked about last week. Perhaps you could sip a little broth, love, to keep up your strength."

A glance at Damon sent him out into the hall, and moments later Blandings bustled into the room, carrying a cup of warm broth. Damon helped his daughter take a few sips, then she turned her face away, her eyelids drooping. "I'm sorry. I'm so tired."

"You should sleep. You can drink more when you wake up again." Damon turned to Meg, smiling, his face hopeful. "She's better now, isn't she?"

"Yes, I think she is. I think we could perhaps pull back the tent for a while so she is not so hot."

As Damon shoved the tent aside, Blandings came forward to take the cup of broth. "This is wonderful news, my lord. And if I may say so . . ."

"Far be it from you to criticize?" Damon guessed, his mouth quirking up on one side.

Blandings sent him a reproachful look. "Now that Miss Lynette is feeling better, it would be a good time for you to rest a bit."

"I could not sleep," Damon demurred.

Blandings turned toward Meg, and she saw the entreaty in his eyes, though his face remained as expressionless as ever.

"Damon, you must rest, " Meg said, going to him. "Now

is the best time to do so. Lynette is more likely to grow worse in the evening and night. If you are exhausted from lack of sleep, you will not be capable of helping me with her."

"You are right," Damon said, surprising Meg. "You should sleep. I told Hudgins to prepare a room for you."

"But you, of course, do not need sleep?" Meg crossed her arms, preparing for a battle. She found herself looking forward to it a little.

"Sir, I will keep watch over Miss Lynette," Blandings put in. "I could awaken you at a moment's notice. It is only sensible for you to sleep."

"You don't understand, Mr. Blandings," Meg said sweetly. "The Earl of Mardoun is not a mere mortal. He does not require sleep, just as he did not require food earlier."

The valet shot her an alarmed glance, but Meg ignored him, facing Damon, her face alight with challenge. Damon's eyes lit as he took a step forward, and for one tingling moment Meg thought he was about to argue.

Then he stopped and set his jaw. "Very well. I will go to bed," he snapped. "But only if you do, too." His words hung in the air, fraught with possibilities, and color flared along his cheekbones. "I . . . that is . . ."

Blandings jumped into the awkward pause. "I will show you to your room, miss."

Meg pulled her gaze from Damon's. "Yes, of course. Let me show you what to give Lynette if she awakens."

Damon stepped aside, carefully not looking at Meg as she went about her tasks. When she was finished, Blandings whisked her out of the room, Damon following.

"Hudgins put you right across the hall, miss," Blandings

said, going to open the opposite door for her. "So you can see I will be able to fetch you in an instant if needed."

Meg thanked him and went into the room, turning to close the door behind her. Across the hall, Damon stood in Lynette's doorway, watching her, a strangely stunned look on his face. She could not imagine why; he had told her himself that Hudgins had made up a room for her. But she was too tired to think about that at the moment. Exhaustion had dropped on her like a hammer. She had an impression of grandeur, of heavy brocade and velvet and looming furniture, but she had no interest in anything but the large, soft bed, its cover invitingly turned down. She paused long enough to take off her shoes, then sank onto the bed with a luxurious sigh and fell deeply and immediately asleep.

—

When Meg opened her eyes some hours later, she stared about her blankly for a moment, groggy and disoriented.

"Oh, Meg! I'm sorry. I dinna mean to wake you up." A girl stood at the dresser, a bag in her hand.

Meg sat up, remembering where she was and why. "That's all right, Annie. What time is it?"

"Almost teatime. I went to your cottage and picked up some of your things. I hope you do not mind; Cook told me to."

"No, indeed, I am grateful. Thank you." Meg shoved back her hair, still trying to clear the fog of sleep from her brain. "How is Lynette?"

"Sleeping, last I heard. Cook says you saved her—she's

ever so fond of Miss Lynette. We all are. She's a sweet wee thing."

"Yes, she is."

"Would you like me to, um, put away your things or . . ." Annie looked uncertain.

Meg realized that she must be something of a conundrum to the staff—one of them, they would have said, a woman they knew by name and had spoken to for years, and yet now she was sleeping in a guest room.

"No. Dinna bother. I'll put them up myself." The truth was, Meg herself was not quite sure how to act, either.

"You'll be wanting warm water for your washstand?" Annie's voice rose slightly in a question.

"Aye, that would be grand."

As the girl left, carrying the pitcher, Meg stood up and took stock of her situation. The bedchamber was large, the furniture dark and ornately carved. A wooden tester hung above her bed, which required a small set of two wooden steps to climb up into it. Dark green brocade curtains hung on either side of the bed, matching the heavy bedcover as well as the drapes on the windows opposite. The room was perhaps not quite as large as her entire cottage, but close enough.

She pulled her hairbrush from the bag Annie had brought and used it as she strolled over to the windows. She opened the drapes to let in the afternoon sun and found to her surprise that one of the drapes covered not a window, but a door. Beyond the door was a walkway, guarded by a stone balustrade.

Meg stepped outside, drawn by the magnificent view. Below her were the gardens, and in the distance lay Loch

Baille, glimmering in the afternoon sun. She could even see the bottom of the path leading down to her cottage. She trailed along the balcony, passing another door and a set of windows. As she approached the third and last door, she heard the murmur of male voices inside, and she came to a sudden halt.

Inside the room one of the voices suddenly sounded nearer and clearer: ". . . the drapes, my lord?"

It was Damon's bedroom. Meg whipped around and hurried back to her room. She closed the door behind her and leaned against it, her heart pounding at an absurd rate. It would be so easy, so quiet, so secret, to slip along the private walkway from one room to the other. No one would ever know. She felt a surge of guilt that she could even think of such a thing at a time like this.

But she could not keep from wondering if Damon had instructed his servant to put her there—and feeling a deplorable frisson of excitement at the thought. But, no, she had seen Damon's face when Blandings showed her to this room; that, she thought, had been the reason for the odd expression on his face. He had been surprised; he had not known what his butler had done. She was glad; she would not like to think that during his daughter's illness he had been coldly calculating how to get Meg into his bed.

But another, less pleasant, thought struck her. Something other than surprise had been in his expression, something perilously close to dismay. Perhaps he had been appalled that the butler had put her here in the wing normally reserved for family and guests. The idea pierced her.

Her thoughts were interrupted by Annie's coming into her room with a pitcher of warm water. Grateful to get out of the clothes she had been wearing so long, Meg could hardly wait for the girl to leave so she could strip off her old sacque dress and the night rail under it. She washed and dressed quickly, twisting her hair up into a serviceable bun, then hurried across the hall to Lynette's room.

"Meg!" Lynette said hoarsely, a smile blossoming on her pale features.

Damon stood and turned toward Meg. He was once again clean shaven and elegantly dressed, even though tiredness and anxiety still limned his features. The look of him, tired or not, was enough to set Meg's heart skittering, and that, she thought, was another entirely inappropriate thought. Sleep seemed to have made her foolish as well as refreshed.

"Miss Munro." Damon inclined his head in greeting.

"Lord Mardoun." Meg wished her voice did not sound a trifle breathless. She turned toward Lynette. "How are you, love? Sounds as if you have a bit of a frog in your throat."

"Yes." Lynette nodded and began to cough. When she stopped, she smiled weakly. "But I am feeling better, truly. I have been awake for half an hour now." She dissolved into coughing again.

"That is wonderful news. I can see that Mr. Blandings has taken excellent care of you. But perhaps you should not try to talk much just yet." Meg went over to lay a hand on the girl's forehead, then listened to her chest. "Your lungs sound better, and your fever is down."

"I hate this cough," Lynette whispered, and was shaken by another spasm.

"I know, dear, but it will help you in the long run. Here, let us shift you in the bed a little."

Meg put her hand on Lynette's arm and back. Damon reached out at the same time to help, and his fingers brushed over Meg's. He slid them quickly away. Meg rearranged the pillows behind Lynette, carefully not looking at Damon, supremely aware of the tingling of her skin where he had touched it. Flustered, she turned away and busied herself with Meg's medicines.

.Damon cleared his throat. "Hudgins tells me he has set up tea for us in the sitting room down the hall. I fear he will take it badly if we do not partake. And Blandings is eager to resume his duties as nurse."

"Oh. Well, yes, of course." Meg's nerves danced a little at the thought of being alone with Damon. It was absurd to feel this constraint; she had just spent almost two days in close quarters with the man, working and worrying together. "Let me just go over Meg's remedies with Mr. Blandings."

She talked to Damon's valet—she was beginning to feel almost friendly toward the man, she thought wryly, and wondered if the change had been in him or in herself. Damon waited for her in the hallway and extended his arm to her formally. Feeling a trifle foolish, she took it and walked with him down the corridor.

He led her to a large and pleasant room with a view of the distant hills. It could not be termed anything but grand in scope and furnishings, but compared to some of the formal rooms downstairs, Meg knew, it was almost cozy. A small table by the windows had been set for them, and serving dishes sat on a low cabinet nearby. The butler stood at the ready to serve them, but Meg was relieved when Damon dismissed him, saying they would serve themselves.

"I fear Hudgins's idea of a 'tea' is somewhat, um, bountiful," Damon said with a wry smile as he seated her. He sat down across the small table from her, his voice was low and earnest. "Lynette *is* better, isn't she? I am not fooling myself?"

"Yes, I think so, though it will take her some time to recover; coughs can linger terribly."

"Will you stay?" Damon's gaze was intense. "I know it is asking a great deal, but I want you here." He hesitated. "That is, I would feel more comfortable, more certain, if you were close by. If you would continue to look after her."

"Yes," Meg said quietly. "Of course, I will stay and care for her."

"Thank you." He sat back, clearly relieved. "Shall we see what Hudgins has in store for us?"

They went to the nearby cabinet and filled their plates. Meg was, she realized at the sight of food, starving. Even Damon tucked into his food with a will. But after they had taken the edge off their hunger, he began to fidget, pushing his plate aside and shifting in his seat. Meg glanced at him, thinking that he was eager to return to Lynette's bedside. But when her eyes met his, he glanced away and began to toy with his spoon. He was, Meg realized, uncomfortable.

Damon cleared his throat and took a sip of tea. Finally he said, "How did you learn all that—the remedies, the herbs . . ."

"My mother taught me, just as her grandmother taught her. I followed her all about when Coll and I were children, learning the plants and the trees. Even when we were at Baillannan, she took us exploring, Isobel and her brother, Andrew, and their cousin Gregory, as well as Coll and me. Though I was the only one who learned the remedies."

"You lived at Baillannan?"

"Aye. My mother was Andrew's nurse when he was little. Isobel and Andrew's mother died, you see, when he was born. So we moved into Baillannan and grew up there until Andrew was old enough to be sent off to school. Coll and I were tutored with Isobel and Andrew." Meg flashed Damon a teasing grin. "That is why, you see, I do not know my place."

"I am certain I never said *that* to you," he protested.

"No. You did not. But it is the generally held view around the glen."

"I am equally certain," he went on drily, "that wherever you were raised, you would not have 'known your place.'"

Meg laughed. "You are probably right about that."

"Meg . . ." He straightened and leaned forward a little, then rose to his feet. "I must tell you something." Yet he did not speak, but turned and went to the window.

"All right." Meg watched him. His expression, his manner, were more nervous than she would ever have imagined Damon could appear. Her stomach clenched—had he decided that he must make it clear to her what her place here was? That she was employee, not friend?

"I'm sorry," he said uncomfortably. "I have little facility with this, and I do not want to make a mull of it, as I seem to do at every turn these days."

"For pity's sake, Damon, just say it and be done with it."

He braced his shoulders. "You are right. I know it does not change what was done, or my culpability, but I want you to know . . . you must believe that I did not know what had happened to those people."

His words were so far from anything Meg had been thinking that she could only gaze at him blankly.

"The Keiths, I mean. And all the others as well. I knew that MacRae was turning the lands to sheep, that the tenants were having to move out, but I did not understand, really, what it meant would happen to them. It is no excuse, I realize. I should have put more thought to it; no doubt a better man would have looked beyond his own concerns. I admit I am to blame for that. But I did not act with malice." He looked at her, his dark eyes fierce. "And I did not condone MacRae's brutality—I would never have. I cannot bear for you to believe that I intended harm to those people, that I am the sort of man who would throw a dying woman out of her home or set fire to someone's house. The thought that you were in that house chills my blood." He went to her, surprising her by dropping down onto one knee so that their eyes were level. "Tell me you do not think that of me."

"I do not. I believe you, Damon." Meg wanted to reach out and stroke her hand across his hair, to take him in her arms and soothe the distress from his face, but she sternly quelled the urge. She could not apologize for what she had said to him. She had meant her words, and they were words that needed to be said. That it squeezed her heart to see him in pain did not change that. Finally she said, "Coll told me you went to see the Keiths and apologized."

"He did?" Damon looked at her in surprise.

"Yes. My brother is a fair man, Damon. And I thank you for not taking any action against him."

"However arrogant I may be, I fight my own battles. Besides, I can hardly fault him for wanting to protect you. Meg"—he wrapped his hand around her wrist—"please, believe this, too: I did not mean, ever, to offer you any disrespect. I wanted only to . . . to express my admiration for you, my happiness, my pleasure." He glanced down, and as if surprised to see he held her wrist, he quickly released it. He stood up and looked away. "I thought the necklace would please you. And I wanted . . . to adorn you. The amber matched your eyes. I wanted to see you in it."

Tendrils of warmth twined through Meg. Her mouth went dry and she could think of nothing to say.

Damon sat back down, clearing his throat. "I do not say this to make you uncomfortable. I assure you that I am not trying to importune you or seduce you. I realize that you are here solely to help Lynette, that there is nothing more between us. But I could not let it remain thus; I did not want you to believe that I held you in low regard."

Meg stared at him, her mind whirling. She could not say anything, she realized, because she did not even know what she thought, how she felt. A knot of anger and pain buried in her chest loosened as a wild mix of emotions rose in her—happiness, eagerness, pleasure, and, overlaying it all, pinning her, a profound dismay at his words: *There is nothing more between us.*

Before she could speak or move, Damon rose abruptly. "I should get back."

"Yes, of course." Meg stood, and they left the room in silence.

⌒

Lynette continued to improve over the days that followed. Her fever abated, and though her cough lingered, she used the tent only at night. Her tiredness remained, and she slept a great deal, leaving Meg with much time on her hands.

After Damon's apology that afternoon, he seemed to withdraw, his manner turning formal and polite. He suggested that he and Meg take turns staying with Lynette, couching his words in such a way that it seemed he was considerately giving Meg time to rest. But Meg could not help but feel he was avoiding her, and the thought made her ache.

He was right, of course. He was being a perfect gentleman, treating her with the utmost respect, as he would any lady, not as a doxy who had once warmed his bed. She should be glad, Meg knew. Relieved.

However much it had warmed her to learn that he had not known about MacRae's rough methods, let alone endorsed them, it did not make him any less an aristocrat. That he was not wicked did not make him good. As Coll had said, he would soon hire another manager, and it would still profit Damon to evict his crofters. Would his regret and guilt over MacRae's actions keep him from continuing the clearances, or would he carelessly, selfishly set them in motion again, even if in a less ruthless fashion?

It would be foolish indeed to love such a man, and Meg was no longer sure she could give her body to him without offering up her heart as well. Indeed, she could not help but think that it would be wrong of her to even try to separate the two.

———

One afternoon as Lynette slept, Meg stood at the window looking out, restless and bored, wishing Damon had not left the room the moment she entered. The main entrance of the house lay before her, with its long drive to the ornate formal gates. This pleasant prospect had a view of the moor, still covered in heather, and the green hills in the distance, though it did not have the dramatic sweep of the staggered gardens dropping down to Loch Baille that was visible from her own room.

As she watched, Damon came into view, and she leaned closer to the glass, watching him. He strolled down the drive between the rows of lime trees, hands in his pockets and head lowered. She wondered what he was thinking, if he was still haunted by the demons of regret and guilt she had seen during Lynette's illness. Meg thought of his drawn, stark face when he came to her cottage, pride stripped, to beg for her help. The expression when he turned to her at his daughter's bedside, his voice thick with emotion as he castigated himself for his failings as a father. A pliant, tender warmth bloomed in Meg's chest, a desire to cradle him to her and comfort him, as strong in its own way as the heat that had speared through her when they came together in passion.

Letting out an exasperated noise, she turned, grabbing up her book and once more plopping down in the chair. She had to stop thinking this way. Damon now thought of her as his child's caregiver, not a woman to be desired. She should prefer it that way. When a nobleman took a peasant girl into his bed, it never ended well for the girl.

She opened the book and began to read determinedly, though after ten minutes she could not have told anyone what the book said. When the door opened and Damon stepped in, Meg's head snapped up and she had to fight back the smile that sought to curve her lips.

"How is she?" he asked, nodding toward the bed.

"Sleeping." Meg was very conscious of Damon's standing beside her, of his long, muscular legs, and she could not help but remember the line of his naked thigh and hip, the hollow there that had invited the touch of her thumb, the smooth glide up over the ridge of his pelvic bone and the latticework of muscle and ribs widening to his shoulders.

Meg pulled her mind away from that treacherous path, realizing as she did so how short and abrupt her answer to his question had been. She began to babble about Lynette's condition, trailing off when she realized that now she sounded nervous and dim-witted. She rose, closing the book on her finger to hold the place.

Damon glanced down at the cover, and his eyebrows lifted. "*A Compleat Historie of the Honorable Name of Rutherford*?" His lips curled, dark eyes twinkling. "You hope to be put to sleep, I take it?"

Meg chuckled. "It was the only thing in my room to read."

"I am certain we can find something more interesting in the library for you." He reached out to take the book, and his fingers grazed her hand. His eyes darkened, and for an instant something so dark, so hungry, was in his gaze that it took her breath away.

She knew then: Damon still wanted her.

The question was, what would she do about it?

22

Damon shrugged out of his jacket and handed it to his valet. His insides were jumping, and it was difficult to sit still as Blandings put on gloves to kneel and slide off Damon's boots, then set them by the door to clean later. Damon knew he should be grateful for his servant's precision and care, for his utter loyalty, and he was, most of the time. But right now he wished the man to the devil. Damon could barely stand his own company, much less that of anyone else.

He was scattered and burning and eaten up with thoughts of Meg Munro, and there was, Damon knew, no surcease for it. She had been in his home for five days now, and he was at his wit's end. At first, he had been so shaken by Lynette's illness, so afraid that his daughter would die, that he had not thought of Meg's beauty or his desire for her—or, at least, those thoughts had merely been part of the whole awkward situation between them, a low, underlying hum of turmoil beneath the dread and pain.

However, when Lynette passed the crisis of her illness the other morning and he swept Meg up in relief and joy, the dam of his anxiety exploded and everything he felt about Meg came rushing back in on him, fierce and bright and free. She was beautiful. He wanted her more than he had ever wanted any other woman. But it was scarcely the time or place to let such feelings show. He felt wrong and guilty even to experience that shaft of longing when his daughter was still ill, still needing him and Meg. Fortunately he had been able to pull himself back, to not give in to the quick, hard urge to kiss Meg or hold her longer.

But when he saw that Hudgins had placed Meg in the bedroom at the end of his balcony, only a few steps away from him, lust had nearly choked him. It was a wonder he had not gone straight to her room and pulled her into his arms right then and there.

Every moment since had been a peculiar combination of pleasure and torment. Even sitting with Meg at the dining table was enough to spark his hunger. Watching as she sank her teeth into a piece of apple and the way her pink lips closed around the fruit, he could hardly keep track of what she said. The scent of her perfume, a subtle hint of lavender, teased at his nostrils; the sound of her light laughter was like her fingers brushing over his skin.

Driven by the razor-sharp bite of desire, he had taken to leaving the sickroom to spend long minutes walking through the gardens. Yesterday he had spent half the morning riding. He had suggested that they start taking turns sitting with Lynette—and then he found himself miserably thinking about Meg the entire time he was away.

It should have been easier now that Lynette, progressing

more rapidly than he had ever seen her do before, no longer needed someone sitting with her all the time. One of the maids would spend tonight on a cot in Lynette's room. He would be able to sleep the night through. But how the devil was he to snag even a minute of ease when all he could think of was that Meg lay soft and warm in her bed only a few steps away from him?

With a low growl of frustration, Damon turned away, yanking at his neckcloth. He felt as if he might choke.

"I beg your pardon, sir?" Blandings said neutrally.

"Nothing." Damon jerked the long, white cloth free and balled it up, throwing it onto a chair. He started on the buttons of his waistcoat, watching balefully as his valet snatched up the neckcloth from the chair, then turned to nimbly grasp the shoulders of the waistcoat and slide it from him. When Blandings moved to unfasten his cuffs, Damon shook his head and waved him off. "That's enough. Go on to bed. I shall do the rest myself."

When Blandings left, closing the door softly behind him, Damon heaved a sigh and ran both his hands into his hair, squeezing his palms against his head as if he might press some calm and reason into it. He walked to the door leading out onto the balcony. Blandings had already pulled the curtain closed, but Damon shoved it open again.

He thought of all the evenings he had stood on the balcony, gazing down at the valley below him, imagining Meg in her cottage, imagining himself there with her. Remembering in vivid detail each moment of the night he had spent with her, until he was full and aching, pounding with the hunger to go find her and take her into his arms, to kiss her until she was as breathless and aching as he.

It was ironic, he supposed, some sort of cosmic jest, that now she was here, only steps away from him down that balcony, and yet as far removed from him as she had ever been. He turned away, cursing under his breath. What demon had possessed his butler to put Meg into a room that lay on the same balcony as his own?

It had been expedient to put her in the room directly across from Lynette's. Hudgins would not have considered that Damon would be so tauntingly close to her. Or, maybe Hudgins had thought Damon wished to have her where no one would know if he slipped along the private balcony to her room. Probably the entire staff was aware of the night he had spent with Meg; servants always seemed to know every detail the instant it happened. Hudgins probably assumed Meg was Damon's mistress; it wouldn't have occurred to the man that Damon would have made such a cock-up of the whole matter. That he would have lost Meg before he had well won her.

Damon leaned his head against one of the panes. The glass was cool against his heated skin and he rested there for a moment, wishing he could as easily soothe his fevered thoughts. But those raced on as though he had no will. He wondered if Meg was already asleep in her bed. He could picture her face relaxed in sleep, lashes shadowing her cheeks, her soft lips slightly open and so eminently kissable. He could imagine her body, soft and warm in a virginally white night rail, the thin cloth covering without really concealing the soft mounds of her breasts, the dark nipples. Or naked, as she had been their one night together, sleeping in his arms, soft and vulnerable and so very much *his*.

He rapped his head softly against the glass a few times.

He could not seek Meg out. She did not want him, spurning him not once but twice and with great vehemence. She was under his roof, his protection. He had invited her, nay, begged her, to come to Duncally to help his daughter, and she had been good enough to do so despite her opinion of him. She had just saved his daughter, and he was more grateful to her than he could express. It would be the act of a scoundrel to pay her back by importuning her.

He turned away and picked up a book determinedly. But as soon as he sat down, it lay unread on his lap. Meg was probably still awake. It was but nine o'clock; time had crawled for the past hour. Perhaps she was gazing out her door, too. Or she might have stepped out onto the balcony. She could be standing at the other end of the stone walkway, the moonlight drifting over her, her long hair ruffled by the breeze.

With another muffled curse, Damon stood up, the book sliding with a thump to the floor. He picked it up and set it back down on the table, rather harder than was necessary, and started toward the door. Swinging it open, he stepped out onto the balcony.

It was deserted, and he the only figure on the walkway. Meg was still awake, he saw; the soft glow of her lamp slanted onto the railing through the panes of glass in her door. It would require only a few steps to go to her; a single, empty bedchamber separated their rooms.

His mouth went dry as he thought of walking to her door. He imagined looking in and seeing her in front of her vanity, brushing out her molten hair. Watching her raise her hands to unbutton her dress, her fingers moving down her back in slow temptation.

Bloody hell! What was the matter with him? He was not going to lurk outside her window like a bloody voyeur. He should just go to her. Open that door and take her into his arms. He was the Earl of Mardoun, for pity's sake. Most women would welcome his attentions. He could give her anything she wanted, offer her much more than a cottage in the Highlands. He could give her the sort of life a woman such as Meg deserved. He could show her a world she'd never seen—Italy, Greece, anywhere she wanted. He would take her to plays and the opera, drape her in jewels, dress her in the finest silks.

All the things Meg did not care about.

She had accused him of trying to buy her, and here he was, wishing he could do just that. Meg did not care what a man could give her. She gave herself only as she wanted. If she came to him, it would be because the same fire burned in her blood for him, because she yearned for his touch, his mouth, as much as he wanted to feel hers. No matter how frustrating that was, it was also one of the many things that made Meg infinitely desirable. She cared not a fig for the Earl of Mardoun. It was Damon whom she would bed . . . or not.

The best course would be for him to go back inside. In truth, the best thing would be for Meg to return to her cottage. That would remove the temptation and end his torment. Yet that was the last thing he wanted.

He gripped the stone railing as he stared out into the night, reminding himself of the many reasons he should turn around and go back into his bedroom. A sharp click cut through his thoughts, and he whirled around. Meg stood in her open doorway.

Meg had told herself she was not going to give in to the feelings that had been tumbling inside her for days. She had a long list of reasons in support of her decision. But she had found that none of those reasons seemed adequate when she looked at Damon. The certitude of his leaving, the impossibility of any future between them, the foolhardiness of wanting a man who would never love her, meant nothing, it seemed, against the way her heart picked up speed whenever he appeared or against the heat that arose in her when she saw him walking toward her, those long, lean legs eating up the space between them.

And when had Munro women ever done the safe thing? When had they trusted their heads over their hearts? Tonight, as she changed into her nightgown, as she took down her hair and sat brushing it out, she kept thinking about Damon in his room. She knew he was there; she had heard him walk past her door.

Meg knew and admitted that she waited—hoped—for Damon to reach out to her, to take her in his arms and kiss away her objections. However weak it was of her, she wanted him to seduce her. She yearned to hear his voice cajole her with soft, low words, to have his fingers tease across her skin, lighting her desire. She ached to feel the heat in him and the rise of exhilaration in herself as she saw the bonds of his control slip away from him.

Meg stood up and began to pace about her room. She was restless and discontent, too hot, too on edge, too eager and melting and full of turmoil, to go to sleep. If she wanted him, she thought, she should admit it, not only to herself, but to Damon. There was nothing to stop her making an advance toward him; after all, she was a woman accustomed to taking charge. It would be humiliating if he turned her down. But that would, at least, make it easier for her to leave Duncally. Still, something inside her quailed at the thought. Was she willing, really willing, to commit herself so blatantly?

A noise disturbed her thoughts, and she turned toward the balcony. Nerves began to jitter in her stomach. She hesitated, then slipped the sash from its knot and shrugged out of her brocade dressing gown, leaving it over the end of the bed. Stepping out of her slippers, she went on silent feet to the door of the balcony and looked out.

Damon stood at the other end, in front of his bedroom door, staring out into the darkness, his hands braced on the stone rail. He wore no jacket, and his lawn shirt hung loose outside his breeches. A breeze stirred the thin material, pressing it against the long, flat line of his chest and stomach. His feet and calves below his breeches were bare, and the sight did curious things to Meg's insides. Taking in a steadying breath, Meg opened the door.

He whipped around and saw her, and he went utterly still. Meg's heart pounded in her chest. She realized that with the low light of her lamp in the room behind her, her form must be silhouetted against it, visible, if only vaguely. She thought of moving out of the light, but she did not.

"Damon."

For a moment she thought he would not answer her, but then he spoke, his voice rusty. "Meg."

He moved closer, and she stepped out onto the balcony to meet him. She should say something, make some sort of conversation to ease the moment. But, she realized, she did not want to ease the tension thrumming in the night air. Damon stopped only a foot away from her. She could see the pulse throbbing in his throat, and she knew a wild desire to press her lips to the spot. Damon's body was taut as an arrow string. Meg reached out and curled her hand around his wrist. He jerked slightly beneath her touch, his eyes going black as pits. She slid her hand up his arm.

His hand lashed out, and he pulled her to him.

23

The kiss was hot, *damp*, desperate. Damon thrust his hands into her hair, holding her still as he consumed her mouth. Meg's arms went around his neck; she offered herself up to him even as she took all he had to give. Finally he pulled his mouth away, breath shuddering out, and changed the angle of his mouth to kiss her once again.

Meg pressed her body into his, reveling in the hard grind of bone and muscle against her softness. She was suddenly trembling with need. She wanted him in her, around her, in every way imaginable. When he tore his mouth from hers again, burying his face in her neck, his breath rasping and his body like fire, Meg dug her fingers into his shoulders, unable to say anything but "Please . . . please . . ."

The words were fuel to the fire in him. Damon hooked his hands into the wide neck of her nightgown, yanking the garment down and off her shoulders. Two buttons went flying off into the night, and there was a distinct ripping sound, but neither of them cared. He shoved the gown down, and it dropped around her ankles. Damon smoothed his hand down her back and over her shapely buttocks, digging his fingers into the fleshy mounds and pressing her against the hard line straining at his breeches.

Excitement bubbled out of Meg in a breathy little laugh. She threw her arms tightly around his neck, springing up from her toes, and he lifted her as she wrapped her legs around his waist. Meg buried her lips against his neck, kissing her way up to take his ear in her mouth. He let out an inarticulate noise, his arms like iron around her.

"You'll have us both off this balcony." He chuffed out a low laugh.

"I don't care," she said boldly, and nibbled at his earlobe. "Do you?"

"No. God, no." He turned his head to take her lips again, walking with her back to his door. Neither of them seemed to mind—or even notice—that they lurched against the doorframe as they passed through.

Tumbling onto the bed, they rolled across it, locked in a kiss. Meg tugged at his shirt, and he reared up, sweeping it off over his head and tossing it across the room. She turned, pushing his shoulders, and he went with her movement, letting her press him onto the bed on his back. Meg straddled his legs, unfastening the buttons of his breeches, and worked her hands inside the trousers and down over the curve of his buttocks, shoving the garment down and off so that he was freed, hard and pulsing.

She sucked in her breath and reached out, running a finger lightly down the side of the engorged staff. He jerked, releasing a low moan, and grabbed her arms, flipping her back onto the bed beneath him. He kissed her face, her throat, her breasts, his mouth and hands greedy upon her flesh, and Meg responded, driven to whimpers of pleasure as he made her his own. The soft noises seemed to spur him to even greater passion, and when she sank her fingers into his shoulders, moving her hips against him in mindless hunger, Damon parted her legs and sank into her.

Meg rose to meet him, shifting to take him even deeper inside her and gliding her hands down the muscles of his back to dig her fingernails into the rounded flesh of his buttocks. He groaned and moved within her, driving them upward with long, desperate strokes. Meg wrapped her legs around him, urging him on, everything within her straining to reach that moment, that instant of perfect pleasure.

Then, at last, it crested within her, shaking her to her core, and she felt the passion take him, too, as he lost himself within her, his arms engulfing her, mouth pressed against her shoulder to stifle his cry of release.

Damon collapsed, and she cradled him, reveling in the weight of his long, hard body. Meg turned her head and kissed his arm, her hands stroking tenderly over his back. She felt consumed, used . . . *owned* in a way that was stunningly pleasurable. She, Meg Munro, who had always prided herself on being her own woman, now belonged to him in a way that was as much possession as being possessed. In that instant and forever, she knew, Damon was hers, and whatever else lay before them, that would never change.

He mumbled something into her skin, an apology for his weight, she sensed, and he rolled over, wrapping his arms around her and cuddling her to him. Meg nestled her head into the crook of his shoulder, finding again how naturally it fit there. They lay for a long time, dreamily touching, caressing, as if their hands were unable to stay away from the other. He pressed his lips against her hair.

"Did I hurt you?" he murmured. "I did not mean to. But I could not . . . I could not stop." He propped himself on his elbow, gazing down at her, and he ran a finger along the line of her collarbone and shoulder, to where his mouth had clamped upon her as his climax raged through him. A red spot was forming there, and he caressed it. "I marked you. I'm sorry." He looked into her face, and Meg saw as much satisfaction there as regret.

"You don't mean that," she said, laying her hand against his cheek and gliding her thumb across his full, kiss-reddened lips.

"I am sorry if I hurt you." A smugly male smile curved his lips. "But I confess I don't mind marking you as mine. I'd like to let every man in the world know you belong to me."

"So I belong to you, too." She frowned at him, but a teasing note was in her voice. "Just like the beach and the standing stones and the—"

He laughed and stopped her mouth with his. "No, not like those things at all, for they have no choice in the matter. You, on the other hand . . ." He caressed her cheek and neck, brushed back her hair. "You have given yourself to me, and that is infinitely more precious."

"And you to me."

"Aye," he said, giving his word a mock Scots intonation. "And me to you."

"That's all to the good, then." Meg grinned up at him. "And to think I wondered if you did not want me." She smoothed a hand down his chest.

He stared at her. "Sweet heaven, how could you possibly think that?" He leaned down, resting his arm on the other side of her so that he hovered over her. He pressed his mouth to the soft top of her breast. "I have wanted you"—his lips traveled over her breasts and stomach, marking each word with a kiss as he said—"every minute. Every day. From the moment I saw you." He circled her navel with his tongue, then slid back up her body. "Each breath I took." He indulged in another long, searching kiss. "Each time I looked at you." He traced her nipple with his tongue. "Whenever I heard your voice." He turned his attention to the other nipple. "I have wanted you so much I thought I'd die of it."

"Well, we canna have that." Meg looped her arms around his neck, her eyes gleaming with the sweet, hot hunger pulsing through her. "But are you sure? Are you able—"

"Oh, I am able." His lips curved up devilishly. "And this time, I intend to take my time about it."

He did so, his mouth and hands roaming over her in slow, lingering caresses that brought Meg to the smoldering brink of ecstasy again and again, only to edge away to taste her in a different spot or caress her from another angle. He touched and probed and caressed, kissing and tasting seemingly every bit of her skin, until at last the breath was sobbing in her throat, her fingers digging into the sheets beneath her, as she arched up against him.

Then at last he eased into her, inch by inch, filling her with a satisfaction so sweet it was almost painful. With a torturous slowness, he stroked in and out, drawing forth each tiny sensation of pleasure. His heat was all around her, coursing within her, and Meg moved with him, so that they seemed almost one in their desire. Finally, the tide of release poured through her, slow and lush and lingering, and he groaned, his fingers digging into the bed, as he poured his seed into her.

Arms around each other, still joined, they slid into peace.

———

Their rooms were a secluded world, set apart from the rest of the house by the private balcony. Meg knew that the servants were aware despite the secrecy of their situation, and she knew that they gossiped, though none dared to be rude to her in Damon's house. She had seen the maids whispering to each other, then going abruptly silent when Meg appeared. Mrs. Ferguson, who avoided speaking to Meg if at all possible, had a frosty glint in her eyes whenever she looked at Meg. But Meg ignored them all. People had always gossiped about her, she told herself. And she was not going to ruin things by thinking about it.

She knew she should return to her cottage, having no reason to stay now that Lynette was better. She said so one evening to Damon, but he quickly pointed out to her that it was imperative that she remain here: "Lynette needs you."

"No. She is doing much better. Why, she has been walking all around, up and down the stairs, and she is even coming down to dinner now."

"I need you," he told Meg simply.

That, Meg thought, was reason enough to stay. She glided through the days that followed, determined to hold on to her happiness. She spent several hours a day with Lynette, talking or reading, sometimes with Damon and sometimes alone. In the stillroom of the kitchens, she toyed with different recipes for remedies to help rebuild the girl's strength and health.

The rest of her time was occupied by Damon. They walked together in the garden and down to the loch. She discovered a number of places about the estate that were secluded enough for an embrace or kiss . . . or more. In the evening, they ate an intimate supper together, their enjoyment of each other's company no longer constricted by the hunger that ran within them. It was still there, humming in Meg's blood, easily stirred to life by a look or a touch, but now it was a feeling to be savored, a spicy undertone to every situation, knowing that soon the need building inside her would be satiated.

They talked—on their walks, as they ate, lying in bed at night. Meg could not believe how much they talked. How was it, she wondered, that two people so different could find so many things to say, so much opportunity to laugh?

He described his home and his parents, their devotion to duty and to family . . . as long as it meant not spending too much time at the estate with their young son. He talked about his older brother, who had died when Damon was five.

"Damon! How awful!" Meg turned to him, horror in her eyes. They were lying in his bed, and she snuggled closer to him, offering him the mute comfort of her warmth. "I cannot imagine what I would have done if something had happened to Coll. What happened?"

"He cut his leg one day when we were playing down in the stables. I remember the head groom going white as a sheet and picking Edward up and running with him to the house. Edward was begging the head groom not to tell anyone because we weren't supposed to play there."

"Oh, Damon . . ."

"They doctored the leg and bound it up, and everyone thought the cut would heal. It wasn't really that terrible a cut, for all it seemed to me to bleed gallons. But then his leg began to swell, and there was the most horrid smell, I'll never forget that."

"Gangrene."

He nodded. "They would not let me into his room anymore. And then Father took me into his study one evening, and he told me Edward was gone. I started to cry, and he said I mustn't. I had to be brave and strong because now *I* was the heir and one day I would be the Earl of Mardoun."

"I'm so sorry." Meg wrapped her arms around him, tenderly kissing his cheek.

"It was so long ago I can't remember all that much about him anymore." Damon smiled faintly. "We had a miniature wooden boat we used to sail on the pond. Our uncle, my mother's brother, gave it to Edward. He was an admiral, you see. We used to pretend it was our uncle's ship."

"And did you want to be a naval man as well?"

"Oh, no. I was dead set on the hussars. Of course, I could not have joined them, being the heir and all, but I thought it would be grand. I must admit that my desire was based mostly on a portrait in the gallery of a long-dead Lord Rutherford. He was a Cavalier, took arms for the king, and died helping Charles escape. I thought it was terribly heroic. Naturally, the hat and the boots were the real enticement."

"I can just see you with a great plume in your hat."

"I'd look quite splendid with a plume, I think." He cut his eyes toward her, grinning.

Meg laughed and kissed him simply because she felt her

heart might swell until it burst when he smiled at her like that. "I can see you now." She settled back into his arms, her head on his shoulder. "It must be so nice to have all those relatives, that history, to know all their names."

"You must have relatives and history. I've heard it said the Munro women have been healers here for centuries."

"Aye, but I don't know their names past my great-grand-mother. You must know each and every ancestor back to William the Conqueror."

"Not every." Humor lit his eyes. "I confess I was not that interested."

"I don't know my grandfather's name. Even my mother did not know who he was."

"That would be a hard thing, not being sure . . ." Damon said carefully.

Meg shook her head. "No, it was not what you are think-ing. It was not that her mother had so many men she could not tell which one fathered her bairn. Faye—my grand-mother—died bearing my mother, and Faye took her secret to her grave."

"No one had any idea who he was?"

Meg related her conversation with Angus McKay, mak-ing Damon laugh with her vivid description of the old man. She told him of Faye and of David MacLeod and his brother Jamie, one dead and the other one living somewhere un-known, all of them lost to her.

"So this David MacLeod fellow could be your grandfa-ther, or maybe your great-uncle."

"Aye. I wish I knew where he was—if, of course, he is still alive. It would be nice to talk to him. If nothing else, he could tell me more about my grandmother. I have been told

I look like her—though not nearly as bonnie, Angus was quick to inform me," she added wryly.

"She must indeed have been a beauty, then." Damon paused to kiss Meg. "Though I think Old Angus's eyesight must be amiss."

She shrugged. "Coll says it makes little difference what our grandfather was like; what matters is what we are. Coll is a very practical man."

"But you are more romantic."

"More emotional, you mean." She smiled faintly to soften her words. "Or perhaps it is just that Coll is more content."

"You are not content?"

"It's not that I do not like my life or who I am; I do. But I always missed—I don't know quite how to explain it—the feeling of background, of understanding who and where you come from." She glanced at him and smiled ruefully. "No doubt it seems an odd thing to you."

"No, not odd. I understand. Though I must tell you—with some relatives, it is better not to know. *My* grandfather, by all accounts, was a proper tyrant and thoroughly disliked by all who knew him."

Meg chuckled. "That, I think, is enough talk about family." She leaned over to kiss him, and the conversation was ended.

Another day, as they walked in the garden, they talked about the places Damon had visited, the sights and people he'd seen, the things he wished to show her. "Italy, I think, should be first. We'll go to Venice and Rome. Florence."

"Oh, we will, will we? And I have nothing to say in the matter?"

Damon laughed. "I'm no fool, Meg. I am sure you'll have a great deal to say." He took her hand and brought it to his lips. "I know you love the Highlands, and if you do not wish it, of course we will not go. But I hope you will not set your mind against it. Say you'll come with me. We'll try London first if you like."

"I do love it here, and I cannot imagine living anywhere else. But that does not mean I wouldna like to visit." Meg gave him a saucy grin.

"Then it's done. We'll go to Italy. In the winter perhaps. It will be good for Lynette, don't you think, to be somewhere warm?"

"I do." Meg's heart contracted in her chest as she looked at him. She ached to believe him, to trust that when winter came, he would still be here with her, that he would want her with him wherever he went. But she feared that he would soon come back to earth; he would see the impracticalities, the difficulties. Damon, she thought, preferred not to see those things, to avoid the realities if they did not suit him. With his wealth and position and charm, he was usually able to have things as he wanted them.

But she could see the pitfalls clearly. Society would not countenance his taking his daughter with him as he roamed about the Continent with his mistress. Damon would discover that, just as he had realized what was being done in his name on his estate. He would see that he was harming his daughter's reputation. He would realize how little Meg belonged in his world.

And what would happen when he wanted Meg to change? When he tired of making the trip back to Duncally? When she embarrassed him by not knowing the proper fork to use or how to address a duke or any of the thousand things she had not been trained for? What would happen when they disagreed?

Meg could not bear to think of it.

"We should get back to the house," she said, slowing her steps. "I should check on Lynette. She was wanting to walk a bit today, and I should be there. She mustn't tire herself."

"I'll come with you." He turned around agreeably to stroll back toward the house. "Though I should look through the names the agency sent me." He grimaced. "I've already put it off two days."

"What names?"

"Men who could manage the estate."

"Oh." Meg tensed. It occurred to her that perhaps one of those moments she feared was about to happen. "What sort of man will you get?"

"That's just it. I haven't the foggiest what to do. I have their names and recommendations. But I don't even know what I want them to do, let alone which one would be right for the job." He glanced down at her. "Don't look at me so. I promise I will not hire another Donald MacRae. I shan't start evicting everyone." He sighed. "But I don't know how the estate can be run if one doesn't do those things, and I suspect that they will all advise me to do just that, including my man of business in London. And, honestly, I would prefer to not run the place at a loss."

"Perhaps you should talk to Jack. Baillannan goes along well enough, I think. And Isobel has invited us to dine there tomorrow evening. You could talk to him then."

"I have talked to him. He tells me Isobel and Coll run the place."

"Then ask Coll."

Damon let out a short laugh. "Thank you, no, I prefer not to start my conversations with a split lip."

She made an exasperated noise. "Coll isn't going to hit you. He promised me."

"Thank heavens I have you to protect me." Damon pulled her against his side and kissed the top of her head. But the look on his face was pensive as they continued toward the house. As they reached the upper terrace, he stopped. "You go on in. I think—there's something I need to do instead."

———

Damon paused for a moment outside the cottage. The door stood open, and he could see Coll Munro sitting at the table, his attention so focused on the wooden object in his hand that he did not even glance up at the sound of Damon's footsteps. Damon rapped sharply on the doorframe, and Coll's head snapped up. Coll's eyes widened and he dropped the awl in his hand, rising to his feet.

"I am here to talk to you," Damon said. "May we begin now, or must you first take a swing at me?"

"I don't know. It depends on what you have to say."

"It is business, nothing personal, and while I am, as always, game for a round of fisticuffs, I would rather get to the matter."

Coll made a disgusted noise, then flapped his hand toward the table. "Oh, come in and sit down and tell me what you've come for. Meg'll have my head if I bloody your face again."

Damon's lips twitched, not quite a smile, and he strolled

over to one of the stools beside the table. His glance went down to the piece of wood on the table before Coll, a chunk of a log, from which a face seemed to be emerging. "You made that?"

"Aye, and the table as well. But I presume you dinna come here to discuss my woodworking skills." Coll sat down across from him, folding his arms across his chest.

"No. I came to offer you a position."

Coll stared at him blankly. "A position? You mean work? For you?"

"Yes. I am in need of someone to manage Duncally, and it seems you are best suited for the job." Damon had the satisfaction of seeing that he had rendered the other man speechless.

After a long moment and a start and stop, Coll said, "Are you daft, man?"

"I may well be." Damon shrugged. "But there it is: I need a steward, and I would like to hire you."

Coll's brows drew together thunderously. "Are you doing this to please Meg? Do you think to pay for her favors by tossing me a job?" Coll rose again, sending the stool grating across the floor. "Or do you think I'll turn my head if you are my employer? That I won't come after you?"

Damon jumped to his feet, his eyes as hard as marble. "First, I don't waste a moment worrying that you might attack me. I can handle a thickheaded Highlander well enough, and if you were not Meg's brother, I would be happy to do so anytime you please."

"I'd like to see you try."

"Secondly," Damon plowed on, ignoring Coll's words, "I would never dishonor Meg by attempting to 'pay' her in any way. And if I were you, I would hope that your sister never hears you suggest that her favors could be purchased by me or any other man."

"Then why in the bloody hell would you offer to make me your steward?"

Damon glared at him. "Foolish as it may be, I thought you would be the best man to do it."

Coll gaped at him, baffled. He turned and walked away, then came back. "Why? Why do you want me? Putting aside the fact that I would never work for you, what makes you think I could manage your estate? I'm a gamekeeper. I carve things. I make furniture."

"You may be all those things, but you also help run Baillannan." As Coll opened his mouth to speak, Damon went on, "Don't bother to deny it. Jack told me that you have helped his wife run Baillannan for years. You know everyone in this glen, and more than that, you are respected here, which, as we both know, I am not—nor any outsider I appoint."

"If you know me so well, then you would know I won't run around enforcing the earl's orders, tossing out crofters and bringing in sheep."

"Good Lord, do you think I'm asking you to? Jack tells me that you are able to manage an estate without ridding the countryside of people. He says that you and his wife have done it here. That is what I want for Duncally. Consider how much you could help the people here by overseeing the place instead of some outsider."

Coll stared at him. "Are you serious?"

"Of course I'm serious. Do you think I would subject myself to a conversation with you otherwise?"

Damon's words startled a short laugh from Coll. "Nae, I would not think so." He went over to the fire and picked up the poker to prod at the embers. He shook his head and sighed, shoving the poker back into its stand. "Are you really so blind? Or do you just choose not to see anything that inconveniences you?" Coll swung around. "Do you really think I could work for you when you've installed my sister in Duncally as your mistress?"

"Meg is at my home to take care of my daughter."

"Surely you cannot think anyone believes that she must stay at Duncally for two weeks because your daughter was ill! Do you think the servants don't talk? Do you think there are not whispers about Meg all over the glen?"

Damon's eyes blazed. "Who talks about her? No one would dare to malign her, and if they did, I would make very sure they did not do so again."

"No doubt they would not—while you are here. But what about when you are gone? What about when you return to London and Meg is left here? Do you think she won't feel the scorn then? That men will not look at her and talk"— Coll's fists tightened until his knuckles popped—"that the righteous women of Kinclannoch will not pull their skirts aside when she walks by so she will not taint them?"

"That is the way of the Munro women; Meg has told me so herself. She chooses to . . . live freely. And people still respect her."

"It is an entirely different thing if the man she chooses is an earl! With an ordinary man, it is . . . not respected, but at least accepted as the oddity of a Munro healing woman. But if that man is you, a nobleman, powerful, then she is just a rich man's plaything."

"That is absurd. Why should it be any different?"

"Because everyone knew that my father, for all his many faults, loved my mother and would have married her in an instant if she would but have taken him. And you would not." Coll turned away. "Now go away from me. I'm not working for you. And I never will."

Damon whirled and strode away without another word.

———

Supper that night at Duncally was quiet. Damon had been silent ever since he returned from his errand that afternoon, and though he smiled at Meg when she teased him, he remained unusually moody, and it affected everyone at the table. Even Lynette had little to say, and Miss Pettigrew's platitudes only seemed to emphasize the lack of conversation. The meal was almost over when the sound of distant thudding was followed moments later by footsteps in the hall. They glanced at each other in surprise.

The footsteps came closer—several pairs of them, it seemed—and everyone turned toward the door. The butler stepped into the room and bowed to Damon, then stepped aside, intoning, "Lady Basham, my lord. The Honorable Mr. Twitherington-Smythe and Mrs. Twitherington-Smythe."

Damon's eyes widened, and across from Meg, Lynette sucked in a sharp breath. Given their reactions, Meg studied the new arrivals with interest. The woman in front was blond, with pale blue eyes, and her stick-thin figure was clothed in a fashionable double-breasted traveling coat of navy blue. An elegant bonnet, kid gloves, and kid half boots completed the sophisticated picture. Behind her stood a bland man and woman, both of them expensively dressed but neither with the eye for fashion of the other woman, whom Meg took to be Lady Basham.

"Hallo, Damon." Lady Basham swept into the room as Damon rose to his feet. "Surprised?" She extended her hand to Damon and turned her cheek for a kiss of greeting.

"That is putting it mildly." Damon took her hand, bowing over it, ignoring her waiting cheek. "Welcome, Lady Veronica." He nodded toward the other couple. "Mr. Twitherington-Smythe. Ma'am."

"Such formality, Damon." Lady Veronica kept her careful smile in place as she swiveled toward the table. "And Lynette. How delightful to see you." Her eyes swept on past the girl to Lynette's governess, giving her a slight nod, before her gaze settled on Meg. "You dine with the help here in the country? How very . . . quaint."

"Meg is our friend, Aunt Veronica," Lynette said quickly, blushing. "She saved my life."

Veronica's brows lifted and she studied Meg coolly. "My. That was fortuitous."

Meg rose to her feet, never one to back down before disparagement.

Damon shifted so that he stood closer to Meg and slightly in front of her. "Pray allow me to introduce you to Miss Munro. Miss Munro, Lady Basham, Lynette's aunt. Mr. and Mrs. Twitherington-Smythe, the late Lord Basham's cousins. I believe, Lady Veronica, that you are well acquainted with Lynette's governess, Miss Pettigrew," he added drily. He gestured vaguely toward the table. "Pray sit down and join us."

"Oh, we are not dressed for dinner, Damon," Lynette's aunt protested.

"We are quite casual here," Damon returned pleasantly.

"So I see." Veronica cast a pointed glance at Meg.

Meg, suddenly very aware of her plain gown, felt a blush start in her cheeks and was irritated with herself. What did she care what this snobbish woman thought of her? But she did; she could not help but feel the gulf between her and the other women, which seemed to be widening by the moment.

"Suit yourself." Damon turned toward the butler. "Show our guests to their rooms, Hudgins. I am sure you must have some prepared for unexpected guests." Damon's tone gave a light stress to the word *unexpected*. "And no doubt they would like their meals brought to their rooms, as well."

Lady Veronica gave a brittle smile. "No, no, Hudgins, I would not put you to such trouble. Since we are so informal here, I am sure we are all happy to dine just as we are."

Without bothering to glance at the other couple for their opinion, Veronica strolled toward the table. Damon quickly moved to pull out the chair beside Meg. Instead, Veronica paused at the end of the table, looking at Meg, and Meg realized that the woman expected to sit in the chair Meg occupied. The aristocracy were seated by precedence; Isobel would doubtless know just how it went.

Feeling the hated blush again, Meg started to move, but Damon clamped a hand on her shoulder, holding her in place. "No need to change places, Miss Munro. As I said, we do not stand on formality here. Veronica?" Damon went on silkily, pulling the empty chair back a trifle more, leaving the woman little choice but to sit or make a scene.

Meg saw the flash of anger in Lady Veronica's eyes, but she gave a regal nod to Damon and sat in the chair he offered. The servants began to serve the new guests immediately, but Meg suspected that the food had grown a mite cold by now. A glance at Damon's carefully expressionless face and cool dark eyes told her that the thought probably gave him some satisfaction. Meg, too aware of Lady Veronica's seething anger beside her, couldn't garner much enjoyment from it. It warmed Meg's heart that Damon had insisted she sit beside him, but she knew it would probably have been better if he had let Meg move and given his sister-in-law the seat of honor. Lady Veronica, however haughty and unpleasant she had been to begin with, firmly hated Meg now.

"I am surprised to find you have become so ruralized, Damon." Veronica fired her first shot. "I suppose out here in the wilderness, it is to be expected. I vow, we quite feared some hirsute sort wrapped in tartan might stop my coach."

Beside her, Mr. Twitherington-Smythe gave a harrumphing laugh and added, "Quite true, my lady. Quite true."

"Mm. The Scots blood does run strong in us," Damon mused. "I confess lately I have felt a distinct urge to grab my ancestor's claymore and venture out to wreak havoc on unsuspecting travelers."

Lynette choked on her drink and hastily covered her mouth with a napkin. Her eyes danced merrily as she looked across at Meg, and Meg pressed her lips together firmly, turning her gaze down to her plate.

"Eh?" Twitherington-Smythe looked confused. "Oh. Ha! Yes, I see. You have some Scot in your ancestry." Meg was not sure whether the man was asking for confirmation or explaining the joke to his wife.

"Damon, you do so love to tease." Veronica's hand clenched around her fork, but she forced a tiny laugh into her voice. "You know I did not mean you. Why, there is scarcely enough trace of Scots blood in you to count."

"I am only one-quarter Scot," he agreed pleasantly. "But I have discovered since I've been here that the Highlands exert a powerful pull. I have been learning to dance a reel. However, I daresay I do not have the fortitude to take up the bagpipe."

Lynette dissolved into giggles, keeping her napkin firmly clamped to her mouth.

"Honestly, Damon, you are a complete hand." Veronica managed an indulgent tone. "You should not say such things or you will alarm Miss Munro. After all, she does not know you as we do."

"Oh, I imagine she knows me well enough."

Meg felt his eyes on her, but she did not dare to look at him, certain that if she did, her face would reveal the underlying meaning of his words.

"Oh! I must not forget—Lord Upchurch bade me give you his regards."

"Indeed?"

"I saw him at the Duchess of Chiverton's soiree. I was surprised to see him; as you know, Lady Upchurch is said to be quite ill. Everyone was there—the Little Season has begun, you know. Cumberland and even Prinny himself graced it with his presence, so I presume Upchurch felt he could not miss it. It was dreadfully boring; you know how her parties are. It was too bad you were not there to keep us all amused."

"I was unaware you found me so entertaining. I fear we are quite dull here at Duncally. Little to do but ride or walk in the garden."

"But you must know that I adore gardens. I have always

enjoyed the gardens at the Hall. Of course, now that my sister is no longer there, 'tis not the same. I was not surprised you found the memories of Amibel too much to bear. Still, I am sure it will heal in time. The Hall is too lovely to spend much time away from it." She turned toward the man on her other side. "Have you visited Rutherford Hall, sir?"

"I don't believe I've had that privilege, my lady. Lovely spot, I've heard. My cousin Lord Harrington has been a guest there on occasion, if I remember right. Good man, Harrington; I was named after him, you know. Of course, he is not a first cousin. I believe the relationship is a second cousin—or is it a first cousin once removed? Do you know, Miranda?"

"No, dear," his wife squeaked out, the first, and only, words Meg heard her utter throughout the meal.

The evening progressed in much the same way, with Lady Veronica continually turning the conversation back to people and places of which Meg had no knowledge, with the wordy help of Mr. Twitherington-Smythe. Miss Pettigrew seemed to hang on the woman's every word, but Damon's responses grew shorter and farther between. Across the table from Meg, Lynette slipped into boredom, pushing her food around on her plate and slumping in her chair, her eyelids drooping.

When at last the dinner ended, Lady Veronica stood, which brought everyone else to their feet. "Come, Lynette, we must withdraw and leave your father to his port. Mrs. Twitherington-Smythe? Miss Pettigrew?" Veronica did not bother to glance at Meg.

"A charming custom I choose not to follow at Duncally." Damon also rose to his feet. "I join the ladies after dinner."

"Oh. My." Lady Veronica looked nonplussed and Twitherington-Smythe goggled.

Meg seized the opportunity the moment of silence presented. "Lynette, I believe the excitement of your aunt's arrival has tired you out." Meg moved around the end of the table to take the girl's arm. "It has not been long since you were unable to leave your bed. I'll take you upstairs."

Lynette started to protest, then snapped her mouth shut, her eyes sparking with understanding. She sagged a bit more, looping her arm through Meg's, and leaned against her. "I *am* a bit tired."

"What? You have been ill?" Lady Veronica said.

As you would have known, Meg thought, if you had bothered to discuss anything but yourself all evening.

"Are you feeling worse?" Damon's eyes darkened with concern and he started forward. Meg, her back toward Lady Veronica, gave him a wink, and he stopped, his face clearing. "Ah, well, then of course you must go to bed." He leaned in to kiss his daughter's cheek, murmuring, "Traitors."

With a quirk of her lips, Meg whisked Lynette out into the hall, leaving Damon to deal with his guests.

Meg was resolved not to pry any information from Lynette about her aunt, much as Meg would have liked to, but she had no need. Lynette began to talk before they reached the stairs. "I am so sorry. Aunt Veronica was rude. She is that way with everyone. Well, never with Papa, of course. Only with all of us who are . . . less than she is. She treats Miss Pettigrew like a servant, and yes, I know Miss Pettigrew is something of a nuisance—she irritates Papa terribly—but Aunt Veronica uses Miss Pettigrew when she wants and then acts as if the woman barely exists."

"Uses Miss Pettigrew? How? Why?"

"To get information. Not so much about me, I think. She is—well, she acts fond of me, but it is not real. And she pretends to have loved Mother dearly, but when she came to visit us, Aunt Veronica rarely spent much time with either of us. She likes the Hall, I think, more than anything. She is a widow, and Lord Basham's estate was entailed, so she has only a bit of income that he left her, and she had to return to my grandparents' home to live. It is Papa she is interested in, really. I think she wants to marry him."

The girl's words stabbed Meg's heart, and for a moment she could not breathe. That was foolish. She knew Damon would be bound to marry again; men were always mad for a son, and with a man of Damon's station, it was a necessity. She had never expected permanence with Damon. Nor fidelity . . . at least not in the long term.

"Papa laughed at the idea, but I do not think I am wrong."

"No, I daresay you are not." Meg thought of the woman's actions, her spite toward Meg and the way she had swallowed her ire when she spoke to Damon, answering him with sweetness, however clearly false. Something hard as iron and fierce as fire raged up in Meg. *That woman will not have him.* Meg knew she would ultimately lose Damon, but by God, it would not be to Lady Veronica.

"He would not marry her, would he?" Lynette asked Meg, frowning.

"I think not." *Not if I have anything to do with it.* "It did not seem to me that your father was well pleased to see them."

"No, he was not." Lynette giggled. "I could hardly keep

from laughing when Papa was talking about being a Scot . . . and then that man had to work out what Papa meant. Mr. Thickerton—no, Twitt—Twittenham—"

Meg could not hold back a chuckle. "Twitterton-Smythe."

"No, no, that's not it either." Lynette burst into laughter. "Twitherington! Twitherington-Smythe."

They turned into Lynette's room. The breathing tent and inhalation bowl were long since gone, but a kettle sat near the fire, and Meg used it to brew Lynette's nightly tisane. Lynette changed into her nightclothes and settled into bed with the mug of tea Meg had prepared.

Quietly, gazing down into her mug, Lynette said, "I thought—I hoped Papa would marry you."

"What?" Meg gaped at the girl.

"I know he likes you." Lynette looked up. "He always . . . brightens when you come into the room."

"Oh, Lynette . . ." Meg frowned a little, searching for the right words.

"No, I know." Lynette sighed. "It isn't done. Though I don't see why; I'd ever so much rather have you for a mother than someone like Aunt Veronica. But Papa always does his duty. My mother used to say so, though she sounded very bitter about it."

Meg firmly swallowed the emotions swirling inside her. "Lynette, love . . ." She brushed a strand of hair back from the girl's forehead. Meg found she had to swallow her tears. "There is no one whom I would love more to have as a daughter than you."

"Do you love him, too?" Lynette gazed into her eyes.

"Mayhap I do." Meg looked away. "But you are right: it is not done. We are so very far apart, your father and I—in birth, in home. Mardoun would not even think of marrying me, and in any case, we Munro women do not marry. I have my freedom and your father has his name." Her words sounded hollow, even to her. Meg let out a breath and tried again. "Don't fret. Your papa will choose wisely when—when he marries again. And you will be uppermost in his considerations, I am sure of it." Meg forced a bright smile. "There now. Enough of this. 'Tis time for you to rest. And dinna worry about your papa. Or me, least of all."

Lynette smiled and handed her the empty cup. Meg set it down and tucked the girl into bed, turning out the lamp as she left the room. Outside in the hall, she stood for a moment, drawing in a deep breath. Then she strode across into her room and began to pack.

24

M eg had been in her own room only a few minutes when she heard the others coming upstairs. Damon's door closed, and the rest continued down the hall, much to her relief. She had feared Hudgins might place one of them in the other room on the balcony, between Damon and Meg.

Damon appeared at her balcony door, and she went forward to greet him, her heart lifting as it always did. He pulled her to him for a long, slow kiss, then took her hand and strolled with her to the comfortable chair beside the fire.

"Thank heavens Hudgins had enough sense to stick those people at the other end of the hall," he said, echoing Meg's thoughts as he sat, tugging her down into his lap. "I cannot imagine what possessed Veronica to come here, much less drag that fool Harry with her. A duller man I've never met, and his wife hasn't two words to say—though I suppose that is probably a good thing since she must be bird-witted to have married the man."

Meg laughed. "I thought they were friends of yours."

"Good gad, no." Damon sent her an appalled glance. "Do not tell me that is your opinion of my taste?"

"No, how could it be?" Meg asked pertly. "When you have a partiality for me?"

"Very true." He kissed the crook of her neck, stroking his hand down her side and along her thigh.

"Lynette thinks Lady Veronica is here to lure you into marriage."

"So Lynette told me a few weeks ago. I find it hard to credit. But if that is Veronica's intention, she has certainly gone about it in a deuced poor fashion, barging in here uninvited, two utter wet gooses in tow." Damon rested his head against hers, idly drifting his fingers over her nape. Suddenly his hand went still, and Meg felt his body tense beneath her. "What is that?"

Meg glanced up and saw that he was scowling at her packed bag.

"Oh." She took a breath. "Those are my clothes. I am returning to the cottage tomorrow."

"No. You cannot."

"I cannot?" She straightened and cocked an eyebrow at him.

"You know what I mean." He grimaced. "Meg, I don't want you to leave." He narrowed his eyes. "Is it because of Veronica? I know she can be—no, she *is* a snobbish bore. I would send her packing, but she is Lynette's aunt. I shall talk to her, tell her that if she wishes to remain here, she must change her behavior."

"In what way? Are you going to ask her to give way to someone far below her in rank? To break bread with the bastard daughter of a Highland healing woman? To live cheek by jowl with your mistress?"

"Stop." The red of anger flared along his cheekbones. "I will not have you talk about yourself in that manner."

"Did I misstate the facts in any way?"

His eyes flashed. "Damn it, Meg, you are not—"

"Not what? The woman whose bed you sleep in?"

He surged to his feet and began to pace, his face stamped with frustration. "Has anyone offered you any disrespect in this house? Have I not treated you with honor?"

"Damon, no!" Meg reached out and took his hands between hers. "You have made me feel nothing but valued. No one has said anything to me. That is not the point."

"What is?"

"I should not be here. I have a house; I have a life. That is where I belong."

"You can do whatever you want here." He waved his hand vaguely. "The stillroom is yours. The herb gardens, the kitchens, whatever you want." He pushed on. "Lynette needs you."

"She is well. And I will check on her—every day if you wish."

"She will miss you." He stopped, then went on in a low voice, "I will miss you."

"And I will miss you." Meg went to him and slid her arms around his waist, leaning against his chest. "But, Damon, we must think of your daughter."

"I am thinking of her. She would tell you to stay as well."

"It is not right for her to live in this situation. What would you say about a man who allowed his mistress to reside in the same house with his young daughter? What would anyone in your society say?"

"She does not know. We have been discreet."

"Do you honestly think your sister-in-law did not know what we are to each other the minute she walked in the room? Do you think the servants don't suspect that you spend your nights in here with me? Does Blandings not know?"

"Of course, he does. It's useless to try to hide anything from his hawk eye. But he would never gossip."

"Others will. It is scarcely the sort of thing you want whispered about your daughter behind her back."

He clenched his fist. "I will not let—"

"Yes, yes, I know, you will force everyone to your will. But the fact is, Damon, you cannot control everything. People will say you raised Lynette loosely, that you brought her up in the company of a hussy. It will reflect not only on you, but on her. I realized it tonight when Lady Veronica and her friends arrived. I saw how it must appear to them. What people would say. And I knew that I have been selfish to stay here this way."

Damon glared at her in frustration for a long moment, then let out a curse and turned away. "Yes, very well, you are right," he said sullenly. "But I do not want . . . I cannot lose you again."

"You won't lose me." A tender warmth blossomed in her chest, and Meg went to him. "Damon, I am not severing myself from you. I am only moving back to my home. I believe you managed to find your way there before." She cast a flirtatious glance up at him, laying her palms flat against his chest. "It may not be as easy, but surely I am worth a bit of trouble?"

He smiled faintly and put his hands on her arms, sliding them up and down. "You are worth a great deal of trouble."

"Then you will come see me?" She curled her fingers into his lapels and went up on tiptoe to brush her lips against his. "At the cottage? Or perhaps the standing stones?" Her eyes sparkled.

"Yes. I will be there." He pressed his lips to hers with more force. "You could not keep me away."

"Good." Meg narrowed her eyes. "But I warn you, if you fall prey to Lady Veronica's wiles in my absence, I will have your lights and liver. And hers, too, for good measure."

"Then I shall be very careful to avoid her." Damon laughed and pulled Meg to him. "I have grown very tired of talking about Lady Basham." Sweeping Meg up in his arms, he carried her toward the bed.

Whatever Meg had said, it was not at all the same without her, Damon thought, gazing glumly down the table at his guests. For one thing, if Meg had been here, he would not be marooned at the most tedious dinner party he had ever attended, with the brainless Harry on one side and Damon's archly flirting sister-in-law on the other. He would have enjoyed talking to Jack and Isobel, but Veronica in her precedent-precise way had stuck the plebeian Jack farthest away from the head of the table, with Mrs. Twitherington-Smythe and the dry-as-dust minister and his wife between.

Jack's eyes, Damon saw, were glazing over as the minister droned on. It was some comfort, Damon supposed, that he had company in his misery. Isobel, on the other hand, was far too stiff, her pleasant gray eyes too hard, to be sleepy. Isobel had never been what Damon would term friendly to him, but tonight, after one encompassing glance at the guests, she had frosted over entirely. No doubt she, like he, wished that Meg were here.

Harry's idiocy might have been somewhat entertaining if Damon had been able to glance over at Meg and see her gold eyes gleaming with suppressed laughter. Any amount of time could be whiled away pleasantly as long as he could watch Meg and contemplate the night ahead.

There would still be the night with her—as soon as he could escape the castle—but it was not the same as it had been when she was in the house. It was a pleasure all its own to lie with Meg in her soft bed, the air scented of herbs—indeed, just stepping into the cottage never failed to subtly arouse him, as if Meg herself were enveloping him—but the result was that he had not spent the night in his own home for an entire week. It brought a fresh reluctance and regret each morning when he had to slip out and leave her sleeping there, soft and warm and sweetly curved. Not to mention that it was a dashed nuisance having to leave early enough so that no one would see him tromping back into the castle at that hour. The only alternative was to leave earlier, right after they had made love, and that was even more unappealing.

The torturous thing, though, was that Meg was not here with him all the time. He missed the sound of her voice. Her laughter. The little tickle of anticipation knowing that he would walk into a room and see her there. He missed talking to her, seeing her. Before when she was not with him, when he had been in his study or sitting with Lynette, he had known that if he wanted to talk to Meg, he had only to walk into the sitting room or the stillroom or the gardens, and he would find her there. Now it seemed that he idled away his entire day, waiting until he could leave for Meg's cottage.

He was relieved when at long last Veronica rose, indicating that it was time to abandon the gentlemen to their port and cigars. Even more fortunately, the minister went with the ladies. Too bad Harry remained, but at least one did not have to mind one's tongue with him. With a sigh of relief, Damon poured brandy into their glasses, and the three men settled back to sample cigars from the humidor proffered by Hudgins.

"Excellent cigar," Harry pronounced, rolling the thing between his fingers and taking a long, appreciative sniff. "I always say, your hospitality is the finest."

As if the man had ever been invited to his house before, Damon thought, but he merely gave a bow of his head to acknowledge the compliment. A bit of devilment then sparked in his eyes. "Perhaps we should have a game of whist later. What say you, Kensington? I am sure Harry is up for it."

"Indeed," Harry responded heartily. "Though I have to warn you I am a dab hand at cards. Cumberland refuses to play with me."

"I am game to risk it," Jack replied carelessly. "But perhaps another night. My wife will likely scorch my ears if I linger too long."

"I am sure time hangs more heavily on her hands in the drawing room," Damon agreed.

"How so?" Then Harry's face cleared. "Oh, I see, because that long-winded chap is in there with them." He chuffed out a hearty laugh. "You have the right of it, Mardoun."

"Isobel was sorry to see that Meg was not here tonight."

"Yes, I thought she was looking daggers at me," Damon agreed. "I can assure you I had nothing to do with the matter. I didn't even know we were entertaining until I walked into the dining room."

"Meg?" Harry asked. "Who is—oh, you mean that bit of fluff you were keeping when we arrived. Quite the stunner, that one, I must say. I wouldn't mind having a go there myself."

Jack's hand went still, cigar halfway to his mouth, as he turned a cold gaze on the visitor.

Damon's eyes turned black as the pits of hell, and he leaned forward. "Do not"—he bit off the words—"speak of Miss Munro."

Harry goggled at him and began to sputter, "No, I assure you, no disrespect meant. I would not dream . . . never poach. Under your protection, of course."

"If I were you, I would stop before you dig yourself deeper," Jack advised mildly.

"Yes. Well, of course." Harry swallowed hard, looking like a rabbit caught in the gaze of a wolf.

"Miss Munro is well respected around the loch," Jack went on. "Something of a sister to my wife."

"Oh! I say. Never meant . . . wouldn't presume . . ."

Damon pulled his gaze away, waiting for the red haze to recede. Harry was a fool, nothing more. Damon himself had put Meg in that position, which, as always, touched a raw nerve in him. "Let it be, Harry." Damon took a long drink of his brandy.

"My lord." Hudgins appeared in the doorway, then came forward at Damon's gesture, saying in a low voice, "There is a man here to see you. The, um, one you hired recently."

"He has news?" Damon's voice rose in interest.

"I believe so, my lord."

Damon shoved to his feet, stubbing out his barely smoked cigar. "Gentlemen, excuse me. And pray give my apologies to the ladies. I have business to attend to."

———

Damon was late. Meg started once again to the door, then stopped, telling herself she was being foolish. It wasn't as if the man had told her he would be here at any certain time. Indeed, he had not told her he would be here at all. Just because he had visited her every evening—and more than once during the afternoon, she thought with a secret smile—did not mean that he would continue to do so every night. He could have something else to do. Jealousy flared up in her as she thought of his playing cards with Lady Veronica or perhaps turning the pages of music while she played the piano.

No doubt he was just delayed. He could knock on her door at any moment. The problem was that she was sitting about waiting for him, as if her life depended on Damon's whims. She glanced about, looking for something that needed doing. But she had busied herself so much this week, nothing was left to do.

She was being a goose, she thought, to be so at loose ends because a man was not here. She should just go ahead to bed, as if it did not matter. But as she started to take the pins from her hair, a knock sounded at the door, and without waiting, Damon walked in. He was smiling, and the glimmer in his eyes sparked Meg's curiosity. She laughed when he swooped her up and whirled her around before setting her back on her feet and kissing her.

"You are very merry." She laughed.

"I am indeed. I have come to get you."

"To get me?"

"Yes, where is that bag of yours? Pack up; we are taking a trip. I have been making arrangements; that is why I am so tardy."

"What are you talking about?" Meg's curiosity was thoroughly roused now. "Damon, you are not making sense. Why would we take a trip?"

"Does it not appeal to you? You and I alone together?" He took her hands and raised them to his lips. "For days." He turned over her hands and kissed the palms, his lips setting up all sorts of quivery sensations.

"But Lynette—"

"I have bid her adieu. She knows what I am about—well, not all, of course—and she quite approves. It will give her aunt, who traveled so far to be with Lynette, ample time alone with her." His eyes danced.

"But I am not ready to leave."

"That is why you need to pack. The boat awaits us."

"The boat!"

"Yes, we are sailing for Aberdeen."

"Aberdeen!"

"You sound like a parrot, my love." He kissed her on the forehead, clearly enjoying himself. "Now hurry." He took her by the shoulders and turned her around, giving her an encouraging push.

Meg was too intrigued to argue, and she went to pack. Damon came up behind her as she pulled things out of drawers and piled them on the bed.

"Nightgowns?" He slid his arms around her waist and kissed her on the neck. "You'll have no need for clothes in bed." His lips trailed lazily down to her collarbone.

"Damon!" She could not hold back a giggle—or quell the sudden heat that snaked through her abdomen. "I thought you wanted me to pack."

"I do. But now that I think on it . . ." His hand came up and slipped inside the front of her dress. "I think you have little need for any underclothes at all." His fingers found her nipple and teased it into hardness.

"Damon!" she said again, shakily.

"Mm?" His other hand moved downward from her waist. "It would be most intriguing, knowing you were naked beneath your dress." His fingers stroked languidly.

"Damon. Stop." She pulled away and crossed her arms, pinning him with a stern look. It was difficult, given the way he was smiling at her, sleepy eyed and mouth heavy with desire. "I will never get this done with you 'helping.' Go sit down there and wait for me." She pointed toward the kitchen table.

His laugh was low and richly suggestive, but he merely kissed her forehead and did as she said. Meg hurried about her business, and soon they were walking along the path past the standing stones to where his carriage waited on the road.

She teased him all the way to the ship to tell her the purpose of their trip, but he just smiled, clucking his tongue and saying, "Meg, darling, have you no patience?"

It was the middle of the night when they reached the wide mouth of Loch Fleet. A ship awaited them there, larger than the small fishing vessel she had imagined. As soon as they were aboard, the ship weighed anchor and slipped smoothly out to sea. It was dark save for a lantern or two, but that did not seem to impede the men on deck scampering about, raising the sails and tying off ropes.

The stars were out in the velvet, black sky, and a breeze lifted the sides of Meg's cloak, making it billow behind her. She looked up at Damon and smiled. "I thought you might want to know that I took your words to heart." She stretched up on tiptoe, her hand on his arm for balance, and whispered in his ear, "I am wearing nothing beneath my dress."

25

With a sweet smile, *Meg* turned and sauntered away. Damon stood as if paralyzed for a moment, then hurried after her.

"What?" He took her elbow. "What did you say?"

"I think you heard me. I took off my underthings while you were waiting for me to pack."

He swallowed. "You tell me this now?" He glanced around. "After we are on the ship? With people about?"

"Patience, Damon, you must have patience."

He laughed. "Vixen." His eyes roved down her. "I never realized you had such cruelty in you."

"Oh, aye, indeed I do. There are some who would call me heartless." She grinned, her eyes sparkling, then turned and continued to the railing.

She stood looking out at the darker shape of the shore receding behind them, her hands on the railing before her. Damon came up behind her and placed his hands on either side of hers. She could feel his hard body against her back, and she moved just a little against him, eliciting a choked noise from his throat.

He slipped his hand inside her cloak. His fingers went to the first few buttons of her dress, and the garment gaped open.

"Damon . . . you mustn't. Someone will see."

"No one can see. We are only standing together looking out at sea."

"Are we?"

"No one knows that I am touching you like this." His hand slipped beneath her dress and cupped her breast, his thumb circling the nipple, light as a feather. "They have no idea what it does to you. What it does to me. They don't know that your flesh is soft as a rose petal, that you prickle and harden for me, that your breath quickens when I stroke you."

She felt the press of his lips against her hair, heard his own breathing turn faster, harder as he caressed her. His hand left her breast and moved down the front of her dress. Beneath the cover of her cloak, he grasped her skirt in his hands, bunching it in his fingers, pulling it higher and higher. The breeze caressed her bare legs, cool and delicate as the touch of silk.

His hand delved between her legs, finding the moisture there. "Sweet heaven, you are so ready. So hot and wet and—" A groan escaped him. Meg felt the hard pulse of his manhood against her, straining for release. She widened her stance, giving his fingers freer access to her, and he let out a breathy little laugh that spoke of a pleasure dangerously close to desperation. "Like honey," he murmured, playing with her, stroking the slick folds of her flesh until it was all she could do to keep from grinding her hips against him.

"That's it, my sweet. You are almost there." He eased a little, teasing her. "Shall I finish, do you think? Or perhaps I should stop. There are people around, after all."

Her response was a low growl, and he chuckled. He pressed more firmly, his expert fingers building her arousal to a fever pitch. "Then come with me. Take your pleasure."

Meg sank her teeth into her lower lip, muffling the cry that rose from her throat.

"That's it," he murmured, his touch prolonging, magnifying the pleasure that flooded through her, so that she jerked helplessly against his hand, moaning softly with her release. After a long moment, he pulled his hand away, letting her skirts fall back to her ankles.

She could feel his breath slamming through his chest, as if he had run a race, and heat fairly radiated from his body, enveloping her. His flesh prodded against her buttocks, hard and insistent.

She leaned back against him for a moment, then slipped out of his arms, looking up and down the deck. Taking his hand, she led him to a spot of deep shadow, behind the small structure that covered the steps below. Sheltered behind this low structure was a chest lashed to the deck, and on the other side of it ropes were piled high, making a small, nearly hidden spot.

"Here. Sit down." Meg pushed him onto the chest, facing her. She straddled his legs and reached down to the front of his breeches, trailing her fingers lightly along the ridge that pushed against the material.

He sucked in a sharp breath. "Meg."

"Damon." She began to unbutton his breeches, her fingers slow and careful. He cursed in a muffled voice, and his hands clenched in her skirts.

She parted the trousers, freeing him. Her fingers slipped beneath him, stroking up the underside, so that desire surged through him, the delicate, soft skin stretched tautly over the fiercely thrusting shaft. "I think perhaps you are ready as well." She teased up and down the length of him.

"I—can assure you—that I have never been so ready," he panted.

Raising her skirts to cover them, she sank down onto him. Damon's breath hissed in as she slid slowly up and down, moving with a languid grace that built the passion within them both to the bursting point. He murmured her name like an incantation, hunger and heat and pleasure mingling into an almost unbearable pressure. Damon dug his fingers into her buttocks, clamping her to him as he thrust into her, and burying his hoarse cry against her breasts, he shook, exploding into his peak.

Meg sagged against him, spent, feeling the aftermath of tremors running through him. Damon took her face between his hands and brought her to him, kissing her hard and slow and long. "Meg, I think you may kill me." He drew in a shaky breath. "But I shall die a very happy man."

She stood up on trembling legs, and he pulled his clothes back together and joined her. "I think it's time we went down to our cabin. I confess that I could use a bit of sleep."

"What?" Meg turned to him, eyes widening. "Do you mean that we have a private cabin? A place to sleep downstairs?"

"Belowdecks, I believe it's called. Yes, we do. 'Tis some distance to Aberdeen."

"Why didn't you tell me before . . . all this?" She gestured vaguely around them.

He grinned. "Because then I wouldn't have had"—he copied her gesture—"all this."

She stared at him for a moment longer, then began to laugh. He gave her his arm, and they started toward the steps.

———

"Do not think I have forgotten that you have not told me where we are going," Meg said the next morning as they lay in bed, having greeted the dawn in a most pleasurable fashion.

"I would never be so foolish."

"And you still won't tell me?" Meg rose on her elbow to frown at him.

He shook his head, a smile playing on his lips.

"Och . . . why are you so annoying?" Meg flopped back onto the bed with a sigh.

"I believe it is one of the fundamental requirements of a man."

Meg laughed. "You have the right of it there."

If his silence on the purpose of their travel was an annoyance, it was the only one Meg found. The voyage was mild; Aberdeen's gray granite buildings sparkled in the afternoon sun; and Damon was by her side every moment. Though he traveled modestly enough as Mr. Rutherford, no one took him as anything but a wealthy gentleman, and everywhere they went, they were afforded the best of service and goods. It was amazingly enjoyable, Meg discovered, to be so coddled and catered to. No wonder a man such as Damon expected to have his own way.

But the respect and the luxury were not what made the journey satisfying, but that away from Loch Baille, no one knew who they were. They had no need to worry about servants' gossip or the spread of rumors. They were assumed to be husband and wife, and no one looked askance if Damon made an affectionate gesture. Meg did not have to watch what she said. They had no need to measure their smiles or be circumspect in their gazes. Best of all, Damon did not have to leave her bed during the night. She could fall asleep in his arms and wake up beside him the next morning. It was pleasant indeed to be roused from her slumber by Damon's soft caresses and kisses, to turn to him, still hazy from sleep, and be brought to full, sharp awareness by his lovemaking. Was this what it was like to be married? she wondered.

The most difficult thing she faced was turning away the gifts Damon tried to shower on her—the shawl with its silky fringe that caressed her bare arms; the bonnet that he pointed out was entirely practical and would not even be noticed by the women of the glen; the pair of soft kid gloves that were, he assured her, a mere trifle; the cameo or onyx ear bobs or lace fichu that she might easily have purchased herself. Had she given him the slightest encouragement, Meg knew, he would have whisked her into a dressmaker's shop and bought an entire wardrobe of dresses too fine for her to wear. She managed to turn him down despite his engaging smile and sweetest blandishments. Still, in the end, she could not resist the shawl of Indian silk, though she knew that it would probably reside, carefully wrapped, in the chest by her bed, too lovely to be worn anywhere except in the privacy of her own cottage.

The second morning in Aberdeen, Damon suggested they take a stroll through town. The look of suppressed enjoyment in his eyes was such that Meg knew it must be time for the unveiling of his surprise. She took his arm and set out with him, expecting—well, she did not know what, but certainly not that their steps would turn toward an area of small, neat houses, well kept but far from extravagant.

She had been determined not to gratify him by asking more questions, but in the end, she could not keep from blurting out, "Damon, where are we going?"

"You'll see. I believe we are almost there. Ah, yes, here it is." He steered her toward a small house built of the ubiquitous gray stone and rapped upon the door. When a young woman opened the door and bobbed a curtsy, he swept off his hat. "I am Mr. Rutherford. I believe David MacLeod is expecting us."

David MacLeod! Meg stared up at Damon in astonishment as they followed the trim girl across the hallway. He merely grinned and winked at her. There was no time for anything else in the few steps it took to enter a small parlor where an old man sat beside the fireplace.

Despite the heat of the room, the old man wore a woolen shawl around his shoulders, and a knitted afghan lay across his legs. If his hair had once been red, no sign of it was now in the thinning, white strands combed carefully across his head. His skin was creased with fine lines, rough and splotched with brown age spots. He looked small in the high-backed wooden chair, though it was difficult to tell his height as his shoulders were bent under the weight of his years.

"Uncle David," the girl said, "here are the folks coom to see you."

The old man started awake and craned his head up and around to peer at them, looking rather like a turtle poking its head out of its shell. He frowned, squinting, and as they drew closer, his eyes widened.

"Faye!" He rose shakily, the blanket sliding down his legs onto the floor, and took a step toward Meg, then stopped, confused. He sagged in disappointment. "You're not Faye." He continued to gaze at her intently. "But your eyes . . . Who are you?"

"I am Meg Munro, Mr. MacLeod. Faye's granddaughter."

"Ah. Ah, yes." He let out a satisfied sigh, holding out his hand to her. "Coom closer, child, let me look at you."

Meg took his hand, and he clasped it tightly, his fingers cool and bony. He continued to gaze at her as if he could not quite believe she was there. "You are very like her. Your eyes—I'd forgotten just how bright they were." Moisture filled his blue eyes and he put his other hand over hers, patting it. "Sit down. Sit down. Would you like a cup of tea? Molly!" he called. "Come bring these folks some tea."

"No, no, that's all right," Meg demurred, but he insisted, and Molly gave another curtsy and left the room.

"She doesna hae much sense, that lass, but she makes fine shortbread, you ken," David told Meg confidentially.

She introduced Damon to the old man. He sniffed. "English, eh? Ah, weel, welcome to you, anyway. Sit doon." He turned his gaze back to Meg as if drawn by a magnet.

She pulled up a stool beside his chair so that she could look directly into the wizened man's eyes. "Weel, lassie, tell me aboot your mither, then. I mind that flaming hair the wee bairn had on her head, like yours."

"My mother's been dead these ten years, I'm sad to say."

"Och, I'm sorry to hear it. Faye's mither passed on many years ago, I ken."

"Aye. I do not remember her well."

"Do you cure folks, too, roaming the woods and picking plants?"

"I do." She nodded.

"Weel, best get to whit you want to know." The old man sighed. "You've coom to hear aboot Faye, I expect."

"I'd like to, yes, if you will tell me."

"She was the bonniest lass I hae ever seen. Michty me! None could touch her. Clever, too, and such a laugh she had. The whole glen was in love with her, and no wonder."

"Who did she love?"

"Ah, now that's a different story. Faye guarded that secret like it was gold."

"Was it you?" Meg asked bluntly.

"Nae." He sighed. "I would hae been the happiest man alive if it was." He glanced over at Damon. "You maun ken what I mean, eh?"

Meg blushed, but Damon smiled faintly. "I do."

"I talked to Angus McKay the other day," Meg told Mac-Leod.

"Angus!" David's eyes lit with memory. "Now there was a guid lad, ayeways up for a lark."

This description of the cantankerous old man took Meg aback. Angus must indeed have been different when he was young. "He was of the mind that it was your brother Jamie who was father to Faye's bairn."

"Jamie?" David let out a little cackle. "Nae, it wasna him; I'm certain of that. The lasses did favor Jamie, it's true, but he couldna get a glance from Faye. If she had picked him, he couldna hae passed up the chance to crow aboot it, at least to me. Anyway, the time was not richt, was it? Jamie was already off following the prince afore then."

"The time? Oh! You mean she was certain about when the bairn was conceived?" Meg asked in surprise.

"Aye. I never heard a woman be so sure about the date. The wee one came a mite earlier than she thocht, but she swore the lassie was early. She maun hae known the exact day, you ken?" David shrugged. "It's said the Munro women hae the sicht, isn't it? They called her gran the spaewife, and I reckon Faye was, too."

"Did her mother know, you think?"

"Who the father was? Nae, I dinna think anyone knew but Faye."

"So you had no idea who he might be?"

"Some said it was wan of the lobsterbacks that forced himself upon her, but . . ." David shook his head. "I dinna believe that. The way she acted about the babe when she was carrying it, the way she talked—I canna think she would hae been that way if the da was a man she despised. But I think it was someone not frae the glen."

"A stranger?" Meg straightened. "Why do you think that?"

"Faye wouldna hae taken up with just anyone. He maun hae been special. Better than the local lads. Sometimes I wondered if it could hae been the prince himself."

"Bonnie Prince Charlie?"

"Aye. Some said it was. But I dinna think so. He was just a lad, that one, and Faye wouldna hae chosen a stripling. It's my opinion he was a ship's captain. She was not wi' him often; she couldna hae been, or else her ma would hae known."

"I guess that is true," Meg agreed.

"Or if he was a Sassenach, he would hae been an officer, a gentleman, you ken, and she fell in love with him despite whit he was. But I think, more like, he sailed in now and then, not just a fisherman, but the captain of a merchant ship. She ayeways used to sit, you see, staring out to sea."

"Angus said she did, that she seemed sad."

"Aye, I saw her there often enough, and she looked fair despairing. It was ayeways in the same spot on the cliff where the loch meets the sea. Above the caves, there's a wide, flat rock just richt for sitting."

"I know where you mean." Meg nodded.

"Weel, it's the way you'd watch if you was waiting for a ship from the sooth. I think she kept watch for him, but he never returned."

"I see." Meg sat back, considering his words.

"I hae—" He paused, looking torn. "Truth is, I hae something to gie you."

Meg looked at him in surprise. "You do?"

"Aye." He nodded. "She gied it me, that last nicht, when she knew she wouldna live. She dinna want to lea' it with her mither, but she wanted her bairn to hae it. She asked me to gie it to Janet when she was auld enough. But I couldna part with it. It was wrong of me, but it was all I had of her. But now . . . weel, I willna be lang for this world, will I? And you should hae it." His old eyes glimmered with tears again. "Looking sae like her as you do."

The old man put his hands on the arms of the chair and pushed himself upward. Damon sprang forward to help lift him and waited until David was steady on his feet before he let him go. The old man gave him a nod, then shuffled across the room and out the door.

Damon turned to Meg. "How are you?"

"I'm fine." She smiled at him a bit tearfully. "I wish I know who Faye loved, what he was like. But I am glad to learn whatever I can. It's a sad story."

"Do you think his notion of the seafarer is right?"

"I'm not sure. It makes sense that it was not his brother Jamie. But he may just not want to think that she was raped by a passing soldier. It could have been that horror that haunted her."

"True. But that would not explain her hair comb. That is the gift of a lover." He reached out to brush her hair. "I know what I feel when I look at her comb in your hair, knowing the feel of your hair beneath my hand, having the pleasure, the intimate knowledge of watching you do up your hair. I know how much more it would be if I had been the one to give it to you. I think whoever he was, he gave that comb to her. And I doubt that it was purchased anywhere around Kinclannoch—probably not even Inverness. The stones are not emeralds or diamonds, but neither are they glass. They are less valuable gems—my guess is peridot and citrine—but they are gems nonetheless, and the workmanship is excellent. I could buy nothing more finely wrought in London."

"But a man who traveled could have bought it in Edinburgh or London or even farther away."

"Exactly. The cost would not have been out of reach for someone such as a ship's captain or a merchant. Yet they are not obviously expensive; people could have easily believed they were mere paste."

"I wonder . . ." An elusive thought teased at the back of her mind, then slipped away as David MacLeod shuffled back into the room.

In one hand, he held a book, tied around with a faded blue ribbon, which he extended to Meg. "Here you are, lass." He clutched it for a second longer as Meg reached out for it, then let it go.

Meg gazed down at the leatherbound volume for a moment, then untied the ribbon and opened it. "Damon!" Her voice was reverent. "This is my grandmother's journal."

26

"**T**his is wonderful!" *Meg held up* the thick, leather-bound journal, opened, to Damon. It was late afternoon, and they were sitting on their bed in the inn, legs stretched out before them and Meg leaning back against Damon's bare chest as she perused her grandmother's journal. "It's full of recipes for her remedies. Here is a drawing of a woundwort, leaves and flowers. And a few lines about a dream she had. This is a treasure. A window into my grandmother." Meg glowed up at him. "I am so grateful. How did you find Mr. MacLeod? Why?"

"I wanted to see you smile like that." His own lips curved up. "You told me his name one day, you remember. So I sent a man to look for him."

"You are very kind."

"It was the only gift I could think of that you might accept from me," he told her lightly. "You are a damnably difficult woman to pamper."

Meg laughed. "I am very glad you did. I cannot think of

anything I would like more than meeting him and hearing about her . . . and this journal!"

He kissed her head, his fingertips idly stroking her arm, and Meg went back to carefully paging through the old book. "She must have done a great deal of writing. It's quite thick."

"Mm. She recorded a lot of things. I think he gave it to her."

"Your grandfather?"

Meg nodded. "Yes, she says something here in the beginning about him giving her this precious gift and only he could know how much it meant to her."

"She doesn't say his name?"

Meg shook her head. "I shall study it thoroughly, you can be certain of that, but the times she's referred to him, it's been 'he' or 'him.' Sometimes she's called him 'my love.' She said something here about leaving a message for him at 'our spot,' but nothing about where that spot is. It's as if she is making a great effort to be secretive."

"Maybe she feared her mother might read it."

"I am not sure her mother *could* read. One of the things that pleases her is that she will be able to write down the recipes for the remedies that have been handed down by word of mouth. Her writing is very plain; she always prints. I think he may have taught her, for she seems to connect it with him." Meg's eyes sent a twinkling gaze Damon's way. "Another man, you see, who understood the way to a Munro woman's heart."

"Ah. A clever sort, then." Damon smiled and kissed the point of her shoulder, his breath teasing over her skin. "Meg, dear, tell me again—why did you put your chemise back on?"

"It seemed a bit improper to sit about reading a book in the altogether."

"I rather like a bit of impropriety." He raised her arm and pressed soft kisses on it, working his way down from her shoulder.

"Do you now?" Meg laughed and closed the precious journal, setting it aside. "It so happens that I do as well." Reaching down, she whipped her chemise off over her head, tossing it aside, and went into his arms.

———

They spent another day in Aberdeen, lingering over their happiness, before they set sail back to the loch. The closer they drew to home, the heavier Meg's heart became, and for the first time she could remember, she felt no joy when she saw the familiar ring of the standing stones.

"Nae," she said, her voice a trifle husky, when Damon started to follow her out of the carriage. "Do not walk to the cottage with me. I—" She swallowed hard; she knew she would start to cry if she had to take her leave of him at home, and she feared she might cling to him and beg him not to go. "It's better here."

She could see the reluctance on his face, but he said only, "Very well."

"Thank you. Thank you so much for everything." Meg grabbed her bag and hurried away.

Damon watched her go, not signaling the coachman to move forward until she disappeared among the trees. He felt . . . lonely. It was silly. It was not as if he would never see Meg again. They would have many days together before he and Lynette returned to London—and the thought of that day gave him no joy. He leaned back against the soft, padded seat, letting out an unconscious sigh.

He and Lynette would have to leave before many months passed. It was September and already turning chilly. It would not be pleasant here in the winter. And yet . . . he thought of Duncally frosted with snow. They would light the massive fireplace in the hall and sit cozily in front of it, the three of them, reading or playing some game or simply talking. Meg would have the shawl he had bought her draped around her shoulders. He smiled faintly.

But, no, he could not leave her. Perhaps Meg would come with them to London—not forever. Meg would not want to live long so far away from all she loved. But she had said she would enjoying seeing other places. For the winter, perhaps. It would be as it had been on the trip. Well, no, not exactly, for she could not live with him in London; they would be far more open to scandal in the city with all the *ton* about. He could buy her a house, though, not far from his and spend as much time as he pleased with her there. Not all the time he pleased, for he could not leave Lynette alone that much. Nor could he could take the two of them together to any of the amusements London had to offer. Italy then, as they had discussed. But Meg was right, damn it—word would be bound to get out and the scandal would haunt Lynette in the future.

He was not in a pleasant frame of mind when the carriage set him down in front of his home, and his mood grew even darker when he started down the hall and heard the sound of Lady Basham and her guests in the drawing room.

Silently, he slipped around to the servants' stairs, startling a passing maid, and went up to greet his daughter.

Lynette was gratifyingly happy to see him, and he spent a pleasant few hours with her. The evening, however, with its overly long meal spent in the company of Lady Veronica and the Twitherington-Smythes brought him back to boredom and gloom, and he hastened over to Meg's cottage as soon as he could escape.

It was balm to his troubled thoughts to lie beside Meg through the night, holding her soft body against him and falling asleep to the sound of her gentle breathing. However, awakening early the next morning to return to Duncally irked him, as it always did, and it set his teeth thoroughly on edge when Harry Twitherington-Smythe decided to join him for an early breakfast. The man then made his day even worse by insisting on joining him and Lynette on their morning ride.

When they returned from the ride, Damon immediately sent a servant to request Lady Veronica's presence in his study. This, at least, was one thing he could remedy.

Veronica swept into his office a few minutes later, her eyes alight with some emotion—he wasn't sure what, but he had no interest in finding out. He rose politely and went around her to close the door. Oddly, this action brought a smile to her lips.

He had spent the last few minutes searching for a tactful way to phrase his words, but in the end he simply thrust nicety aside. "It will soon be fall, Veronica. I am sure you will wish to get started back to London before the weather turns cold."

Veronica looked taken aback. She lifted one brow. "Life in the country has made you distressingly blunt, Damon."

"No doubt. You said you came here to see your niece. Now you have. Lynette is healthy and happy, so you can be at peace with yourself, knowing that my daughter is not ill cared for."

"Damon, really, you act as though I thought you were a bad father."

"I see no other reason why you would come haring up here—though I cannot conceive why you chose to bring that mutton-headed Harry and his wife. It's doing it too brown to pretend you missed your niece's company, given that you had seen her in London only a month before—not that you spent much time with Lynette there."

"I am quite fond of Lynette. She is my niece, and as her closest female relative, I find it incumbent upon me to see that she is prepared to take her place in society."

"Good gad, the girl is only thirteen. She's hardly about to make her come-out."

"Turning a young girl into a lady is not done overnight. Lynette needs feminine guidance, Damon—and I do not mean traipsing about the Highlands with your latest paramour."

His mouth tightened. "Have a care how you speak about Miss Munro."

"Spare me the pretense of defending her honor. It is clear you are having an affair with the woman. However, that is the way of men. What is alarming is that you allow your daughter to spend time with her. Lynette acts as if she were a member of the family."

"Lynette is very fond of Miss Munro. I believe I mentioned that she nursed my daughter through a difficult illness."

Veronica forced a smile and went toward Damon, smiling and extending her hand. "Come now. Let us not quarrel. You and I both have Lynette's best interests at heart. And we have always dealt well with each other, I think."

"I have no interest in quarreling with you, believe me." Damon avoided her hand, linking his own behind him. "I appreciate your concern for Lynette. It is gracious of you to offer to help my mother bring her out."

"Of course. I look forward to that day."

"However, I still do not understand why you are here."

Veronica let out a little laugh. "Really, Damon, you do put a woman to blush." She paused, walking a few steps away, then turned back, an ingratiating smile on her face. "I suppose I must be equally blunt. I hoped you would come to realize how well we suit."

"How well we suit what?"

She made a moue of annoyance. "I am talking about marriage."

"Marriage!" Bloody hell, Lynette had obviously been much more perspicacious about the matter than he. "Veronica, if I have ever given you any reason to suppose that I had hopes of marriage . . ." He stopped, then said more firmly, "Indeed, I am very certain that I have not! You are Amibel's sister!"

"It is not as if you and I are related. There is no reason to have any hesitation in that regard. It is one of the things that is so advantageous. Lynette is my niece, and I am already fond of her. I am quite prepared to take up the task of raising her correctly. And she, already knowing me, will have none of the fears or jealousies that often afflict a girl when faced with a stepmother. We shall get along admirably."

"Veronica, no. Stop. I have no intention of marrying."

"I know the wounds of Amibel's death are still too recent. Certainly we would not even announce it until the full year of mourning is over, and—"

"It is not a question of propriety or how long it has been since your sister died. I do not plan to marry."

"What nonsense! You must marry someday. You have no heir. I am two years younger than Amibel, and I was never one to indulge in the sort of ill health my sister did. I have a number of childbearing years left. Basham was far older than I and never in the best of health; you must not regard the fact that we did not have children as an indication that I am incapable of producing an heir."

"For God's sake, Veronica, I am not looking to purchase a brood mare," Damon snapped. "*If* I should decide to marry, I have a number of years to do so."

"Do you intend to wait for some silly chit making her first come-out to catch your eye? A romantic goose who will cry and complain about your affairs? Who would expect you to dance attendance upon her? I have no such delusions. Give your carte blanche to your little barque of frailty if you wish. I will make no objection."

"Veronica!" he snapped. "Enough. I do not love you." He dropped each word like a stone.

Veronica stared at him. "Good heavens, Damon, what does that have to do with anything? I am speaking of marriage, not love. I have no expectation of love nor any need for it."

"Perhaps I do."

She let out a trill of laughter. "Do not tell me you have turned into a romantic! I had thought you were a man more ruled by his head than his . . . other parts."

"I married once for family and duty; I tied myself to almost fourteen bloody years of misery and boredom. I do not plan to do so again."

"What *do* you intend to do, marry your little Highland fling? I should love to see you introduce your witch-woman to the *ton*. Lord, Damon, tell me you have more sense than to marry someone common?"

"Meg Munro is anything but common, I assure you," he shot back. "But I know such a thing is out of the question." He whirled and stalked over to the fireplace.

"Thank God for that, at least."

"Good day, Veronica," he grated out, not turning around.

With a little huff of outrage, Veronica turned and left. Silence smothered the room. Damon rubbed absently at his chest. It felt heavy and sore beyond measure. He stared into the low flames of the fire. Picking up the poker, he stabbed viciously a time or two at the coals.

What bloody good was being an earl if he could not marry the woman he loved?

The woman he loved.

Suddenly everything inside him eased. What a fool he was. He'd been one from the first with Meg. Of all the blundering, idiotic things he'd done, of all the kinds of narrow-minded simpleton he'd been, this last bit of blindness had been the worst.

But no longer.

He slammed the poker back into its rack. It was time to put things in order. Retrieving a box from his desk, he turned and hurried to the door.

27

Meg sat at the table, the late-afternoon light slanting onto the open book before her. She had steadily been working her way through her grandmother's journal ever since she got home. It was almost enough to distract her from the pain in her heart.

How ironic that her joyous trip should leave her in such sadness and turmoil. Meg had learned several things, but first and foremost she had discovered what she wanted most in life. And it was the one thing she could not have.

She loved Damon. Loved him as her grandmother had loved the man she kept secret, a love so fierce and consuming it pierced her heart and soul, blazing up in the core of her being. There would never be another love for her; she was certain of that. Her mother had never wavered; had Faye lived, she would have remained true to the lover who never returned to her. Like them, Meg would love only one.

Unlike them, she did not think she could be content with the love she had. In Aberdeen, she had glimpsed what she truly wanted, a life with Damon. The peace, the joy, the easy comfort, of a life truly commingled with her lover had captured her. She wanted marriage and all that came with it, not just children or the pleasure of his bed, but the shared life. The vaunted independence of the Munro women paled in comparison. She knew she had no real freedom when her heart would always be chained to his. A life with him was what she ached for, and as long as she had only a part of him, she would continue to ache.

But he was an earl, and she could be nothing more than his mistress. His occasional mistress. It would be better when he went back to London. She would miss Lynette, and the pain of parting from Damon would be searing. But only then would she begin to heal. She would not have the love she wanted—indeed, she thought she needed it like she needed air to breathe—but the wound of parting would scar over. Without the constant reminder, the continual pull of Damon's presence, she could pull her life together and move on. She would have . . . contentment.

Until then she would live in this state, yearning and happy and sad, fearing the moment of parting.

A crackle of a branch underfoot brought her head up, and Meg looked outside to see Damon coming up the path to her door. Hands in his pockets, he walked with his head down, frowning. Her heart began to pound, and she rose a little reluctantly to her feet. What was he doing here at this time of day? And what had put that sober expression upon his face?

She pulled open the door before he could knock.

"Meg!"

"Yes. Who did you expect?" She smiled, determined to maintain a light manner.

"No one. I mean, well, you, of course. I was just thinking. Meg . . . I want to talk to you."

Her stomach turned to ice. "Of course. Come in. No, wait, I have a better idea. I was just about to leave. We can go together—Damon, I think I've found where they used to meet." She took his hand, real excitement tingeing her voice, and pulled him over to the table where the book lay.

"Really? Where? Did Faye say his name?" His attention was caught.

"No, never. But he *did* give her the hair comb, as we thought; she mentions it late in the journal. There were two of them, but one must have gotten lost over the years. He gave her something else, as well, only she will not say what. It's terribly frustrating. All she writes is that he entrusted 'it' to her and she has hidden it and will keep it till he returns again. After that, the entries grow farther and farther apart in time. He hasn't returned, and I can hear the sorrow in her. I think she lost all interest in her life. She was just waiting for the baby to arrive. Toward the end, she writes about a frightening dream she had; she fears that it means she will die soon. And of course she did. Then, there is obviously a page torn out of the book. Maybe more than one." She held out the book to him, showing him the ragged tear.

"Why?" He frowned, running his finger down the tear.

"I don't know, but after that there is only one more entry." Meg turned the page, pointing to the words. "She says she went to their 'spot' again to leave him a last message. I wonder if that missing page was what she left there for him. If we went to that place, we might be able to find it."

"After all these years?" He looked skeptical.

"It's possible. I presume it is where they met, but she refers to leaving their messages for each other there. So it must have been some place that was protected. Where she knew it would not be damaged."

"Where is it?"

"She doesn't say outright. She calls it the 'spot' or 'the cave' or 'the place.'"

"A cave?" He groaned. "There are hundreds of them. And they're all dank and cold," he added darkly.

Meg laughed. "But, you see, I know exactly which dank, cold cave she's talking about. She says right here that she went there to leave him the message and to fetch Irish moss for a tonic." Meg smiled triumphantly. "There's only one cave where the Irish moss grows, where the Munros have always picked it. That is where she left the message. Damon, she might have put his name on it or told him where she hid whatever it was and that might give us an indication of who he was." Meg started toward the door. "Come, I'll get the lantern and we can row over there. You can reach the cave only from a boat."

"Wait." He pulled her to a stop. "First I want to talk to you."

"No!" Anxiety clawed at Meg. She knew in the depths of her heart that he was about to tell her he was leaving, and she could not bear to hear it. Not now. Later, when she had prepared herself. . . . "It's a sea cave. The moss grows there because it is submerged in seawater. The sea is just below the entrance, and when the tide comes it, it fills the place with water. We have to go now, before the tide, or else we won't be able to get in until tomorrow."

"Very well." He sighed. "We'll find your cave first. But *then*, we are going to talk."

———

They rowed out of the loch through the narrow channel to the sea, their speed aided by the flow of the river. The sun shone on them from the west, negating the chill of the water, though off in the distance gray clouds gathered over the gray sea. A storm might blow in with the tide, Meg thought. But they would be gone by then.

Damon rowed up to the dark entrance Meg indicated, and she lashed their rope to a large rock at the entrance. She stepped up into the cave, and Damon followed her with the lantern.

"Where do you think this place is?" Damon moved forward into the cave, lifting the lantern to illuminate the dark space. It was not large, for he reached the end in only a few strides. The walls were damp to the touch, and water pooled here and there in depressions in the stone shelf beneath their feet. Fallen rocks of differing sizes decorated the floor, and lichen grew on most of them. "This is your Irish moss?"

Meg nodded. "Yes. The water will cover these rocks when the tide is in, so their messages would have to be up high."

"Seems a peculiar place anyway. Even if it's not directly in the water, it's bound to be damp."

"It's secluded. No one ever comes here that I know of, except for me."

"They went to great lengths in their quest for privacy. I'm beginning to think he must have been an Englishman. Only loving an enemy would have required such secrecy."

"Sometimes no one knowing about you is a very pleasant thing," Meg said, remembering the feeling of Damon and her existing in their own world, the cozy intimacy that had been theirs when they were away from the loch.

"That's true." Setting down the lantern, he went to her, placing his hands on her hips and smiling down into her face. His eyes sparked with light, and Meg knew he was remembering the same thing. He tugged her forward gently until her hips rested against him. The familiar heat started deep in her abdomen, and Meg felt his response. Damon's eyes took on a dark and heavy look, and he bent to nuzzle her neck. "Privacy is a pleasant thing indeed."

For the next few minutes they were lost to everything else, but finally Meg pulled away with a sigh. "This is *not* finding what we want."

"I believe I am finding exactly what I want." But he gave her a final kiss and let her go. "Very well. The sooner we find it, the sooner we can get back to a comfortable bed."

Meg laughed. "Is that all you think about?"

"Not entirely. Only a large portion of it."

He reached out a hand to her. Meg's heart ached in her chest, thinking how soon this would all be over. Firmly she pushed the thought aside. Leave the sorrow for when that happened. She laced her fingers through his, and they strolled around the cave, lifting the lantern to peer into holes and crevices. They got distracted once or twice and spent a few more minutes locked in an embrace, but each time they pulled away and continued with their thorough search. Damon felt along the walls as high as he could reach.

"You know, this looks like a waterline, where the tide comes to." Damon pointed. "The only place I can see that wouldn't be covered with water would be that narrow shelf of rock that runs along this wall."

The shelf was too high for Damon to see to the back of it, so he lifted Meg up to look at it. It was empty save for grit. When Damon set her down, she dusted off her hands and glanced around disgustedly.

"Nothing. Perhaps she came back and took away the message. That notation was several months before she died. Or maybe the tide came in higher than usual and it did get washed away. The storms strike this headland hard, and there is bound to have been a ferocious storm or two in the past fifty years."

"What about that hole?" Damon pointed to a large black opening just above the floor at the far end of the cave.

"Surely they would not have left messages there. It is far too low; obviously anything there would be washed away."

"Yes, but as I recall, the caves are like a rabbit warren."

"You think it leads to another cave?" Meg's interest was piqued.

"Or opens up inside to something higher." Intrigued, Damon went to the hole and knelt, holding the lantern inside. "It doesn't open up, but I can't see the end of it." He started to crawl forward. "Blast. There *would* be water on the floor."

"Water?" Meg glanced down and saw that a shallow trough of water was indeed running along the center of the floor. She turned, looking back, and saw that near the entrance of the cave, water sloshed on the floor. "Damon, look! I don't understand. The tide doesn't rise for another hour."

"Just a minute." His voice was muffled, his body entirely inside the hole now. "This is a tunnel. It goes back some distance."

"What is that noise?" It had been going on for some time, Meg realized, hovering in the back of her consciousness, an irregular knocking that she had paid no attention to, wrapped up as she was in the search. Her heart began to thud, and she started toward the entrance. "Damon, come back! Something is wrong."

The water was over Meg's feet by the time she reached the entrance, and she had to hold her skirts up to avoid getting them soaked. Behind her, she heard Damon moving about and the clink of the lantern on stone, then he exclaimed, "What the devil!"

Wind whipped into the entrance, making her skirts swirl, and Meg braced her hand against the cave wall and peered out. The gray clouds they had seen earlier over the ocean had moved in with alarming speed, and the sky had darkened to a deep, threatening gray. Rain came down in a heavy sheet, moving swiftly toward the cliff. The wind had kicked up the waves and sent their dory, on its mooring rope, clattering against the cliffside again and again. The water, which had been a foot below the base of the cave when they arrived, now lapped freely over its edge, water sloshing in and spreading across the floor.

"It's that storm," Meg said, her throat tight. "The tide hasn't risen yet, but the storm is sending water in. Once it starts rising . . ."

"Damn and blast!" Damon said as he came up behind her. "How could it have blown up so quickly?"

"It does," Meg said grimly. "I should have paid more attention." She had seen the clouds on the horizon, but she had been too eager to find the place her grandmother wrote about, too eager to flee from the words she knew must come between her and Damon, and so she had ignored the warning signs. "We must leave immediately."

Meg glanced past Damon toward the loch. The passage from here at the mouth, where the water emptied into the sea, narrowed as it stretched back to the loch. Between the high cliffs, it would be somewhat protected from the high ocean waves crashing against the cliffs here. It would be rough going, but they could make it into the loch and from there to shore. Provided that they managed to get into the dory and into the neck of the passage, away from the higher waves. They could not stay here, for the cave would fill up with water.

Damon edged around her and grabbed the mooring rope, which was soaked and pulled taut, the wind shoving the dory toward the loch. Damon leaned out to haul it in, the wind whipping his hair and billowing out his jacket. Water splashed up onto his breeches and lapped around his boots.

"Damon, be careful." Fear clutched at Meg's heart.

Picking up one of the oars they had laid aside on the rocks, she squatted down, ready to use the oar to draw the dory to them as soon as Damon pulled it within reach. Damon let go of the anchoring rock so that he could haul at the rope with both hands. The dory moved toward them, and Meg stretched out the oar, hooking it inside the boat and tugging. She pulled as hard as she could from her awkward position, and after a moment the dory eased toward her. Then everything went wrong.

The wind suddenly swirled, shooting the boat toward Meg and on past the entrance, knocking the oar from her grasp. She grabbed at the wooden paddle, and a gust of wind shoved her in the back as she twisted. Feeling herself overbalancing, Meg let out a shriek and grabbed frantically at the rock beside her, but her hand slipped across the slick stone, and she fell. She heard Damon's shout, and his arm locked around her waist, but the momentum and the force of the wind were too strong. The two of them tumbled together into the churning, dark water.

28

The sea covered her head, but Meg kicked up with all her strength. Damon's arm was still tight around her, and his strength helped propel her upward. As they broke the surface of the water, the waves slammed them against the cliff face, knocking the breath from her. Miraculously, Damon had retained his grip on the rope with his other hand, so that they had not moved from the entrance to the cave, but the storm tossed them about, threatening his hold on their anchor.

Meg clawed at the side of the cliff and grabbed the lip of the entrance. The thick of the storm was upon them now. The rain shot down, stinging their faces, but at least the fierce wind helped plaster them against the rock. Holding on with all her strength, Meg climbed up the cliff beneath the surface of the water, her feet slipping and sliding but always moving upward. When another strong wave lifted them up, she was able to stretch out her arm and wrap it around a large rock. She pulled herself upward until her upper body was mostly in the cave. She felt Damon's arm leave her waist, sending a surge of panic through her, but his hand went under her and gave her a hearty shove upward.

She scrambled into the cave and whirled around, terrified she would find that Damon had disappeared under the water. But she saw that he had grabbed the rope with his free hand as well, giving him a more secure purchase. However, she knew that his hold could not last long in the cold force of the storm. Meg crawled forward and grasped his jacket with both hands, tugging at him. He swung one foot up onto the ledge, and she clamped her hands around his leg and pulled with all her strength. He reached out to the rock anchoring the rope, and then, with another sweep of a wave, he was inside the cave.

They sat up, panting. The last surge of the ocean had finally torn the dory's rope from Damon's hand, and the little boat whipped away, slamming against the rocks. Rain slanted in upon them, pushed by the wind, and they crawled away from the entrance. Damon lurched to his feet, wrapping his arms around Meg's waist and hauling her up with him. They staggered to the back of the cave and collapsed on the floor beside the lantern.

Damon leaned back against the wall of the cave. "I am never, *ever* going into the caves with you again."

Meg began to giggle. He cast a jaundiced glance at her, then he began to laugh as well. Unable to stop, they guffawed until their sides hurt. Finally, their laughter died away, and Damon reached out to curl his arm around Meg's shoulders and pull her close. She leaned against his chest, listening to his heartbeat, steady and comforting beneath her ear.

A shiver ran through her, and Damon rubbed his hand

up and down her arms in an attempt to warm her. Meg sighed and sat up, turning to look at him. "What are we to do now? The tide will start rising soon."

He looked out over the cave, now underwater at the entrance, with a shallow stream creeping up the slight hollow in the middle of the cavern, then up at the watermark over their heads. "You might try praying," he suggested drily. He stood and picked up the lantern. "I think our best course is to trust that your ancestor was not foolish enough to leave her messages in a waterlogged cave and that this hole leads us to some place higher where we can wait out the tide."

Damon carried the lantern to the entrance of the low, dark hole and got down on all fours. Picking up the lantern, he started forward. Meg crouched down and followed him.

The noises of the storm receded behind them, and the tunnel was silent save for the shuffling sounds of their progress. The lantern light cast flickering shadows on the narrow walls of rock, adding to the eerie atmosphere. Meg could see nothing of what lay before them, as her only view was of Damon's legs and muscled buttocks. It was, she reflected, rather a nice view. That showed exactly how foolish she had become, that she should be thinking of such a thing at a time like this. Or perhaps it was simply the mind's nature when death was looming—turning with fervor to the essence of life.

The ground began to slope upward sharply, but alarmingly the ceiling did not have the same tilt, so that the passage grew more and more narrow. Just as Meg began to fear they would have to turn back, Damon let out a low cry of triumph, and in another few steps he was on his feet as the cave ballooned out around him. Reaching down, he pulled Meg up and wrapped his arms around her.

"Meg, Meg." He rained kisses over her hair and face. "I was so bloody frightened. I thought I was going to lose you."

She let out a little laugh. "That is what scared you? You would have died, too."

"That made it slightly less unbearable."

"Damon . . ." Tears welled in her eyes and began to spill down her cheek. "Don't say that."

"No, no, don't cry," he said tenderly, wiping her tears away with his thumbs. "You will unman me entirely." He kissed her lips, and in a flash the gentle touch turned scorching. "I want you," he growled, breaking their kiss. "I want you more than I've ever wanted anything. I know this isn't the time . . ."

"It is. It's exactly the time." Meg's hands went to the lapels of his jacket, gripping them and pushing the garment off his shoulders. "All through that tunnel, I kept thinking of this. Wanting this." She dropped his jacket on the ground and ran her hands down the length of his back. "I was watching . . . this." Her hands curved over his buttocks, and she smiled wickedly up at him.

He made a low, inarticulate noise, fire flashing in the depths of his black eyes.

"And thinking about doing this." Her fingertips dug into the hard, muscled mounds of flesh. "Touching you."

She went to his breeches, busily working at his buttons, and whatever control he still had broke. He dug his hands into her hair and tilted up her face to kiss her deeply. They tore at their clothes, pausing in their rapid disrobing only to touch and kiss, unable to keep their hands or mouths off the other for long. It took too much time, it seemed, to divest themselves of all their clothing, so they came together still trailing bits of half-discarded clothes. Damon lowered Meg to the ground, his arms beneath her back to shield her from the stone and grit of the cave's floor, and he plunged deep within her.

His movement wrenched a soft cry from her lips as Meg convulsed against him, immediately brought to her peak. Light flared in his eyes at the sight of her pleasure, and Damon bent to take her mouth with his as he began to thrust inside her. His lovemaking was as wild and fierce as the wind and rain they had escaped, and Meg clung to him, riding the storm. Her fingers raked down his back as another wave of pleasure washed through her, slow and piercingly sweet.

Damon stared into her eyes, his mouth tight and his eyes alight with some deep, primitive need, as he continued to stroke in and out. "Again," he grated out. "I want to see it take you again."

Her breath shuddered out in something almost like a sob as he reached his hand down between them and found the small, sensitive nub of flesh between her legs. Meg arched up against him, her hips grinding in a mindless, breathless race to fulfillment. Finally, it took her, and she let out a groan as the heat poured, engulfing her. Damon's voice mingled with hers as he erupted within her, his body shuddering. At last they went still, their labored breathing the only sound in the utter silence.

Meg buried her face in the crook of his neck, filled with

such completion, such bittersweet pleasure, such love, that she began to cry, tears spilling from her eyes as she shook with silent sobs.

"Meg, Meg . . . are you crying? Did I hurt you?" Damon rolled onto his back, pulling her on top of him, and his hands roamed over her anxiously. "I'm sorry. I was out of my mind. I didn't mean to hurt you. Please, tell me what's wrong."

She shook her head, sucking in her breath and struggling against the tears. "No, no, you didn't hurt me. I'm fine. I'm just . . . happy." She began to cry again.

"Happy!" His taut body relaxed, and he laughed weakly. "You're crying because you're happy?"

"I love you." She kissed his skin. "I know you will not want to hear it, but I have to tell you. I love you so very much."

His laugh turned deep and rich, and he skimmed his hands over her. "Not want to hear it? I love to hear it." He kissed her ear. "Say it again."

"I love you, blast it." Meg pushed away, sitting up astride him and wiping the tears from her cheeks.

Damon crossed his arms behind his head and grinned up at her. "I love you, too, blast it."

He reached up to tug at a sleeve of her dress that draped down low on her arm. Her bodice was unbuttoned, and the other side of her dress had fallen completely off. Her chemise was untied and shoved down so that both wide straps hung around her elbows and the neckline cupped her breasts.

"I like this fashion." He covered one of her breasts with his hand.

"Of course you do." Meg snorted and shoved his hand

aside, rising lithely to her feet. Her wet dress slid down to plop onto the stone. "As if you look any better."

"I am sure I look decidedly worse." He languidly lay there and watched her as she pulled off the remainder of her garments and began to wring them out. "But since I get to look at you rather than myself, I am quite enjoying it."

His eyes widened suddenly and he grabbed up his jacket to paw at the inside of it, then relaxed visibly.

"What's wrong?" Meg eyed him curiously.

"Nothing. Just thought I'd lost something." He, too, began to pull off his remaining garments and wring them out. "What the devil shall we do with these?"

Meg shrugged and spread her dress out on one of the rocks. "Let them dry, I guess. They won't dry out completely, but perhaps they won't be entirely soaked."

"It's fortunate that I'm feeling quite warm at the moment." He grinned suggestively, laying out his breeches and shirt. "No doubt we'll need to repeat that several times to keep from catching cold."

Meg rolled her eyes, then glanced speculatively around the room. "Do you think this was 'their place'? Where Faye left . . . whatever it was?"

"Not to criticize, but your grandmother might have been a bit less cryptic." Damon walked around, inspecting the walls of the cavern.

It was much like the one they had left, albeit rounder, but there seemed to be even fewer places to hide anything. Along one wall a small ledge jutted out, almost like a seat, and Damon knelt to look under it, but saw nothing.

"If anything was here, I think it's safe to say that it's disappeared." He reached out and encircled her wrist. "Come, let's rest."

He went to the low rock ledge and sat down upon it, stretching his legs out in front of him and pulling Meg into his lap, his arms around her. Meg rested her head against his chest, his warmth all around her.

Damon stroked his hand down her arm. "We've plenty of time to talk now. I have something to tell you."

"No." Meg sat up, turning her face away. "I know what you're going to say, and I don't want to hear it. Not now. Please." She stood up.

"I see." Damon's voice turned distant, and he let her go.

She turned and saw his face. His eyes were cool, his face blank, his lips pressed firmly together in the haughty mask that was his customary retreat from emotion. From hurt, she had grown to realize. Why should he be hurt? she thought resentfully. She was the one to be left behind. Crossing her arms, she walked away, feeling supremely vulnerable, to pick up her dress. Even wet, it would be preferable to this intimacy while he sliced her heart in two.

Suddenly Damon surged to his feet. "Damn it! What is it that is so displeasing to you about me? You seemed to like me well enough there." He gestured toward the floor where they had lain only moments earlier. "Why do you run from me at every chance?"

"What?" Meg whirled, astonished, then angry herself. "Me? You hold me at fault?"

"And how the devil do you already know?" He scowled. "Did Coll tell you?" He frowned. "No—how could he have—"

"Coll! You told Coll? You let *him* know before you talked to me?" Her eyes blazed. "You told my brother you were leaving? That you were casting me aside?"

She had, she saw, stunned him. He stared at her in a frozen way, then started to speak, but only a strangled croak came out. He cleared his throat and said tightly, "You think I am casting you off? Is that what Coll told you?" His face turned grim. "I'll tear that bloody bastard limb from limb."

"Coll has told me nothing!" Meg's voice rose to a shout. "I'm not stupid. I'm not blind. I know you must return to London. I know this is all"—she waved her arm around vaguely, her voice rough with unshed tears—"temporary."

"*That* is what you think I wanted to talk to you about? Of all the single-minded, pigheaded—" He broke off, stalking over to his jacket and scooping it up off the floor. He dug into an inner pocket. "If I were not trying to woo you, I would point out that you are indeed stupid and blind."

"Woo me? You have an odd notion of wooing, I must say."

"And you have an odd notion of me." He flung the sodden jacket back on the floor with a splat and turned to her, jaw set and eyes flashing, holding out a box.

Meg eyed the box suspiciously. Her insides were in a turmoil, dread and hurt and hope and astonishment all swirling around in her like a hive of bees. "I don't . . . what is that?"

"Well, it bloody well isn't a parting gift, I assure you." Since she made no move toward him, he went to her and took her hand, plopping the small box into her palm firmly. "Open it."

Her fingers closed around it, shaking, and Meg shot another wide-eyed glance at him. She opened the lid and stared at the glittering ring inside, a large, clear, yellowish stone with small green gems on either side of it. "Damon . . ." She raised her eyes to his, huge tears welling in them. "I don't know what to say."

"Yes. All you have to say is yes, Meg." The irritation of a moment before was gone from his voice, replaced by something warm and gentle and a trifle uncertain. "Tell me you will marry me." He plucked the ring from the box and slid it over her finger, holding her hand up to admire it. "Doesn't it look splendid there?" He folded her fingers down, as if to prevent her from removing it, and brought her hand up to kiss the knuckle below the ring. "Say yes, Meg, and end my misery," he murmured, his voice slightly unsteady.

"But, Damon, think. You are an earl. You cannot marry me."

He smiled, a gleam entering his eye that told her he knew he had won. "Your mistake, my love. I *am* an earl. And I do as I please."

"But I am nobody!"

"You are Red Meg Munro."

"All your friends . . . your mother . . . everyone will be appalled. You know what your sister-in-law thought of me. And the others, the Honorable Harry Twitting-something and his wife."

Damon chuckled. "It may surprise you to learn that my first requirement in a wife is not the approval of either my former sister-in-law or Harry Twitherington-Smythe." He bent and nuzzled the crook of her neck. "Say yes, Meg."

"But Lynette—"

"Adores you. She will think I am a clever fellow to have caught you."

Meg could not hold back a breathy laugh as his lips nibbled across her collarbone. "Stop. You make it hard to think."

"I intend to." He took one earlobe between his teeth and delicately worried it.

"Damon . . ." Meg sagged against him, the sweetly familiar throbbing beginning between her legs.

"You needn't think. Just feel." He skimmed his fingertips down her spine and teased along the line of her buttocks, slipping in between her legs. "I want you. I want to have you with me always." The stroke of his fingers was almost unbearably light, and she shivered. "Say yes, Meg. Tell me you want the same."

"Yes," she whispered, kissing his skin. "Yes, oh, Damon, yes."

He took her to the ground with him, and where before their lovemaking had been all fire and heat and urgency, this was all tenderness, love given and taken in equal measure. Their kisses were sweet and lingering, pleasure delayed as they aroused and explored, building the hunger within them, and when at last he slid inside her, he laced his fingers through hers, pulling her arms above her head, and he gazed into her eyes as he slowly pushed them both to the shimmering peak. When at last he saw the ecstasy haze her eyes, it seized him, too, and they both soared into the joyous fire.

They lay nestled on the floor some hours later, having dozed, then wakened. Damon had turned the wick of their lantern low to conserve the light, and the room was barely lit. Meg had no idea what time it was or how long had passed, and she did not care. She could have lain like this forever, she thought, cradled in love.

"I wonder if they lay here," she mused, stroking her hand idly up and down Damon's arm. "Faye and the man she loved."

"I would not be surprised." He rose on his side, bracing himself on his elbow, and gazed down at Meg. He trailed his thumb down the center line of her chest. "If he felt as I do, he would have doubtless seized the opportunity whenever, wherever, it arose." He traced the rise of her hip bone. "Though I cannot believe she could have been as beautiful as you."

"More so, according to all who knew her."

"Memory is kind."

"Damon . . ."

"Hmm?" he murmured, watching his finger circle her nipple, making the pinkish bud tighten.

"Why did you talk to Coll?" She took his chin, turning his head so that he looked in her face. "Did you ask his permission to marry me?"

"Oh, that." Damon's expression turned wary. "Well . . . yes. I know you pride yourself on your independence, but, dash it, there are just some things one has to do. I could not ask for your hand without telling him, could I?"

"And what if he had said no?" She cocked her eyebrow.

"I would have had to resign myself to your brother's

dislike, I suppose." He grinned at her. "You cannot think I would have given up if he disliked it."

"What did Coll say when you asked him?"

Damon tilted his head consideringly. "I believe his exact words were 'Not another bloody Sassenach.'"

Meg burst into laughter. "That sounds like Coll."

"Then he said that if I hurt you, he would break me, bone by bone. You are a violent lot, you Scots."

Meg snorted. "Says the man who threatened to tear Coll limb from limb a little while ago."

"Yes, well . . . you can drive a man to his breaking point. After that, Coll informed me that what he thought meant nothing, as you would do exactly as you pleased. Of course, I knew that already. But still, one must observe the proprieties. And he and I had talked about—well, I wanted him to know, to see, that I intended to treat you with the utmost honor."

"What do you mean, you and he had talked? Have you had another bout with him? And the two of you kept it hidden from me?"

"No, no, you need not scold. We did not fight. We did not even argue, not really. I offered him the position of estate manager at Duncally."

Meg said nothing, merely gaped at him.

"I thought of it that day you and I talked about it. It seemed the obvious thing. All that stood in the way was my pride—and I've learned since I came here to swallow that. He'll take it eventually. People will say I am a lovesick fool whose wife rules him, no doubt. But I shall have to put up with it, I suppose, since it's the truth." He cast a sideways grin at her and bent to kiss the tip of her breast. "I am, after all, a slave to your wishes."

Meg placed her hands against his chest, holding him off as he leaned toward her again. "Wait. Are you saying Coll accepted the job?"

"Of course not. He said no, along with a number of other, more uncomplimentary things. But I daresay I will persuade him eventually. I have a way of wearing people down. And it is, after all, his duty to the people of the glen, isn't it?"

"You *are* sly." Meg laughed.

"I have learned how to handle a Munro."

"Oh, have you now?" Meg cocked an eyebrow at him.

"I have." He slipped his hand down her body and in between her legs, gently teasing until she was slick and throbbing. "You see?" He grinned at her.

"You're very cocksure." Meg rose, pushing him onto his back. He went with her movement, his eyes sharpening in anticipation. "Two can play at that game, my lord."

She took him in her hand, stroking him, and he let out a soft hum, his lids drooping. He looked at her with hot, dreamy eyes. "I yield, my lady. You are the master of this game."

Damon pulled her head down and kissed her, rolling her onto her back.

"Ow!"

Damon's head snapped up and he pulled back. "What? Did I hurt you? Or are you merely happy again?"

"No." She grimaced at him. "Something jabbed me." She reached behind her, feeling along the dirt. "There is something here."

Her eyes lit, and she sat up, turning to look at the ground

where she had lain. A thick layer of dirt and grit covered the stone surface, and poking up from it were the tips of two metal tines. Meg bent closer, rubbing with her finger at the dirt caked on them. "Damon, look!"

A glitter of pale yellow and green and gold peeked out of the dirt. She dug at the earth around it until she had exposed the object, and they both stared down at what Meg had uncovered. A piece of parchment lay there, folded and stuck between the tines of a filigreed, golden hair comb.

"My grandmother's comb!" Meg breathed. "There *were* two of them." She picked up the comb and gently pulled the paper from its tines. Carefully unfolding the fragile paper, she read the faded lines of ink.

"'My love, I pray you find this well and happy. What you left me is safe; I have hidden it, and you will know where and when to find it. If you have gone on, as my heavy heart fears, it will be there for our child. My time is coming, and I do not fear it, for I pray I will find you waiting for me. I love you with all my heart. Faye.'"

"Oh, Damon! How sad." Tears welled in Meg's eyes, and she sat back on her heels.

"It is." He brushed his knuckles across her cheek tenderly, then turned back to the spot of earth. "But not, unfortunately, terribly enlightening. Who was this love? And what did she hide? Do you suppose your mother did find it?"

"I don't know." Meg brushed away more soil, and Damon joined her.

He dragged his fingers like a rake across the floor beside him. The dirt and silt had built up more beneath the little stone ledge. He touched something smooth and supple. "I found something." Excitement pulsed in his voice.

"What?" Meg moved over beside him, her tone eager.

"I don't know, but it feels . . . well, it doesn't feel like rock." He clawed at the dirt. "It's cloth—no, leather." He carefully worked the object free and held it out to her.

This pouch, thoroughly smeared with mud, was open, the tie that had once closed it gone.

"There's something here. A mark or something." He rubbed gently at the mud, and slowly an emblem emerged, a stylized flower.

"Rose!" Meg gasped. "That is the rosette, the symbol on, well, on everything at Baillannan."

"Oh. So it was just dropped here sometime by one of the Roses."

"I suppose it could have been. But . . ." Her brain was whirring. She began to dig beneath the ledge, scattering the dirt. "Hah!" She pounced on something, and when she pulled her hand back, it held two round pieces of metal, smeared with dirt. Gold winked from a corner of one. Meg scrubbed at them, clearing the flat sides.

They stared at the coins, large and gold, with the silhouette of a man with flowing hair on one side, Latin words stamped around it. On the other side was a crown and two ovals containing patterns. One pattern Meg recognized as a fleur-de-lis.

"The louis d'or. Gold Louis," Damon translated. "It's Louis the Fifteenth; those are the coat of arms of France and Navarre on the back."

"French coins."

"French coins from the *last century*." They looked at each other.

"Oh, my Lord." Meg sat back on her heels. "It's the treasure. Malcolm Rose's treasure." She waggled the remains of the money pouch with the Rose emblem stamped upon it. "There *was* a treasure, and my grandmother hid it."

Damon nodded. "And your grandfather was—"

Meg whispered, almost in shock, "Malcolm Rose."

29

Though they searched the rest of the cave till their fingernails were broken and their hands caked in dirt, they found nothing else. It was impossible to tell the time, but as their clothes had mostly dried and the lantern was burning precariously low, they dressed and made their way back down the tunnel to the original cave. The tide had gone out, though water still stood here and there in puddles. It was dawn, the sun just edging above the horizon, and the sea was so calm it was hard to imagine that a violent storm had been here earlier. A soaked rope still wrapped around the rock at the entrance, but all that was left of the dory was a single piece of wood.

Damon sighed and looked down at the water lapping a few inches below the lip of the cave. "It appears it's a good day for a swim."

"The water's calm. But it's a long way to the loch."

Damon tossed his jacket on the cave floor beside the lantern, along with his neckcloth and waistcoat, then sat down to pull off his boots. He studied the cliff that stretched toward the ocean. "Where does that path go?"

Meg followed his pointing finger to the narrow path that ran along the cliff several feet above their heads. "It curves around the headland. See that promontory?" She pointed to the end of the cliff. "That's the rock where David MacLeod said Faye used to sit and watch the sea. The cliff turns there and runs northward. The land comes down as it goes along and the path turns up a bit, so that it actually comes out atop the cliff. Not far from where you rode down to the beach that day." She smiled a little at the memory. "But we'd have to get to the path first. It's above us and a good way away, as well."

"There's a bit of a ledge." Damon gestured toward the cliff face near their feet. "Not wide enough to walk on, but I can hold on with my hands and make my way along it until I reach that rock that juts out. I can climb out there and take the path around the headland."

"You! And what am I supposed to do while you're out there clambering about?"

He slanted a look at her. "Sit here where you're not wet or breaking off a bit of rock and falling into the ocean. I'll get a boat once I reach the shore and come back for you. If I don't, then you'll sit here till someone comes looking for you."

"Or I'll go with you."

"It could be dangerous. I'm a good swimmer."

"As am I. I grew up beside the loch, and I've spent half my life climbing over these rocks. And being smaller, I'm less likely to break off any piece of rock than you are."

"Oh, the devil." He scowled. "Come along then; I'm not going to waste my breath arguing with you."

"That's a wise decision."

"But I will go first," he said darkly.

"Of course." Meg smiled sweetly. She skinned out of her underlying petticoats, wrapped up their newfound treasures inside the garments, and with Damon's help stowed them on the ledge above the waterline. Then she pulled the bottom of her skirt up between her legs and firmly hooked it in the waistband.

"At least I shall have a pleasant view as I die," Damon said, eyeing her bare legs.

With a kiss, he took hold of the rope and slipped into the water, letting out a curse at the chill. With the rope for security, he made his way to the small ledge and tossed the rope back to Meg. She followed. Damon's plan, as it turned out, was surprisingly easy. Buoyed by the salt water and with fewer clothes weighing them down, they "walked" their hands along the ledge and climbed out at the wider jut of rock. The worst part came as they made their way up to the narrow path that led around the cliff, but Meg found if she faced the cliff and did not look down, it was amply wide to sidle along, and after a time, the path broadened as it curved around the headland and started north.

They soon emerged at the top of the cliff. Meg pulled down her skirts and took the hand Damon held out to her. The sun was fully up now, and everything sparkled, clean and fresh. It was, Meg thought, a lovely day.

She gestured in front of them. "That was a fierce storm.

Look at how much land has been disturbed. Even up there, where the water does not reach."

"The wind was vicious; it probably blew the sand off."

"That used to be a hillock there." She pointed. "Now all you can see are some stones." She narrowed her eyes. "How odd. They look almost like a wall."

"Perhaps it is."

"Why would anyone put a little wall there?" She started toward the spot, intrigued. "Look! There's more than one."

They stood looking down at the low line of flat stones, peeking up above the sand. They ran in regular lines, forming three-fourths of a square, and beyond them stretched another line and still another set of walls in an L-shape.

"It looks almost . . ."

"Like a house that's been torn down," Damon finished. "Or a shed, I suppose. It's rather small."

"Small! It would make my cottage seem grand. But why would anyone build a house here? Or a shed, for that matter." She frowned. "No one's ever lived here that I've heard of. It's been just a hillock all my life."

"I think this is much older than that. Perhaps even older than your tales." He squatted down beside one wall. "This reminds me of some things I've seen in England. I had a professor—" He looked up at her with a grin. "The one who would have flayed me for letting those standing stones be moved. He took some of us students to a place that had been excavated. Not Roman ruins, older than that."

"Older than Roman?" She looked back at the exposed stones. "You think these are ancient ruins?"

"Could be." He shrugged. "They had a similar look, so old the earth had grown up around them. There were barrows and standing stones not far from those ruins, just like here." He stood up. "I'll have to write Lionel; he'd be very interested in a holiday at Duncally, I imagine."

They regarded the partially buried stones.

"It seems there are a number of secrets in this place," Damon mused.

Meg pulled the gold coin from the depths of her skirt pocket and rubbed her thumb across it meditatively. "Far more than I've known of." She turned to Damon. "Do you think Malcolm Rose was really Faye's secret lover?"

"Well, we have French coins from that time in the place where she likely left messages and/or met with a man whose identity she was extremely careful to keep secret." Damon began to tick the points off on his fingers. "We have a married man—whose wife sank a knife into his back, by the way, not an unlikely end for an unfaithful spouse—a married man of some stature and wealth who is rumored to have brought back treasure from France, a treasure no one has ever been able to find. Cryptic messages from your grandmother about holding something that belonged to her lover, an expensive hair comb given to her by said mystery lover, and the mate to it with the love letter she wrote him. And she referred to 'our child.' I think it would be far more unlikely if you were *not* Malcolm Rose's granddaughter."

Meg shook her head and took Damon's hand again. "It is hard to imagine. I never dreamed it could be him because he was in France during that time."

"But you told me this story before. Malcolm came back, and his jealous wife killed him because she discovered a letter he'd sent to another woman. It all fits. Your grandmother was that woman."

"Yes, but his wife intercepted his note asking his lover to meet him. So Faye would never have gotten that letter. So he and Faye would not have met."

"Obviously she did see him somewhere. Somehow. How else would she have the treasure he brought back with him? Being a man eager to be with the woman he loved and whom he had not seen for weeks—and I think I have some knowledge of that position—I suspect Malcolm went to Faye as soon as he arrived. He was reunited with her, gave her the money or told her he had left it in their secret place, and then he hied off to Baillannan, where he then decided he could not leave without seeing his love again. So he sent her a note, and it was that which his suspicious wife found. And she paid him back for his infidelity with a bit of cold steel."

"A high price." Meg gave a little shiver. She went up on tiptoe to kiss Damon's cheek. "I am very glad that I do not have to hide your identity." She held her hand out, turning it this way and that, admiring the glitter of the sun on its gems.

Damon took her hand and brought it to his lips. "It looks lovely on your hand. But this is only a frippery thing, just citrine and peridot, that I had already ordered to match your hair comb. It was all I had at hand to use as an engagement ring. We can replace it with a finer one in London, emeralds and a yellow diamond, say."

"But, no, I love this one! It is . . ." She rubbed a finger over the stone. "It is from your heart." She looked up at him, suddenly serious. "Are you sure, Damon? Really, really sure? I love you with all my heart, but I do not need to have your name for that."

"I *do* need for you to have my name. My name, my

heart, everything I am or possess. I love you, Meg." He took her mouth again in a long, tender kiss. When he pulled away, he grinned. "And how else am I to get you to accept a gift?"

Damon looped his arm around her shoulders. Meg laughed and leaned against him as they turned toward home.

Don't miss the third book in the delightful

Secrets of the Loch series

by *New York Times* bestselling author

Candace Camp

Enraptured

Coming Summer 2016 from Pocket Books!

The coach lurched through another rut, and Violet grabbed the leather strap above her head, hanging on grimly as the vehicle bounced and swayed. She was beginning to think this journey through Scotland would never end. She tucked her hands back inside her fur muff, deciding that sliding about on the seat was preferable to frozen fingers, at least for the moment.

Thank heavens for the muff, a remnant of her life in her father's house. After all these years, it was a mite bedraggled, but it still kept her hands toasty. Her practical flannel petticoats and woolen carriage dress were warm enough as well, at least inside the chaise. She wished she could say the same for her ice-cold feet. She wriggled her toes inside her half boots and thought regretfully of the wrapped heated brick their butler had tucked under her feet in the past. It was not that she was unused to difficult weather or rough travel; she had accompanied Lionel to other sites throughout Britain, subjecting herself to cold, heat, and rain. But none of those occasions had been in winter . . . or in the Highlands of Scotland.

Still, she was sure that she had been right to come early instead of waiting for spring as Uncle Lionel would have done if he were still alive. Her situation was entirely different now. Violet swallowed hard at the thought of her mentor and blinked away the tears that threatened. She would *not* cry. Lionel himself would have pointed out that it was ineffective and unnecessary. Her tears would not bring him back, and she must not arrive at her future patron's home looking woebegone and red-eyed. She had to be firm and strong, professional, if she hoped to convince the earl that she was the person most fit to take her uncle's place.

It was vital that she seize this opportunity before other antiquarians heard of it. Before the Earl of Mardoun learned of her uncle's death and offered the ruins to someone else he deemed more worthy—in short, to a man.

Violet suppressed a sigh. It was no use thinking of the inequities of life. She was accustomed to the ways of the world. She had long since learned that she must struggle for everything she accomplished. Only Lionel had accepted her abilities.

At a muffled shout, the carriage halted abruptly, sending Violet sliding from her seat and onto the floor of the post chaise. She sat up, a trifle stunned, hearing more voices and then a loud crack. Was that the sound of a gun? Violet jumped to her feet, and flung open the door.

"What in the—" She stopped, her mouth dropping open at the sight before her.

It was dark, for evening fell early here in November, and the scene was illuminated by only the lantern in the postboy's trembling hand. The lad was huddled on the lead horse, bundled up so against the cold that only his reddened nose and wide, frightened eyes were visible above his woolen scarf. Two men stood across the narrow roadway, facing the post chaise, four others to the side of the road. They were attired in similar bulky clothing, hats pulled low on their heads and thick woolen scarves wrapped around their necks and lower faces, making it almost impossible to discern their features in the poor light. It was easy enough to see, however, that one of them held a musket trained on the postboy and two more carried pistols.

Anger surged in Violet, sparked by the cumulative aggravations of the trip. "What do you think you're doing? Stand aside and let us pass."

"Och! A little Sassenach," one of the men cried in a gleeful tone, his words muffled by his scarf.

Between his thick accent and the cloth covering his mouth, Violet could make little sense of what he had said, but she had understood the word *little* well enough, and it added fuel to the fire of her anger. As if because a woman was petite, she was the same as a child! It was another attitude she had had to endure all her life.

"Get out of my way." Violet's eyes flashed. "I do not think the Earl of Mardoun will be pleased with you detaining one of his guests." *Guest*, of course, was stretching the truth a bit since Mardoun had no idea she was coming, but the principle was the same.

"Oooh, the Earl of Mardoun, is it? Now I'm shaking in my boots." He laughed, and the men around him joined in. "Throw doon your jewels, lassie, and your purse, too. And then we'll let you gae on your way . . . if you ask nicely."

"I haven't any jewels." Her chin jutted stubbornly. She had precious little money in her reticule either after paying the expenses of this journey. If she gave it up, she would be utterly penniless.

"What's those bobs in your ears, then!" He gestured at her with his pistol.

Violet's hands flew up to her ears, knocking her bonnet back. "My grandmother's drops! No! Absolutely not."

The man's jaw dropped in surprise at her defiance and so did his pistol hand, so that for an instant Violet thought she might have won the day, but then he scowled and started toward her. "Maybe you're wanting to pay me some ither way, then."

Violet knew that her fury and, yes, fear had carried her too far, but though her stomach clenched with dread, she reached back inside the carriage and grabbed up her umbrella, turning to face her opponent. Again the man halted in astonishment, but then one of the men let out a hoot and began to laugh.

His face darkened and he rushed forward. Violet swung with all her might and the umbrella met the side of his head with a loud crack. He let out a screech and stumbled back, one hand going to his head. The umbrella had snapped beneath the blow, and Violet had no idea what she would do now. She braced herself. Suddenly there was a shout and a large man hurtled out of the darkness into the circle of light cast by the postboy's lantern and charged straight toward her.

Startled, Violet swept her hand back to meet his charge, but the dangling end of the umbrella only rapped him on the arm. In the next instant, she realized that the newcomer was reaching out to grab her attacker, not her. He turned his head to her in shock, growling, "Blast it! I'm trying to help you!"

Turning his back on her, he seized her attacker and jerked him up, lifting the smaller man almost off his feet. "What the bloody hell do you think you're doing?"

Violet gaped at her apparent rescuer, a behemoth of a man, almost as tall as she, even though she stood on the top step of the post chaise. His wide shoulders owed little to the heavy jacket he wore, and his broad, long-fingered hands held the other man up with ease. Unlike the brigands who had stopped her post chaise, he wore no muffler or cap, and his jacket hung open down the front. His thick tousled hair glowed golden in the light of the lantern.

He flung the other man toward the side of the road, saying disgustedly, "Is this what you've come to? Preying on travelers like a band of brigands! Robbing innocent women! I'm ashamed to call you Highlanders. Look at her." He swung his hand toward Violet. "She's just a wee lassie! Hardly bigger than a child."

"Wee!" Violet bristled at his description of her, the anger still pumping through her. "I am not a child. You will not dismiss me as *wee*. Just because I am not . . . a . . . a *giant* does not mean that I am not capable of taking care of myself."

He turned and stared at her in astonishment. His gaze swept down her in one swift, encompassing glance. At some other time, Violet suspected she would have found his strong features handsome, but at the moment, she saw nothing except the scorn in his eyes. His mouth quirked up on one side. "Oh, aye, I can see that you are doing quite well so far. No doubt your broken umbrella would hold off any number of men."

"I don't need your help." Violet knew she was being foolishly stubborn, but her nerves were stretched to the limit and she wanted nothing more at the moment than to hit someone.

"Do you not?" His brows, darker than his light hair, drew together sharply. "I dinna ken whether you're blind or just foolish, but there is only one of you—one small one, I maun say, and you wouldna have won this fight."

"I did not ask for your help." Violet drew herself up to her full height, crossing her arms in front of her. One of the men on the side of the road chuckled, spurring her aggravation.

"Nae, you dinna," her rescuer shot back, "and in truth I am beginning to regret offering it. Now would you cease this arguing and get back in your carriage and let me handle this?" He swung back around, effectively dismissing her, and addressed the other men again. "Begone, all of you. And cease this kind of idiocy before the lot of you wind up with your necks in a noose." He gestured toward the men blocking the carriage's way, and they dropped their gazes, shuffling over to the side of the road.

"That's fine for you to say, Coll." The man whom Violet had hit sent the newcomer a sulky look as he pressed his scarf to his bleeding cheek and ear. It gave Violet a little spurt of satisfaction to think that she had clearly inflicted some damage on the blackguard. "Now that you're one of *them*. Sitting all snug and pretty, aren't you? Carrying out his lordship's orders. You used to be one of us."

"I am not one of *them*," Coll retorted in a goaded voice. "I'm of this glen, the same as you. Same as I've always been. I dinna take on this job for him. I did it for you, for all the crofters. There willna be any more families tossed out of their homes now."

The other man let out a snort of disbelief. "For how long?"

"For as long as I've breath in this body. Dinna try me, Will. I have no hope for you any longer; you're on your way to the gallows as fast and straight as you can go. But I willna let you take any of these others with you. Is that clear?" Coll took a long step forward and grabbed the man's shirt and shook him.

Violet watched with a jaundiced eye. It must be handy to be able to roar over everyone else's voice and to shake them into submission. Authority came so easily to a man like this. He had saved her and she was grateful for that—indeed, with every passing second, the fury that had swept her along was seeping out of her and she realized what a dire situation indeed she had been in—but she had too often been shoved into the background by men who were louder, larger, and stronger than she. She was not going to faint or dissolve into tears or gaze at this man in feeble, feminine awe.

Turning, she gestured sharply to the postboy and got back into the carriage, and the vehicle rumbled away. She settled back against the seat with a sigh. What a ghastly day! Well, at least, she knew now that they must be nearing the earl's estate. The highwaymen had obviously recognized his name.

Violet wondered who that other man was, the one who had charged in, tossing people about. The would-be high-wayman had called him something—it had sounded like *call* or *cull* but that could not be his name, surely. Perhaps it was some Scots term. If she understood what the ruffian had been saying, he must be someone who worked for Mardoun. But not one of the earl's English employees—that deep rumbling voice had been softened by a Scottish burr. What, she wondered, was so appealing about the Scot accent? It seemed to roll through a person like warm honey—or, at least, this man's had.

The voice had fit the man—outsized and solid, reassuring. She closed her eyes, remembering the scene again. The glint of his hair in the low light—too long and untidy to be fashionable. Nor had his clothes been those of a gentleman. They had been rougher, plainer, like a worker's garments. Yet there was something about his speech that had set him apart from the other men.

It was not just that his accent was less thick; there was something in his words, in his turn of phrase that spoke of . . . gentility? No, that was not quite right; he had clearly called himself one of them. Education, perhaps? Violet smiled to herself. No, there was nothing of the narrow, hunched academic in his broad shoulders or massive hands.

Her thoughts lingered for a moment on those shoulders. She remembered the way he had looked her up and down. What had been in that look? Contempt, she supposed, given the way he had dismissed her. And yet . . . there had been a glint of something on his face, in his eyes. She wished she knew what color his eyes were. It had been far too dimly lit to tell. But she had seen that firm chin well enough . . . the square jaw. . . .

What a silly thing to be thinking about! Violet sat up, opening her eyes. It scarcely mattered what he looked like or who he had been. Or how rich or deep his voice was. She was curious about him, of course; she was always curious—her mother had called it her besetting sin. He did not easily fit into a category, which made him intriguing. But it was absurd to be thinking about how he looked or what he said.

The post chaise soon pulled into a village, and the post-boy hopped down to question an ostler at the inn. They passed through the village and continued on the road, which, Violet noted, grew even more narrow. Turning off, they started up a smaller road, but one that was smoother than the road they had just left. The path rose steadily, and the tired horses began to slow, but then at last they reached a tall pair of ornate gates, and the post chaise turned and passed through them. Relief swept through Violet. This must be the estate.

Pushing aside the corner of the curtain, she peeked out. At first she could see nothing but trees, but they emerged onto a wide lawn and she could see the enormous dark bulk of a house looming before them. She had to crane her neck to look up at the ornate towers atop it as the post chaise pulled to a stop in front of the set of massive double doors.

For a moment, Violet feared her courage might fail her. Duncally was massive. It obviously sat atop a hill, for the post chaise had climbed almost from the moment they left the main road, and the castle—there was no other word for it, with its crenellations and turrets, all of them for effect not use—sat at the very top, looking out over the country-side. The manor house in which Violet had grown up was large, but it would have been dwarfed by Duncally's splendor. Though she had known Mardoun was a man of great wealth and consequence, for the first time it sank in on her how powerful Lionel's patron was. It would be seriously detrimental to her career—her entire life—if she offended the man.

She straightened her shoulders and drew in a deep breath. She was here. There was nothing for it now but to go on. Picking up her cape, Violet wrapped it around her shoulders, and stepped down from the carriage. The postboy, who had slipped off his horse, stood holding the reins as he gaped up at the house before them.

"You may unload my trunks," she told him with a great deal more assurance than she felt. It would be humiliating indeed if Mardoun sent her packing now.

She tied her cloak as she walked up the steps to the grand doors. There was more wind up here than there had been in the valley below, and it sliced through her, tugging at her hat. The house was utterly dark; no lights shone in the myriad of windows, not even a glow through the drapes or around the edges. It was too early for everyone to have retired, surely.

Violet raised the ornate knocker and banged it firmly against its plate. After a long moment with no response, she gave it several more sharp raps. What seemed an eternity passed, and she was beginning to despair of an answer when at last, one of the heavy front doors opened, revealing a young man, obviously hastily dressed, holding a lamp in one hand. He raised the light and stared at her blankly.

"I am Lady Violet Thornhill," she said briskly. She had learned long ago that one could not show any sign of hesitation or lack of confidence if one hoped to be taken seriously. "I am here to see Lord Mardoun."

The young man gaped at her, looking—if such was possible—even more incapable of speech. A woman's voice sounded faintly somewhere in the house behind the man, and with a look of relief, he turned away. "Mrs. Ferguson! Some lass is here tae sae the earl."

"What nonsense is this?" The female voice was closer now, and the lad stepped back as an older woman appeared at the door. Mrs. Ferguson was a square, substantial woman wrapped in a heavy flannel dressing gown. Her hair, liberally sprinkled through with iron gray, hung braided in one thick plait over her shoulder. She held up a lamp and regarded Violet suspiciously. "What do you think you're doing, pounding on people's doors at all hours of the night?"

"It is barely eight o'clock." Violet returned an equally steely gaze, refusing to be intimidated. "I am here to see Lord Mardoun."

"Well, you have nae chance of that. Gae on with you noo." She made as if to close the door, but Violet hastily slipped inside.

"I am here at the express invitation of Lord Mardoun," Violet went on. That was stretching it a bit, but the man *had* invited Lionel, and Lionel would have brought her with him if he had been able to come.

Mrs. Ferguson crossed her arms, blocking Violet's way. "That's a puzzle, then, since his lordship is not here."

"Not here!" Violet's stomach sank. She had been counting on Lord Mardoun recognizing her as Lionel's student. "What do you mean? Will he be gone long?"

"Aye. He's gang to Italy on his honeymoon. As you would ken if you were really a friend of Lord Mardoun's." With a triumphant expression at having bested her opponent, she began once again to move the door forward. "Now, gae along with you."

"No, wait." Recovering somewhat from her surprise, Violet dug in her reticule and pulled out her silver-chased card case. She extracted one of her calling cards and held it out. "I did not say I was a friend of Lord Mardoun. But he is acquainted with me. I am Lady Violet Thornhill."

The mention of her title had the desired effect, for Mrs. Ferguson paused, then took the card and perused it, frowning. Violet dug in her reticule again and pulled out the earl's letter.

"This is Lord Mardoun's invitation to my mentor, Mr. Lionel Overton, to visit and examine the ancient ruins he found. You can see that it is written in his hand. Here, read it."

Mrs. Ferguson drew herself up and said frostily, "It is not my place to read his lordship's letters."

"Then surely it is not your place to turn away Lord Mardoun's guests, either," Violet pointed out and was pleased to see uncertainty flicker across Mrs. Ferguson's face. She pressed her advantage. "If his lordship is not in residence, who is in charge of Duncally?"

"I am the housekeeper here," Mrs. Ferguson said.

"Then you are the one who reports to the earl?"

"Well, to the butler, of course." The older woman began to look a trifle flustered. "But he has gang back to London with his lordship."

"So that leaves you responsible for deciding whether or not you will refuse Lord Mardoun's hospitality to his acquaintances? He delegated such authority to you?" Violet felt a twinge of remorse at browbeating the woman; she had always despised her father's aristocratic bullying of all those in lesser positions. But she had no idea what she would do if Mrs. Ferguson cast her out of the house. She could not fail after she had come so far.

With a final glare at Violet, the housekeeper turned to

the footman, still hovering with his lamp in the background. "Bobby, gae fetch Mr. Munro."

The young man beat a hasty retreat down the shadowy hall. Mrs. Ferguson turned and regarded Violet stonily, her arms crossed over her chest. Violet, affecting a false air of unconcern, sat down on the hall bench as if prepared to wait there forever. Minutes dragged by. There was no sound but that of a large clock striking the hour somewhere down the hallway. Violet wondered who Mr. Munro was, but she was not about to give the other woman the satisfaction of appearing curious. Finally, there was the sound of a door closing somewhere in the back recesses of the house, and soon heavy footsteps came toward them along one of the hallways.

Violet turned as a tall blond man strode into the entry. He came to an abrupt halt. "You!"

Violet's stomach sank. Mr. Munro—the man who would decide whether she stayed or left—was the man who had rescued her on the road. The man with whom she had just quarreled.

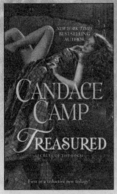

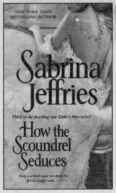